A LIFE OF ADVENTURE

I0664290

G. Allen Wilbanks

Deep Dark Thoughts Publications LLC

A Life of Adventure

Published by: Deep Dark Thoughts Publications LLC

Visit my website at www.gallenwilbanks.com

Paperback: ISBN 978-1-952630-00-2

Digital: ISBN 978-1-952630-01-9

Cover design: Arcane Covers

Contributing artist: Jason Jacobo

To Gwen, the inspiration for Sonja.

I hope you found your life of adventure.

PART I

THE GIFT

CHAPTER 1

Sonja Drommer perched on the corner of her bed, legs folded under her, glaring at the clock on her dresser. With elbows propped against her knees and her chin resting in her hands, she tried to force the time to change through sheer will and the intensity of her unblinking gaze. The blue, digital display staring back at her read: 3:52 PM.

Outside, the sun seemed frozen in place, refusing to budge any further across the cloudless, blue, March sky and reinforcing the impression that time had suddenly ceased to function properly. It would be easy to believe the whole world was stuck in amber or had somehow slipped into Limbo, if not for the harsh, cold wind whipping at the bushes and trees and reminding everyone that winter had not yet fully released its icy grip on the weather.

"Fifty-eight. Fifty-nine. Sixty," Sonja whispered, then snorted a soft breath of impatience. The clock refused to corroborate her timing. "Sixty-one. Sixty-two..." she continued reluctantly. At "sixty-eight," the lighted numbers at last flickered and changed to 3:53.

Sonja dropped her hands into her lap and picked up the small, wrapped box she had placed there earlier. Only three inches across on any side, the tiny package barely covered her open palm as she held it up to examine it for perhaps the one thousandth time since receiving it a few days ago. Green and blue tissue paper covered the box, tied neatly with a slender, white string; hardly an elaborate decoration but still tidy and obviously put together with great care and effort at presentation.

It weighed very little as it sat in her open hand, and she briefly wondered if there was actually anything inside. Either way, she would find out soon enough.

"Fifty-nine. Sixty. *Shit!* Still too fast."

Three days earlier, Sonja had entered the house after walking home from school, as she did most weekdays. Her high school was three miles from home, and since her dad only had one car, getting to and from school was by necessity on foot or on her ten-year old Huffy bicycle. Frankly, she preferred walking to riding on that rusted-out, pile of scrap metal.

She dropped her backpack on the small bench in the entryway and headed directly for the kitchen, planning to browse through the refrigerator for something to calm the growling in her belly. As she passed the dining room, she paused as she noticed a brown, paper-wrapped package about the size of a shirt box sitting unopened on the dining table. It was tied together with a crisscross of twine, and a large white label had been affixed to the otherwise plain brown surface. Across the label, in blocked, hand-written letters, was her name, "SONJA DROMMER." Beneath her name, although in much smaller printing, was her home address written by the same careful hand.

There was nothing else. She picked up the package and turned it over but found no return address, no postage, and no other markings that might suggest where it had come from or how it had gotten to her house.

Sonja raised the package to her ear and shook it gently. She heard and felt something small and light sliding around, loose inside. Tucking the mysterious box under one arm, she marched into the kitchen and fished a pair of scissors out of the utensil drawer. She dropped the package on the marble-tile counter of the kitchen island, snipped the twine away with the scissors, then began to pick at the meticulously taped edges of the paper wrapping. After a few seconds, she gave up on the polite approach and tore the paper away in ragged strips, revealing glossy white cardboard underneath.

The box itself, like its covering, also had no distinguishing markings. The top was loose, not secured with any tape or adhesive, and Sonja flipped the cover off in one smooth motion, letting it drop to the counter on top of the discarded scissors. Inside the larger box, Sonja found a smaller, blue-and-green tissue-shrouded present and a single sheet of white paper.

The paper was a note, scrawled in the same neat, handwritten letters as the address label. It read, "Under no circumstances is this gift to be unwrapped and opened prior to four o'clock in the afternoon on the date of your birth."

5

Odd, Sonja thought. And not helpful at all. She still had absolutely no clue as to who might have sent the package. She was tempted to open the little box immediately despite the note. Who would know? If the sender revealed themselves and asked if she had waited, she could just tell them she had. There would be no harm in that.

"Hey, you. I see you found the package."

Sonja startled and turned to see her father standing in the hallway. He was using a rag to wipe at a rainbow smear of colors on his hands. He had been painting, a hobby he had loved his entire life, but one that he devoted much more time and effort into during the past few years. His growing obsession with art seemed to coincide, uncoincidentally, with his divorce from Sonja's mother. It had been a bad breakup, and although everyone had known it was coming, he still held a lot of anger and resentment against her mother for abandoning the family and leaving him alone with two kids. Painting had become his way of dealing with the issues he refused to talk about.

"Hey, dad," Sonja called back. "Yeah, I found it. Any idea who sent it?"

He shook his head and wiped at his forehead with the back of one hand. The gesture left a narrow streak of blue paint above his right eyebrow.

Sonja's father was tall and slender; well over six feet tall and weighing under two hundred pounds. His full head of blond hair had begun to thin and recede over the past decade, though it did not seem to bother him. Sonja had always thought her dad was handsome, but he was never vain about his appearance. In fact, today he was still wearing the t-shirt and pajama bottoms he had probably slept in. He must have gotten up that morning and gone straight into the den to paint.

"Who brought it over?" she asked her father. She tapped a finger to her forehead to indicate the paint smear he had placed there.

"No idea," he responded, dabbing the cloth to his head in response to Sonja's pointing. He succeeded only in adding a patch of green and white to the blue streak. "Doorbell rang and that was on the porch when I opened the door. I never saw who left it. Did I get it?" her father asked, pointing at his forehead.

Sonja ignored the question, focusing back on the note she had found with the gift box. "What is it?" she wondered aloud, turning the paper over to the blank side to make sure she had not missed an important clue as to its origin. "And who would send it like this? Do you think maybe mom dropped it off?"

"I have no idea," her father replied. His tone grew cold and the smile he had been wearing slipped from his expression. "Does she even know when your birthday is?"

Sonja flinched. Even four years later, her father still reacted poorly to any mention of Sonja's mother. She normally knew better than to bring up the topic of mom whenever dad was in the room, but the question accidentally slipped out.

"Do you recognize the handwriting?" Sonja asked, offhandedly, trying to redirect the conversation before it became yet another heated lecture about that "thoughtless woman" that walked away from her marriage and her own children.

"I don't," he replied, flatly. He flipped the paint rag over his shoulder, walked past Sonja into the kitchen and retrieved a plastic cup from the cupboard beside the refrigerator. He filled the cup with water from the sink faucet. "Why don't you open it up and let me know what you find out."

Her father strode past her again with his water and disappeared down the hallway.

Sonja winced again. She had dodged the speech, but she had also thoroughly wrecked his good mood for the day. He hadn't even waited around long enough to see what was in the package. Shaking her head, she picked up the colorfully wrapped box and grasped the string between her thumb and forefinger, preparing to pull the covering off.

At the last moment, however, she decided to wait. After all, how many times did a girl get to turn seventeen? And, who doesn't want a little mystery and intrigue to celebrate their birthday? Three days was not so long to be patient. It just made the whole endeavor more exciting.

3:58.

Sonja was starting to second guess her decision not to open the box. With just two minutes left, maybe she had waited long enough. It was only two lousy minutes.

Nope, she told herself firmly, closing her hand around the box so she no longer had to look at it. She had waited this long; two more minutes were not going to break her. She would see this through to the end.

"This stupid thing had better not be empty," she muttered.

Sonja still had no idea who sent it. Since the package had turned up on their doorstep, she had questioned everyone she knew. No one expressed any knowledge of the gift or where it had come from.

Her younger brother, Philip, told Sonja she was being stupid. He had flashed a wide smile full of braces at her and explained that only a complete jackass would wait for three days simply because a piece of paper had told her not to open her own present. His statement only made her more determined. If her brother – who was always wrong no matter what he said – believed she should open the present early, what better sign could the universe give her that she should wait.

Sonja had even called her mom to ask if she sent the present, though she knew the answer to that question before she started dialing her mother's number. Her mother admitted the surprise had not come from her, then muttered some excuse about not forgetting Sonja's birthday. The present she had selected was somewhat difficult to wrap, she explained, so she had not yet had an opportunity to mail it. Before hanging up, Sonja reassured her mother that a present was not important, and she could mail it or just hang onto it until the next time they saw each other. She knew there was no present, but there was no reason to make an issue of it.

By this time, anyone she thought might potentially give her a birthday present had done so or already been questioned by her about the mysterious box. Or both. Sonja was as in the dark now as she had been when she first read the anonymous note.

At last, the clock flashed four o'clock and Sonja's self-imposed torment was officially over. Still, she hesitated a moment longer, bracing herself against potential disappointment.

"You really better not be empty," she reiterated. In emphasis, she shook the box next to her ear. Something shifted inside, clicking audibly as it rattled back and forth against the sides of the container. Sonja looked at the package in surprise. It had not made any noise like that before, and this certainly wasn't the first time she had shaken it trying to gauge what was inside. Had she broken something?

The box felt a little heavier as well. Not a lot, but there was a new sense of mass to the gift. "Stop it," Sonja whispered to herself. The box could not possibly be any heavier than it had been a moment before. She was being irrational and starting to make herself a little crazy over a ridiculous birthday gift. Perhaps the sudden noise had triggered something in her brain and subconsciously made the package seem more substantial.

Regardless of whatever silliness was going on in her head, guessing was no longer necessary. Sonja had promised herself she would wait until four o'clock and she had done just that. There was nothing left but to open the box and end the suspense.

Sonja did not bother trying to unwrap the package, instead she snapped the string with a quick pull of one curled finger, then used her fingernail to tear and strip the paper away. Under the colorful paper she discovered a small, brown, plastic box. It was a jewelry case, with a tiny metal hinge on one side connecting the two halves. Applying a small amount of pressure, Sonja forced the mouth of the box apart and was rewarded with a soft click as it snapped open on its hinge.

A delicate, silver ring rested on the cushioned pad inside. The head of the ring was a figurine of some sort of mythical creature Sonja had never seen before. The upper half appeared to be a flying horse, complete with wings and tiny hooves, however the snout on the animal's head was much too long. It looked like the toothy maw of a crocodile rather than the tapering lines of a horse's muzzle. The lower half of the thing's body was reptilian as well, consisting of the long, scaly torso and tail of a serpent looped around itself into a glittering, silver coil.

The design was odd, but still quite beautiful. The details were remarkably clear on such a small figurine. Sonja sighed in delight. It was lovely, but it still offered no clue as to who had sent it.

Taking it from the box, Sonja put the ring onto the middle finger of her left hand. It slipped easily onto her finger like it had been sized to fit her. Poking a fingernail into the now empty jewelry holder, she verified there was nothing else inside. No folded paper note, just the empty slot where the ring had rested.

"Now," she said, admiring the ring and the silver creature adorning it, "I wonder who you belong to."

"Isn't it obvious? I belong to you."

Sonja froze at the unexpected voice, choking down on the surprised scream that threatened to escape. When she was sure her heart was going to keep beating, she spun toward the bedroom door to find whoever had wandered in uninvited. The door was closed and no one else was in the room with her. She shot a look toward her window, but that too was closed, and there was nobody looking in at her from outside.

When she recovered enough to find her voice, she stammered, "W-who said that?"

"I did."

The voice was high pitched, but melodic rather than squeaky or piping, like the ringing of a small chime. Sonja turned around, covering a full circuit of her room, but still she found no source for the voice. She thought of checking her phone in case someone was playing a practical joke. Before she could reach for her cell, however, her eyes settled on the ring on her left hand.

The silver figurine on the ring moved. Its tiny wings fluttered. Once. Twice. Then they blurred into full motion, lifting the creature clear of the band around her finger. The miniature beast rose to hover before Sonja's staring eyes, its tail unfurling beneath it and lashing back and forth.

"I said that," the creature repeated clearly. "After all, you asked me a question and answering it was the only polite thing to do under the circumstances."

This time, Sonja did scream. Throwing herself backward, she tripped over the corner of her bed before stumbling as far away as she could manage in the confines of her bedroom. Sonja scrambled to escape, only to find she had trapped herself in a corner. The bedroom door and any hope of freedom lay on the other side of her room, past the hovering creature.

No rescue would be coming, either, despite her scream. Her dad had gone out to pick up dinner, and Philip had gone straight to a friend's house after school. The house was empty. Empty, except for Sonja and whatever she had just let loose in her bedroom.

"Oh dear," said the flying figure. "You're afraid of me, aren't you? I mean, I figured that because you're huddled in the corner and I've never seen anyone huddle in a corner unless they were afraid, or maybe sick, and although you look a little pale, I don't think you're sick. Ergo, you are afraid of me. See how simple that is?

"Now, we have to find a solution to this problem, because it is a problem. I don't want you to be afraid of me, but you obviously are. That is a problem. But all problems have solutions. So, let's find it."

The creature zipped through a pattern of three wild loops in the air before settling back to hover in its previous location. Sonja flinched at the sudden activity, but the little beast did not seem intent on attacking her.

"What is the best way for two people, or more specifically a human and a hippoganth, to become unafraid of each other?" it asked. But whether the question was directed at Sonja or merely rhetorical, she could not tell.

"I know! We must become friends, and the first step to becoming friends is to find out each other's names. I'll go first since I'm already the one talking, and you don't look like you are completely done huddling just yet. My name is Rithagarianaff, but you can call me Rith. Everyone calls me Rith because most people can't remember Rithagarianaff. What's yours?"

"Sonja," answered Sonja hesitantly, stepping away from the corner to get a better look at Rith. Despite the unnaturalness of the situation, she found herself warming towards the garrulous little creature. Still, to be safe she slowly worked her way around the creature as it talked, giving herself a clearer path to the door.

"Yes. Sonja. I already knew that, but I asked anyway because that's the way it's supposed to be done. It's more polite letting you say your own name. Anyway, Sonja, I'm your birthday gift. So now that you know my name and a little bit about me, are we friends yet?"

Sonja laughed, nervously, still eyeing the closed door on the far side of the room. "Yes, I suppose we are," she agreed, not wanting to upset the creature, although feeling as if friendship with it was still far from a sure thing.

"Good," said Rith, doing another series of aerial somersaults.

"Rith?" asked Sonja. "Do you know who sent you?"

"Of course. I was there, wasn't I?"

"Well, who was it?" she asked, fascination and curiosity beginning to overcome her fears.

"I can't tell you," said Rith. "Let's just say it was an admirer. Besides, you know what they say about looking a gift horse in the mouth."

Rith nickered in a manner vaguely resembling a laugh, then he opened his mouth, revealing rows of pointed, silver teeth. Sonja frowned at the tiny animal; not completely sure she understood the joke.

"Can you at least tell me why I wasn't supposed to open your box until four o'clock, today?"

"Oh, I can answer that," said Rith. "Curiosity. I just wanted to see if you could do it."

"Curiosity?!" Sonja choked on the word. "And if I didn't wait?"

"Nothing. I would still have been in the box when you opened it."

"So, there was no reason for me to…" she trailed off.

"Nope. No reason." Rith nickered again.

Sonja laughed, too. This time, her amusement was more genuine. It was hard not to like the flighty hippoganth. "So, you're my present. Does that make you my property, or my pet?"

"Pet?" huffed Rith. "I'm not a pet. And I'm not property, either. I'm just Rith."

"Well, 'just Rith,' whatever you are, you're absolutely incredible. I mean, you're clearly a bit of a jerk for making me wait to open the box, but I think I'll get over that. I've never seen anything like you before. I can't wait to tell my friends about you."

"No," said Rith, his tone turning serious as he moved closer to Sonja for emphasis. Sonja jerked backward a step and Rith immediately retreated. "Sorry. I didn't mean to scare you again, but you must not tell anyone the truth about me. I was gifted to you, and because of that I can reveal myself to you, but to others I must remain simply a ring. Magic and the creatures of magic, like myself, are wonderful things, but they are very rare in this world. They must be safeguarded, protected by those who still believe in them. People who do not accept magic would want to trap me and study me; to figure out how I work. Their unwillingness to believe their own eyes would cause them to destroy me, whether they meant to or not. That's why I was sent to you; because you believe, and with you I can be safe.

"Someday, you will have to pass me on to someone else who believes enough to keep the magic in me alive. Just as I was passed on to you. But until that time, no one must know about me. You have to promise you will keep me a secret."

"I promise," replied Sonja solemnly, although reluctantly. She frowned, disappointed at not being able to share something so remarkable with her friends, but she resolved not do anything that might put Rith at risk. "At least now I'll have someone to talk to when I'm bored and there's no one around."

"Yes, there is that," agreed Rith, brightening again. "I'm very good company and I love to talk."

"I noticed that," laughed Sonja.

"Oh, and I almost forgot one little thing." Rith fluttered in excited circles. He kept up his aerial acrobatics for almost a minute, and Sonja began to think he had forgotten whatever he had planned to say. He came to a sudden stop and started talking again as casually as if he had never paused. "There is a benefit to having me around. Other than having a great friend, that is. Because I am currently yours, and because of all the wonderful things that magic can accomplish, you are entitled to one wish."

"What?!" exclaimed Sonja, unable to believe what she was hearing. "A wish. A real wish? You can grant wishes and you're just now getting around to mentioning it? You know, that might have been a real good place to start this conversation when you popped up out of that box and scared the shit out of me."

"I suppose you have a point. But, to answer your question, yes, I can give you a real wish. Le desir de ton coeur. You ask for it, I deliver. See how simple it is? But think about it carefully," Rith cautioned her. "Be absolutely sure you really want what you wish for, because once you use it, it's gone, and you're stuck with what you get."

Sonja hesitated a moment, then asked, "This isn't a trick, right? I mean, if I ask for a million dollars, you're not going to kill my parents so I collect the insurance money? You won't twist my wish into something horrible?"

"N-no. No, no, no," Rith stammered. The little creature's flight pattern became erratic and his tail lashed wildly back and forth. He seemed genuinely horrified by Sonja's suggestion. "The wish is real. It's a reward for taking care of me, and I would never kill your parents. Even if you wished for me to do it, I don't think I could. You're not going to wish for me to kill anybody, are you?"

"Stop," said Sonja, holding out her hands in apology. "I'm sorry I suggested it, and no I don't want you to kill anybody."

"That's good," said Rith, visibly relaxing. "That's very good."

"Okay. I wish for–"

"Wait! Wait!" blurted Rith. "Don't you want to take some time to consider what you want?"

Sonja shook her head. "I already know what I want. I've known for a long time. I want to live a life of adventure."

Sonja paused and waited for the thunderclap, or a flash of brilliant light to let her know her wish had been granted. Nothing changed. She and Rith were still in the middle of her cluttered bedroom. She watched Rith closely, but he only hovered quietly, pondering what she had told him.

"What kind of adventure?" he finally asked. "That wish was kind of broad. I'm going to need a little more detail."

"Um, any kind. You know, the kind of adventure that heroes have in novels. I want excitement and I want to know that I'm doing something amazing with my life, not just exchanging oxygen for carbon dioxide like most of the people on this boring planet."

Rith took another moment to consider Sonja's request. "This," he said at last, "could really be a promising wish. If it is handled correctly. Do you have anything more to add?"

"I'll leave all the details to you. I trust you."

"Good. Then, I deem your wish granted."

Another long awkward pause followed. Rith placidly drifted in front of her, occasionally zipping off in one direction or another before returning to his original spot. Sonja watched Rith's antics with growing impatience as she waited for whatever was going to happen next.

"Well," she asked when her patience failed her.

"Well, what?" replied Rith.

"When does the adventure start?"

"Start? It starts whenever you want it to start. I thought you understood. But no. I guess I never actually told you that, did I? So, the confusion is understandable. That would be my fault. It starts when you say it starts. Go ahead, pick a time."

"Why not now?" asked Sonja.

"Why not?" agreed Rith.

CHAPTER 2

Sonja stood alone in the middle of a forest. Towering trees and sparsely foliaged bushes surrounded her where her bed and furniture had been seconds before. She spun in a circle, trying to orient herself to her new, unexpected surroundings, but it did not help. All she found was more trees and no hint as to where she was or how she had arrived here. The odor of rotting leaves and vegetation reached her nose, kicked up from the ground beneath her feet as she moved. The strength of the smell argued that this was not an illusion or, if it was, it was an incredibly thorough one.

The sun hung low on the horizon, filtered heavily by the surrounding woods, but despite the shadows, Sonja felt comfortably warm. The pleasant temperature was a nice contradiction to the miserable weather she had endured earlier that day, but it only confirmed what the woods around her were already telling her.

She was far from home.

To her added dismay, her clothes had changed as well. Instead of the jeans and button-up blouse she had worn moments ago, she now had on a plain, ankle-length dress of gray cloth. A laced, felt bodice cinched the shapeless material of the dress tight against her waist and torso. Her wavy, light-brown hair, previously hanging loose on her shoulders, had been pulled back into a tight braid and covered with a white, linen bonnet. The outfit, complete with calf-high, cross-laced ghillies on her feet, gave her the appearance of a country peasant girl from some Renaissance Faire.

"And what, pray tell, is a young lass like yourself doing so far from the protective walls of the city?"

Spinning again at the sound of the voice, Sonja found herself confronted by a tall, lean, young man of about twenty-five years of age. His face was tanned and weather worn, and he would have appeared much older except for the boyish grin lighting his expression and revealing his youth. Locks of thick, black hair covered his forehead and all but hid his soft brown eyes, which also seemed to be smiling at her. He wore well-tanned leathers, hand stitched and carefully fitted to his slender frame, and strapped to his back was a quiver containing the protruding, feathered ends of several arrows. In one hand he held a long bow; in the other, a worn felt cap with a quail feather affixed to it.

"Ahh, and such a pretty thing, at that," he said, approaching and getting his first good look at Sonja. His eyes traced her from head to toe, but the look was not lascivious; merely appraising. "The deep woods are truly not a place for one such as yourself. Have you lost your way?"

Sonja was too stunned to do anything other than nod in agreement.

"What is your name, fair one?" asked the young man.

"Sonja," replied Sonja. "Sonja Drommer. Please, can you tell me where I am? And, who are you?"

"I think you can figure out where you are. After all, you don't look like you've traveled very far. As to who am I? Well, I am called Robin. Robin of Locksley. Although, I have no real name or title to speak of other than those bestowed upon me by that black-hearted Prince John Lackland. He does at times refer to me as Sir Robin the Scoundrel, or Robin the Outlaw, or–"

"Robin Hood!" blurted Sonja. "You're Robin Hood!"

"Then you have heard of me," said Robin with a bow and a flourish of his hat. His impish grin reappeared. "I am honored that my reputation is growing."

"Of course, I've heard of you," said Sonja, amazed. "Everyone has heard of you."

"Many have, yes," he agreed. "But not everyone, and not nearly enough to help me remove Prince John from his cruelly won throne."

"And this is Sherwood Forest?"

"Indeed," said Robin. "I knew you were not as lost as you claimed. It is late, however, and I do not think you can be out of these woods before dark. If you have no other lodging for tonight, will you be a guest in our camp? There are nine of us at present and sleeping room is limited, but I'm sure we can find you someone willing to share their tent."

"Wait a minute," said Sonja, suddenly suspicious. "Whose tent, and what are you thinking?"

Robin stared at her for a moment, before an amused comprehension dawned in his eyes.

"I see your worry," he laughed. "And it is a needless one. My party is not exclusively male. In fact, if you wish, you may spend tonight in the company of Marian, my wife to be."

Sonja fairly glowed at the thought of meeting Maid Marian, and she agreed immediately to the suggestion.

"Very well." Robin brushed the hair from his face and pulled his cap on with a small flourish. The tall, quail feather jutted cockily behind his head. "Come then, for we have a fair walk before we reach camp."

Robin started off at a comfortable pace and Sonja fell in step behind him. This was not what she had expected when she voiced her wish, but then, honestly, she had not really known what to expect. She needed to ask Rith...

Rith!

Sonja glanced at her finger, panic kicking her heartbeat into high gear and causing a painful pounding in her chest. Relief rushed in to replace her concern as she saw the ring was still where she had placed it on her left hand, and Rith was once more perched comfortably on top of it. He fluttered a tiny wing at her in acknowledgment. *Good,* she thought. *He's still with me.*

Sonja allowed herself to fall back from Robin another pace, then brought the ring close to her mouth. She whispered, hoping she was quiet enough that the young man would not hear her.

"Is that really Robin Hood?" she asked. Rith did not reply, but Sonja saw his head move up and down in a nod. "How did we get here?"

"Pardon?" asked Robin, keeping his gaze forward as he maneuvered through the trees. "Were you asking something?"

N-no," Sonja stammered, awkwardly. "I was just talking to myself. It's nothing."

She dropped her hand and turned her attention back to keeping up with Robin, who had increased his stride with the fading light of day. This conversation was going to have to wait for a more opportune moment.

21

A LIFE OF ADVENTURE

The trek toward camp covered almost two miles of forest but took only about a half an hour at the pace Robin set for them. He kept clear of obvious paths or roads, forcing Sonja to watch her footing as she ducked through brush and dodged around trees. Her toes painfully discovered several protruding roots and stones along her route, and she nearly fell on more than one occasion. Robin, on the other hand, seemed unaffected by the terrain, moving smoothly across the uneven ground as if he knew every step by memory. His long stride had Sonja almost running at times to stay with her guide as each one of his steps made up almost two of hers.

At last, with Sonja sweating and thoroughly out of breath, they broke through a final screen of tree limbs into a small, man-made clearing. Several immature trees had been cut down and the forest floor was cleared of the usual detritus to make room for five tents pitched in a circle and an open fire pit at the center of the grouping. Robin strode confidently through the encampment to a group of six people gathered in front of one of the larger tents. Sonja hung back at the edge of the clearing. She found a large smooth rock outside the ring of tents and sat down. Her feet hurt; the soft leather ghillies she wore did little to protect them from the rocks and rough terrain. If this was adventure, maybe her wish had not been such a good one, after all. She closed her eyes and breathed deeply to slow her heartrate to something more closely resembling normal, and she remained this way until Robin called to her several minutes later.

"Sonja," he said as she approached the group of figures gathered around him. "Here are those I wish you to meet. These are my comrades." Robin proceeded to introduce Sonja to the group, listing each of his companions by name. He also mentioned two missing members of his band who were at present on watch outside the camp.

Sonja nodded to each in turn but paid little attention to the names, realizing that five minutes from now she would probably not remember them anyway. Except for one. When Robin introduced Marian, Sonja saw one of the most beautiful women she had ever met. She was dressed like the others, in a leather vest and breeches, and stood perhaps an inch shorter than Sonja's own five foot six. Her hands and face were dirty from hard work, and though most of her dark hair was tied back into a long braid, several strands had escaped and hung limply across her face. Despite the layer of sweat and grime, her beauty still shone through. Sonja saw a fierce intensity in the light brown eyes, a mirror of Robin's own in both color and determination. They seemed to say that nothing short of death would ever keep her from achieving something she desired. But those eyes were kind as well, and currently they looked at Sonja with only compassion for her plight.

"Sonja, dear, come with me," said Marian after introductions had been completed. "I'll show you where you'll be sleeping tonight. Bring your things."

"I don't have anything with me," answered Sonja, realizing the statement was the absolute truth. Rith had given her no time to pack or prepare for … whatever this was.

"Robin always says it is good to travel light, but for a girl to not even have a single change of clothes is unacceptable," said Marian, smiling kindly. "We will have to find some way to rectify the situation."

Marian led Sonja to one of the five standing tents and ushered her inside. The interior was empty except for an elaborately decorated, wood travel trunk and several rolls of blankets. Pulling open and digging through the wooden chest, Marian pulled out a set of clothing similar to those she was wearing.

"Here," she said, studying Sonja carefully. "These are mine, but they should fit you well enough. Go ahead and change. I'll give you some privacy, and when you are finished, call me. I'll be nearby."

Marian left the tent, closing the flap behind her. Sonja watched her leave, then eyed the clothes draped over the trunk. Slowly, she began to strip out of her dress.

"Rith," she whispered as she pulled and tugged at the lacing of her bodice. "Rith, what's going on?"

"I thought you knew already," answered the hippoganth, fluttering off the ring to hover in front of Sonja. "I mean, it isn't really that hard to figure out. You're in Sherwood Forest, and outside is Robin Hood and Maid Marian, and–"

"Yes, I know all that," interrupted Sonja. "But this isn't what I wished for. I wanted a little excitement and adventure in my own life. I don't know what all this is, but I know it doesn't have anything to do with *my* life."

"Well, you're alive, aren't you?" retorted Rith. "And you're having an adventure, aren't you?"

"Yes, but it isn't real."

"Oh, but it is!" answered Rith. "It's very real. Anything that happens to you here is permanent."

"Permanent?" asked Sonja, pausing as she worked the last of her laces free. "What do you mean? Like, I could die here, permanent?"

"Hopefully, not," said Rith. Sonja assumed he was trying to be reassuring, although he was doing a terrible job of it. "But I suppose that yes, you could die if you let someone kill you."

"Then, I really am in the middle of a forest, surrounded by people I don't know. I'm not at home asleep in my bed and dreaming this whole thing."

"Nope. Not at home. Not dreaming. You are really here."

"Happy birthday to me," Sonja breathed, then almost started to laugh despite the fact she found no humor in anything Rith had told her. "What about getting home? If I stay here much longer, my dad will flip out. He'll call the police, and when I do get home, I'll be in more trouble than I've ever been in my entire life."

"You said you wanted some excitement," said Rith.

"*Rith!*" growled Sonja.

"I'm kidding, I'm kidding, I'm kidding," squealed Rith, flying sporadic little circles in the air and nickering. "Really, you have nothing to worry about. Nobody will miss you. They won't even know that you've been gone. Trust me." Rith settled back down on the ring. "Trust me," he repeated.

Sonja shook her head. "I guess I don't really have any choice."

"That's the spirit!"

"Shut up."

Sonja finished changing, deciding at the last minute to remove the bonnet and leave her head uncovered. She wasn't certain what was proper for this time period, but Marian had not been wearing anything over her hair, so it was probably fine. She dropped the white lace hat onto the pile of clothes she had placed on the chest and pulled open the front tent flap. Marian stood about twenty feet away, between two of the other tents, talking to Robin. Or maybe "talking" was not the proper word for it. Embarrassed, Sonja closed the flap again and called out for Marian from inside the tent. A moment later she heard the woman's voice call back.

"Come out by the fire so we can look at you."

A LIFE OF ADVENTURE

Stepping outside, Sonja noticed the sun had fully set and darkness claimed the clearing. Everyone in camp had gathered around the fire pit and a cheerful blaze now emanated from it, casting warmth and a comfortable glow upon their faces and outstretched hands. As she joined the group, Marian approached her and critically examined her new clothing. The blouse and vest were a little loose, and the breeches a couple inches too short. "But," concluded Marian, giving the vest one last motherly tug, "they will do fine until we have time to make some that fit better. At least the boots look right."

"They're very comfortable," said Sonja. The calf-high, tanned leather boots felt much better on her feet and offered more protection than the high-laced slippers she had arrived in.

"She won't be staying long enough for new clothes to be made," interrupted Robin. "Tomorrow, I am taking her back to her family in Nottingham."

"I don't come from Nottingham," Sonja told Robin. "And I don't have any family anywhere in this world." It was not a lie. She did not know anyone here and, if she were cast out, she really had nowhere to go. "I'd like to stay here if I could, at least for a while. Please?"

Robin paused, watching Sonja carefully before shifting his gaze to Marian. He next glanced questioningly at each member of the group, but none offered any objection. "I guess I was wrong. It appears that the Lady Sonja will be staying. For the nonce she cannot go home. But remember, lass, you must do your share here. It is not an easy life and there is always plenty of work to be done."

Sonja nodded, afraid to speak for fear of saying something foolish that would give Robin a reason to change his mind.

"With that settled, I welcome you to our merry band of thieves."

Sonja spent the next several days adjusting to the rhythms and regular work schedule of the camp. Being the newest member of this small group, she received the more menial tasks as they required no specific expertise, and no one else wanted to do them. She washed clothing and kitchen utensils in a nearby stream, collected firewood, cooked – although admittedly not very well – and did anything else that needed to be done that others could not spare the time to do. The work was hard, but Sonja never felt unfairly treated. She considered tired muscles and a few blisters to be a small price for spending time with Robin and Marian and the others. Evenings, after eating and clean-up, was her time to relax and enjoy the conversations around the fire. She listened with amusement at the various stories and boasts of impossible accomplishments, as well as the rowdy jokes or good-natured retelling of others' misfortunes during the day. Sonja did not want to miss a single moment of her time here, and it was Marian who frequently dragged her to her tent each night, insisting they both needed their sleep.

Sonja questioned Rith several times about her family and friends back home, and what they must be thinking about her being gone so long. Rith assured her each time that no one would miss her and, when she returned, everything would be fine. She finally abandoned her concerns and decided to put her trust in the hippoganth. Even if he were wrong, there was nothing she could do about it. She might as well enjoy this experience.

On the morning of the third day, Sonja was presented with new clothes. Marian had spent the past two nights stitching and altering one of her older outfits until they now fit Sonja beautifully. Blouse, vest, breeches, and boots; everything was perfect. Sonja was also given a brand new, handmade, green felt hat identical to Robin's own, although this one had no feather. Squealing with delight, she slapped the hat on her head and twirled in a brief dance of joy. Marian laughed at her unbridled response to the clothing.

Also, on the third day, Robin decided it was time to teach Sonja how to use a weapon. "Everyone who stays with me," he told her, "must know how to work, to hunt and, when necessary, to fight."

He handed her a bow, smaller than the weapon he carried for himself. The limbs of this bow were slender and flexible so she could draw the string fully without much difficulty. An arrow fired from Sonja's weapon would not have the same velocity as one launched from Robin's, however Sonja doubted she could draw a bow like his back far enough to use it. The lost power of her smaller version was an acceptable compromise.

Next, Robin presented her with a six-foot, wooden staff. It was hand-carved and had probably still been a tree branch the day before as the wood was green and slightly damp. She hefted the staff in both hands, trying unsuccessfully to hide the wild grin that pulled at her lips.

From that moment her training began. She watched, and learned, and practiced until, over time, she gained nominal proficiency in both weapons. Sonja spent an hour or two each morning practicing with her bow, sticking arrows into the nearby trees from varying distances. She enjoyed the meditative quality of the routine: Knock, draw, release. Knock, draw, release. It was soothing, and there was the immediate gratification of hearing the *chunk!* of each arrow as it struck the target she had chosen for it.

Sparring with the staff in the afternoons was decidedly less enjoyable as training with the weapon left her battered and bruised. Her training partners were not trying to injure her, but even their "friendly taps," as they called them, were unpleasant reminders of her own ineptitude. She persisted despite the discomfort and, through the dogged desire of self-preservation, she improved.

Barely four days passed since she received her bow, when Sonja brought down her first game during a hunt. While following a well-worn animal trail, she flushed three pheasants from the bushes when she passed their hiding spot. At the sound of the birds taking flight, Sonja raised her weapon, arrow already nocked and ready, and drew the string until the feathers of the arrow's fletching brushed her cheek. The frightened birds fluttered away in a staggered line and she fired at the lead bird in the trio. Her arrow struck the animal in the rear of the fleeing group, bringing it down to the forest floor in a tumble of feathers and leaves. The shot had been blind luck. Sonja, however, was not about to admit that to anyone. If somebody asked, she would tell them she had had hit precisely where she was aiming.

"A right fat pheasant," laughed her hunting companion, a man called Will Stutely. He pulled Sonja's arrow from the bird and returned it to her to replace in her quiver. Looking the fowl over carefully, he selected a black and white, banded tail feather and plucked it out. He leaned over Sonja and placed the feather securely into the material of her hat. Stepping back to admire the overall effect, he told her, "You will make a fine bowman, someday, but you have to remember to shoot in front of a moving target, not at it."

Sonja's face fell as she realized she had not fooled Will with her lucky shot. He knew exactly where she had been aiming. Yet, when they returned to camp, he stayed quiet. He stroked his beard thoughtfully when the others questioned him and stated simply, "She shot it clean through the middle. I saw it with mine own eyes."

The days passed in this manner for a week, then two, then three. From sunup to sundown Sonja attended her chores or practiced with the staff and bow until she fell asleep exhausted at the end of each day. Despite the grueling schedule, she found herself enjoying life with Robin and his outlaws.

A few days before the end of her third week, Robin brought the routine to an end. Calling a meeting one night of all those in camp, he made an announcement.

"We have rested here for many a day as we have awaited the return of Little John and the rest of our companions with word from King Richard. Their return is still a month hence yet rest we can no longer. I have news that come the morrow the Sheriff of Nottingham, under orders of Prince John, begins a sweep of these woods in hopes of ending the lives of me and all those who would stand with me. We can run, or we can hold our ground, and I fault no one for choosing either path."

Robin spoke to the group, although he looked directly at Sonja. "If your choice is to go, then go now, and my prayers for your safety go with you."

Sonja's heart raced, but she did not want to appear to be a coward. More importantly, these people had taken her in and sheltered her when there was no reason for them to care what happened to her. She considered them friends, and she would not abandon them.

Besides, where would she go?

Sonja raised her head and stuck out her chin at Robin's implied question. He smiled at her defiance then nodded. It seemed everyone was staying.

"My suggestion is simple: a trap for our dear Sheriff. It must be done quickly and ruthlessly to discourage any such brash quests in the near future."

Robin explained his plan of action in detail. It involved speed, stealth, and above all, complete cooperation. Knowing the importance of the coming confrontation, every step was threshed out thoroughly. The group recounted the plan multiple times around the central fire that night to be sure everyone knew what was required of them. Robin offered Sonja the opportunity to remain behind, but when she learned Marian planned to participate, she insisted she wanted to do her part as well.

By the following morning, all preparation had been completed. Spies sympathetic to Robin's cause had notified him that the Sheriff planned to march the main contingent of his troops in a straight line, while sending out scouts through the surrounding woods to search for Robin. If a camp were located the scouts would return to notify the rest of the soldiers.

Robin had sent out scouts of his own to monitor the Sheriff's progress. There were only a few roads in and out of the forest that were wide enough for a contingent of soldiers to move upon easily, so as soon as the Sheriff committed to one of these roads, Robin's men could position themselves to meet the oncoming threat.

Robin's scouts returned just before daylight and upon hearing their reports, Robin, Sonja, and the others positioned themselves in the trees along the path on which the Sheriff's men had been reported to be traveling. Although coordination between the members of Robin's group required some timing and precision, the overall plan was simple in nature. The archers would loose a volley of arrows into the ranks of soldiers at a signal from Robin, scatter while the soldiers ran for cover and tried to reorganize, then reconvene at a predetermined point further down the path. With any luck, the Sheriff's guardsmen would begin their retreat after the second or third volley. If not, there were plenty of arrows in each quiver.

Sonja waited from her position in the lower branches of an oak tree forty long paces to the north of the road the soldiers would take. She wedged herself into the vee between two separating branches using her legs and back to brace her in place while keeping her hands free to wield her bow. Her hands shook slightly as she heard the heavy tread of the approaching men. She took several shallow breaths and tried to will herself to calm down.

The first of the soldiers marched into view. Arrows, already knocked, were now drawn, and Sonja picked out a target among the brightly colored ranks of armored men.

An officer fell, a feathered shaft planted through his heart. As the first soldier toppled and died, seven more arrows flew in reaction to the agreed upon signal. Each found a home in chest or throat, bringing down their intended victims. Sonja's arrow never found its mark. Instead, she let it and her bow drop to the ground in horror as she realized for the first time since she had arrived in Sherwood Forest that this world was real. She was not involved in a game or a fantasy. Blood spilled red and wet onto the ground and men died violently in front of her eyes.

She screamed.

Several of the surviving soldiers attempting to regroup after the initial surprise heard her scream, dropped to their knees, and began firing in Sonja's direction. Most missed, arrows flying far wide of their unseen target, but one flashing arrowhead managed to graze her left shoulder, tearing through the cloth of her sleeve and leaving a long, though fortunately shallow, cut in her flesh. The sudden pain jolted Sonja and she reeled back in unthinking reaction. The movement overbalanced her, and she fell from the branches she had been straddling, plummeting to the ground. Luckily for Sonja, the location she had chosen was not exceedingly high and the fall only knocked the air from her lungs, causing no permanent damage. She lay on her back, stunned and fighting for air for several seconds before a strong hand grabbed her good arm and jerked her to her feet.

"Get up and run," came Robin's angry voice. "The soldiers are moving fast."

Sonja, with Robin pulling her along behind him, ran harder than she had ever run in her life. Bushes and tree branches blurred past her, grabbing at her clothing and scratching her face and arms. A painful stitch tugged at her right side and her throat burned raw from trying to pull enough oxygen into her laboring lungs to fuel her flight, but she continued running as fear spurred her on. The sounds of the soldiers' pursuit faded behind them, and Robin permitted them to slow their pace. Just as Sonja convinced herself they had reached safety, a curse from Robin stopped her short. He stumbled and fell, throwing out his hands in a failed attempt to catch himself. As he struggled to push back to his hands and knees, Sonja dropped to the ground beside him. She opened her mouth to ask him what had happened but closed it again when she spied the wooden shaft of an arrow protruding from his lower back.

"Go on," he yelled. "Don't let them get you. Find the camp and we'll come for you."

Sonja watched long enough to see Robin drag himself behind the cover of a nearby fallen tree and draw an arrow, knocking it to his bow in anticipation of the men pursuing him.

Choking back a sob at her cowardice, Sonja fled for the relative safety of the outlaw camp.

She ran, pushing herself to move as fast as possible for as long as possible. Though she stumbled and fell numerous times, she slowed to a walk only when she absolutely had to pause to catch her breath. When she could breathe again without gasping, she would break back into a lurching, headlong rush through the forest.

She reached the clearing what felt like hours later, coughing and gasping. Tears tracked down her face, shiny and wet on her cheeks. She had no weapon and she was worse than useless in a fight, but she hated herself for running away and leaving Robin alone. He was most likely dead by now, and all because he had stopped to help her. If she had only been able to shoot and run like the others, he would not have been hurt. Instead, she had panicked and ruined everything. Climbing inside the tent she and Marian shared, Sonja crawled to a corner, curled up into a ball and cried herself to sleep.

Sonja awoke to the sound of voices. She carefully poked her head out of the tent, ready to bolt back inside if the sounds should prove to be made by the Sheriff's men. When she recognized the people around her, she came out into the open to join them.

The faces gazing back at her were grim. Two of the men carried a make-shift stretcher between them, and Marian stood nearby with tears in her eyes. Lying on the stretcher was the still form of Robin Hood. The arrow had been removed but the blanket covering him was stained red with his blood. The men carrying him carefully set him down at the center of camp by the fire pit. After kicking away the cold ashes from the night before, they hastened to kindle a new fire.

Sonja rushed over to Robin who still had not moved. His face was pale and waxen, and his breathing seemed much too shallow. She dropped down beside him. Marian watched her, but otherwise did not react to her presence.

"I'm sorry," she sobbed. "I didn't mean..." but Sonja choked on the next words.

Robin opened his eyes and covered her hand with his own. He smiled slightly, though Sonja could see in his face the effort it required.

"It's no shame to be unable to take the life of another human being," he said. "That is not your fault. I never should have allowed you to be there." He paused to draw in another careful breath before continuing.

"But screaming was a bad decision."

His hand dropped and his eyes closed once more.

CHAPTER 3

Sonja stood alone in her room. Her bed, furniture, and everything else was back where it had been before she left. The blanket at the corner of the bed was still crushed and rumpled where she had been sitting on it and staring at her clock. Nothing was different.

Nothing, except for her.

Tears streaked down her cheeks and she wiped at them with her sleeve as she looked around, making sure that she really was back; that this was truly home.

"It's over," she sighed.

"It's over," echoed Rith.

Sonja reached a hand to her left shoulder to probe at a lingering stiffness. She winced at the touch and her hand came away sticky with blood.

"Oh my God!" she cried. "It was real!"

"Of course, it was real," said Rith, flying up to hover at eye level. "I told you that. Why didn't you believe me?"

"I could have been killed," she yelled angrily at the little creature.

"I told you that, too. Not exactly in those words, but that's what I meant. Why don't you start listening to me? I said it was real, and I said whatever happened to you there would be permanent. I thought you understood. Besides, isn't that what you wished for? Adventure?"

A thought occurred to Sonja, pushing away all concerns for her own welfare. If her injury was real, then what about...?

"Robin! What happened to him? Did he ... die?"

"Eventually, yes," said Rith. "But not from an arrow wound, and not because of you. He was in pretty bad shape, but he must have made it, because all the legends say he died when he was murdered by a relative, not shot with an arrow by a soldier."

Sonja heaved a sigh of relief at the news. "I guess," she said reluctantly, "that I should go tell my dad that I'm alive. He must be worried to death after I disappeared for three weeks."

"No, he's not," reassured Rith. "He doesn't even know you've been gone, which in this time frame is the truth."

"What are you talking about?" asked Sonja, thoroughly confused. "Time frame?"

"Do you see what I mean about not listening to me?" Rith's voice carried a slightly annoyed tone. "I'll try to keep this simple. When you made your wish, you said you wanted to live a life of adventure. 'The kind of adventure that heroes have in novels' is what you said. Do you remember? I do. I have a wonderful memory. That's how I know what you said. See how simple it is? So, you wished for a life of adventure like a novel's hero and that is exactly what I gave you.

"Now, where I think your problem is, when you made your wish you didn't think about the phrasing of it. You must realize that the hero in a novel has no actual life of her own other than what the author gives her during the adventure. In short, when the adventure ends so does the hero.

"You already have a life of your own, so in order to fulfill your wish I had to do one of two things: First, I could remove you from this existence completely and just phase you in and out during each adventure. Second – the one I chose – was to allow this life to continue and draw you temporarily into a different timeline to live out your adventures. When each adventure ended it would put you back into your normal life which would then continue as if it had never been interrupted.

"The first option would be much too difficult because in order to totally wipe out your existence I would have to go back in time and make sure you had never been born. That isn't really an option since messing with the past gets tricky and it's much too easy to mess up other events by accident. The bigger the changes you make, the more likely you will create some unintended and very unpleasant consequences.

"It's all theoretically possible, of course, but it would be such a difficult undertaking I chose the second option. It's not only easier, but it's so much more fun. I get to be the author and set up your adventures and drop you right in the middle, then bring you back when you're done with no changes to this reality. But remember, once you are there, you're on your own. I create the situation, but when you enter the story, it is your responsibility to work your way through it. It's not an adventure if I just swoop in and help any time you get into trouble. See how simple it is?"

"So, I have two lives in two separate timelines?" asked Sonja. "One I was born into, and one that you are creating. And

38

they are both completely separate. While I'm in one timeline, the other stops moving."

"That's good," said Rith. "You followed all that pretty well. Maybe you're smarter than I thought."

"Okay," continued Sonja. "If I'm living in two timelines, how come I got hurt in one timeline and when I came back here, I'm still hurt?"

"Forget what I said about you being smarter than I thought." Rith's tail lashed back and forth in agitation. "Let's see if I can clear this up. You aren't living in two timelines. You are jumping back and forth between them, but it is still you no matter where you are at that moment. Any injuries you have move with you regardless of where you got it or where you're going. You're living both lives, but you aren't living them at the same time. You are alternating from one to the other. That's very important for you to remember because while you now have two lives, you have only one body to live them with. If you get killed during either existence, you are dead in both."

"All right. Stop talking and give me a minute to think. If I'm alternating between these two time lines," said Sonja, trying to get everything straight in her mind, "that means each time I jump to one from the other I'm always returning to the same instant that I left from the time before."

"Yes!" chirped Rith happily. "Now you've got it. See how–"

"–simple it is? Yes," interrupted Sonja. "But that means that the next time I go back to my second life – the one you created – I'll be kneeling next to Robin, and he will still be bleeding to death. Right?"

"Wrong."

"Wait a minute," complained Sonja, losing her patience with all the apparent inconsistencies in Rith's explanation. "I thought you said I would be returning to the same spot that I left."

"No, no, no," said Rith. "You keep forgetting that your other timeline doesn't run in a smooth series of events like this one here. It's a story book life, and a story book ends at the end of the adventure. The next instant after the finish of one story is the beginning of a brand-new story. The sequel, if you will."

"And when I go back it will be the beginning of a brand-new adventure, not just more of the last one?"

"Yes. Correct! I'm becoming optimistic about your intelligence again."

"Great. Is there anything else you feel I should know while you have my attention?"

"Just one more thing. When you are in your other timeline, you will not grow any older regardless of how long you stay there. If you spend a lot of time away from home, I didn't want you appearing to age too quickly to the people on this timeline. It would not do at all for you to suddenly age twenty years in a single moment. To prevent this problem, your age is one factor that I will keep consistent while you are away. Magic does have some advantages."

"That's nice to know. Anything else?"

"That's about everything, I think. Do you understand it all?"

"Probably not," admitted Sonja. Her head was spinning, but she was fairly sure she had followed most of what Rith told her. "I want to talk about this some more tomorrow, but right now, I'm going to take a shower and clean up my shoulder. I don't think the cut is too deep, but it probably needs a bandage. Then I want to lie down and sleep for a week."

"Good, because I'm tired, too. Good night."

G. Allen Wilbanks

With that, Rith settled back onto his ring.

rt: `1`

CHAPTER 4

Sonja awoke to the whisper faint touch of feathers against her cheek. She lay curled in a tight ball in a bed of soft earth, covered by a blanket of white down. Remaining motionless, she listened for any sounds that might give clues as to her location, but she heard only the movement of a light breeze blowing over and past her huddled form. The feathers draping over her were warm and comfortable, so she burrowed deeper into them, enjoying the momentary peacefulness of her new surroundings.

A heartbeat ago, Sonja had been sitting at a tiny wooden desk, listening to her math teacher lecture on material that was so far above her head she could no longer see it. The past half hour had left her so lost that she stopped even trying to follow along with the figures appearing and disappearing on the white board at the front of the classroom.

Glancing at her notebook, she saw it had twice as many little drawings and doodles in it than it did math notes. All this, coupled with the fact that she had to do well on tomorrow's test in order to bring her grade back up above a C, had Sonja frustrated enough that she wanted to cry. In desperation, she held Rith close to her mouth and whispered, "Get me the hell out of here." She wasn't certain it would work, yet suddenly here she was, lying on an open plain in the middle of who knew where, buried in feathers.

From the sun's position in the sky, Sonja figured she had arrived sometime in the mid-morning, assuming of course that the sun was rising instead of setting. With no other frame of reference, she could only guess. A quick exchange with Rith confirmed her suspicions. Lying on the ground under a warm pile of feathers with no one around for miles to bother her was certainly an improvement from the stuffy, overheated classroom she had come from. Sonja did not want to budge from her cozy little bed, but she figured she had to get up at some point or this adventure could never begin.

Upon rising, Sonja discovered a couple of shocking facts. First, was her dress; or rather the lack of it. Other than a white, skin-tight leotard which covered her from hips to ankles, she was naked. The air around her was warm enough she did not feel chilled, still she felt somewhat self-conscious about her exposure. Bare feet and bare everything else from the waist up was not her typical choice of outfits for going outside the house. She quickly scanned her surroundings for some sort of shirt or jacket but found nothing of use in the immediate vicinity.

Her second surprise came during her hunt for additional clothing. Figuring she should grab the white blanket until something more suitable to wear could be found, Sonja grabbed a handful of feathers and tugged. Immediately, all considerations of modesty – or anything else for that matter – completely left her mind. The wonderfully warm blanket of feathers she had been lying under was not a blanket at all. It, or rather they, were two magnificent, snowy-white wings.

And they were *hers!*

Reaching a hand awkwardly behind her, Sonja felt the junctures where each wing merged with the smooth skin of her back. It was an eerie feeling realizing that the feathered limbs were actually attached to her. An extension of her. In response, part of Sonja wanted to run, screaming at Rith to get rid of them, to make this freakshow he had created go away and send her back to math class. Another larger part was fascinated and excited about what a pair of wings might mean. Did having wings mean she would be able ... to fly?

Focusing her attention on the muscles in her back, she was able to slowly extend her new appendages to their full length. Each wing spanned about eight feet from her shoulders and they spread out and up until the feathered tips reached to just above the height of her head. She flapped them once experimentally, to see if she could control their motion. They responded to her thoughts as easily as if she were moving her outstretched arms. She flapped them again a few more times, then drew them back in where they tucked and draped like a cloak down her back.

Sonja continued to extend and retract her wings while standing in place for almost ten minutes before she felt confident that she could reliably control them. Afterwards, she spent another twenty minutes practicing flapping motions; first slowly, then gradually with more speed and power. Before too long, she was ready to try something a little more daring.

Taking a deep breath to calm her nerves, Sonja began to beat her wings in a steady downward motion, building the speed of the movements until she could feel herself being pulled upward. She increased the strength of her strokes, creating a dust cloud that billowed around her like a miniature storm. The dirt stung her face and caused her to cough as she inhaled it into her mouth and nose, but she only flapped harder. As Sonja felt herself lifting from the ground, she kicked off with her feet to give herself some added momentum. A moment later she was in the air, breathing easily as she gained altitude and rose clear of the suffocating cloud of dirt and debris she had created during her liftoff.

Sonja altered the angle of her wing strokes slightly, changing her direction from straight up to a more forward path. She watched the ground glide along beneath her and disappear behind her dangling feet. With a little more practice, she figured out how to travel freely in any direction, including backwards and side to side. She was careful not to go too high while she experimented, lest a momentary lapse of concentration cause her to fall.

"Rith," she said as she hovered in position about six feet off the ground. "I was just thinking."

"About what?" replied Rith, who was also hovering, although with less apparent effort.

"You said that anything that happens to me in either time frame is permanent in both. Right? I was just wondering does that include the wings? When I go back to math class will they still be part of me?"

"Oh, no. Oh, no," nickered the hippoganth. "Anything that you do to yourself is permanent. The wings are magical. I put them there and I'll take them away when I send you back."

Sonja nodded. She was both relieved and a little disappointed that the condition was temporary. The wings were beautiful, and it was thrilling to be able to fly, but it would be extremely difficult to keep them hidden or to find clothes that would fit comfortably over them. This fact probably explained her present attire, she figured. Sonja laughed as she pictured herself explaining to her P.E. teacher that the wings were real and she could not take them off, which was why she was not wearing a gym shirt.

She shook her head to stop the daydreaming and focused her attention back on her exercises. It turned out, flying was the easy part. It was the landings that caused Sonja the most difficulty. The first time she tried to land, she slowed her flapping too soon, causing her to fall and crash painfully to the ground. The speed of her unarrested plummet sent her sprawling into a jumbled ball of arms, legs, and feathers. Rather than give up, Sonja dusted herself off, wincing slightly at the scrapes on the palms of her hands from trying to catch her fall, and launched herself back into the air. With a little coaching from Rith on the next few attempts, she managed to not only hit the ground and stay on her feet, but she figured out how to do it without looking like someone had pushed her down a flight of stairs.

While mastering the basics of flight with her new wings, Sonja took the opportunity to scout out her surroundings. Taking the risk of climbing a few hundred feet, she saw only dirt, dried grasses, scrub brush, and a few stunted trees for miles around. It wasn't quite a desert, but not far from it. To the north of her location, assuming the sun was travelling in an east to west direction like back home, she could see the dark shadowy outline of mountains on the horizon.

Rith had not provided any provisions at the beginning of this adventure, so Sonja figured it was up to her to find water and something to eat. With that goal in mind, she set out toward the mountain range, hoping that a change in location might mean a change in scenery.

In the late morning, or perhaps early afternoon, while Sonja was experimenting with how high and how fast she could go, she attracted the attention of a large blue and white bird. It looked like a blue jay except for the sheer size of it. The bird was two feet long from the point of its beak to the tip of its long slender tail. Although Sonja wasn't certain this world had blue jays, she figured the label was close enough.

The bird screamed at her. It even sounded like a blue jay. A very loud and agitated one.

"Hi," Sonja answered back.

Again, it screeched. This time, sounding off with a tirade of angry sounding squawks that lasted over half a minute while it flew along beside her.

"Don't worry," said Sonja when the jay finally quieted down. "I'll be fine, Dad. And I'll be home in plenty of time for dinner."

With a final over the shoulder chirp that seemed to say, "see that you do," the blue jay turned and flew off in the opposite direction. Sonja watched it go, giggling quietly to herself.

For the rest of that day, Sonja practiced with her new wings, stopping only for brief rests. As she travelled, the dry, barren terrain below gradually changed. Dirt and dying scrub gave way to prairie grass and wildflowers. Trees and larger shrubs began to fill the landscape and foraging animals became more plentiful.

When she found a small stream meandering through the prairie grasses, Sonja dropped down to take advantage of the available water. She was tired and growing dehydrated from a long day of flying. After swallowing several handfuls from the running brook to slake her thirst, she sat down on the shore and dipped her feet into the cool, flowing liquid, reveling at the feel of it on her skin. She even discovered a few wild blackberry bushes growing nearby and, after checking with Rith to be sure they were safe, ate several of the plump juicy fruits. Another drink and a quick splash of water on her face and neck, and Sonja was airborne once more.

By the time the sun set that evening, she was soaring freely and easily through the air as if she had been born to it.

Darkness loomed as the sun descended beyond the horizon, and Sonja was forced to search for a place to settle in for the night. She figured she had covered over fifty miles by air, and she was now far from the open plain where she had begun her journey. She did not reach the mountains that were her initial goal, though she traveled far enough to find an area of foothills and small rock peaks. She selected a shelf of rock under a protective overhang about two hundred feet up the face of a sheer cliff. It appeared to be safe from any predators and a perfect place to hide should there be any rain during the night. No storm clouds threatened the currently pleasant evening, but Sonja knew nothing about the weather patterns here, so it was better to be safe than sorry and soaking wet.

She sat with her knees tucked under her chin and drew her wings around her for warmth. The ledge she had selected was wide enough there was no real risk of falling off while she slept. Not unless she picked tonight to start walking in her sleep.

"Rith," said Sonja as she huddled with her back against the cliff face.

"Yes."

"I'm hungry and thirsty. I haven't had anything to eat since this afternoon."

"That's not my fault," replied Rith.

"I know. But can you do something about it?"

"I could. But I won't," said Rith. "It would interfere with your adventure. Go to sleep, and in the morning, you can look for food and water."

Unhappy, but unable to do anything about it, Sonja did as Rith suggested.

Sonja woke early the next morning. The warmth and light of the morning sun low on the horizon struck her full in the face and temporarily blinded her when she first opened her eyes. Blinking away sleepy tears to clear her blurred vision, she looked out over the landscape hundreds of feet below her. The sunlight had interfered with her sleep, but it had been something else entirely that roused her.

A noise startled her out of her dreamless sleep, but it had been too brief for Sonja to identify the source. She sat up and waited patiently, head cocked and breathing slowly so as to make no sounds herself, wondering if the noise would repeat.

In the stillness, she heard it a second time. Someone was calling out, the voice sharp and high pitched. It was a cry for help coming from directly above her. She scrambled to the edge of the rock shelf where she had spent the night. Trying to lean far enough out on the ledge to see past the overhang of rock above her, Sonja promptly lost her balance and slipped out into open air. Her arms and legs windmilled for solid supports that did not exist, and a few seconds of panicky freefall followed before she remembered her wings. Unfurling her feathered appendages, Sonja opened her wings to their full extension to break her fall.

She righted herself and stopped the uncontrolled downward plunge.

After a moment to calm her racing heart, she climbed back upward in search of the source of the calls for help. Her shoulders and back ached and cramped from the workout they had received the day before, but she felt the knots loosening as the muscles warmed from the exertion of flying again.

Scanning the cliffside, Sonja spotted the problem. A boy, maybe fourteen years old, clung to the face of the cliff, stranded and in immediate danger of falling. One hand held desperately to a crack in the rock while the other attempted futilely to grab a rope dangling just out of reach.

Sonja reacted instinctively. She sped toward the boy and grasped his free hand with both of hers. Bracing herself against the additional weight, she shouted at him to release his hold on the cliff. Reluctantly, the boy did so. He was not particularly heavy, but his weight combined with her own was more than Sonja's newly acquired wings could carry. Her attempt to lift him to safety became a struggle to keep them both from falling helplessly out of control. With her teeth clenched and the already sore muscles of her back straining with the effort, she gave up trying to get him to the top of the cliff and instead concentrated on controlling their descent.

It was a long way down. Sonja could feel the fatigue in her back muscles as her wings fought against the increasingly tenacious pull of gravity, but she persevered and, somehow kept the two of them in one piece. The landing was a bit jarring, but still infinitely better than it might have been for the boy without his rescuer's timely intervention.

When they were safely on the ground, Sonja, puffing from the unplanned morning workout, allowed herself to plop down in the dirt and catch her breath. Sitting at the boy's feet, she got her first good look at the unfortunate climber and was shocked to discover he was not completely human.

He appeared mostly normal, with one head, two arms and two legs, and he was about the right size for a young human boy, but it was still very clear that Rith had brought Sonja someplace far from Earth. The boy's skin sparkled in the sunlight with the deep metallic color of yellow gold. In addition to the odd skin color, there was something not quite natural about his eyes. Long blond hair tumbled across his face, almost, but not quite, covering two large almond-shaped pools of pale lavender that stared back at her.

The boy wore a simple black and yellow, cloth skirt wrapped about his waist and tied in place with a leather cord. A long, pointed dagger hung at his right hip, the blade resting in a metal ring attached to his belt.

"What were you doing up there?" asked Sonja when she was certain she could speak without panting. She climbed to her feet and set her hands on her hips, still a bit shaken from the ordeal. This morning's wakeup call was not something she would ever care to repeat.

The boy did not meet her eyes. He dropped his head and stared at the ground in front of his feet. When he spoke, his words were hesitant, as if choked by guilt or shame. He wiped at a tear that tracked down one dirty cheek. "I... I was trying to get to you."

"Get to me? Why?"

"Because I wanted to ... kill you." The boy peered up at Sonja, gazing at her through the curtain of hair hiding the top half of his face. He watched her closely, perhaps to gauge her reaction to his admission. His wide, expressive eyes shone with remorse and another tear traced a wet line to his chin.

"I saw you last night when you settled into the cliff. I thought you were a demon, so I took the path to where it crossed just above you. I waited for enough light this morning to climb down the cliff and kill you in your sleep. I thought I could then take your wings as proof I had killed an evil spirit and return home a hero." He bowed his head again, unable to meet her eyes any longer. "But I know now that you are a good spirit and not a demon. You saved me instead of letting me fall, and a demon would not care if I lived or died. Please, don't be angry with me."

Sonja could not see his face, but his shoulders began to shake, and she could hear his quiet sobs.

"I'm not angry with you," she said, placing a hand on the boy's head and stroking his hair. "In fact, I'm glad you're here. If you don't mind, you can do me a big favor."

The boy looked up, instantly hopeful and eager.

"First," said Sonja, "tell me your name."

"I am Ma-orph," he said, proudly puffing out his chest. "I am a hunter for my village."

"Well, Ma-orph, I'm Sonja, and I am very hungry. Will you take me somewhere I can get something to eat?"

"Of course," said the boy without hesitation. "Follow me and I will take you to my village. They will feed you there and treat you with respect. They would not dare offend such a great spirit."

Sonja would have explained that she was not a "great spirit," but she was afraid she might hurt Ma-orph's feelings. Besides, what was wrong with a little hero worship if it got her something to eat?

They set out for Ma-orph's home. The boy led on foot and, while Sonja could have walked with him, she preferred to glide overhead. It gave her a better view of her surroundings and she figured it allowed her more to time to react to whatever they happened to stumble across on their journey. Occasionally she glanced down and saw Ma-orph with his head crooked back, watching her in wonder. Each time, she laughed and waved at him. He would wave back to her then quickly drop his head, embarrassed to have been caught staring.

From her vantagepoint, Sonja spotted the collection of grass huts and houses several minutes before they actually arrived in the village. When she saw the homes and the well-worn path that Ma-orph was now following, she decided the area was probably safe, so she landed beside the boy and walked with him the remaining distance.

Upon reaching the first of the houses, Sonja and Ma-orph were met by a crowd of curious people. Someone had seen them approaching and word had spread quickly. The people gathered all had the same golden coloring as Ma-orph, and their over-sized eyes shone in the sunlight with differing shades of purple varying from Ma-orph's pale lavender tint to a darkness that was almost black in some of the older villagers. They all wore handmade clothing, the men dressed in only a skirt wound around their hips, while the women were draped from neck to ankle in clothes of brightly patterned yellows, oranges, and reds. The only decoration or adornment worn by anyone that Sonja could see was a dagger carried on the hip of each of the men.

After seeing the women in the village, Sonja was reminded that she had nothing covering her above the waist, however it was much too late to do anything about that now. Ma-orph had not seemed bothered by her lack of clothing, so she had to hope none of the villagers would have an issue with it either. As they walked into the crowd, Sonja raised her chin and smiled. If she acted like this was all totally normal, maybe everyone else would, too.

"Clear a way!" shouted Ma-orph into the crowd. Sonja walked with the boy leading her forward by the hand. "Run and bring your best offerings of food and drink for a good spirit who desires them. Go!"

Most did as the boy demanded, returning almost immediately with offerings of a multitude of foods on trays of wood or woven grasses, as well as water and fruit juices in clay pots. Sonja was ushered to a large open ground in the center of the village, and there she was given a blanket on which to sit. Ma-orph waved an urgent hand at her, indicating she should not wait to partake of the feast that was being laid before her.

"Eat," he insisted. "There is more if this is not enough."

Sonja indulged whole-heartedly. She sampled an amazing assortment of jerked meats, fruits, and nuts; some delightful to the taste, and others which, after one sample, she carefully avoided touching again. Besides the water and many types of fruit juices, there was also an abundance of one sweet, milky drink that, from the sharp aftertaste, Sonja was certain was fermented at least to some degree. The taste was pleasant, however, and she helped herself freely to it whenever it was offered.

After perhaps thirty minutes of non-stop eating and drinking, Sonja found herself feeling sated and relaxed. Her belly was pleasantly full, perhaps a little overfull if she were being honest, and she found herself waving away additional dishes as they were held out for her to try.

"Thank you, no," she said to a woman trying to hand her a small bowl of dried fruit. "I'm so full. That's enough. Really, I'm good."

Sonja leaned back and propped herself up on her hands. The sharp, milky drink was starting to affect her, and she smiled blurrily at the people gathered around her. For no reason, she began to giggle helplessly. The whole idea of being here among these people suddenly seemed hilariously funny.

"You are pleased with our offering?" asked a voice from behind Sonja. Up until now, the villagers had merely placed items in front of her then stepped away respectfully to quietly observe as she ate. This was the first person besides Ma-orph to speak to her since she had arrived in the village. She looked around and saw an older man – he looked to be about her father's age – looming over her. He was not tall, but he was stocky and powerfully built. He stood in a manner that suggested he was used to being in a position of control. His face was stern, though more thoughtful than threatening as he peered down at her. Perhaps he was merely appraising the intentions of the visiting spirit in his home.

"Yes. Everything is wonderful," said Sonja, forcing herself to stop laughing but unable to completely wipe a smile from her face. "Who are you?"

"I am Chamere," replied the man. "I am the chief of the Tribe Council."

So, you're sort of in charge then." Sonja staggered to her feet, realizing as she did that the drink had affected her more than she previously thought. "You did a wonderful job. Nice skin color. I've always loved gold." Her comment sent her off on a new round of giggling.

Chamere did not seem offended. He merely smiled at her, as though he too understood the joke.

"It is early in the day," he said. "But perhaps you would like to lie down and rest."

"What? Alone?" Sonja winked at him. Then, realizing what she had just said, she cleared her throat and amended, "Yes, maybe I should lie down before I fall down."

Chamere smiled again and, taking her arm, he led her from the clearing and away from the gathered crowd. He brought her to a small slat-walled building with a grass roof, much like most of the other buildings she had seen since arriving here. He motioned for Sonja to enter, then followed her inside. There were no lights inside, but the interior of the hut was well illuminated by the sun coming through numerous cracks and gaps in the walls. Sonja could see everything in the room clearly. There was not much to see, however: only a bed of straw with cloth bindings to hold it together on one side of the room and a hand-made wooden chair beside a small table on the other.

Sonja turned to thank Chamere. She froze with the words only half out of her mouth as she watched him close and latch the door. He removed his belt and skirt and dropped them to the ground.

"In spite of your color, your face is very beautiful," he said, though his gaze never reached her face. His eyes were focused several inches lower. "I will enjoy the touch of a spirit."

Sonja screamed as Chamere moved toward her. The door remained closed and secure. No one rushed to her rescue.

"Screaming will not help. No one would dare enter this place without my permission."

He leapt forward and caught Sonja, grabbing her by her shoulders. With an iron grip he pulled her to him, caressing her roughly. Sonja screamed again and fought back, flailing with her fists and slashing at him with her fingernails, but the stocky man pinned her to one of the flimsy walls of the hut. In desperation, she brought her knee up to his groin, fast and hard. With a hiss of pain and surprise, Chamere took one step back before crumpling to the dirt floor.

Free of the man's grasp, Sonja stumbled to the door, pulled loose the latch, and bolted for freedom. As soon as she was outside, she searched for Ma-orph, panting and staring wild-eyed at the villagers once again clustered around her. Chamere staggered out after her, hastily refastening his skirt. His dark, amethyst eyes burned with rage.

He glared at Sonja, contemplating terrible murderous thoughts. Then, suddenly, unexpectedly, he smiled. It was not a pleasant smile. It was a smile that said some sort of battle had been won.

"You bleed, Spirit," he said, gesturing to Sonja's shoulder where she had been injured only two days ago in Sherwood Forest. The cut was healing, but when Chamere grabbed her, the scab had cracked and torn away. Blood ran down her left arm in small but steady drops.

"Spirits are not supposed to bleed. Devils bleed, however, because they draw blood from their human victims."

The village leader turned to face his people. "Take up weapons," he screamed, pulling his dagger and motioning for others to do the same. "Kill this demon that has come to destroy us."

Several men followed his example, drawing their own weapons. They advanced on Sonja, at first hesitantly, then, as she backed away, with more purpose. Her retreat and the obvious fear in her expression emboldened her attackers, and she could see others drawing weapons and joining the men she already faced.

"Rith," she cried. "Do something!"

Rith was immediately by her, hovering in front of her face. "I told you," he said sadly, "you have to do this yourself. I won't help you."

"A *little* demon," shouted Chamere, spying Rith. "Kill them both and punish the boy who brought them among us."

In her panic, Sonja had momentarily forgotten her magnificent wings. Seeing Rith in the air beside her reminded her of what she could do. On the ground, she was helpless, but she did not need to remain on the ground. Sonja spread her wings and launched herself skyward, rising above the level of the wooden huts and circling above the angry villagers. Fortunately, these people did not seem to have advanced sufficiently to invent bows or any other projectile weapons. For the moment, she was safely out of their reach. She decided not to stay and gloat, however. It was time to go.

A terrified shout wrenched Sonja's attention away from her escape plan.

Searching the ground for the source of the cry, Sonja saw Ma-orph fall at the hands of another man. The boy's throat had been cut; his body cast aside and left to spill its life out onto the sand. Not pausing to think about what she was doing, Sonja dove toward Ma-orph. She drew her wings back against her body and let gravity pull her down as fast as it wished. She did not attempt to slow her fall until the last possible instant. Her wings billowed out, reversing her orientation, and driving her feet into the man who had cut Ma-orph and now stood over him, watching him die. She felt her heel strike the back of his neck; a jarring impact that vibrated up the entire length of her leg. With a sickening popping noise, the man's head snapped back from the force of the unexpected blow. The speed of Sonja's fall drove them both to the ground, and she was forced to roll across the hard-packed earth, somersaulting once before bouncing back to her feet, prepared to follow up her initial attack. There was no need. The man she had struck made no attempt to move.

Sonja scrambled to Ma-orph's limp form and grasped one of his hands in her own. She gazed into his unfocused eyes and searched for signs of life. For an instant, she saw recognition dawn in the golden face and she felt his grip tighten. He tried to speak, but he had lost too much blood already and she could only watch helplessly as the boy's body relaxed for the last time, and his beautiful lavender eyes closed forever.

Sonja wanted to cry, to scream out her pain at the sky, but she was given no time to grieve. Chamere continued shouting orders and urging his mob onward. While she held Ma-orph's lifeless hand, the villagers once again managed to surround Sonja. She considered taking to the air, but that thought disappeared only half-formed, drowned under a red haze.

She was done with running.

Anger now ruled her actions, and Sonja was not going anywhere until she vented the hot ball of hate that burned inside her. Everything she considered unimportant faded from her consciousness: the noise, the heat, the villagers pressing in on her, even the dull ache in her injured shoulder so recently reawakened. All that existed in her mind at that moment was herself and the man responsible for Ma-orph's death. Not the one who had wielded the blade; he was only a tool. Sonja wanted the one who wielded the power.

Grabbing the dagger from Ma-orph's belt, Sonja launched herself forward at her target. Chamere's voice, still bellowing threats and spewing venom, acted as a guide, allowing her to home in and locate the source of her outrage. It required only a moment to orient herself and fly directly for him. She held the dagger in both hands, straight out in front of her; a gleaming silver arrow pointing the way.

Sonja could not see the last moments before impact. Tears of rage and loss effectively blinded her. It didn't matter, Chamere's shouts were enough to tell her where to go. There was the slightest instant of resistance against the point of her knife before she felt it push through flesh, and Chamere's bellowed orders became a scream of pain. His final cry was cut short as the steel blade found his heart and Sonja's hurtling body crashed into his.

CHAPTER 5

Sonja screamed and lurched to her feet. Her chair and desk combo tangled around her hips, throwing her off balance and spilling her to the floor with a loud crash. All eyes in the classroom turned toward her as she scrambled to separate herself from the school desk and stand up. Turning her back to all the surprised faces, she wiped at the tears on her cheeks with a shaking hand.

"Sonja?" asked her teacher with a concerned tone to his voice. "Are you all right?"

She turned to face the math teacher, her face flaming hot with embarrassment and leftover adrenaline. "I'm... Yes, I'm okay! I ... I must have leaned too far back and fell. I'm really sorry, Mr. Wilson."

It was a lame excuse, but it was the first thing that came to mind. Several students in the class began to laugh, but at least they had turned back to the front of the room and were no longer staring at her.

Her teacher continued to stare at her oddly. He pointed a finger toward her and said, "You hurt yourself. You should go to the nurse and get that looked at."

Sonja glanced down, trying to understand what her teacher was pointing at. It took her a moment to realize the problem. The left sleeve of her t-shirt was turning a dark red, and a thin trickle of blood had escaped to run down her arm. She clapped a hand to the injury, trying to stop any further bleeding.

"I will," she blurted. "Go see the nurse, I mean. I'm sorry about... I just... I'm sorry!"

Grabbing her backpack, Sonja threw her math book and note pad inside, zipped it shut and fled the class. She had no intention of going to the nurse and trying to explain how she had cut herself. Instead, she left the school campus and half walked, half ran home. Math was her last class of the day and there had only been twenty or so minutes left before the bell. No one would miss her.

When she got to her house, she let herself in the front door. She was earlier than most days, but with any luck, her dad wouldn't notice the time. She called out to him to let him know she was home, and her dad responded from his den. He did not come out to greet her. Relieved, Sonja went directly to her room.

She dropped her backpack on the floor, grabbed her bathrobe and some extra clothing, then locked herself in the bathroom that she and her brother shared. Less than five minutes later, she was lying in a tub of water heated as hot as she could possibly stand it. She let the heat and steam soak the blood from her arm and sooth her shattered nerves.

Her clothes lay nearby, heaped on the bathroom floor where she had tossed them; her shirt stained with the drying blood from her shoulder. She knew she would have to do something eventually to try to clean the shirt, but at the moment, blood on her clothing was the absolute last thing on her mind. The hot bath let her relax, but it also gave her time to think about what had happened.

"Damn it, Rith. Why are you doing this to me?" Tears spilled down her cheeks again as visions of Ma-orph's death, and everything that had followed began to surface in her mind. She had successfully suppressed the memories while she was at school, focusing instead on getting herself out of class and away from the campus, but now that she was safely back home, they all came flooding back.

"I'm not doing anything to you," said Rith. He sat on the edge of the tub, relaxing in the steam from the hot water. He seemed oblivious to her discomfort. "You're doing it all to yourself by making mistakes."

"Mistakes?!" cried Sonja angrily. She sat up and glared at Rith, the water in her bath sloshing almost to the edge of the tub at her sudden movement. "What mistakes?"

"First," said the tiny figure calmly, "you never should have screamed when the Sheriff's men were so close. You should have known they were going to hear you. Second, you should not have been drinking so much of that native booze in the village. If you had kept your head clear you would have seen what Chamere had in mind a lot sooner. You made some bad mistakes, and they came at a cost."

Sonja opened her mouth, then closed it, unsure what she was going to say.

"But don't worry," continued Rith. "You learn from making mistakes. As you go on, you will become much better at making decisions and weighing the consequences of what you do. Just try to remember to think about everything you do before you do it."

Sonja listened to Rith's explanation and felt the energy slowly drain out of her. She was still angry, but she was also emotionally exhausted. She nodded reluctantly as she realized that Rith was probably right. She had no reason to lay the blame for what happened anywhere but at her own feet. If she had considered the results of her actions more carefully, she might have avoided the tragedies that followed.

So far, Sonja had treated her adventures like a game rather than recognizing the seriousness of the situations she found herself in. She vowed not to make that mistake again. She sighed and wiped the tears from her face with the back of her hand.

"Those were lousy situations you put me in," she told the little hippoganth.

"They were adventures, just like you wished for. If that wasn't what you wanted, you should have wished for something else."

Sonja nodded again, too tired to argue any longer.

"Did you have to return me to math in such bad shape, though?" she asked.

"The adventure was over, and it was time to send you back," explained Rith. "All I could do for you was put you back in your own clothes, clean off some of the dirt, and maybe straighten your hair a little. I can't change any emotional or physical injury."

"I'm tired," she said, stating the obvious.

"You are probably still a little drunk, too."

Sonja covered her face with her hands and began to cry again. Her sobs were silent, but her shoulders and chest heaved with the exertion of staying quiet. She did not want her father to hear her as she tried to choke out the burning knot that had formed in her throat.

"I killed them, Rith," she whispered when she felt she could safely speak. "I let the boy die, then I killed two people. I killed two people."

"Yes, and no." Rith fluttered over to hover next to her. "Yes, you killed them. But, no, you didn't really kill people. I created the adventure. I created all the characters in it. They did not exist before you got there, and they no longer exist now that you are gone. What happened while you were there, does not change any of that."

"That helps," said Sonja, though her eyes still glittered with forming tears. "But I didn't know that at the time. What does that say about me? That I could be so angry I could kill someone?"

"It tells me that you cared very much for a boy you hardly knew. It tells me that you are very protective of people close to you and you would do anything to help them."

Sonja coughed and sniffed noisily. "So, they weren't real?"

"Not this time," Rith agreed. "To be clear, sometimes they will be. Some adventures I will create, but for others, I may take you places that already exist. You won't know the difference unless you ask me, so you may just want to assume it's real every time. The worst part..."

Rith paused a moment as if gathering his thoughts, or perhaps deciding if he should continue.

"The worst part?" Sonja prompted.

"The worst part is that in some adventures, there will be people who try to hurt or kill you, and you will have to make the same decision again. Can you do that?"

Sonja shrugged. "I don't know," she admitted. "Do I have to decide right now? Can I think about it?"

"Of course!" piped Rith, a little too cheerfully considering the conversation they had been having. He dove straight down to plop into the water. Sonja watched his rippling form swim to her hand and settle onto his ring. She sighed and closed her eyes.

She needed to wash her bloody clothes and try to bandage her cut so it wouldn't open again. She also had homework and a math test to study for.

But not now, she told herself. All those things could wait a few more minutes. Just a few more minutes. Sonja let herself slip deeper into the tub and the soothing embrace of the steaming water.

CHAPTER 6

Two months passed after Sonja's disastrous experience with flying. The chill, sporadic rains of late winter surrendered to the warmer, sun-filled afternoons of spring, and Sonja's normally positive outlook returned with the improving weather. The death of Ma-orph and her own killing of two men still echoed within her, making her hesitant to try any further quests, but as time soothed the initial shock of the event, the growing allure of setting out upon another adventure could not be denied.

This time, Sonja selected a day in which she was home and completely alone to initiate her request. She did not want a repeat of the scene she had created in class after returning so abruptly last time. She also asked Rith if it would be possible to create an adventure that was not quite as intense as her meeting with Ma-orph. Maybe he could come up with something a little more light-hearted. Rith agreed, but only after pointing out that it was not going to be his fault if her next trip turned out to be boring.

"Boring doesn't sound too bad," she told the little hippoganth as she flopped back on her bed and stared up at the ceiling. "No. I take that back. If I really wanted boring, I could just stay home." She sighed dramatically. "Okay, we'll do it your way. What have you got in mind?"

The next instant, Sonja found herself dressed in the flowing pink robes of a princess, complete with silk slippers and a tall conical hat with a veil draping down the length of her back. Her house had been replaced by a formidable stone castle, although Sonja had the immediate impression that it was not her castle. She might have been dressed like a young lady of royal privilege, but Rith had not deposited her among the comforts of the castle's throne room. Instead, he had placed her inside a small, windowless room surrounded by walls of rock and mortar.

She was in a dungeon.

Carelessly strewn hay unevenly covered the floor, and through gaps in the straw covering, Sonja could see the glistening of damp paving stones. She wrinkled her nose at the dank smell of rot and mildew pervading the air around her. There was another more sweetly acrid smell in the room as well, but she tried hard not to think about what it might be.

Sonja attempted to take a step forward but was brought up short. Rusting steel manacles bound her wrists and ankles, holding her firmly in place. She pulled against the restraints a few times, testing their strength and discovering she was securely bound.

"Shit," she breathed, giving her right hand one last frustrated yank.

The only light in the chamber came from a single oil lamp suspended on a metal bracket beside the cell door. The door was only a few feet away at the far end of the cell, but the short lengths of chain between her manacles and the metal bolts fastened to the wall behind her kept her from reaching either it or the lamp nearby. Not that it would have done Sonja much good if she could get to the door. The heavy wooden slab reinforced with wide bands of hammered iron looked more than capable of resisting any efforts she might make to escape.

The surrounding gloom pressed in on her, barely held at bay by the flickering flame of the lamp. The unstable light source caused everything in the room to appear to move in jerky uncontrolled motions, including two large rats huddled in one corner. The vermin peered at her, apparently undecided as to whether Sonja was a threat or food.

The stone cell measured about nine feet by nine feet; normally plenty of space to move around were she not so securely clamped to one wall. Sonja typically did not have issues with either dark or enclosed spaces, but the dreary atmosphere of this cell had her feeling more than a little claustrophobic.

"What the hell is going on?" she asked so suddenly the rats bolted off through a crack in the wall. She shook her right fist, making the chain links ring against one another. "Are you trying to get me killed, Rith?"

Rith appeared in front of her, buzzing from side to side in excited bursts of motion. "Of course not," he reassured her. "If you die, it will be due to no effort on my part. Of course, you could certainly put yourself into a more dangerous situation with your penchant for making poor decisions, but I would recommend against it."

Sonja blew out a slow breath through her nose, calming herself. She knew getting upset with Rith was pointless and, especially right now, counterproductive. "Can you at least tell me a little bit about what's going on? Why am I here?"

"I suppose you are entitled to a little of the backstory," Rith allowed. "You are a princess. You are in a cell in the castle dungeon."

Sonja rattled her chains again. "I've figured that much already. Anything else?"

"Yes. You have been captured by an evil sorcerer who wants you to marry him. You, of course, have refused, and so he locked you up here. See how simple it is? Now, in about five minutes – give or take for unforeseen circumstances – a handsome prince is going to break in here and free you from your shackles. That is when your adventure begins. You must get out of the castle before either the sorcerer recaptures you, or you get stopped by one of his guards."

"Isn't that story line a little old?" asked Sonja. "Damsel in distress? Stuck in a dungeon waiting for rescue?"

"Maybe. But if you do it right, it should still be a lot of fun."

Sonja did not argue. Even if the premise was trite, this was still an adventure and she figured she should get into the right mindset. Rith had been correct about her making poor decisions before when she had not taken his scenarios seriously. This adventure might prove exciting. It could also prove extremely dangerous. Dungeons. Guards. And how was she supposed to protect herself from whatever magic this unknown sorcerer might have? Rith would probably be no help. He had already demonstrated his lack of desire to get involved once a storyline was underway. All she could do now was wait to be freed by the prince and then face each situation as it came. At least it wasn't too cold and, aside from the uncomfortable manacles, she wasn't in any real distress.

Sonja heard footsteps outside her cell door. A hushed voice reached her ears. "Lady Sonja. Are you in there?"

"He knows my name," whispered Sonja in surprise. Then louder, "Yes. Get me out."

"Of course, he knows your name," said Rith. "Do you think he would risk his life for someone he doesn't know?"

"But I don't know *him*."

"Sure you do," answered the hippoganth. "That is your fiancée. You are getting married next month, assuming you live that long. His name is Kevin."

"Prince Kevin," said Sonja, and giggled. "Okay. I'm being rescued by Prince Kevin. My fiancée, Prince Kevin."

The lock disengaged with an audible click and the cell door swung open. Through the opening stepped a tall man who looked to be maybe a year or two older than Sonja. Long, curly black hair framed equally black, sparkling eyes. His nose curved slightly left from having been broken at some time in his life, but rather than detracting from his appearance, Sonja thought it made his face handsome rather than merely boyishly pretty. Dressed in gray and black, Prince Kevin resembled a thief, or maybe a pirate, and the rapier sheathed at his hip completed the image. He was currently fumbling with a ring of keys, searching for a particular item.

"Who else is in here?" he asked, still focused on his keys.

"No one," answered Sonja.

"Who were you talking to?"

"Oh. I was just, um … the rats. I was talking to the rats. Did you know they make great pets? They really know how to listen."

"No, I did not." He gave Sonja an odd look before holding up a slender, brass-colored key and reaching for her chains. The shackles fell away one by one as the key slid into each lock and popped them open. As soon as she was free, Sonja flung her arms around the prince's neck. If a helpless princess was the role Rith wanted her to play, then she was determined to play her part to the hilt.

"Thank God you've come to rescue me, Kevin," she wailed. "I thought surely I was going to die in this horrible place."

"If for one moment you believed I would not come for you, then your faith in me is less than I would have hoped." He disengaged her arms from his neck. "But come. We must move from this place quickly."

Sonja felt a momentary twinge of guilt as she realized how sincere Kevin was. Whether Rith had arranged it or not, this man seemed to genuinely care for her and was currently risking his own life to save hers. She mentally chastised herself for playing games and resolved to take her situation more seriously.

Leaving the cell, Kevin led her by the hand down the corridor to the right. His touch was firm and warm, and suddenly Sonja found herself very much concerned for how this adventure turned out. Kevin was only here because of her, and that meant she had a responsibility to make sure he stayed safe. Sonja promised herself nothing would harm Kevin while she was around. Not if she could prevent it.

"Do you know where we're going?" she asked, trying hopelessly to keep her headpiece from falling off as she ran. The tall hat behaved as though it would prefer to be on the ground rather than on her head.

"Yes. This is the way I came in. I don't know if it's the most direct route, but it is the only one I know." Kevin noticed Sonja's difficulty. He paused to pluck the cap from her head and toss it aside. "Leave it. Anything that distracts you from our escape is a hindrance and not worth holding onto."

G. Allen Wilbanks

Sonja did as Kevin suggested. She did not want to leave the hat behind – it was beautiful, and the princess outfit just did not seem complete without it – but she knew Kevin was right. She left the lovely nuisance where Kevin dropped it and moved on.

After only a few seconds more of fast traveling, Kevin brought them to an abrupt stop. Sonja slid to a halt behind him.

"What's wrong?" she asked.

"Quiet," whispered Kevin. "I dropped a guard somewhere near here, but I don't see his body."

Drawing his rapier and motioning for Sonja to stay behind him, Kevin inched forward. The passageway they occupied stretched before them, empty and silent. Although no visible threat existed, they approached two closed doors, one on each side of the hall. Either door could be hiding an ambush.

Kevin positioned himself opposite the first door. The handle was an iron bar, twisted into an 'L' shape and adorned with spirals of silver and gold thread. Kevin laid a tentative hand on the latch and applied gradual pressure. It turned without effort. With a sudden push, he threw the door inward while skipping back and bringing his blade between himself and anyone that might come rushing out. He stood poised for a long moment, ready for an attack, then Sonja saw him relax and smile slightly.

"So, this is what he was guarding," said Kevin, lowering his weapon to peer inside the room.

Sonja went to her tiptoes and peeked around his shoulder so she could see what he had found. It was a library, but like no library she had ever seen before. Scrolls and books of all sizes lined every wall. Two massive wooden desks placed on opposite ends of the room were littered with yellowed papers and tattered, leather-bound volumes. Various documents covered every

73

available free space along the entire circumference of the room, but what caught Sonja's eye was not the items along the walls.

In the middle of the room, a tall, elaborately carved, wooden stand held an enormous leather-bound tome. The book was easily four feet wide and equally as tall. It had been left open on its pedestal, as though someone had been reading a passage from its pages and only recently stepped away. Sonja wondered briefly what information she might find in a volume like this one, but her main interest wasn't in the contents, rather it was the object suspended directly above the monstrous book that fascinated her.

A spherical gem, as large as her fist, hovered seemingly unsupported in the air, casting an eerie, diseased green light. Sonja leaned forward to get a better look, but Kevin's hand on her arm stopped her.

"Never enter a Sorcerer's library without permission," he said. "It could easily prove fatal."

Sonja started to reply but Kevin stepped away, already moving towards the second door in the hallway. As he reached for the ornate iron handle, the door swung open on its own. Kevin had only enough time to retreat several steps and assume a defensive crouch before four men rushed out to block the corridor. All four held weapons; two handling rapiers like Kevin's, while the others gripped long black spears topped with duel-edged blades. None of the men looked particularly friendly.

"Only four?" asked Sonja, mildly surprised.

"I think four is quite sufficient," said Kevin. He cautiously began to back away.

"But I would have expected more."

"A magician as powerful as Moribus has very little need of human minions. I would say we were lucky to be facing men instead of … something else."

Kevin continued to retreat, keeping Sonja behind him as he did. His eyes never left the four guards, so he was prepared when the two spearmen lowered their weapons and charged. They lunged forward, spear points balanced level with Kevin's heart, hoping to kill him quickly. They gauged him to be the greater threat and figured with him down, they could deal with Sonja at their leisure. The young prince was not so disposed to dying as they had hoped.

Kevin moved as though he had been trained all his life for just such an encounter. He slid forward and to his left, avoiding the first attacker's spear thrust. With an upward slash of his blade, he deflected the second. Another step brought him within sword range of the two men. Without hesitation, he took the offensive and initiated an attack of his own. With his free hand, Kevin grabbed the shaft of the second man's spear. A sharp jerk and twist wrenched it free from the surprised guard's grasp. Tossing the captured weapon behind him he shoved the unarmed man back with a lowered shoulder, then used the momentum of his attack to drive him toward the first spearman. He countered another clumsy strike with a parry from his sword and followed up by driving a bootheel into his armed opponent's knee. Sonja heard a loud pop, and the man screamed once before the tip of Kevin's rapier found his left eye.

The two swordsmen, who up until now had stayed clear of the fighting, decided their comrades no longer had control of the situation and the time had come for them to join the melee. Their approach distracted Kevin long enough for the remaining spearman to roll aside and collect his fallen partner's weapon. The odds had improved slightly, but Kevin remained at a decided disadvantage.

Sonja figured two against three would be better still and stepped in to help. Grabbing the spear Kevin had discarded, she stepped between the prince and the man rising to his feet.

"Go for those two," she ordered Kevin, motioning toward the advancing guards with a nod of her head. "This one is mine."

"But, how can you...?"

"I can. Trust me."

"Sonja..."

"Do you want me to drop you to prove it? Move!"

Kevin paused, obviously wanting to say more, but he realized there was no time. He did as she directed. With a last glance in her direction, he turned forward to meet the two swordsmen.

Sonja did not see the look. All her attention was on the man in front of her. She had never fought with a spear, but the weapon roughly equaled the length and mass of the staff Robin had given her. While the spearman held his weapon near the butt end with the point leveled at Sonja's chest, she held hers roughly horizontal to the floor across her body. She placed her hands near the middle of the shaft about a foot apart, right palm up, left palm down.

"You've never handled a spear before, have you, girl?" leered the guard, eyeing her unfamiliar stance.

"Nope," she admitted.

Sonja made a feint with the spear point. When her opponent moved to intercept her strike, she leaped forward while reversing the direction of her spear, allowing the solid wooden butt of her weapon to rotate 180 degrees and strike his left arm. The guard winced and jerked back from the contact. She did not have an opening for a follow-up attack and did not wish to risk being grabbed, so instead Sonja danced out of range of the man's reach.

"Bitch!" he shouted. "I'll cut you wide open."

He charged, running his weapon straight toward her heart as he had done with Kevin. Sonja stood ready. Holding her spear perpendicular to the floor, she sidestepped and blocked so the dagger-sharp point passed harmlessly by. With a quick flick of her wrist, she struck the guard once to the groin with the bladed end, reversed rotation as his momentum carried him past her, and cracked the shaft of her spear across the man's left temple with enough force to splinter the wood. The guard slumped lifelessly to the floor.

Tossing aside the cracked spear, Sonja hurried to join Kevin as he continued to battle for his life. One swordsman lay on the stone floor, stabbed through the chest, while the other remained on his feet. Even to Sonja's untrained eye, it was obvious the two dueling men were closely matched. Neither seemed to be able to gain an advantage over the other.

Determined to tip the balance, Sonja pried the rapier loose from the hand of the dead swordsman on the floor and, with a wordless cry, she plunged into the fight. She managed to make only one attack, clumsily attempting to stab the point of her sword into the guard's leg before the man cleanly disarmed her. Her interference served as just enough of a distraction for Kevin to find his opening and run his blade through his opponent's throat.

"I thought I would turn around to find you dead," said Kevin when he had checked to be certain all four assailants were no longer a threat. Holding his sword in his right hand, he pulled Sonja to him, wrapping his left arm around her waist.

Sonja thought that in this pose she and Kevin could be a picture on a romance novel. Laughing at the image, she happily returned the embrace, burying her head against his shoulder and enjoying the warmth of his body against hers.

"You should have a little more faith in me," she said somewhat smugly. "I can take pretty good care of myself when I have to."

Kevin looked down at her, and Sonja cocked her head to meet his gaze. "Green," he said with an almost surprised tone. "Your eyes are green."

"Grey, actually," Sonja corrected him. "But there is some gold and yellow in there that make them look green. Or sometimes even blue, in the right light."

"Grey, green or blue, they're beautiful."

Unsure how to respond, Sonja leaned her head back against his shoulder. Although she always enjoyed a nice compliment, Kevin's comment had left her surprisingly pleased. She felt heat rise into her cheeks and she was afraid she might be blushing.

Kevin held her a moment longer before stepping away. "We are not safe yet," he warned. He knelt briefly to clean his blade on the tunic of one of the fallen guards. As he did, he paused to examine something he discovered suspended around the dead man's neck. The man wore some sort of gold or bronze pendant. The centerpiece was the size of Kevin's palm and was shaped like a triangle with horns protruding from it. Etched inside the triangle was an image of the sun.

"What is it?" asked Sonja, happy for the change of topic.

"A talisman," answered Kevin. He removed the chain from around the dead man's neck, then stood up, holding the item triumphantly out to where Sonja could see it plainly. "This is the shield we need. This talisman can ward off demons and protects the bearer from hostile magic."

"Do you think we'll need it?"

"I don't know. But I think finding this says good things about our chances of escaping."

"How much further do we have to go?"

"Another few hundred feet along this corridor and we will come to another doorway. This one will lead to the castle's ballroom. That chamber is huge, but on the opposite side of it we reach the main exit and then we'll be free of this dismal place. I can't wait to breath clean air again." Kevin replaced his sword on his hip and slipped the amulet over his head. He held out a hand toward Sonja and she accepted it.

Together, they jogged along the remaining stretch of hallway and soon reached the ballroom entrance Kevin had mentioned. Like the previous doors, this one was also unlocked and it opened easily, revealing the cavernous castle ballroom behind it. The room was cavernous not only in its size, but in appearance.

Granite walls curved, stark and austere, climbing to meet each other and forming an expansive dome overhead. Marbled stone ribs provided support but did nothing to mitigate the menacing appearance of the space. A darkness clung to the room that no number of torches could dispel, and in every corner, black patches of shadow danced and shifted ominously.

The hall was bare of any decoration except for a pedestal and throne carved from a single piece of stone and placed in the center of the floor. Gray and rough-cut, the rock centerpiece was a foreboding feature despite being draped and surrounded by cushions and blankets of all colors imaginable. Rather than lending cheer to the chair, the massive stone furniture seemed to leech the color away from the items adorning it.

At the far end of the imposing room towered fifteen-foot tall, twin oak doors representing freedom for Sonja and Kevin. This was their way out. Unfortunately, the throne was directly between them and their planned exit, and lounging in that chiseled, stone chair stretched the brooding form of Moribus himself.

The sorcerer was incredibly thin; his flowing, purple robes hung on his emaciated figure like a sheet modeled on a skeleton. His hair fell straight, long and snowy white around his bony shoulders, and a pointed beard the same color of ivory fell to the center of his chest. Icy blue eyes sparkled from under the sharp lines of his brow, focusing on the fleeing pair. He smiled, and the expression on his skull-like visage was more frightening than any threat he could have made. The sorcerer unfolded from his throne to greet his two visitors, rising to his full stature of six and a half feet. Standing on the stone dais, he towered above Sonja and Kevin.

"I had a feeling you were going to get through," he said. His voice was strong and firm despite his frail appearance. "In fact, I was hoping you would. Now, I can deal with you myself."

"If you can, wizard," growled Kevin, pulling Sonja once more behind him. He removed the pendant from around his neck and held it toward the towering figure of Moribus. "Talisman, I invoke thee!"

A pale blue light emanated from the pendant, faint at first, but quickly growing brighter. The sun in the triangle appeared to move, beginning to rotate as the talisman flared and a spear of white energy blazed forth toward Moribus. The beam struck the sorcerer, bathing him in its luminescence, but the man merely laughed as the light surrounded him. He stood in the center of the burning corona, outlined by its brilliance but otherwise untouched and unaffected.

"You think a weapon of my own creation could ever harm me?" he crowed, contempt twisting his features. "You have made a grave mistake."

He held out a skeletal hand and the wild energy surrounding him focused through his outstretched arm and returned to the talisman.

Kevin cried out in pain as the pendant's glow changed to an angry red color before turning to molten slag in his hand. He dropped to his knees, throwing the melting remains of the pendant aside and clutching the injured hand to his body. Sonja knelt beside him, grabbing at his arm to see how badly he was hurt. The skin of Kevin's palm was red, blistered, and raw.

Sonja tore a strip of cloth from the hem of her dress and tried to wrap the injury, though she knew little about first aid and was unsure if a bandage would help.

"Yes, Princess," said Moribus. "Tend to your brave prince. But who will tend to you when you lie writhing on the cold stone floor, still alive even as your flesh is stripped from your delicate little bones?"

Moribus lifted his hand once more. Sonja hunched her shoulders and shifted to shield Kevin with her body from whatever the sorcerer had planned. After all he had done for her thus far, it was time to repay the debt, even if the effort was futile.

A flash of brilliant white light jumped from the sorcerer's fingertips. Sonja covered her eyes with one arm and extended her other hand in a vain attempt to block the blast of searing white fire. She felt the impact along her outstretched arm and a slight heat warming her palm, but there was no pain. In amazement, she looked at her hand and saw her ring was glowing a dull orange color. Rith launched into the air, his fast, sporadic flight announcing his agitation.

"This is my fault," Rith told her. "You aren't ready for this. You don't know anything about magic. Okay. Okay. Okay. I'm going to fix this, just tell me what to do."

"Do? What do you mean, tell you what to do? I guess, do anything. Get us out of here."

Moribus released another bolt of light, but again Rith moved to intercept it. The attack flared and winked out of existence still several feet away from Sonja. Her eyes stung and watered from the bright light, but she suffered no other injuries from the sorcerer's assault.

"Pretend you know magic," Rith explained. "You just blocked an attack and it's your turn to fight back. What would you do?"

"I don't know," shouted Sonja. "Can I use fire?"

Rith buzzed up beside Sonja's left ear so he knew she could hear him. "Hold the ring out toward Moribus and yell, 'Fire!'"

Feeling silly, but trusting Rith's direction, Sonja closed her left hand into a fist and held it out so Rith's ring faced the sorcerer. She clenched her teeth and cried out, "Fire!"

A snake of fire uncoiled from her outstretched fist. It struck too fast for Sonja to follow, stretching across the distance between her and the sorcerer and coiling around the emaciated figure on the dais. Moribus did not even have time to scream before the flames extinguished and his empty, smoking robes folded harmlessly to the floor.

Kevin stared at Sonja, his mouth hanging open. "How did you do that?" he asked, trying to regain his composure.

"I didn't. I mean, it's a magic ring," she explained, just as surprised as Kevin by what had happened. "Like your talisman, only stronger, I guess. Look, I think we can talk about it later. Right now..." Sonja pointed at the unguarded double doors.

Kevin did not argue. He grabbed Sonja's hand once more and they fled for the exit. When they reached the mammoth castle doors, they had to push together to get the barricade to move, but there were no further obstacles and the heavy portal slowed them by only a few more seconds before they were able to break free of the castle.

Sonja stepped out onto a dirt path that lead several hundred feet from the castle entrance before disappearing into the trees of a nearby forest. Kevin followed close behind. As soon as she felt the sunlight on her face, Sonja spun around and threw herself into the young prince's arms. He winced slightly when, in her haste, she bumped his injured hand.

"Kiss me, quick, Prince Charming," insisted Sonja. "There isn't much time."

"What do you mean?" asked Kevin. "Now that you are free, we have all the time we want."

"You don't understand. Please, don't argue. Just kiss me."

He did.

CHAPTER 7

Sonja lounged on her bed, hands behind her head, staring at the ceiling. Music blared loudly throughout her bedroom from speakers that she had linked to her phone. The song currently playing was a heavy metal love ballad by a group whose name she could not remember and who had probably broken up years before she had been born. She paid no attention to it. Instead her mind wandered back to a dank castle dungeon, a sorcerer named Moribus, his guards, and Kevin.

Especially Kevin.

Sonja relived the kiss they had shared after their escape, moments before Rith snatched her back to her own timeline. It had begun light and tender, his lips barely brushing her own, but it had quickly grown more passionate. She could almost feel the pressure still on her mouth as she remembered how he pulled her tight against him, one hand sliding up her back to cup her neck, fingers tangling into her hair. The fierceness of her own responding passion had caught her by surprise. Arms wrapped hard around his waist, she had felt like she could never get close enough to him.

And then … he was gone.

"It would have been nice if you had let me stay just a little bit longer," she said, wistfully. Sonja inhaled a long, slow breath and released it in a regretful sigh.

"At least this adventure turned out better than the previous ones," consoled Rith. "It had a happy ending."

"It did. It was a storybook ending," agreed Sonja. "But the story is over, and Kevin is gone. I suppose that's okay, though. It wasn't as if he was real."

"Oh, he was real," said Rith, flying a leisurely circle around the perimeter of Sonja's bedroom. "As real as both of us. It shouldn't be a big surprise to you that there are other people out there making wishes. I wouldn't say he's gone, either. Let's just say he's been shelved for a while. I mean, haven't you ever reread a good book?"

Sonja propped herself up on her hands to stare at the hippoganth drifting lazily from one corner of the room to another. A gleam of surprise and hope shimmered in her eyes. "Real? As in he lives around here, somewhere? So, I could find him and see him again if I wanted to?"

"Yes, and no. Yes, he's real. Yes, you can see him again. But no, not whenever you want. You will see him when *I* want you to see him. Don't worry. I might throw him into another adventure with you, but it probably won't be soon. Especially since you have other things which will be keeping you very busy. Maybe for a long time."

"What things? Like, school?"

Rith nickered his musical little laugh. "School. Yes, like school. But not like the kind of school you are thinking of."

Sonja wrinkled her nose in annoyance. "You're being mysterious again. I don't like it when you hint at stuff. Just tell me what you're thinking."

"When I put you in the castle, I made a mistake. You weren't ready for that. You faced a sorcerer, but you don't know anything about magic. You also fought with several castle guards, but you don't know how to fight."

"Hey!" Sonja interrupted, feeling a bit defensive at Rith's comment. "I think I did pretty well against the guards. I won, didn't I?"

"No. Kevin did pretty well. You just got lucky that the spearmen I put there were slow and clumsy. Next time, your opponents might be a little better at their jobs. I would like to see you be better as well."

Sonja flopped back onto her pillow. "Whatever," she muttered. "I still won."

"I have an idea for what your next adventure will be, but you are a long way from being ready for it. You need specific training that will help you not get killed or mangled no matter what you encounter. I never want to drop you into a situation again that you are not prepared to handle. I mean it. But this part is going to take time. A lot of it."

"I don't mind a little training," said Sonja. "When do we start?"

"I think you should finish the school year, so you don't forget everything you need for your finals. Then say goodbye to your friends. Do something fun with them because you won't be seeing them again for a while. Maybe a year or two."

"A year?!" Sonja sat up again. She swung her legs over the edge of the bed and stood up to face Rith. "What are you cooking up in that little head of yours, buddy? Where am I going, and why is this going to take so long? Am I leaving home?"

"You don't have to go anywhere, and you don't have to leave home. You will be gone, but it will be like all the other times. No one else will realize you were missing."

"I'll be gone for a year, but no one will know," Sonja repeated, making sure she was following Rith's explanation correctly. "And, where will I be all this time?"

"Maybe two," Rith said, either missing or ignoring Sonja's question.

A new thought occurred to Sonja and she held up a hand toward Rith. "Stop. Okay, if I'm gone two years and come back to the exact same spot, won't I still be two years older? You don't think anyone will notice that."

"Only your attitude will be two years older. I mentioned before that I can stop your body from aging while you are away from this reality. How long you are in another place doesn't affect that. You could be gone two hundred years, and you will not age a day."

"Like Peter Pan in Neverland," said Sonja, more to herself than Rith. "But, still. Two years? I don't know if I'm ready to be away from home that long. Where are you planning on taking me?"

Rith flew several excited loops, racing and diving left and right. "I'm not telling," he said, nickering again. "That would spoil the surprise."

CHAPTER 8

The last weeks of school passed much too quickly in Sonja's opinion. Each day seemed to melt unnoticed into the next. Before she knew it, May had gone and June had arrived. Sonja completed her finals with respectable grades – even in math – and school let out for the summer.

As soon as the break began, Sonja expected Rith to whisk her away to whatever unknown destination he had in mind, but that did not happen. The first week of vacation passed without a single word from him on the topic of leaving. Then the second. And the third. During that time, Rith told Sonja nothing about his plans. When she finally broached the subject with him, he simply repeated what he had already mentioned: that she would be gone for up to two years and it was to "prepare" her for the future. He offered her no further enlightenment.

The little hippoganth could be remarkably stubborn.

Two years of living another life. Two years of not seeing friends and family. Sonja was fascinated but also more than a little scared. Several times, she found herself moments away from backing out, a heartbeat from telling Rith that she had changed her mind and she did not want to leave, but each time she opened her mouth to tell him, she remembered running through castle corridors with Kevin.

And sharing that wonderful kiss.

She wanted adventure in her life and Rith had given her exactly that. It had been her wish. How could she throw away this amazing new world that she had only so recently discovered? Two years was a long time, but it was nothing compared to a lifetime of tedium in a world devoid of magic.

Despite her resolve to go wherever Rith deemed necessary, Sonja did not push him to hurry up. There was no rush. If he wanted to take a few more days before whisking her away from everything familiar in her life, she was okay with waiting. If he wanted to wait a few more months, that was fine, too.

Sonja resolved to be patient.

In the last week of June, at two o'clock on a Saturday afternoon, Rith told her it was time to go. Sonja, wearing a pale blue bikini, reclined in a lawn chair on her backyard patio. The mid-year temperatures had at last clawed their way up into the nineties and she decided it was time to take advantage of the warmer weather. She had just finished applying extra sunscreen to her nose and face and was settling back to enjoy the opportunity to erase some of the winter pallor from her complexion when Rith made his announcement.

"Right now? I just got comfortable," Sonja complained. Then, more seriously, "I don't know if I'm ready."

"Of course, you're not ready," replied Rith. "There is no 'ready' for this. There is only go, or don't go. See how simple it is? So, are we going?"

"What skills do I need, and why can't I learn them here?" Sonja asked, though she realized she was stalling for time.

"You'll see when we get there," Rith said, unhelpfully.

Sonja looked toward the back door of her house. She stared for several long seconds, taking a mental picture to carry with her. She would not see home again for a long time and she wanted to remember this moment. At last, she closed her eyes and braced herself mentally.

"I guess I'm ready. As much as I can be, anyway, since you haven't told me anything. Wherever 'there' is, let's go."

"There" turned out to be the walled courtyard of a medieval castle, similar to the one she had escaped from not too long ago. Although the previous structure had been surrounded by forests, and there had been no wall around the courtyard, the similarities were still greater than any differences.

Spaced sporadically throughout the castle yard, over a dozen men were paired off in combat. They fought with swords, daggers, and staffs, but as fierce as the fighting seemed to be, no one appeared injured and Sonja did not see any casualties lying about on the ground.

After a few moments observing the melee, she began to discern some order in the confusion. One man took a fall in front of her, and Sonja watched as his opponent lowered his sword and reached out a hand to help him to his feet. Understanding dawned. These men were sparring; trying to score points on their adversaries rather than actually trying to kill one another. She watched the activity with fascination until a voice rang out, drawing everyone's attention.

"Hold! Rest period." The command boomed through the courtyard.

The fighters relaxed, some taking a knee while others paced in small circles shaking out tired muscles and keeping themselves loose. In an instant, the men went from trying to cave in each other's skulls to laughing and chatting amiable amongst themselves.

Sonja searched the grounds for the source of the voice and discovered a large, powerful looking man at the far end of the courtyard. The impressive figure stood well over six feet tall and must have weighed at least two hundred and fifty pounds, none of it fat. His eyes and hair were black, as were his thick eyebrows and closely cut beard. The few visible features on his wide face seemed to be locked in a permanent scowl. He wore only a baggy pair of cloth pants, exposing the blocky slabs of muscle covering his arms and chest; the kind of muscle that comes from years of hard labor rather than the carefully sculpted lines a body builder would cultivate in a gym. Strength and confidence emanated from him. This was a man who expected to be obeyed.

In his right hand he carried a long, curving, battle-marked sword. The blade appeared to have seen more than its fair share of combat, just like its wielder.

"Go over to him," said Rith to Sonja, noticing the direction of her gaze. "His name is Cejack, but always refer to him as Master Cejack or Teacher. Tell him you want to be taught the ways of battle and you want your training to start as soon as possible."

Sonja's stomach fluttered, threatening to turn inside out. The last thing she wanted to do was walk through this gathering of training warriors and approach the brooding monster in charge of them. She would much rather go back home and get back to her original plan for the day: lying around in the backyard. She was not prepared for this.

Setting her reservations aside, she did as Rith requested.

She approached Cejack, pausing a few, respectful feet away but still close enough to draw his attention. Not wanting to speak first, she waited for him to acknowledge her. The brooding giant did not so much as glance in her direction.

While she stood silently, hands clasped behind her back to hide their shaking, she observed two tattoos on Cejack, one on each massive forearm. On his right arm was a bear, although its teeth were somewhat longer than those of any bear she had ever seen. On his left, was some type of lean, cat-like animal, with a bony ridge running along its skull and down its back.

A full minute passed and Cejack still refused to recognize her presence.

Sonja realized she was going to have better luck waiting for a stone wall to speak. Running out of patience, she cleared her throat and addressed her, hopefully, soon to be teacher. Her voice was not as steady as she might have hoped when she spoke, but the words were clear as she requested his help learning how to fight with the sword.

Cejack glowered in her direction, then began to laugh.

"A girl, who wishes to be a man," he said, gesturing at her clothes.

Fortunately, instead of her blue bikini, Rith had thoughtfully provided Sonja with calf-high boots, leather breeches and a light wool tunic. From Cejack's reaction, this was apparently not the standard dress of a female in this place.

"You wish to learn to do battle? Do you have any potential?"

"I don't know," she replied honestly.

"Have you ever handled a weapon?"

"The bow, and the staff."

Cejack looked her over one more time, this time more thoughtfully. "What is your name?"

Sonja told him. By this time, a small crowd had gathered around the two of them. Several of the resting fighters left their assigned places in the courtyard to wander closer and get a better look at the spectacle occurring in their midst. Cejack called to one of the onlookers.

"Misha, hand Lady Sonja your staff." The identified student rushed forward immediately and surrendered his staff to Sonja. When Misha retreated into the crowd, Cejack raised his sword, leveling the point at her. "Let us see what you know, girl. Attack me."

Sonja hefted the staff in both hands, testing its weight, then assumed a comfortable stance. She leaned forward, balancing on the balls of her feet. Letting her vision go slightly out of focus, she used her peripheral vision to watch for movement from Cejack's hands and feet. As Robin had taught her, she did not let her eyes settle on any particular part of his body.

"If you are focused on the left hand, you cannot see the right hand coming," Robin had instructed her. *"Watch all of him, and none of him, and react to your opponent's movements."*

At the moment, however, Cejack was not moving at all.

Sonja briefly met the large man's stare before dropping her attention back to the middle of his chest and unfocusing once more. Cejack's eyes revealed more confusion and curiosity than anything else. She had obviously intrigued him with her request. She just needed to follow through and let him know she was serious.

Still, he did not move.

"Don't take a defensive stance with me," he roared. "If I strike first, I'll cut your head off. Now attack!"

Sonja complied. Thrusting the end of her staff forward, she aimed for Cejack's massive chest. It was such a large target, she figured she couldn't possibly miss. He swept her attack aside with his sword, as she expected he would. She rotated the pole with the momentum of his block to strike at his head. Again, he blocked without even seeming to try. Sonja struck again and again, and each time Cejack countered her so easily it appeared as if he were repeating a choreographed scene. The gathered soldiers began to laugh and call out to her to give up, increasing her frustration. As her desperation grew and pushed her to greater effort, she lashed out with more power, but her control suffered.

"Enough," cried Cejack, catching her staff in his left hand and tearing it from her grasp as if he were correcting a toddler who had picked up a stick. "Your attacks are clumsy and your stances are awkward. You have no discipline. How do you expect me to teach you anything? There is no reason for me to take you as a student."

He turned his back to Sonja and walked away.

Sonja stared at the ground, fighting back tears of humiliation. Embarrassing herself further in front of all these people would not happen, she told herself, angrily. She heard Rith's voice moving away from her, and she glanced up to see him confronting Cejack.

"Take her Master Cejack. Please. As a favor to me. Teach her what she can learn."

"She is with you?" asked the swordsman.

"She is," agreed Rith.

"Like the other one?"

"Yes, Teacher. Like the other one, only I believe she can be much better than he was."

Other one? Sonja thought. *What the hell is Rith talking about?* But she had no time to ponder the question further.

"Then I will teach her, because you requested it." Cejack peered around the yard until he located a particular student. "Derrik, take Sonja to the weapons room and have her outfitted properly. Then take her to have quarters assigned to her."

The boy addressed as Derrik stepped forward. "Come along," he said to Sonja as he passed by her, not waiting to see if she followed.

Sonja hurried after him as Derrik's long legs carried him briskly through the courtyard. He moved too quickly to allow an opportunity for questions, and she only caught up with him when he paused at a stone shed abutting the castle wall at the North end of the yard. The main gates of the castle entrance loomed nearby; twelve feet tall from the ground to their rounded top. The shed had a sturdy looking wooden door mounted on heavy metal hinges. There were no windows in the structure, and no other openings which might allow access. The single door could be secured with a latch and padlock, but these were currently unfastened, allowing Derrik to swing the barricade aside easily.

Stepping into the shadowed depths of the building, Derrik removed one of two burning candles mounted in a bracket near the door. He used the candle to ignite several oil lamps around the room. As firelight flickered and illuminated the interior of the shed, Sonja had a momentary flashback to the cell in Moribus' castle. This room was much larger than her cell had been, and there were no chains on her wrists this time, so she pushed the memory aside and focused on what Derrik was showing her.

Weapons of all types and shapes covered tables, filled shelves, and hung from hooks on all four walls. Swords, knives, staves, and bows surrounded her in dismaying numbers. Sonja turned in a half circle, her eyes tracing the perimeter and trying to take everything in. This unremarkable little structure held an amazing arsenal of lethal items.

"Choose a sword, which you can carry easily," instructed Derrik pointing to a wall bristling with swords of differing lengths and widths. "If it is too heavy you will tire quickly, and the first to falter is surely the first to die. When you find one that suits you, bring it and its sheath to me, and then choose a mace from this table. I think a morning star would be your wisest choice."

Sonja thanked him and bowed awkwardly, not sure how to properly respond. The amused look on Derrik's face told her she had erred yet again. Ears and cheeks growing hot from embarrassment, she turned and went to examine the sword-covered wall. She hefted several of the weapons and found them all clumsy to wield. The blades were either too long, or the grip of the handle was too wide for her hand. Although the swords weighed only three to four pounds, and she could lift them easily, she knew even that slight weight would be too much if she were forced to use the weapon for more than a few minutes at a time. She took Derrik's warning seriously. She needed to find something smaller and lighter than those she had examined so far.

Moving further down the wall, she found a collection of smaller weapons. They were probably designed for children,

Sonja realized. She almost stepped away and returned to the larger swords, her pride urging her not to pick up a child's weapon, but she forced herself to stay where she was. Practicality needed to win out over ego. She was a small person; she needed a small weapon.

Sonja selected a slender, tapering broadsword with a grip petite enough to be comfortable in her hand. It was half the weight of the other weapons she had tried and therefore should be easier to handle over prolonged periods of time. She cut the air with the sword a few times and, satisfied with the feel, resheathed it and brought it to Derrik.

Next, she examined the mace table, immediately finding one she liked. The weapon had an eighteen-inch metal shaft connected to a spiked steel ball about the size of a baseball. Raising it without much effort, she guessed it weighed no more than a pound and a half. Sonja swung it through the air a few times, experimentally. It was probably a remarkably effective tool against a human opponent, she mused, picturing the spiked ball striking someone in the chest or head.

"Good. You took my advice and chose a morning star," said Derrik when she brought her choice to him. Sonja merely smiled. She had no idea what a morning star was, but if Derrik was happy with her choice, she wasn't about to admit her ignorance.

"Hold still a moment."

Derrik slipped a belt through the loop on Sonja's sword sheath and placed it around her waist. He positioned the leather strap so the weapon dangled from her left hip. "Right handed?" he asked, before fastening the clasp. Sonja nodded confirmation. "Good. I won't have to reattach your sword.

When the sword was secured to his satisfaction, he knelt and affixed a metal scabbard into her left boot. In the scabbard, he placed an eight-inch, duel-edged dagger so that the handle protruded over the top of her boot and lay flat against the side of her calf. The narrow blade appeared wickedly sharp, and the sides gleamed in the lamplight before the weapon disappeared into its sheath.

Derrik peered up at her while he secured the boot dagger. "Always keep a weapon accessible to your left hand. If your sword arm is ever injured, you will be glad of the precaution. Does that feel okay?" When Sonja nodded again, he stood up and brushed the dirt from the knees of his breeches.

"Now you need a bow. What is your draw?"

"My what?" asked Sonja.

Derrik ignored her question and scrutinized her for a moment, focusing on her arms and chest. Sonja felt momentarily self-conscious, but from the look of concentration on his face, she was relatively certain he wasn't just checking out her breasts.

"About thirty pounds I would guess."

He stepped over to the wall on Sonja's left and pulled down a bow and a leather quiver holding ten arrows. Setting the quiver on the ground at his feet, he unwound a length of string from around the bow's wooden frame. He secured the string to one end of the weapon before bracing the bow between his feet. Next, he flexed the curved limbs until they were close enough to secure the string to the unsecured end. He handed Sonja the newly strung bow.

"Try to pull the string all the way back."

With a little effort, Sonja braced the weapon's riser in her left hand, grasped the string in her right and pulled the bow to its full extension. She held it a moment, then tried to ease it back. The bow jerked painfully at her shoulder as it sprung back to its resting shape. Derrik nodded in approval. "Thirty pounds is not a lot of force," he explained. "But as you get stronger you can move up to a heavier draw."

To complete her arsenal, he directed Sonja to choose a quarterstaff, which she did quickly, already knowing what length and weight felt most comfortable. Satisfied that she had all she needed, Derrik ushered her out of the weapons room.

He led her into the castle proper, up two flights of stone stairs and into the student barracks. A stooped, elderly man in charge of housing all of Cejack's numerous students – Sonja later learned his name was Merind – assigned her a room.

"Usually new students are partnered with a roommate," explained Derrik as he located her quarters and ushered Sonja inside. "As you are Master Cejack's only female student, we cannot do that with you. So, you get a room of your own. Someone will be assigned to come get you for meals and call you for drills until you become more acquainted with the routine."

"Will you come get me?" asked Sonja with a nervous smile. Derrik was the only person she had met here, and so far he had been, if not friendly, at least not completely dismissive of her.

Derrik's face flushed slightly, and for the first time his eyes directly met hers. They were blue, which surprised Sonja because his hair was so dark. It gave him a feral look. He was much younger than Sonja had originally thought, as well. They were probably close to the same age, although several days-worth of heavy stubble on his face made him appear much older. He lowered his gaze and quickly regained his soldier's composure.

"Perhaps. For now, stay here and wait for Master Cejack to summon you. I have to go tell him you've been armed and quartered."

"Thank you," said Sonja, but Derrik had already gone, closing the door behind him as he left.

Sonja paced the limited space, examining what was to be her home for the next two years. It looked more like the weapons storage shed than a bedroom: a stone walled cube, fifteen feet across with a bed in one corner and a clothes chest in another. One window, currently open to alleviate some of the daytime heat, allowed in pale yellow streams of afternoon light. A colored tapestry on the far wall added a small touch of much needed cheeriness to the mostly drab decor. There were four oil lamps in various wall sconces about the room, but there was still enough ambient light she didn't need to use them just yet.

Sonja placed her selected weapons on the floor at the foot of her bed. Next, she removed her sword and belt and propped it standing up against the wall. After a moment's consideration, she decided to leave the dagger in her boot for now. She was not completely sure she could properly reaffix it if she removed it.

A random, terrifying thought made Sonja check her door. It swung open easily when she tugged at the handle. She was not locked in. The students were not prisoners here and remained free to come and go. Closing the door once more, she noticed a bolt lock on the inside which would enable her to secure the door and keep others out. A nice feature. She felt she would sleep better at night knowing it was there.

"Rith," said Sonja, still looking around the room even though there was nothing more to see. "Cejack knew you. How come?"

"Master Cejack," corrected Rith. "Don't forget that."

"You didn't answer my question."

"You are not the first student I have brought to Cejack," explained Rith. "We have met before."

Sonja turned to Rith excitedly. "You mean other people have made the same wish I made?"

"No, and technically this is not part of your wish. You see, what I haven't told you yet is that I didn't create this place. It really exists on a different world and timeline. We have skipped over. That's the reason you will be here so long. I can return you home to the exact moment that you left, but time will keep moving here. If you go home and try to come back, everyone here will notice you were gone, and Cejack does not allow students to leave the grounds while they are in training. If you leave for any reason without specific permission, you won't be allowed to come back.

"I need Cejack to train you so you will be ready for your next adventure. What I have planned would be too dangerous for you to enter unprepared, and I promised I wouldn't do that to you again. Once I am sure that you are competent with the necessary weapons, I will continue to fulfill your wish and begin the next adventure. See how simple it is?"

"Simple. Sure," Sonja agreed without enthusiasm.

"Don't worry, though," continued Rith. "You will still get home exactly when you left, and you won't age at all while you are here. Plus, any time you need help, I'll be here with you."

Sonja continued exploring the confines of her new home while Rith talked. When she lifted the lid to look inside the clothes trunk, she waved a hand at the hippoganth to get his attention. "Help," she said.

"What?"

"There aren't any clothes in this trunk. What am I going to wear for two years?"

"I'll take care of that. I'll make sure you have a change of clothes each day. They'll all look pretty much the same, but at least they will be clean."

Sonja let the trunk lid fall. "That works, I guess," she said, flopping backward onto the bed. "Hey. At least the bed is comfortable."

She closed her eyes, figuring if all she could do was wait for someone to come get her, she could at least get in a short nap.

Her hopes for slumber quickly faded, however. Too many thoughts misfired through her mind and she was unable to quiet them enough to fall asleep. She thought about her family and friends and how far away they were. She would not see them, talk to them, or even get an occasional letter or message while she was gone. They would never realize she had been missing. In addition, the people around here so far did not seem overly friendly. Would she be able to get along with them, or would she spend the entire time alone and feeling sorry for herself?

Most of half an hour passed with Sonja lying on the bed trying to force her thoughts aside far enough to let her sleep. It was almost a relief when a soft knock on the door caught her attention and brought her back to full awareness. She sprang to her feet thinking it must be Derrik coming back for her, but when she pulled open the door, a boy of about fourteen stood in the hallway. Brown eyes under a mop of light, brown hair peered back at her.

"Master Cejack wants to see you," he said. "Get ready and I'll take you to him."

Sonja stepped outside and closed the door behind her. "I'm ready. Let's go."

The boy stared at Sonja's waist and his mouth popped open as if he were going to object to something. With a shrug and a rueful shake of his head, he appeared to change his mind. "If you say so."

Sonja followed him out of the barracks area, down the same two flights of stairs she had climbed before, to a large lecture hall on the main level. The ceiling of the hall was not high – the candelabras providing light hung down to just a few feet above her head – but the room was enormous. There was also little furniture filling the available space. The meeting hall could probably hold a hundred people and still provide easy access for a wild bull to run through without touching a soul. Today, it was completely empty except for Cejack sitting cross-legged on a table at the far end, running a whetting stone expertly over the edge of his sword blade. When he saw her, he motioned with the hand holding the stone for Sonja to come to him, at the same time shooing the boy away. As she timidly approached, she saw Cejack's ever-present scowl deepen.

"Where is your sword?" he growled.

"I took it off in my room," Sonja told him, suddenly frightened, although she was not sure why. "It's still there with my other things."

"If you intend to remain here for any length of time, there are a number of rules that you will follow. The first is: no student shall leave his quarters without sword, dagger, and any other weapon I request be carried at the time. You are not wearing your sword. For this, you will not eat with us tonight. You will remain in your room until you are summoned for breakfast in the morning."

"But that's not fair," blurted Sonja. "I didn't know the rule. How could I–"

"Rule number two," interrupted Cejack. "No decision of mine will be questioned. Continue and you risk a second penalty."

Sonja stared at Cejack for a moment, not knowing whether to scream or cry. Realizing neither reaction was going to help, she forced herself to reign in her emotions and, through clenched teeth, she said, "Yes, Teacher. Will you please tell me the other rules so that I do not offend you further?"

Cejack nodded. "Three: orders received from me, other Teachers, or ranking students will be unquestionably obeyed. Four: personal disputes will be settled by sword under my supervision. Five: first blood decides the winner of all such matches. Six: punishments will be dictated by me or those appointed by me. No exceptions."

"Is that all you wanted to see me about?" asked Sonja.

"No. I called you to tell you that although you are the only girl at this school, and you are under Rith's guidance, you can expect no special privileges from me. Do you understand?"

"If I didn't before, I do now," said Sonja, her jaw muscles flexing as she ground her teeth.

"Go back to your room. Though you cannot eat tonight, you can at least get some sleep. Breakfast is early tomorrow, and your training begins immediately after."

Sonja turned and left. She walked slowly to the door, with her back straight. As soon as she left Cejack's sight, she ran the rest of the way to her room, locked herself in, and threw herself on the bed. This time, she had no difficulty falling asleep as she cried herself into an exhausted slumber.

As Cejack promised, the next morning came early. Sonja awoke to a pounding on her door and rose groggily to answer it.

She found Derrik waiting on the other side and became suddenly very aware of how she must look. Her clothes were disarrayed from sleep, her hair was uncombed and unwashed, and she knew her eyes must still be red from crying.

When Derrik saw her, he simply nodded a greeting and handed her a large cloth towel and a bar of soap. In his left hand, he held a glowing lantern for illumination in the pre-dawn dark.

"Follow me," he said, "and I'll show you where to find hot water for a bath."

He led Sonja down a short series of hallways and into a stone-walled room about half the size of the hall where Cejack had spoken to her last night. *Lectured me, actually*, thought Sonja, still angry about how she had been treated. Most of the floor at the center of this room was paved with marble tiles in a concave shape designed to act like a basin, catching steaming hot water that poured from a pipe set in one of the walls. Derrik explained that the water was pumped in from a hot spring a quarter of a mile away. As the pool overflowed, the water ran out through a series of drains placed on the opposite side of the room from the inflow pipe. Derrik showed her how to stop and restart the water flow using a twisting valve and two manual pumps.

He had started the hot water flowing before going to her room, so the pool was ready when she arrived. He had also lit several of the wall lamps to give her enough light to see in the windowless confines of the bathing room.

"Normally the students bathe after training or after evening meal, but I thought you might like some privacy until you adjust to the idea of being the only female here. The room is usually empty at this time of morning. You have to hurry, though. Breakfast is in less than half an hour. I'll come back in about ten minutes to get you."

"Thanks, Derrik," said Sonja, turning the valve he had shown her to shut off the rush of steaming water. "When you come back, do you think you could bring me a comb?"

Derrik smiled. The smile warmed his face and Sonja caught herself wishing he would do it more often. "I'll try and find one," he said.

Sonja watched him leave, then hurried to start her bath. She stripped off her clothing, settled into the hot water, and began to scrub with the rough bar of soap.

The pool appeared large enough to accommodate two dozen people at a time with plenty of room to move about. The deepest point in the middle was about four feet deep, almost deep enough to swim. Having the whole thing to herself seemed an incredible luxury to Sonja and she decided to take advantage of the opportunity. When she finished washing, she took a moment to lie back and float in the soapy warmth. All the anger and humiliation of the night before seeped out, leaving her completely relaxed for the first time since Rith had brought her to this place.

Unfortunately, Sonja only had a limited time to enjoy the peace and quiet. She had just decided to climb out and dry off when she heard Derrik returning. She glanced around to where she had left her towel, and saw it was too far away for her to reach in the time she had to grab it. With no other options, she ducked down in the middle of the pool, hoping he could not see too much through the murky water.

"I brought your comb," said Derrik, entering the room and holding up a wide-toothed, metal comb.

"Thanks," replied Sonja. "But I also need my–"

"Towel," finished Derrik. He picked up the towel from the floor and held it out for her.

"Um, would you mind just setting it down again and stepping outside for a second while I dry off?"

"Sure," he said, placing the towel and comb on the floor. "But you are going to have to get over your shyness eventually if you expect to be here for any length of time."

"Fine. Okay. We'll take up this topic again when you're the one naked and wet. But for now…" Sonja waved him toward the entrance with a dripping hand.

Derrik laughed, not unkindly, and stepped back outside. "Grab the soap," he told her over his shoulder as he exited. "They're hard to come by, and if you leave it here, someone will steal it."

Sonja floundered out of the pool in a rush and grabbed her towel. Taking only enough time to wipe the majority of water from her body, she pulled on her sleep-wrinkled tunic, which draped her torso to mid-thigh. Next, she grabbed the comb, towel, soap, and remainder of her clothes before joining Derrik in the hallway. He walked her back to her room, strolling casually at her side.

Back at her dormitory, she apologized and asked him if he could again wait for her in the hallway. He agreed, handing her his lantern.

"Excuse me," she said closing the door so she could remove her tunic and finish drying off properly. She found a clean change of clothes in her trunk, as Rith had promised, and she used her new comb to get her hair at least mildly under control. When she opened the door again, Derrik was still waiting patiently.

"When is breakfast?" she asked him.

"We should be leaving now."

"First, I have a quick question. Where do I ... go to the bathroom?" Sonja blushed. She hoped Derrik would not notice in the flickering lamplight.

Derrik stepped into her room, knelt, and reached under the bed, pulling out a hammered metal bowl two feet in diameter. "After you use it," he explained, "take it outside the castle gate and empty it and clean it. Some of the students choose to ignore the pot and simply relieve themselves outside." He put the bowl back under the bed. "Are you ready to go?"

"Yes."

"No," countered Derrik. "You are not wearing your sword and dagger."

"Shit!" Sonja swore. Not wanting to miss another meal, she strapped on her sword belt and, with a little assistance from Derrik, her boot sheath. She holstered both weapons. Now, at last prepared to meet the day, Derrik led her to breakfast.

Sonja waited on the hard-packed dirt and clay of the school's courtyard. She shivered once, but it had little to do with the outside temperature. The sun had barely begun to lighten the morning sky to a pale blue cast, but the day ahead already promised to be hot one. *Nerves,* Sonja told herself. *I'm scared because I have no idea what to expect. I just need to calm down and follow everyone else's lead.*

At least her stomach was full. Breakfast had been simple – bread, cheese, fruit, and some type of hot cereal – but very filling. After missing dinner the night before, Sonja helped herself to as much as she could pack down without making herself too sick to leave the dining hall when the students were ordered outside. Now, as her stomach threatened to turn over and climb into her mouth, she questioned the wisdom of her strategy.

Sonja stood in a group of about fifty new students, all waiting to begin their first day of training. Most looked to be in their teens or early twenties, although one man pacing quietly off to the side did seem to be somewhat older. She thought he might be about her dad's age. Sonja wondered what might bring a person like him to this school. Perhaps a mid-life crisis of some kind. Instead of fast cars and younger women, maybe he had opted for weapons and warfare.

At breakfast, Sonja overheard a student saying that Master Cejack only took one new class every six months. The unfortunate speaker explained he had shown up at the school one week after the last class started and was refused admittance. He was told to come back for the next group and not to be late or he would be turned away a second time. Sonja figured it was no coincidence that Rith had brought her here one day before this class was to begin.

While a few hushed conversations rippled through the group, most of the assembled students remained anxiously mute as they observed Master Cejack speaking to a small gathering of men a few yards away. Sonja could hear Cejack speaking, although she found herself too far away to make out what was being said. The private conversation continued a few moments more, then six stern-looking individuals separated from Cejack's group to approach Sonja and the other students.

Sonja experienced a moment of surprise when she noticed Derrik among the six. He eyed the assembled group dispassionately, his gaze flicking past Sonja's face with no hint of recognition. Nothing of the smiling figure she had spoken with this morning remained. Now, he had a job to do, and he clearly took that job seriously. The four men remaining with Cejack turned and observed the proceedings with almost bored expressions.

The six instructors – as Sonja guessed them to be from their manner and attitude toward the assembled students – lined up facing the new class and waited for their attention. The last few mutterings died away. When they had complete quiet, one of the instructors stepped smartly forward one step. Sonja recognized him as the boy who had loaned her his staff yesterday in her ill-fated first match with Master Cejack. He was shorter than the other instructors by a few inches, with a wide chest and broad shoulders. Long, shaggy black hair fell wildly around his sun-darkened face and all but obscured his equally black eyes. He had soft, round features that appeared to still be harboring some baby fat, although the rest of him looked lean and trim. He was also the only one of the six without a beard or at least some type of facial hair. His cheeks and jawline were as smooth as Sonja's own.

Misha, she remembered he had been called.

"Listen closely," Misha began, letting his gaze take in the entire crowd before him. "Your training begins today, and it starts with finding out how well you follow instructions."

Sonja expected Misha to begin pacing back and forth as he spoke, stopping occasionally to yell in someone's face like a drill sergeant in some military movie. He did not move. Instead, he stood comfortably at ease, remaining one step in front of his fellow instructors. His voice carried enough to be heard, but it held no emotion in it, except perhaps the patient tolerance of a teacher speaking to a particularly dim student. *Okay, one more time: one plus one is two. Two plus two is...*

"You will be separated into six groups. Each of us will instruct one of these groups, and I expect that you will follow our orders as you would Master Cejack's. If you disagree with our training methods, you are free to leave the school at any time. There will be no discussion and there is no middle ground. Complete obedience or leave. And remember, once you leave these grounds, you will not be welcomed back.

"When you hear your name called, answer by stating 'aye' and line up next to the instructor calling the roll. Are there any questions before we begin?"

"Is lunch going to be any better than breakfast?" called out some wit from behind Sonja.

Misha's demeanor and voice did not alter as he responded. "While humor is always appreciated here, stupidity is not. If you are unhappy with any accommodations the gate is less than one hundred yards away. Anyone else? No? Good. Davar!"

"Aye," called a boy who rushed over to stand near Misha.

"Marian!"

"Aye."

"Evan!"

"Aye."

When Misha had called out nine names, he gathered his students and ushered them to an isolated area of the courtyard. The second instructor in line shuffled one step forward and continued the roll call. Sonja's name came up in the third group.

Sammon, a boy even younger than Misha – although unlike Misha, he had a few thatches of hair on his face that might one day become a beard – instructed Sonja's group. He carried himself with the same self-assurance as the other instructors despite his age. Sammon was slender with a narrow face and long blade of a nose, giving him the appearance of a puppy still growing into its features. His voice was clear and high when he spoke, as puberty had not yet fully lowered its register to what it might be in a few more years. The sound of his speech only added to his youthful appearance.

While he appeared at first glance to be physically unimposing and easily dismissible, Sonja noticed the hard, definition of muscle in his forearms where they protruded from the cloth sleeves of his shirt, and she was forced to reassess her opinion of him as an opponent.

Sonja's group consisted of eight individuals, including the older man she had noticed earlier. He had responded to the name Tanner during the roll call. Sammon lined up his charges so they faced him in a single row and immediately began training. He gave no introduction or information about himself as an instructor, he didn't have the students interact to get to know each other, and he did not bother explaining any rules or expectations. This wasn't like the public-school system back home, Sonja realized, with a week of orientation and easing into a learning routine. This was follow along and keep up or don't let the gate hit you in the ass on the way out.

"Draw your swords," ordered Sammon, removing his own weapon smoothly and leveling it in front of him. "There are four basic defensive positions, each protects one quadrant of the body. Watch, and do as I do. One!" Sammon lifted the sword point to shoulder height and moved the blade left across his body.

"Two!" The blade moved back to center, then glided right.

"Three!" Sammon's blade dropped in a sweeping motion, stopping just as the tip passed his right knee.

"Four!" He fanned his blade past his left knee.

"Okay," he called, as he replaced his sword in its sheath with a distracted, seemingly unconscious ease. "Again. One. Two. Three. Four. One. Two…"

Sammon continued counting off each movement, strolling among his students and making adjustments to their stances and movements. Sonja repeated the motions, endlessly and without reprieve until her shoulder and arm trembled with the effort of just keeping the sword upright. Sweat streamed from her brow and fell stinging into her eyes, blurring her vision. Her palms grew slick and she thought the weapon might just slip from her grasp and fall into the dust, with her body following soon after. Still Sammon counted.

One. Two. Three. Four.

After what felt like a lifetime of pain – but was probably only about twenty minutes – Sammon called for them to stop. Eight sword tips dropped simultaneously to the ground, and eight tired sighs of relief rushed from panting lungs.

"Pick those blades up!" Sammon's eyes flared as he kicked a student's sword point out of the red courtyard clay. "Never lay your weapon in the dirt. Someday it may be the only thing between you and a messy painful death, and you will not dishonor it by dragging it through the mud. Sheath it or carry it. Never drop it!"

"Lighten up. It's just a piece of metal."

The comment, from the student standing on Sonja's right, was not meant to be overheard, but Sammon moved lightening quick to confront the speaker. He faced his pupil almost nose to nose, his body tensed like a snake about to bite but waiting for just the right moment. Sonja forced herself to again reevaluate her opinion of their instructor. The boy was not just formidable, he was downright dangerous. She decided she never wanted him angry with her, and she figured following directions and keeping her mouth shut was a good start at keeping on his good side.

"Name!" snapped Sammon, his voice rising another half an octave in agitation.

Sonja almost answered until remembering he was not speaking to her. She closed her half open mouth with a click of her teeth.

"Brion," responded the boy next to her.

"Brion, you are too new to be called into the Circle. But if you ever insult me with a comment like that again, I will see you on the end of my sword or out of this school. Maybe both. Do you understand?"

"Yes, Master Sammon."

Sammon drew his sword and held it to eye level in the limited space between himself and Brion. The student flinched, but to his credit he did not back away.

"Look at my blade and tell me if you see anything on it."

Brion glanced down at the sword balanced so close to his body. A puzzled look crossed his face. "I don't understand. Is there ... what?"

"Do you see anything on my sword?" Sammon spoke slowly and deliberately. Contempt oozed from each syllable. "Is there something etched on my sword? Specifically, a bear perhaps? Or a ceravit?"

Brion looked again, this time more carefully. "No," he said. "I... No. Nothing."

"Precisely." Sammon sheathed his weapon and stepped back to address all of his students. "Do not give me titles I do not deserve. I have earned my sword, but the metal is still bare. You may refer to me as Mister Sammon, or Sir. Any other titles belong to those who have reached levels above mine. Am I understood?"

No one responded, but Sammon nodded as though he had heard the answer he wanted.

114

"Now," he continued. "When you leave this school, I expect you to be able to handle a sword in either hand with equal skill. Draw your weapons and hold them in the hand that does not currently feel like it is about to drop off. Begin defensive drill number one. One. Two. Three. Four. One. Two…"

Sonja lay on her bed in her chamber, too exhausted to move. Every part of her body hurt. Her legs felt like dead meat. Both of her hands were curled into painful claws, too weak to either open fully or close into fists, and her forearms and shoulders still burned from the effort of holding her blade through the endless drills. Swinging two pounds of metal a few inches at a time did not seem like much of a task, but when doing it thousands of times over several hours, the effort of simply holding the sword off the ground became herculean.

There had been moments today that Sonja feared she had died and gone to Hell. She believed that her eternal torment was to swing a sword in front of her over and over until her arms dropped off and she cried blood. She had never been so tired in her life.

She knew she wasn't the only one. All the students that had started the morning with her looked equally spent, although many of them had fared a bit better as they had more muscle than she did and had practiced with a blade prior to arriving at Cejack's school. Still, every one of them had been pushed to their limits.

When Sammon finally called an end to the day, Sonja had been almost too tired to eat her dinner. She was also too hungry to skip it. She had vomited about an hour into the morning exercises, losing most of her breakfast. It had been embarrassing, but fortunately she wasn't the only one to suffer that particular discomfiture. It gave her a bit of satisfaction to know she wasn't the first one to have to step out of line and be sick, either. That dubious honor had gone to a student in Derrik's group. He had given up his morning meal a few minutes sooner than she had.

Lunch had been a brief, meager affair, consisting of mostly water, a few dried biscuits, and some more hard cheeses. That coupled with her evacuated breakfast had left her ravenous at the end of training. Now, fed and worn out, she simply waited for sleep to take her as her mind wandered over the trials of her day. She wondered what tomorrow would be like. Probably more of the same grueling punishment, she decided.

After working the sword all morning, Sammon switched to training with the dagger in the afternoon. Thankfully, the dagger weighed significantly less than her sword, so her poor abused arm muscles had some opportunity to recuperate. As if to make up for this fact, however, Sammon had focused on stances, both offensive and defensive. He drilled them over and over on squat, lunge, and retreat. Squat. Lunge. Retreat. Down, forward, up, and back, until Sonja's legs burned as badly as her arms and she feared she would topple over at any moment.

Sammon interspersed his exercises with periodic, but all too brief, stretches of lecture. The students had gratefully listened to his diatribes, as they were perfect excuses to rest rapidly failing muscles. Lying on her bed, Sonja could almost hear him droning on in that high, clear voice of his:

"...two primary methods of fighting with a knife or dagger. One is to lead with the knife hand. This is a more defensive method with the dagger being used to cut and slash

and generally keep your opponent at a distance. Fatal wounds are difficult to inflict and these often become battles of attrition, trying to slowly wear your enemy down. The second is leading with the open hand, with the knife held in close to your body. This method is more offensive. The fighter is attempting to move in close and grapple with his opponent. The idea is to hold on long enough to bring the knife into play and drive it in for one killing blow. There is a middle ground, but I don't recommend it. It can lead to some awkward stances. When your balance is compromised..."

With Sammon's words still echoing in her head, Sonja drifted off to sleep.

Living at the school was hard work. It did improve as Sonja adapted to her schedule and gained in strength and stamina, but it took time. Thirteen students left in the first week. Brion, from her training group, had been one of them. Eight more disappeared in the second week. Sometime during the night, they had packed up the few items of gear they owned and walked away. Several times in those first few weeks, Sonja wished she too could go over the wall with them, but with Rith as her only door back home, leaving early was not an option. The instructors never discussed the disappearances. It seemed that at least some attrition was commonplace, and so was not unexpected. Classes were simply shuffled so at least five students remained in each group.

As the weeks passed, Sonja fell into a routine that made existence at the school, if not easier, at least bearable. The days did not consist entirely of drills and training. The instructors realized students needed opportunities to rest and recover, both physically and mentally, so there was some minimal downtime allotted to them. Students were permitted one morning and one afternoon off each week. They also had their evenings after dinner to spend as they saw fit. However, as morning drills began early each day, most chose to go to bed and sleep after the evening meal.

Each morning began with sword practice. In the afternoon, the instructor ran drills with either the dagger or the staff, depending on where he felt the students needed more practice. After a month, the bow and mace were worked into the rotation.

Also after one month, the students were allowed into the Combat Circle for the first time. Each received a bamboo sword and dagger, to prevent them from causing or sustaining any serious injuries, and then one by one they were brought into the Circle and given their first taste of armed combat. Initially, students sparred only with instructors. As their skill and control improved, they were permitted to compete with one another. The instructors supervised these student bouts carefully and stepped in whenever they felt it necessary.

Because of the nature of the weapon and its inherent dangers, only instructors were permitted to carry a mace into the Circle, and they did so only to permit their students to practice defensive tactics with the sword or staff. Master Cejack did not like the mace as a training weapon. *"It is a weapon of force, not skill,"* he had told them once, early in their training. *"Any horse's ass can swing a mace."* And so, their education remained unsurprisingly brief regarding the subject.

Sonja's skills improved dramatically with time and practice, and before long she started to enjoy parts of her training. She looked forward to archery and discovered she was surprisingly good at it. As she had learned in the woods with Robin Hood, the constant draw and release of the bowstring, along with the steady hum of the vibrating string as each arrow took flight, could be quite therapeutic. Sonja treated archery practice as her meditation time; a place to quiet her scattered thoughts and set aside the worries that plagued her during the early hours of the night when she could not fall asleep.

Her teachers noticed her love of the bow as well. While Sonja needed to work on building up to a heavier draw so she could shoot with more accuracy at greater distances, when working with targets at shorter or middle ranges, she held her own with the best archers in the school.

While her training progressed mostly without incident, Sonja did suffer two potentially disastrous mishaps in her first couple of months at the school. The first involved an instructor named Tavares, who approached her after lessons had concluded one evening during her fifth week.

"Sonja," Tavares called to her as she gathered up wooden swords from the afternoon's Circle training to return them to the weapons shed.

"Yes, Mister Tavares?" she responded, turning to face him.

"When you finish this task and after you have a chance to eat, I want you to report to my quarters."

"Your quarters?" Sonja asked, a small knot of concern settling in her stomach.

"Yes, my quarters. And plan on staying the night. The room needs cleaning and my bed needs warming. You're not much to look at, but there are not a lot of choices around here so, you will have to suffice."

Tavares turned without further comment, heading for the main entrance of the school keep. Before he took more than two steps, Sonja blurted out, "No! I'm not doing that."

Tavares spun about immediately, his features screwed up in anger. He stormed back to confront Sonja, attempting to stare her down. "You're refusing my directions?" he asked.

"Those directions? You're goddamned right, I am." Sonja was frightened; scared by the physical threat of this man looming over her, and terrified at the possibility that while at the school she might not have the right to refuse such a demand. But she was also angry at being treated like property, at the idea that she could be used like this without her permission. She let the anger fill her and root her to the ground so Tavares could not see the fear that was just beneath the surface of her defiance.

"I'm not your toy," she told him. "You don't get to play with me then throw me away when you're done."

Tavares' eyes narrowed further, and he tapped a hard finger into the center of Sonja's chest. The jab hurt, but Sonja did not step away. "The only person done, is you," he said softly, then again headed for the castle entrance.

Sonja did not call after him. Her blood ran cold, and her eyes burned with unshed tears from the adrenaline coursing through her. She clutched the practice swords tightly against her stomach to hide the shaking of her hands and mentally ordered herself not to cry. She knew she had made an enemy, and her life at the school was about to get much harder because of it. She also knew there had been no alternative. She was not going to sleep with Tavares just to avoid extra chores.

She expected Tavares would plot something terrible to get back at her, something embarrassing or demeaning, or perhaps even physically painful, but she did not expect what came next. Within ten minutes of Tavares leaving the courtyard training grounds, Sonja was approached by another student and directed to meet with Master Cejack in his study.

When she arrived, she knew she was in trouble. Sonja had only been to Cejack's personal study on one other occasion. That had been to deliver a sealed message from a teacher, and after which she had departed immediately. Cejack had barely acknowledged her presence. This time, however, she had his full attention.

As she entered and closed the door behind her, Cejack sat rigid in an uncomfortable-looking, rough-cut chair behind a long wooden table. The table was stained a dark maple color and polished to a mirror finish. Sonja could see Cejack's reflection glowering at her in the glossy surface as the table was currently empty except for a stack of heavy, leather-bound books pushed to one side. As she approached, he rose to his feet to address her.

"Is this true?" Cejack asked, his voice low and ominous. "You refused to take direction from an instructor?"

Sonja did not ask for clarification. She knew what he was asking. That little weasel, Tavares, must have gone directly from the courtyard to Cejack's study.

"Yes," she answered. "But he–"

"No! I will not hear excuses. You could be removed from the school for refusing an order. You know that."

Sonja realized she was expected to keep silent. Talking back could only aggravate Cejack further, which would make everything worse, but she was still upset by Tavares' actions. She was still *angry*. Besides, she had never been known for staying quiet when she felt she was being treated unfairly.

"He ordered me to sleep with him!" she spat back. "Is that the way this school works? Is that acceptable to you?"

Cejack paused, though his face revealed nothing of his thoughts at that moment. He sat down, eyeing Sonja intently. In a calmer voice, he said, "Please tell me what happened and why you refused."

Sonja explained how Tavares had approached her and the conversation that followed. She repeated what she had told him to the best of her recollection, not denying that she had flatly denied his directions, but explaining why she had done so. Cejack nodded, his brows drawn together and his lips pursed tight in contemplation. He cursed under his breath, and Sonja hoped his venom was not solely directed at her.

After listening to her story, the schoolmaster told her he was assigning her to the kitchens for the next three days to do food preparation and clean up after the morning and evening meals. She would be permitted to train each day, but only when her duties in the kitchen allowed it.

"Three days?" Sonja asked, surprised to still be receiving a punishment.

"Do you wish more? Perhaps an additional week for challenging my decision?"

Sonja at last remembered her earlier commitment to keep her mouth shut and not draw avoidable attention down on herself from the instructors. This was bad, but she had not been removed from the school. She reigned in her temper before giving Cejack a reason to throw her out. "No, Master Cejack. I'm sorry for my outburst. Of course, I accept your punishment. Am I free to leave? Dinner starts soon and I should go help serve."

"Yes. You may go," said Cejack. Then as an afterthought, "Although today is almost over, I will accept this as one day's service."

Sonja was stunned. Cejack never changed a punishment once he had made a decision. Reducing her time by almost a full day was the equivalent of a pardon from anyone else. She quickly left the room before he had time to reconsider his largesse.

The next morning, Sonja finished scrubbing the last of the breakfast pots and hung them from their ceiling hooks to dry before hurrying out to the courtyard where training was already well underway. She had just joined her group, apologizing to Mister Sammon for being late, and began practicing a series of "Clash" drills with another student, when Master Cejack entered the yard. With a word, he halted the morning training and called for everyone's attention.

Cejack pointed and waved Tavares over to him. The students and instructors looked on with curiosity at the unexpected break. The four masters who assisted Cejack with the daily running of the school stood quietly behind him. They frowned unhappily; even more so than usual.

"Give me your sword," ordered Cejack when Tavares approached him.

The instructor complied. Cejack reversed the weapon in his hands and drove the point of the blade into the red soil at his feet. He released the handle and the sword remained upright where he had placed it. The slender sword swayed slightly back and forth between Cejack and Tavares. Sonja felt a dull headache building behind her eyes as she watched it move. To her, the weapon standing in the courtyard resembled a narrow metal cross, the kind one might find symbolizing an important ceremony.

Or marking a grave.

"I strip you of your right to carry this sword," stated Cejack so all assembled could hear. The students stood rigid, afraid to move or speak. Cejack could have whispered and no one would have missed a word.

"You have disgraced yourself in the eyes of the school. When you leave you are entitled to take nothing with you. If I ever learn that you have claimed my name or the school's sigil, I will hunt you like an animal and I will kill you. I will kill you with this blade." Cejack touched the pommel of Tavares' sword where it stood between them as a graphic token of his promise. Tavares opened his mouth to speak, but Cejack silenced him with a shake of his head.

Two of the masters escorted the former instructor from the grounds. He was not even permitted to return to his room to gather his belongings.

After Tavares left the school, stories and rumors circulated for months, speculations on why he had been removed so abruptly. The school masters offered no explanation, and Sonja felt no need to share with anyone her part in his expulsion. It was nobody else's business.

Sonja's second incident occurred in the middle of her second month, barely a week after the first. It was not so dramatic as her confrontation with Tavares, but it was physically much more dangerous.

The conflict began over a game of dice. Several students had gathered during one of their rare free afternoons and decided a little friendly game of chance was what was needed to pass the time. Although no money was permitted to change hands at the school, there were no rules about divesting oneself of tiresome chores on a less fortunate classmate. Sonja joined the others in the game and quickly found herself on a prolonged lucky streak.

One of the losing students, Mekhil, did not appreciate her luck and accused her of cheating.

"Don't be ridiculous," she told him, preparing for her next throw.

"Are you calling me a liar?" he fumed, rising to his feet.

"You're damned right I am," Sonja shot back.

Mekhil drew his sword and pointed it in her direction. "I will address your insult in the Circle."

Mekhil was technically in the same class as Sonja, but he had been through training with Cejack once before. At the end of his first year, he had failed his final test to earn his sword. Many students failed the first time they tested, and all were offered a chance to repeat the training and test again. Most refused, unable to stomach the idea of repeating the hellish drills and workouts required of beginning students. Mekhil, however, returned to try again.

At this stage of her training, Sonja's experience in the Circle included slightly more than two weeks of practice sparring; and that was with a wooden sword. Mekhil had completed a year of study and had not failed his exam by a great deal.

Sonja knew she was in trouble.

She had been challenged and she could not refuse. Not if she wanted to stay. A student ran to request Master Cejack as the rest of the group moved outside to the courtyard. Cejack arrived to find both Sonja and Mekhil already waiting in the Circle. Mekhil understandably appeared more pleased than Sonja at the prospect of the duel.

"This match will be decided by first blood," said Cejack. "Do both of you accept this condition?"

Sonja nodded, subdued.

Mekhil was more vocal, "I accept! Remember, little girl," he continued, lowering his voice so only Sonja could hear. "First blood could be fatal."

"Draw your blades," Cejack directed. Then when both had taken a ready stance, "Begin!"

Sonja avoided Mekhil initially, knowing his skills far exceeded her own and not wanting to give him too easy of a target. She considered stepping out of the circle and accepting disqualification, but Cejack had made it very clear on numerous occasions that he considered deliberately exiting a combat a personal insult to him and the school. Sonja had seen him deal with personal insults before, and she wanted no part of it. In desperation she tried to figure a way out that did not end in expulsion, death, or serious injury.

One possibility occurred to her, though she was unsure if it was wise to attempt it. Even if her idea worked, this duel could still end badly for her. With no better plan in mind, however, she figured it was worth trying. If she did nothing, Mekhil was going to try to cut her in half.

Mekhil shuffled in close, driving his weapon straight forward in a simple test of Sonja's defenses. Instead of parrying the easy jab, Sonja surprised everyone by holding her ground and reaching out with her empty left hand. She grabbed his sword, pushing it aside as she did. Startled by the unexpected maneuver, Mekhil jerked backwards, pulling the sword from Sonja's grasp and cutting her across her palm. The cut did not go deep, but a crimson line of blood welled up from the injury. Sonja held her open hand out toward Cejack so the wound was visible.

"First blood," called Cejack when he saw her bleeding palm.

Mekhil cursed, commenting loudly and angrily about women not knowing enough to keep their hands off a weapon's edge before he stomped away to resume what was left of his free afternoon. Sonja watched him go, relieved she had escaped with nothing more than a cut hand.

The following morning, Sonja tried to apologize to Mekhil, but she discovered the offer was unnecessary. The young man's memory seemed as short as his temper was fast. He had smiled and waved off her attempts to discuss the incident.

"My fault entirely," he assured her. "Sometimes I let my pride make me stupid. I never should have put you in the Circle. I'm glad you were not hurt."

"You … aren't mad?" asked Sonja.

"You don't get mad at a fox that avoids your trap. You can only admire it for being smarter than you." With a wink, Mekhil moved on to begin the day's training.

Sonja shook her head, a bit bemused by Mekhil's jovial attitude regarding their duel. There was no time to dwell over it however, as Sammon called her group into line.

Time blurred for Sonja as day after exhausting day passed. Weeks slipped by and she all but forgot she had another life waiting for her when she finished her training. She began to feel as though she had never known anything other than sparring, training, and the Combat Circle. Her speed, strength and skill improved, and she began handling heavier weapons with more proficiency. Many of the men were stronger than she, but few moved as swiftly or as deftly.

In addition to her speed, Sonja was building a reputation for being a smart fighter. Light on her feet, and able to take advantage of repetitive patterns or weaknesses in her fellow students, she won more often than she lost in the practice circles. Her successes in her training also translated into greater acceptance from the other students. She had gone from merely being an anomaly – the only female student at Master Cejack's school – to being an included member of the greater group.

She enjoyed the feeling of belonging, and Sonja no longer felt out of place at the school. Still, there were moments of homesickness that left her desperately missing her family and friends.

At the end of Sonja's third month, Rith gave her some surprising but welcome news.

She had just finished the evening meal and returned to her room to grab the pitcher and basin Merind had provided her during her first month in the dormitory. In addition to assigning rooms, the old man was responsible for procuring reasonable necessities, and a few comforts when possible. Sonja requested these specific items after several early mornings of slinking off to the bathing room before any other residents had begun to stir.

After a fatiguing day of training, having to wake up earlier than everybody else so she could wash and still have time to get breakfast was wearing her down. She needed sleep as much as anyone, but her circumstances were making it difficult to get enough rest. Her baths dwindled from every morning, to every other day, then finally to about twice each week. Although this frequency was not atypical of most of the other students – in fact, some visited the bath much less often – it bothered Sonja that in the evenings when she stripped off her clothing and gear, she could smell the sharp reek of her own body odor.

Now each evening, after the last meal of the day, she took her pitcher and basin to the bath to dump the previous day's water down the sluice and refill the pitcher from the wall spout. This allowed her to perform a "bird bath" cleaning in the privacy of her own room, using a rag to wipe away the worst of the grime and sweat from her body before crawling into bed.

On this particular night, Sonja paused as she collected her pitcher from the battered bedside stand she had foraged out of a discard heap. She hesitated as she noticed that the ring on her left hand was empty. Only the thin silver band remained around her middle finger. Rith was gone.

"Rith?" she asked softly, trying to ignore the flutter of panic growing in her chest. "Where are you? You didn't just leave me, did you?"

There was no response.

"Rith!" she called again, as loud as she dared without risking drawing attention from anyone wandering the halls outside her room.

"I'm here!" piped Rith's tiny voice as he blinked into sight in front of her. "Sorry about that. I didn't think I'd be gone long enough for you to notice. Sorry."

Sonja exhaled a small sigh of relief. "That's okay, buddy. I saw you were missing and started to flip out a little bit. Where did you go?"

"I went to see Cejack. I had a question for him."

When Rith did not immediately continue, Sonja rotated a finger in the air, indicating that he should keep talking. "You're dying to tell me something. I can see you're pretty worked up by it, too, so just spit it out."

"Okay. I noticed that many of the students get messages and gifts from home. Some even are allowed visitors during their free time. I went to ask Cejack if there is something we can do for you, since you are kind of stuck so far away from anyone you know."

Sonja banged the pitcher back onto the stand. She tried to reign in her sudden excitement. Rith had only said he asked the question. The answer might still be no. "And, what did he say?" she asked with a hopeful gleam in her eyes.

Rith dipped and leapt in a series of aerial flips. "Cejack said that you can take one day each month, as long as you keep up your training and don't get into any trouble."

Sonja blinked, confused. "One day? To do what? A day off?"

"One day to go home," explained Rith. "Didn't I say that? No, I guess I didn't. Yes, well, one day to go home."

Sonja screamed, no longer caring who might hear.

"I can go home. I can see my family," she gushed. Then, whirling back to face Rith. "When? When can I go?"

CHAPTER 9

Sonja jerked upright in the reclined lawn chair. After three months away, she was back in the familiar surroundings of her own backyard. She stared joyfully at the patio and back door of her home, trailing her eyes over the rusted barbeque grill and faded padding of the wicker furniture pushed up against the house. It all remained exactly where she had seen it last. Although she had been gone for what felt like an eternity, here it had only been the blink of an eye.

As she reveled in the view of her yard, breathing it in like the first fresh smell of rain after a long dry summer, she realized that although no time had passed, there were some things that had most definitely changed. The light blue bikini she wore felt oddly tight around her chest. The string that tied around her back was digging into her skin as though it had been cinched down two sizes since putting it on.

Months of endless workouts and brandishing bulky weapons had added layers of muscle that had not been there before she left. Her back and shoulders were heavier; broader. Her arms and legs had also gained size and a roundness of definition that had not previously existed.

Sonja discovered one more difference that, although not a big deal, might be more difficult to explain to her family. The skin along her exposed body remained as pale as the day she left, but her arms from the biceps down were the deep brown of someone who had been out in the sun for months. She giggled as she admired the tan. Well, she *had* been in the sun for months. Not here, but that didn't change the reality of her new farmer's tan. She gave a mental shrug. Once she had a shirt on, nobody would know the difference.

"There's no one home, is there?" asked Sonja, trying to remember where everyone had been before she left.

"No," agreed Rith. "They left earlier this morning."

That's right, Sonja thought. *It's still morning here.* At the school, it was early evening. Despite the time difference and a long day of sword practice and knife drills, Sonja was no longer tired. She was wide awake and eager to see her dad again. She also looked forward to seeing Philip, even if she did still consider him a pest.

Try as she might, Sonja could not recall where they had gone or when they might be coming home. No matter. She knew exactly what she wanted to do while she waited for them to return.

"I need a shower," she announced. "I want to wash my hair with real shampoo for a change. Not that sandy block of lye they call soap at the school."

Grabbing her beach towel from the lawn chair, Sonja skipped into the house and went straight to the bathroom. She paused in front of the bathroom mirror, taking a moment to examine herself in the reflection. In the past three months, Sonja had not so much as seen a mirror at Cejack's school, much less found an opportunity to observe herself in one.

The girl staring back was familiar, but in many ways seemed like a stranger. The new muscle in her arms, shoulders and back made her look wider, stronger, and maybe even a bit more confident than the Sonja who had disappeared three months ago.

"Hey, Rith. Check it out. I have abs."

It was true. While Sonja had always been slender, and her stomach had always been flat, she had never had much to brag about in terms of muscle tone. Today, she was rocking the beginnings of a really nice six-pack. She ran a hand over the curves of her belly, admiringly. Then, with a comical grunt she raised her arms in a body builder's pose, flexing her biceps and grimacing at her image in the mirror.

"Oh, dear," she mused, catching sight of the hair under her arms. "That's a bit more Bohemian than I'm used to. We'll have to do something about that after I wash my hair."

"You know something, Rith?" Sonja asked as she stripped out of her swimsuit and turned on the hot water for her shower. "Those movies are complete bullshit."

"What movies?"

"Those movies where women end up in the jungle or lost in the woods for weeks, but their mascara is always immaculate, and they always have perfectly smooth pits. I wish I could have whatever magic spell they have that stops their hair from growing and their makeup from smudging. Do you think you could...?"

"No," said Rith at the implied question.

"Yeah, I didn't think so."

Freshly washed and shaved, Sonja applied deodorant and a small spray of perfume. Within a couple of days, she would be just another smelly, unwashed body at the school, but even if it was just for a few hours, she wanted to feel like a twenty-first century, human being again.

She got dressed, trying on several pairs of jeans that no longer fit before resorting to baggy, blue sweatpants and a blousy green t-shirt that hid the dramatic tan lines on her upper arms. She needed to go on a shopping spree when her training with Cejack was over so she could find clothes that would fit her new body shape. Most of the items in her closet were going to be a bit snug, if she could get into them at all.

Her father and brother had not yet arrived home. Tired of waiting, and growing desperate to hear a familiar voice, she called her mom on the phone. When her mother picked up, Sonja mentioned her need to go shopping for clothes as her excuse for the call.

"Sweetheart," her mother objected, "I don't have any money to buy you clothes."

Sonja quickly reassured her mother, "No, Mom. I don't need money. I just want to take you with me. It might be nice to have a woman's opinion on some new outfits."

"Oh. Well then, of course," her mother said, cheerily. "I'd love to go with you."

The two of them talked for almost an hour and, other than a few tense moments when her mother asked how her dad was getting by without her, the conversation stayed light and pleasant. Sonja had been slightly hesitant about calling but was ultimately glad she did. She hung up with a final, "I love you, Mom."

Her father and brother arrived home not long after the phone call, and Sonja met them at the door with a hug and a kiss for each.

"Where did you go?" she asked, trying to keep her voice neutral.

"To the store," said her father, holding up the bags of groceries he was carrying. "I told you before we left. I even asked you to come with us. Don't you remember?"

"Oh, yeah," said Sonja hastily. "Of course, I do." She grabbed one of the bags out of her dad's hands and carried it into the kitchen.

"Are you all right? You seem a little anxious about something."

"No, I'm fine."

And she was. It was joy, not worry that had her so wired, but how could she explain to her family how exited she was to see them? To be home? They would think she had lost her mind. Instead, Sonja contented herself with enjoying their proximity as she helped put away canned goods in the pantry. She had one day with her family before she needed to go back to the school. She wanted to make the most of it.

"Hey, I have an idea," Sonja said, folding up the last empty grocery bag and setting it aside on the kitchen counter. "Let's go out and get some ice cream. I feel like it's been forever since we got ice cream."

"Ice cream?" her dad asked, skeptically. "You really want ice cream? We just got back home. I'm not sure I want to go out again."

"Wait a sec."

Sonja dashed down the hallway to her room. After a brief hesitation, as she attempted to remember where she had last dropped her purse, she snatched the handbag out of her closet and rummaged through it to find her wallet. Praying it wasn't empty, she snapped it open.

"Yes!" she hissed, pulling out thirty-five dollars in cash and skipping back to the kitchen.

She flapped the money in the air where her father and brother could see it. "I'm buying. But, it's a one-time offer. We go now, or you guys lose out on free ice cream."

Her dad laughed; his mood buoyed by her own. Glancing at Sonja's brother, he said, "Your sister's buying, so I guess we're going to get ice cream."

"And pizza," Sonja amended as her dad pulled the car keys from his pocket. "I think we should do pizza for dinner. Definitely, pizza for dinner."

CHAPTER 10

Sonja's first year of training at Cejack's school passed more comfortably after the initial few months. The opportunity to return home for one day each month eased the loneliness of missing friends and family and gave her something to look forward to. It was also good motivation to perform. She did not want to disappoint any of her instructors or get into trouble that would cost her that one day of leave she had been allowed.

In addition, she made a few friends at the school. While there were several students that felt a woman learning to use a sword was a waste of time and chose to keep their distance, there were plenty of others who either did not care or decided she was novel enough they wanted to get to know more about her.

Still, when the first anniversary of Sonja's arrival finally came, she awoke that morning feeling as though she had successfully endured the most difficult year of her life. Which was probably true. Today marked her final day as a student at the school. When the sun set this evening, she would have earned her sword, or she would be sent away. Of course, Cejack would probably offer her a chance to return and attempt the training again, just as Mekhil – the boy who had tried to kill her in the Circle – had done.

Mekhil had earned his sword six months previously, when Cejack allowed him to test with an older class. Despite the original agreement that he would complete the entire year of training, the instructors all agreed that he was ready, and he had proved them correct. Even if she were to be offered the same abbreviated training period, Sonja did not have the stomach or the heart to start over after the trials of the past twelve months. She admired Mekhil's determination, but she knew if she failed today, she would go home.

Of the original students in her group, only eighteen remained to take the test. Not all of them would pass and, by tomorrow, that number would be smaller still. She hoped she would not be one of the day's failures.

Too nervous to eat, Sonja skipped breakfast, instead opting for an early morning bath. Three others testing that day had the same idea and were already lounging in the pool when she arrived. Evan, Khal, and Arvin sprawled, spaced out around the edge of the filled basin, soaking in the warmth of the water and trying to appear relaxed. Sonja knew better. Her stomach was churning as she contemplated the day ahead, and she could only assume these three were feeling the same way.

Long over her initial shyness of being undressed in front of the other students, she stripped her towel off and hung it on one of the wooden racks affixed to the wall, then stepped into the steaming water to join them.

Sonja waded to the center of the bath and began to lather soap into her hair in the deeper water. While she scrubbed away the previous day's grime, she joined in on the boys' conversation, which consisted mainly of what they believed Cejack would be looking for during the test and how they could best perform to his expectations.

Evan, who began the year training under Misha, shook his head slowly. "I don't know," he said in answer to another's inquiry. "Master Pott still doesn't like the way I transition from right to left hand in the seventh form. It's too late to fix it now, so I just have to hope it isn't enough to stop me from passing."

Sonja finished rinsing the soap out of her hair and ran her fingers through the wet strands to work out the worst of the tangles. "You'll be fine, Evan. You should just slow it down a little bit. You move through that transition so fast you don't have a chance to check your grip before you move into the next attack. Just take a breath and you're not going to have any problem."

"Easy for you to be so relaxed," Evan told her. "You were probably ready to test two months ago. This is going to be simple as taking a piss for you."

Sonja fought a smile, hoping the redness in her face would be attributed to the hot water. Embarrassed by the compliment, she was also secretly pleased at Evan's assessment of her abilities. "Quit complaining. You are going to have a shiny new sword by tonight and you know it."

"I guess we'll all know the outcome in a few hours," Evan said, rising to his feet and stepping out of the pool.

Khal and Arvin followed him out of the water, grabbing towels and proceeding to dry themselves at the edge of the bath. When they finished, they wrapped the towels about their waists and all three exited the room, waving to Sonja and wishing her luck.

Sonja finished up soon after they left. Wrapping her own towel around herself, she returned to her room to dress and prepare to meet whatever this day had to offer.

To earn a sword from Master Cejack, the schoolmaster demanded that the students learn eight practice forms, ten clash drills, six extended drills, and four melee drills. The forms were demonstrated solo and required the student to perform a series of movements considered necessary for basic sword use. Beginning forms consisted of twenty-five techniques in combination, while more advanced forms could take over two-hundred moves and several minutes to perform properly.

Clash drills utilized two or three basic sword attacks and defenses with a partner. Extended drills were ten moves or more and sometimes required the use of several opponents to execute. Finally, the melees each consisted of no less than thirty techniques with a partner in a choreographed sparring simulation. Once a student mastered all of these, they were still considered by the Masters of the school as merely "competent" at the use of a sword. However, competency at a training facility such as Master Cejack's still carried quite a bit of prestige to those who were familiar with his name.

Competency carried privileges as well. Students carried their own weapons rather than the battered relics from the school armory. They were also given their own classes to teach. Novices, brand new to the school, were grouped up and trained by advanced students who had earned their swords but had not yet achieved the level of Teacher or Master. Sammon, had been new to his sword when Sonja began her training with him.

The first two hours that morning, Sonja and the remaining members of her class performed the eight practice forms. One by one, they stood before Cejack and three other school masters, and demonstrated the choreographed techniques. If even one movement was not perfect, Master Cejack would see it immediately. The unlucky student would be stopped and directed to begin again. Sonja could feel her hands shaking when it was her turn to perform, however, as she worked through the familiar motions of the first few moves, her body calmed and slipped into a comfortable rhythm. She completed each of the forms cleanly and without significant error.

The remainder of the morning, following the forms, the students completed all required drills. By the time they were allowed to sit and enjoy a lunch break, Sonja's legs and shoulders felt leaden with fatigue. Sweat soaked her shirt and plastered it across her back, and she felt trickles of moisture running from under her arms and tickling down her ribcage. Despite the muscle aches and uncomfortably wet clothing, Sonja did not feel tired as she was called back into line following the brief meal. Excitement over how well she had performed so far, as well as nervousness about what came next, kept her energy and adrenaline high. The next two phases of the exam would only last a few minutes each, but they remained the most important segments of her test.

Sonja's head snapped up when she heard her name announced. One of the masters ordered her to the front of her group and she hurried to comply. It appeared she was going first this afternoon. Perhaps that was for the best as it gave her no time to ponder and worry over her performance.

"Derrik," called Cejack, as Sonja stood patiently at attention. "You will partner with Sonja for the next phase."

"Yes, Master Cejack," responded Derrik, without hesitation. He drew his sword and stepped forward. Derrik was a year ahead of Sonja and had already earned his sword, his bear, and the title of Teacher. Tomorrow, he was scheduled to test for the highest rank at the school, which would earn him the title of Master and give him the right to carry the ceravit emblem etched into the blade of his sword.

Sonja faced him and drew her own weapon. This test was a series of five movements called the Contact Frays. One opponent would step forward and initiate an attack of their choice, the second would take appropriate defensive action then follow with an attack of their own. On the fifth move, the original aggressor would initiate a fatal blow while the defender was required to drop his guard and allow the contact. The two combatants would take turns initiating the Frays. Back and forth, until one of the masters called a halt.

Sonja shifted her right side forward, aligning herself to create a smaller target, and raised her sword to the ready position. Her weight rocked forward to the balls of her feet as she waited for the signal to begin.

"One!" called Cejack, and Sonja lunged, her sword driving forward to impale Derrik through the heart. His blade met her thrust with a loud clash, easily turning it aside. He followed her attack with a cut of his own across Sonja's torso, waist high, right to left. Deflecting the slash, Sonja opted for another thrust, this time angled low to threaten her opponent's thigh. Derrik did not even counter the move. Instead, he shifted his leg a fraction to the side, allowing her attack to miss by its own momentum. His counter was an upward jab at her belly that would have disemboweled her if it had been delivered with any speed. He slowed his blade to allow Sonja to recover and deflect the cut. As metal rang against metal, Sonja caught Derrik's eye and the look of disappointment in his gaze shamed her. She had overextended on her second attack, and she had done it during a damned practice fray. If this had been actual combat, it would be over already, and Sonja would be bleeding out in the dirt.

Sonja shuffled forward and finished with a slash meant to remove Derrik's head from his neck. She stopped her blade inches from her intended target to show her control in the confrontation and demonstrate the win.

Despite the ending, anyone with any knowledge of battle could see clearly that Sonja had lost this encounter. She did not look around for fear of what expressions she would find plastered on the faces of the masters. Staring straight ahead at Derrik, she clenched her teeth, determined to keep control.

"Two!" Cejack ordered immediately.

Sonja continued. Three. Four. Five. Attack, parry, attack. Attack, parry, attack. The masters considered repeating an attack that had already been attempted to be poor form, so Sonja worked diligently to vary her assaults. She used simple, basic strikes, then worked her way through gradually more intricate movements, careful not to let her focus on attacking cause her to overextend again and allow another of Derrik's offensives to break through.

After a couple tense minutes, she stopped worrying about who was watching or trying to think ahead to her next move, and at last let herself relax. Sonja stilled her mind, and the countless hours of practice took over, carrying her along as she settled into the flow and rhythm of the fray. As fast or as hard as she moved against Derrik, he met her with equal force, never tiring or showing any effort either in his face or in his body. He moved with a liquid grace, letting Sonja set the pace and then matching it. Sonja envied his skill and, with each successive fray, found herself watching Derrik's technique and trying to mimic it in her own movements. She realized that even should she earn her sword today, there was still a great deal for her to learn.

Twenty-four. Twenty-five. Twenty-six.

Then it was over.

Cejack called out for Sonja to hold and sheath her blade. She raised her sword in salute as protocol demanded – and out of true respect for Derrik's ability – then returned it to her belt. Sweat dripped from her face and she panted heavily. Derrik returned her salute and smiled. Other than a sheen of sweat forming at his brow and dampening the edges of his hair, he looked no more disheveled than when he had first stepped forward at Cejack's request.

"Very nice," Derrik commented, replacing his weapon.

"Don't make fun of me," Sonja retorted. "Next to you I looked like an idiot. A clumsy, slow idiot."

"Sonja! Derrik!" Cejack allowed no more time for conversation. "Into the Circle. Time to earn your sword."

Sonja accepted a boiled leather vest and leather helmet from one of the teachers. The helmet covered the top and sides of her head, but left her face open so as not to obstruct her view. The vest and helmet were the only protective clothing permitted in the Circle and, while the leather would protect fragile skin from accidental brushes against the sharp edges of a sword, it would do little to stop the impact of a well landed blow. As she fastened the laces of her vest, Derrik donned his own gear.

When all preparation was completed, Sonja moved to her position inside the Combat Circle and watched as Derrik entered from the opposite side. Because Derrik tested for his ceravit tomorrow, Sonja knew this final test was as important to him as it was to her. Possibly more so. She needed to demonstrate her ability to maintain a sustained, armed confrontation. Her skills would be assessed by Cejack both on offense and defense. Despite her performance so far this morning, she could fail this test completely in the next few minutes.

Derrik also had a great deal to lose. Although this combat was not part of his test, if he allowed Sonja to cut him, he would be seen as incapable of defending himself from a student. Similarly, if he injured Sonja, he would be demonstrating an inability to control his own weapon. He had nothing to gain and everything to lose.

Sonja soon realized she need not concern herself with Derrik's performance. He was fully prepared for anything she might throw at him. Seconds after the combat began, she found herself wishing she did not have to be in the arena with him. She would have loved to simply take a step back and watch his performance with the rest of her class. She wanted to be a spectator for this moment. His movements with the sword were so natural and fluid, flowing smoothly from one position to the next, that the weapon did not seem to be an object in his hand, but rather an extension of his body. The blade moved as though it were reacting directly to his thoughts.

Despite her admiration for Derrik's abilities, Sonja did not have the luxury of merely observing. Her performance was critical to earning her sword, and she reminded herself to stay focused on her part of the fight.

Shaking away the distracting thoughts in her head, Sonja shuffled forward, taking the offensive and trying to drive Derrik backward. She worked basic techniques at first, using simple, controlled movements to poke and prod at his defenses as she searched for an opening, looking for some crack in his armor.

Derrik offered nothing. Sonja varied her attacks and gradually pushed herself to faster and more complicated maneuvers, hoping to create an opportunity. Derrik turned every thrust and deflected every cut. On two occasions, she forced Derrik to disengage and retreat, but Sonja knew he only backed away because his choices were limited to creating space between them or a more aggressive parry that might have led to an injury. Hers.

Derrik blocked, parried, and fended Sonja off dutifully, allowing her to display her full offensive repertoire for her evaluators. When he decided she had sufficient opportunity to showcase her offensive ability, he pushed his own attack, bringing her defensive skills into play. Sonja found herself quickly pushed to her limits keeping Derrik's blade from its intended targets. His attacks came fast and precise, exploiting any weaknesses or hesitations and highlighting them for the masters to see. Every stumble and blunder stood out in stark relief compared to Derrik's flawless defensive performance against her. Whenever Derrik's blade cut completely through her guard – as it did on more than one occasion – he would stop, holding his weapon inches from her throat, heart, or some other vital organ, before beginning a new series of attacks.

Sonja danced to her left, panting, and narrowly avoided a cut to her sword arm. She felt her defenses slipping yet again, pushed to desperate, panicky counters before Derrik's merciless assault. Each block she made felt just a heartbeat too slow, or an inch too close, and she knew, at any moment, he would claim another vital piece of her anatomy. Before he could solidify his next victory, Cejack called an end to the exercise.

"Enough," he announced. "Put away your weapons."

Sonja stood shaking and defeated, completely drained of energy and ego. She glanced at Derrik and saw with some satisfaction the sweat running off his face. His breathing seemed a little elevated as well. *Oh well,* she thought. *At least I made the bastard work for it a little bit.*

"Sonja," said Cejack. "Remove your sword and go replace it in the armory."

Stunned, Sonja did not move immediately. Turn in her sword? Her first thought was that she had failed and Cejack was kicking her out of the school. She almost started to plead in protest, begging Cejack to give her another chance, when Derrik's hand clapped down on her shoulder, jarring her out of her shock.

"You did it," he said. "You earned your sword. Now, go turn in your student weapon like he told you, and hurry back."

Sonja ran to and from the armory, pausing only long enough to drop her sword onto a pair of hooks on the wall. When she returned, she was directed to sit with the rest of her class. For the next few hours, she rested and observed as the other students each had their turn in the Circle. On occasion, as she sat, a hand would clap against her shoulder and someone would mutter a quiet congratulations.

At the end of the day, with the sun hovering a few fingers' width above the courtyard wall, Sonja lined up before the masters and instructors of the school with ten other students. Seven people had gone home in the past eight hours. Cejack offered each of them the opportunity to return in the next class and test again, but all refused and instead chose to leave. Only eleven, out of fifty-four original students, earned the right to carry the school's sword.

Sonja waited, basking in the warm glow of her accomplishment. She had rested long enough that the sweat on her and in her clothing had dried, so although the evening air was chill and a breeze had recently picked up, she was not cold. A few of the students, having tested more recently, shivered slightly beside her as the wind cooled their damp skin. They did not seem overly bothered by the weather, however.

Content in her success and smiling broadly, she soaked up the moment, privately wishing that it could last forever.

"Congratulations. I am very proud of you all. Today, you have earned your swords." Cejack paced slowly up and down the line of students, holding eye contact momentarily with each of them as he talked, making his speech all the more personal. Several feet behind him, the assembled teachers and masters of the school observed the ceremony, trying to appear solemn and dignified, though a few were obviously enjoying the moment as much as the students.

"Each sword carries on its cross guard the sigil of this school: an open eye in the palm of an iron gauntlet. The image symbolizes strength and control. Strength is meaningless without the will and intelligence to guide it. You have each demonstrated to me, today, your understanding of this concept.

"Wherever you go, I give you the right to carry this symbol with you, so that all who see it will know what you have accomplished here. I also now give you the opportunity to stay and continue your studies. So perhaps one day you might earn your bear."

Cejack drew his sword and held it up to eye level. On one side of the blade was etched the image of bear shambling on all four paws. "The bear symbolizes power. It is the emblem of a teacher at this school, and it requires great dedication to achieve it. Many who try, fail. But nothing worthwhile is ever gained easily.

"As a teacher, your next step may be the ceravit." Cejack turned the blade over to display, on the opposite side, an etching of a small feline animal with a bony ridge running the length of its head and back. The animal matched the tattoo on his left arm.

"This animal has been known to kill creatures many times its own size. It uses not just the weapons the gods gave it – teeth and claws – but guile and cunning. To display the ceravit is to claim the title, Master. I do not grant this right lightly, as I jealously guard the standards and reputation of this school. A master representing my school must show superior moral character as well as skill and intelligence."

Cejack sheathed his sword. "Today, the blades you receive are bare, but they are no less important for it. You are still a representative of this school and I expect you to comport yourselves as such. Should you choose to leave today, you go with my blessings and wishes for success. If you stay, I look forward to seeing how much more you may achieve."

Two school masters, Master Gregor and Master Amarand, approached Cejack, each holding several scabbarded swords bundled in their arms and held tightly against their chests. Master Gregor was tall and wiry, with a heavily grayed beard, though the close-cut hair on his head remained as black as night. Blond, short and fat, with a cherubic face that he kept neatly shaved, the younger master, Master Amarand, was Gregor's polar opposite. Sonja had frequently wondered how anyone could be a part of Cejack's school, working as hard as they all did, and still be so round.

The two positioned themselves to either side of Cejack as he paused in front of the first successful student in line. Sonja noted with pleasure that the first student was Evan. His worries that morning had been baseless, as she had told him, and she was happy to be proved correct. The boy's grin covered his entire face, and his ears were flushed red with excitement and pleasure. His face probably matched her own, she thought.

Cejack held out his left hand and the master instructor closest to him placed the grip of a sword into his palm. Master

Cejack raised the weapon, holding it out toward Evan laid across his open hands like a gift. As the boy received his sword, Cejack clapped a hand to his shoulder. "Wherever you carry that blade, your reputation is no longer solely your own. You represent me, and you represent this school. Remember that always, and never take action that may diminish us both."

Evan nodded, clutching the sword tightly in both hands.

Master Cejack moved down the line. Handing each student a new sword and repeating the words he had spoken to Evan. Sonja was in the middle of the lineup, with five people to either side of her, yet when Cejack reached her, he simply stepped past, moving from the student on her right to the one on her left. Surprised, and more than a little hurt by the snub, Sonja wondered why she had been skipped. Was this a new school tradition? Girls get their swords last? Master Cejack had never before given her any indication that he considered her more or less than any other student, so why this odd treatment? Or, maybe, he had no plans to give her a blade at all. Maybe Cejack did not think a girl was an appropriate representation of his precious school.

Sonja's thoughts grew heated, although she knew better than to speak up. Interrupting the ceremony with an angry accusation would only get her into trouble so, she waited silently to see how Master Cejack planned to end this farce. She vowed she would be patient, but she also promised herself if Cejack came back and handed her a bunch of flowers or some other lame bullshit like that, she was going to kick the pompous asshole square in the balls.

When Master Cejack finished working his way through the line of assembled students, he walked back to stand in front of Sonja. He smiled as he took a moment to look at her, his dark beard bristling around the corners of his mouth. Cejack did not smile often, and the expression was a bit off-putting to Sonja. It didn't seem natural. A smile on Cejack's face looked more predatory than pleased, making her feel like an injured bird staring up at a cat. Sonja attempted to smile back, but the expression only devolved into one of awkward confusion.

"Today, something very special happened," said Cejack, not taking his eyes from Sonja. "Today, I was given an opportunity to honor my father."

Cejack snapped his fingers and a third master, Master Colin, broke ranks from the group behind him.

He better not have flowers, thought Sonja again, though it was already clear Colin held another sword in his hands.

Cejack accepted the weapon from Colin, who jogged back to his place with the other teachers and masters. He held the sword up to show it to Sonja but did not hand it to her.

"When a new sword is made for one of my students, I commission the work only to weaponsmiths I know and trust. I do not personally have the skill to make these weapons, but I set the standards for how they are to be forged and created. Each of them is stamped with the emblem of this school only after I have approved the finished blade."

Cejack tapped a thick finger to the image on the guard. Sonja saw the open gauntlet she had become so familiar with in the past year, however in the center of the palm the design was different. Instead of the open eye she had expected, she found a stylized letter 'R.'

"My father had no such limitations," Cejack continued. "When he desired that a very special sword be created, he made the blade with his own hands. He made each of his weapons with great care, love, and skill, and he gifted them only to those students he felt would appreciate them."

Grasping his own sword, Cejack held the two weapons side by side so Sonja could see the cross guards together. Master Cejack's sword carried the same stylized 'R' in the gauntlet.

"His name was Rinalli. The R was the way he signed his blades. It was a small joke of his that most students received an eye, but there were always a few who deserved an R." Cejack pronounced the letter so it sounded closer to the word, "ear." "He passed away many years ago, but I still have one or two of his blades hidden away.

"This one," and Cejack held up the sword so all the students could see it, "he made quite a long time ago. It is smaller than his typical blades. Lighter. I remember when he forged it, I told him it was too small. I thought he had made a mistake or failed to use enough material when he started. I teased him and asked him who it was for. He told me, 'I do not know the answer to that question, yet. But when I find the proper bearer of this blade, I will know him.'"

Cejack's gaze became momentarily sad and distant. "He never found the person who was meant to carry it. But I believe that I have."

With no more ceremony, he thrust the sword toward Sonja. She took it from his hands, stunned by his speech. She wanted to thank him or say something meaningful to show Cejack that she understood the significance of his gift, but he gave her no time to form a response.

"This morning you were students. That is true no more. Swordsmen!" Cejack shouted, then paused, eyeing Sonja. "And Lady," he amended. "Draw your weapons!"

Eleven blades cleared their scabbards and flashed in the late afternoon light of the sun. The sound was not the ringing of metal across metal – again the movies had lied, thought Sonja –

but rather the hissing rasp of sharp edges against leather and wood.

Sonja admired the sword in her hand. As Cejack had said, it was smaller than the blades given to the other students. It was several inches shorter and narrower near the point. The base where it met the guard was flat and wide, giving the blade an overall triangular appearance. In addition, the grip was narrower and slightly longer than many of the swords with which she had trained, allowing her hand to close comfortably around it. The shape and weight seemed perfectly matched for her and could not have felt more natural in her grasp if Cejack's father had built it specifically with her in mind.

She hefted it in one hand and took a few slow practice cuts through the air. It moved as if it wielded itself and Sonja was merely hanging on for the ride. The weapon balance was ideal for one handed combat, yet the extended grip also allowed for a more powerful two-handed strike. After a year of carrying the bulky student swords from the main armory, Sonja felt like she had just passed her driver's test in a busted-down station wagon, then been handed the keys to a brand-new sports car.

The other students – no, swordsmen now, she reminded herself – had begun to wander off the practice grounds. Bunching into small groups of two or three, heads together chatting excitedly about their new status, they headed for the castle to eat, drink, and celebrate. Sonja sheathed her blade and turned to follow them in.

A light touch on her arm, stopped her.

"A moment, please," said Cejack, watching the others moving away. "I have one more thing to ask, but I wanted some privacy to say it."

"Of course, Master Cejack," Sonja responded. "And thank you for the sword. It's beautiful. Your father was amazing. It's so... I don't know how to... Thank you."

Another smile pulled at the corner of Cejack's mouth. This time, it did not seem so dangerous to Sonja. It looked more natural.

"That sword is some of the finest work my father ever did. I have rarely seen its equal. A blade like that deserves more than just the right person to carry it. It needs a name. That is what I would like you to do for me. I am asking that you name my father's sword."

Sonja's mouth popped open in surprise. "I ... of course. I would be honored to name it."

She drew her sword again, holding it in the evening sunlight, looking carefully at the blade.

"Don't just give it a name," cautioned Cejack. "It has to be the true name. You will have to..." he paused, searching for the correct words, "to discover its name. Take your time and I know you will find it."

The dual edges of the sword were slightly paler than the heavier center, with an odd wavy pattern forming in the darker steel. Sonja remembered reading somewhere that this coloration was the result of a heating and cooling process that left the edges hardened while allowing the middle to be slightly softer and more flexible. The color variation made her think of waves on the ocean.

Should the name be about the water? she wondered. For a weapon, that would be an oddly peaceful image, however it did seem appropriate. The ocean was passive and calming despite the power and strength behind it. A tsunami could level a city, yet waves on the beach could sooth a person to sleep. Water felt *right.*

As Sonja contemplated, she rotated the blade from one side to the other. A flash of sunlight glinted along its length, briefly blinding her and causing her to squint against the brightness. It again reminded her of water, or more precisely of the way sunlight danced across the uneven surface of moving water.

Light on water, she thought. Fire and water. Something about fire on the water. Ocean Flame? No, she stopped herself. Fire and water was a little derivative, and yet, she felt she was close to something.

"Sun and sea," she muttered. "Ocean light?"

Ocean was too big, Sonja realized. This blade was not an ocean. It was tiny, delicate. Made for someone who would wield it like the piece of art that it was, rather than swing it like an axe trying to take down a tree. So, not ocean. Something with more finesse, but still as implacable as any flow of water. River? Stream?

Then, without question or doubt, Sonja knew. Reflected sunlight flashed across the metal surface once more, and she took it as confirmation of her decision.

"Master Cejack," said Sonja, and Cejack, who had stepped a few paces away to give her a moment of privacy, moved closer. She held the sword across her palms as he had done when handing new blades to his students.

"Yes, Sonja?"

"Her name is Brookstar."

The following day was a free day for Sonja, but she rose early and made her way out to the courtyard as the sun crested the horizon. Five instructors were scheduled to test for their bear this morning, and two teachers were attempting to earn their ceravits. Sonja wanted to see the trials she herself might one day be undertaking. Derrik was one of the teachers trying to win the title of Master, and Sonja specifically looked forward to watching him take his test.

To earn her sword, Sonja had needed to demonstrate the forms, drills, and melees that proved competency with the weapon, while also demonstrating that she was familiar with the basic use of the staff, dagger, bow, and mace. For her bear, she would need to learn two more forms, each over a hundred and fifty moves, and fight again in the Circle. If she succeeded, the school would then recognize her mastery of the sword.

In addition to mastering the sword, she would also need to achieve competency with two other weapons.

For a ceravit, she would next have to demonstrate mastery of the sword and one other weapon, as well as competency in two more. Along with demonstrating her own personal ability, the ceravit required that she teach at least one beginning student all the way through to earning their sword. It was difficult, and required dedication to achieve, but as Cejack had said, *nothing worthwhile is ever gained easily.*

All five instructors performed for the assembled masters before Derrik's name was called. He, like the previous five men, executed the advanced sword forms Sonja would need to learn over the next six months. To her inexperienced eye, he shifted from one motion to the next without error or hesitation. Though each form lasted several minutes, and there was no rest between them, Derrik completed the intricate maneuvers without visible difficulty. He raised his blade to salute the masters when he finished before moving on to demonstrate a similar familiarity with his knives. When at last he returned to his seat with the rest of his group, he was breathing only slightly faster than when he had first stood up.

After forms, the remainder of the morning was spent demonstrating competency in other weapons. Derrik tested with the staff and bow, although Sonja elected not to stay and watch. Instead, she wandered back into the castle for a late breakfast and short nap. The next part of the test she really wanted to see came later that afternoon.

Half an hour past lunch, Sonja returned to the testing grounds. She arrived in time to see the first bear candidate enter the Circle. Mekhil had been selected to begin the afternoon session, and as soon as he heard his name, he leapt up from his seat on the ground and loped into position. Two masters greeted him with drawn weapons.

Mekhil attacked first, shifting from left to right, engaging one opponent then the next. His feet never ceased moving as he fought to keep both masters in sight at all times. It did not matter how skilled a swordsman might be, if an opponent successfully found your back, the fight was over. While Mekhil never allowed himself to be pinned between them, occasionally one of his two opponents would break his defense and deliver a rough tap with their sword. From his reaction, Sonja guessed they touched hard enough to hurt, although the contact did not draw blood. Despite these lapses, Mekhil did not show any signs of frustration or defeat. The sound of metal ringing on metal continued without pause.

"Are you ready to leave?" Rith flew up to Sonja's ear, startling her with the question.

"What do you mean, 'leave?'" she asked, reluctantly pulling her gaze from Mekhil's performance in the Circle.

"I told you in the beginning you would be here for one or two years. Two years would be better, but I think you have learned enough to move on if you wish, so I'm offering you a trip home."

Sonja considered the offer carefully. Home sounded very tempting, but she also liked the idea of finishing what she had started at Cejack's school. "Can I come back, later? Maybe do my second year some other time?"

"No. Sorry. Once you leave, you are not welcome back. Or, rather, you are always welcome back to visit. Not as a student."

"If I decide to go home, do we have to go right now?"

"Of course not. You can stay as long as you like. But don't you want to go back?" asked Rith.

"Yes. You know I do. I miss my family like crazy. But first I want to learn that," replied Sonja, pointing at the three men dancing their deadly ballet in the Combat Circle.

"I am really glad to hear you say that. I was hoping you would stay, but I wanted it to be your choice. Okay. We stay. See how simple it is?" Rith flew circles around Sonja's head and nickered with joy.

"Settle down, Rith. I want to watch this," Sonja admonished the hippoganth before returning her attention to the two-on-one contest.

When his turn came, Derrik earned his ceravit easily. Although asked to remain as a master teacher at the school, he declined, explaining that his strengths lay in performance, not teaching. The next day he gathered his few personal possessions and left the school. Sonja never saw him again. She and Derrik had never been particularly close – teachers did not tend to socialize with students – but she had always liked his calm, easygoing manner and she considered him a friend. She appreciated his quick, wry smile and still recalled his kindness towards her the first day they had met. His sudden departure left her feeling empty and a little bit abandoned.

Mekhil also left. He had failed to earn his bear and was offered the chance to try again in six months. He refused. When Sonja cornered him in the dining hall the evening after his test, she asked why he didn't want to stick around. He shrugged, then gave her the same open, boyish grin he always used when trying to lighten the mood.

"I spent a year and a half working for my sword when everyone else here needed only a year. I have no desire to remain and spend the rest of my life trying to achieve something I may never have. Even if Cejack should one day give me my bear, I am quite sure by the time I got it, my sword would only be good for trimming my long white beard.

"No, I'm content with my sword, bare though it is. Remember, even without the bear, Cejack's students are still some of the best swordsmen in the world. I will have no trouble finding work after this."

"Swordsmen and women," amended Sonja.

Mekhil laughed into his beer. "Of course. Forgive me for misspeaking. And you will have your bear in six months. I would wager my right arm on that."

"We'll see," said Sonja, trying to hide the sudden pleased flush in her cheeks behind her beer mug. "I wish you were staying. We could get our bears together."

Mekhil draped a companionable arm about her shoulders. "Oh, don't be so maudlin. We are celebrating, tonight. Besides, the world is small. I am sure we shall meet again."

"It's larger than you think," said Sonja, softly.

"Hmm?" asked Mekhil over the rim of his cup as he took another long drink.

"Nothing. And you're right. Tonight is for celebrating." Sonja raised her own mug again, taking a much more modest sip. The beer at the school was potent, and there did not seem to be any minimum drinking age, but she had learned her lesson long ago about compromising herself in questionable surroundings.

As the evening progressed and the celebrating students became louder and a bit more raucous, Sonja decided to call it a day. Taking a last sip of her beer, she said goodnight to those closest to her and headed for her room.

Of the ten students who earned their swords with Sonja, five elected to remain with her and train for their bear. Among the students opting to leave were Tanner and Evan, two of the people with which she had spent most of her off time. Sonja asked Evan why he didn't stay, telling him she felt he was one of the best in their class and could easily earn his bear in six months. Evan explained he had learned all he wished to know. He cryptically commented on a duty that waited for him at home and explained that he had put off his responsibilities long enough. He said nothing more on the subject, and no amount of questioning or drink could pry another word out of him.

The months that followed seemed more lonely with her closest friends gone, but they were no less busy. Sonja took her place among the school's instructors and assisted in training Cejack's incoming new students, as well as continuing her own lessons. Four days each week, she taught, and the remaining three were devoted to sparring and training with the teachers and masters. Somehow, she also managed to squeeze in her one day off each month to visit home.

Six months almost to the day after she earned her sword, as Mekhil had predicted, Master Cejack granted her the bear. Again, Rith asked if she was ready to leave and return home, and again she elected to stay, realizing there was still more she wished to accomplish.

Six months after receiving her bear, near the end of her second year, Cejack surprised Sonja by asking to borrow her sword.

"Borrow, Master Cejack?" she asked, confused by the request. Sonja was one week away from testing for her ceravit, and the thought of practicing with a student sword again instead of Brookstar made her nervous. "How long will you need her?"

"Only a few days," he assured her. "I need to speak with the weaponsmiths about a new sword design. Brookstar is the first of her kind, as are you, but that will change."

Cejack gestured at the two female students training in the yard. One was quite young, only fifteen-years old, with pale, freckled skin and fiery red hair. The other was closer to Sonja's age; a tall, lean girl with an ebony complexion and jet-black hair and eyes. The older girl spoke infrequently, and always wore such a serious expression that Sonja had made it a personal goal to get her to smile at least once. So far, her attempts had not met with any success.

Both women had arrived six months ago, asking to be accepted into the new group of students. After hearing rumors of a female warrior at Cejack's school, they had come to see if it was true and, if possible, join the training facility. Sonja hoped they were only the beginning of a new trend at the school that would see many more like them arriving in the future. The women were currently running clash drills with the other students.

"If they earn their swords, they deserve blades designed for them. Don't you agree?"

Sonja did, handing over Brookstar reluctantly. Letting the sword out of her hands felt like a betrayal, yet she knew if anyone would treat the blade with the respect it deserved, it would be Cejack.

For the next three days, Sonja walked the grounds of the school constantly feeling like a piece of her was missing. She carried a blade from the school armory, but after wearing Brookstar for the past year, it may as well have been a rusted iron bar hanging in her scabbard.

At last, on the morning of the fourth day, Cejack called a halt to the day's training and asked all the students and teachers to gather. Next, he ordered Sonja to approach. Surprised, but obedient to the direction, she stepped out of the group to stand in front of the school Headmaster.

Cejack held up Brookstar in his right hand. Sonja breathed a sigh of relief at the sword's return. She saw the familiar gauntlet on the guard and the etching of a bear in the metal of the blade.

"This is yours," he said.

"Thank you, Master Cejack."

"No, wait."

Sonja paused, her arm partially raised to reclaim her sword.

"*This*," Cejack emphasized, turning the blade in his hand to reveal the form of a lean, feral cat etched into the side opposite the bear, "is yours."

"A ceravit?"

"You have earned it."

"But, I never… I never tested for it."

Cejack waved a dismissive hand in the air. "You did. I saw you meet every requirement months ago. I have only been waiting for one of your students to earn their sword. That will happen in two days."

"That was just practice!" Sonja blurted, then covered her mouth as she realized she was arguing to give back something she had spent two years trying to achieve.

"It is all just practice, isn't it?" he said. Then, turning serious. "Sonja. You are finished here. You have come as far as I can take you."

"So … I graduate today?" she asked, happily. Her eyes began to water forcing her to blink rapidly to clear her vision.

"You graduate today," agreed Cejack.

"I would gladly accept you as a permanent teacher here, but Rith explained you must leave. Should you ever decide to teach students, wherever you may go, you do so with my blessing and my confidence that you will uphold the honor of my school."

Cejack held out Brookstar again, and Sonja closed her hands around the grip. It was warm where Master Cejack had held her.

"Thank you for everything," said Sonja, overwhelmed that all the time she had spent at Cejack's school was coming to an end. "I'll always remember what you taught me."

"Are you ready to go?" asked Rith, hovering at Sonja's eye level. "The next adventure can begin now."

"No. Not yet, Rith. There's one thing I would like to do before we leave." She turned her attention back to Cejack. "When I first came here you called me clumsy and awkward. You embarrassed and insulted me. When I became your student, you never missed an opportunity to criticize me or make my life miserable. Today, I get even."

"You want a rematch," said Cejack, running a hand across his beard. Sonja saw white teeth exposed as he gave her the predatory smile that had always unnerved her before. She did not back down.

"I want a rematch."

Sonja unbuckled her belt and removed it, setting her practice sword on the ground. She scanned the gathered crowd and found the older of the two new female students. "Gallia," she called and gestured to her. The tall girl moved immediately to Sonja's side.

"I will need this, thank you," said Sonja, claiming the staff the girl was holding. "And you will hold Brookstar. I don't trust any of these boys anywhere near her."

"Yes, Teacher. Um ... no. I mean, Master Sonja."

Sonja laid Brookstar in Gallia's hands. The girl's eyes grew wide, and she handled the sword as delicately as though it were made of glass.

Ah, there it is, thought Sonja. *I finally got my smile out of you.*

Turning back to Master Cejack, Sonja set her feet into a comfortable stance and angled the staff to point at her mentor. She bounced the smooth, comfortable weight of the weapon briskly, almost cockily, in her hands. "Draw your sword, if you would be so kind."

164

Cejack unsheathed his blade and the surrounding students and teachers scrambled to give the two contestants room. This was not the controlled boundaries of the Circle and no one wanted to end up underfoot when the battle started.

Neither Cejack nor Sonja advanced for several seconds. Finally, Cejack pointed a thick finger in her direction. "Don't take a defensive stance with me. I warned you before. Attack!"

"Not this time," Sonja replied. "Today, I give you first move."

Cejack laughed, a great booming roar. He raised his sword in a salute, and marched toward Sonja in slow, deliberate steps. She backed away at an equivalent pace. Cejack laughed again. "I could keep backing you up until you bumped into the far wall, then leisurely cut you to pieces."

"You could," replied Sonja. "But I don't think you will."

After allowing Cejack to push her one more step, Sonja lunged forward, driving the end of her staff down toward the sensitive instep of Cejack's foot and forcing him to hop back to avoid a painful injury. Moving in to press her advantage, Sonja swung the length of the weapon to strike across his ribs. Cejack dismissively blocked the attack. "Simplistic. I thought I taught you better than that."

Instead of replying, Sonja rotated her staff and swung again for his torso on the opposite side. Again, the strike was deflected, but Sonja used the momentum of the block to reverse the staff once more, striking with the opposite end low across the legs, focusing on his knees. Cejack flashed his sword down and caught her attack at the last instant. He looked up at her in pride and admiration.

"That was dirty. You know I have bad knees. Now, I hope you can protect yourself as well as you attack because it's my turn."

The crowd ebbed and flowed around the two combatants as the spectators scrambled to stay close enough to watch the battle as it progressed, while still remaining out of striking range of sword or staff. Shouts and cheers rang out for both contestants. Bets were even placed, with the odds in Cejack's favor, certainly, but not by a great deal. Although Cejack's swordsmanship was unequaled, Sonja had also earned a reputation for herself. She had not been beaten with the quarterstaff in her hands in several months.

Cejack moved with a speed belying his heavy stature, and his attacks were powerful and sure. The sunlight glinted off his weapon as he struck and parried, slashed, and blocked. Small wood chips and splinters flew from Sonja's staff with each blow she deflected and still Cejack hammered his attacks home. Sonja briefly pictured a lumberjack, grimly determined to cut through one last stubborn tree. Except in this situation, she was the tree.

Neither fighter gave nor asked for quarter. Several minutes passed as the two battled, with neither gaining an advantage over the other. Every step of ground gained on either side was soon surrendered. Sweat gleamed on Sonja's face and arms, and she tasted salt as droplets leaked into the corners of her open mouth. She was panting, she realized, partly from adrenaline and partly from growing fatigue. She wanted to wipe the stinging moisture from her eyes, but she had no time to waste on anything other than the conflict at hand as she fought to keep Cejack at bay.

Cejack's power and experience seemed perfectly balanced by Sonja's speed and the reach advantage the staff afforded her. Eventually, Cejack's greater stamina began to show. His attacks moved closer to their mark, and Sonja became harder pressed to defend herself. The struggle would end soon, and she knew it would not finish in her favor unless she did something unexpected.

"How do you expect to win?" asked Cejack, trying not to sound as tired as he was. "Everything you know, I taught you."

"Not everything," she replied. Sonja remembered her brief time in Sherwood Forest with Robin and his band. She had learned a few tricks there and in her time with Cejack, she believed she had improved on them.

Sonja stepped back to give herself some breathing room, then when Cejack moved to close the distance, she swung her staff directly at his sword hand. Surprised by the move, Cejack avoided the attack by dropping his hand and letting the pole pass harmlessly by. In dropping his guard, he left his upper body open. Sonja leapt at the opportunity and struck hard for the chest, knowing Cejack could never raise his sword fast enough to protect himself. Cejack knew it, too. Instead of dodging, he stepped directly into her swing, taking the blow on his outstretched forearm before Sonja could build enough momentum behind it to be fully effective.

As the staff contacted his arm, Cejack took advantage of the brief moment of time that Sonja's staff was not in motion. He rotated his sword in a tight loop to drive a downward blow at Sonja's head. With no opportunity to avoid the attack or deflect it, Sonja could only raise her staff and meet the blow full force. Weakened and damaged from the repeated contact with Cejack's sword edge, the staff broke under the assault with a crack like a gunshot.

The damaged staff held up long enough to permit Sonja to leap back and avoid the follow through of Cejack's swing, but as she regained her footing and prepared for the next attack, she realized the fight was over. Sonja held a three-foot length of wood in each hand. The pieces could still function as weapons, but with the lost reach advantage Cejack would cut her apart in seconds.

Cejack also recognized the situation. He saluted Sonja with his sword. "I assume you yield. Yes?"

Sonja responded eloquently. "Shit."

Cejack saluted again before sheathing his weapon. "I have not enjoyed a duel like that in a very long time. Thank you for reminding me how good my students can be."

"Shit," Sonja repeated. "You took away my staff. Again. You chopped it in half."

"Yes," he agreed. "But last time I took your staff away because you did not know what you were doing. This time I won because steel will always win out over wood given enough time. I did not beat you. I simply outlasted you. And I will have a few bruises for it." He winced dramatically and held out his forearm to show where Sonja had connected.

"You are a fine warrior, Sonja. I am proud to have been your teacher and to be able to claim a small part in what you have accomplished."

On an impulse, Sonja tossed the broken pieces of her staff aside and threw her arms around the big man's neck. She pulled herself close and kissed his hairy cheek. Surprised and embarrassed by the display, Cejack merely stood still and accepted the unexpected show of affection. She released him after a moment.

"Goodbye, Master Cejack. I will miss you."

"Cejack," he told her. "You need no longer address me so formally. We are equals, are we not? Master Sonja?"

CHAPTER 11

Sonja lay on her back, sprawled upon a wide cotton blanket. The blanket was thick and soft, and more comfortable than any her family owned, so she knew immediately that she was not yet at home. She cracked open one eye and discovered open blue sky above her, with a single sun shining warmly down from its vantage point high in the sky. Propping herself on one elbow and raising a hand to shade her eyes, she took her first look at her new surroundings.

She was on a beach. That was immediately obvious, but which beach it might be, she had no idea. Except for herself, there were no inhabitants along the sandy shore in either direction. As far as her eye could see to the right and left, sand covered the landscape, its smooth whiteness broken only by the occasional clump of dark seaweed or driftwood settled along the shoreline. Directly in front of her, was an endless expanse of water the color of blue topaz. Sunlight sparkled on the rippling surface in sporadic flashes of dazzling brilliance as small, lazy waves, barely three-feet high at their peak broke into a white froth and curled forward to lap softly at the sand a dozen yards away from her bare feet. The rasping sound the water made as it rolled up onto the beach and slid back was steady and comfortingly hypnotic.

Craning her neck, Sonja discovered the beach ended at a cluster of palm trees and what appeared to be the beginnings of a tropical forest a hundred yards or more behind her. The foliage was thick enough she could not discern anything beyond the first few feet of growth.

A sharp, piercing cry startled her. She glanced up in time to see a group of five sea birds flying overhead, calling out to one another. Besides herself, the birds were the only immediate signs of life anywhere nearby.

To Sonja's right, next to the edge of her blanket, rested a picnic basket wedged into the sand. More than three feet wide and two feet tall, the wicker container was much larger than most picnic baskets with which she was familiar, and it gave the impression that it would not be easily picked up or carried off. It was currently closed, giving no hints as to its contents.

Propped into the sand next to the basket, was a brown, plastic bottle of sunscreen.

"Hey, Rith," said Sonja, looking down the length of her torso and legs. She held up one foot and wiggled her toes.

"Here!" came the immediate reply.

"Do you remember back home, where I had my blue bikini?"

Rith launched himself from his ring and flitted over to a position a few inches above the picnic basket. "Of course, I do," he announced.

"Can you tell me why it isn't here with me, now? I seem to be all kinds of naked at the moment. What if somebody shows up?"

Rith nickered in amusement. "There isn't anyone else here. Nobody is going to show up. This is a private beach. *Your* private beach. I thought you could use a little rest and relaxation after you finished your training. I could have just taken you home, but that wouldn't really be as relaxing as here, so I created this place to be ideal for you to hang out and do absolutely nothing."

"So, this isn't another adventure? There isn't anything that's going to come rushing out at me from the jungle, or climb out of the water?"

"Nope. Absolutely not. Nothing dangerous anywhere in the water, land, or sky. Just vacation time. Think of this as a pre-adventure respite. Nothing will bother you here, and all you have to do is enjoy yourself. See how simple it is?"

"Nothing dangerous, except maybe skin cancer, I guess," Sonja responded, reaching out to grab the bottle of sunscreen.

"Not even that," assured Rith. "I gave you the lotion because I didn't know if you would feel more comfortable if you had it. You don't really need it. Lie out in the sun all day, every day for a year out here and you won't burn or have any problems. The sun is plenty warm, but it isn't real. Of course, you won't get tan, either. Sorry about that."

Sonja shrugged, brushing away the sand sticking to the bottom of the brown bottle in her hand. She popped the cap and squirted a large puddle of creamy liquid into her palm, then began working the thick lotion into her skin, starting with her shoulders and arms, and working her way down. Totally unnecessary, perhaps, but what was a beach day if you didn't end up with sand sticking to every part of your body?

When she finished covering all the areas she could reach, she snapped the cap closed and dropped the bottle back into its former divot in the sand. Curious, she flipped open one of the top flaps of the picnic basket to peek inside. A variety of wrapped and packaged food and drinks filled most of the available space inside the basket, easily enough to last the day and probably a few days after that. Sandwiches, chips, water, sodas, and various other snacks assured her she would not be going hungry or thirsty while she enjoyed her time here.

The sun was currently positioned directly above her, shining down bright and hot, burning away all memories of the endless sparring and harsh training she had so recently completed. No more sore muscles, bruises, and blisters, and no more rules and regulations to follow. More importantly, no more having to smell sweaty, unwashed bodies packed together in the enclosed spaces of the castle. She inhaled deeply of the clean, salty air, then released the breath slowly.

Sonja gazed up at the cloudless blue sky and laughed. Rith had gifted her with her own private little piece of summer paradise that no one else could touch. A beachside haven for her alone. She flopped onto her back, arms and legs akimbo in the joy of absolute freedom.

"Rith," said Sonja after a moment. "You forgot just one thing."

"What?" he asked, a slight edge of concern in his voice.

"Sunglasses. The sun is hurting my eyes. I need a pair of glasses."

"Oh, that. Check the basket," Rith replied. "Anytime you need something, tell me what you are looking for, then check the basket. It will probably be there."

Sonja did. While she was positive there had been nothing but food and beverages inside before, now a pair of green-framed sunglasses rested on a paper-wrapped sandwich at the top of the basket. She grabbed both items, dropped the wicker top back into place, then settled again onto her blanket.

"How long can I stay?" she asked, slipping the glasses onto her face before unwrapping her sandwich and taking a bite. Ham and cheese. One of her favorites; but of course, Rith would know that.

"A little while. We need to leave tomorrow, or maybe the next day. This is just a break before moving on to your next adventure."

"Next adventure?" she asked, her cheeks full of bread, ham, and cheese. "We're not going home?"

"Not yet. Most of the training you went through during the last two years was specifically to prepare you for this next challenge. Remember, I promised you that I wouldn't put you in any more situations that you weren't properly prepared for? Well, now you're properly prepared. Don't worry, though. This will be a quick trip, and you will be home immediately after we're done."

Sonja nodded. She had waited two years, she supposed she could handle a few more days before getting back home.

"It's a beautiful beach," she said around another large mouthful. "And it's so huge."

"This whole island is a beach, with a little bit of jungle in case you wanted a shady spot to hang out. In fact, if you walk ten miles east of here," Rith indicated the line of trees behind her, "you will run into another ocean. I figured you might like a rest so I thought to myself, what would be the most restful situation I could think of. Answer: a private island. An island with a great big beach. After all, everyone says that life is a beach." He nickered appreciatively at his clever pun. Sonja simply ignored it.

"Do you like it?" he asked.

"Yes," said Sonja, rewrapping the rest of her sandwich and depositing it back into the picnic basket. She stretched luxuriously, yawning loudly before she rolled onto her stomach, laying her head across her forearms.

"I really do."

For the next few hours, Sonja did nothing but lie on the soft blanket and sunbathe. Occasionally she would fall into a light sleep, wake, roll over, and doze again. After so much time baking under the sun's rays, she was surprised she had not gotten burned. She wasn't even any noticeably darker. Rith had warned her the sun was not real, but it was one thing to hear him say it, and quite another to observe the results. Or rather, the lack of results. It still felt real. The warmth of the sun and the sounds of the waves, the feel of the sand shifting beneath the blanket as she moved were all perfect. If none of this was real, Sonja was completely content living in a fantasy world.

A few times during the day, when she grew too warm, Sonja went for a swim in the cool salt water of her own private ocean. The temperature was ideal for swimming, not too chilly and not too warm. Playfully, she dove into approaching waves only to pop up on the other side. At Rith's suggestion, she tried a few times to bodysurf the waves, launching herself forward as the water peaked and crested, then letting the momentum carry her towards shore. She took a few tumbles and even swallowed a bit of salt water early on, but she quickly learned the trick of it.

Later in the afternoon, as the sun moved further out over the ocean, Sonja decided to take a long run along the shoreline just to burn off some excess energy. The feel of wet, hard-packed sand under her bare feet as she ran was exhilarating. The waves slid past her, splashing up onto her legs as she raced through them, then receding, erasing her footprints and all evidence of her passage.

Sonja reveled in every moment. It was a wonderful feeling to be free of all responsibility, to be able to relax or play as she wanted, and to simply waste time. There was nowhere she needed to be and nobody she needed to report to.

In this manner, the day passed and, all too soon, ended. Sonja sat on her blanket, eating another sandwich and watching the sun set into the shifting liquid horizon. The dying orange-red ball seemed to submerge into the ocean, dousing itself in the expansive greenish waters. The sky commiserated with the sun's tragic end by staining itself blood red, and the few visible clouds blackened in empathy. As a hungry sea swallowed the last of the light, the timid stars that could not be seen during the day began to show themselves.

Sonja finished eating and drank a small amount of water from a bottle. As her eyes adjusted to the night, the emerging stars and a full moon rising above the forest of trees behind her provided plenty of light to see. Placing the bottle and sandwich wrapper back into the basket, she settled onto her blanket for a moment of stargazing; hands behind her head and her elbows out, looking for familiar constellations. Not expecting to find any, she was not disappointed. Just as the stars told sailors hundreds of years before how to find their way across the forbidding oceans, these clusters of distant solar systems were telling Sonja that she was very far from home.

"Hey, Rith?" Sonja spoke softly, trying not to disturb the peaceful, evening surroundings.

"Still here," came the reassuring response. Rith's voice was also more hushed than usual.

"Thank you. For this place, I mean. It's amazing, even if it is a bit lonely."

"You aren't alone. You have me."

Sonja felt a small smile pull at her lips. "Yes, I do," she agreed. "I was just thinking, though. Is this a one-time thing? This beach? Or can I come back here sometimes?"

There was a short pause as Rith considered the question.

"I don't see any reason you can't come back here. I made this place for you, and I suppose it would be sort of silly to never use it again."

"Good. I agree. Can you do me a favor, then?"

"Maybe," said Rith. "What's the favor?"

This time, it was Sonja's turn to pause. She took a moment trying to figure out the best way to explain her request. "Do you remember the time you gave me wings? Then, when you brought me back home, what happened in the classroom at school?"

"You fell out of your desk and everyone laughed at you," Rith recalled.

"Yes. That," she agreed. "That was embarrassing and very upsetting for me. It would be nice if we can avoid something like that happening in the future."

"I can't always control how an adventure goes or keep you from getting hurt—"

"No, no," Sonja interrupted the hippoganth's explanation. "I don't expect you to. If I get hurt or do something stupid, I don't expect you to rescue me. But, if you don't mind, is it possible that the next time I go through something really traumatic like that, that you don't bring me straight home? Can you bring me here, first? You know, that way I can cry, or scream, or bleed or whatever I have to do right here. I can have some time to prepare myself before I go back home. I don't have to fall down again in front of a classroom full of people."

"That sounds like a good idea. I like it."

"So, we can do that?" Sonja asked, hopefully.

"Yes, I think we can do that."

Sonja sighed, a long exhalation of contentment. "Thank you."

Despite a small breeze that blew in from over the water, and her complete lack of any cover, Sonja did not feel cold. The temperature had dropped very little since the sun had set, and she decided against searching the basket for additional blankets or clothing. In addition, the sound of the surf rushing in and out, whispering over the sand, was an effective lullaby. Sonja's eyelids grew heavy and the distant points of light in the sky above her began to blur in her vision. With no conscious effort, Sonja's breathing slowed, and she drifted off into a dreamless sleep.

CHAPTER 12

A small rundown shack stood forlornly at the top of the hill, an ugly splotch of brown on a backdrop of green. Sonja paused on the gravel path leading up to the wooden blight on an otherwise perfect landscape, and only at Rith's urging did she move toward it. Sonja's left hand caressed the pommel of Brookstar hanging at her hip, a nervous habit she had acquired while training under Cejack. The feel of the cool metal under her palm soothed her. It was solid and real, reliable in times when she felt uncertain about her immediate future.

Rith rode along with her, perched on his ring around her finger. His calm presence reassured Sonja somewhat. If the little creature was at ease, she felt she could relax as well. Still, it was a comfort to feel the weight of Brookstar at her side

As she climbed the hill, Sonja noticed the first signs of life about the ruined house: an open window with a blue curtain waving in the slight breeze, and a thin wisp of grey smoke rising from the chimney. With each step, more evidence came into view, including a small but obviously well-tended garden trailing along one side of the structure and wrapping around to the back. At last, as she stood on the termite-eaten porch, the sounds of someone or something moving around inside proved conclusively the building was occupied.

"Now what?" she asked Rith.

"What do you usually do when you stand on someone's doorstep?" he answered, still motionless on her hand.

Sonja rolled her eyes at the unhelpful reply, then reached out to knock tentatively on the aged and sun-faded wooden door. The door rattled about on its hinges, and for a moment she feared it might break loose and fall down. It held however, and after a short wait, she heard a soft click from inside, the sound of a latch being turned or perhaps a bolt sliding back. As the door swung inward, the open doorway revealed a hunched little man dressed in a drab, sack-like cloth robe. The sleeves were cut away just past the shoulder, allowing Sonja to see that his left arm terminated above the elbow. His face and remaining hand were covered by a mottled layer of thick, ridged scars that testified to a terrible fire he had survived at one time in his life. There was no hair on the exposed parts of his body, and the only expression his tortured, frozen face seemed capable of displaying came from his lively, pale blue eyes.

"Yes," he said. His voice sounded strong and alive compared to the wasted body it came from. "Can I help you?"

"I don't know," said Sonja.

The man paused, peering about his yard as though searching for any additional unexpected guests. Finding no one else, his piercing gaze returned to Sonja.

"Do you care to come in for a moment?"

Sonja nodded and the man stepped aside. Before she could enter, he leveled a pointed glance at her sword.

"Would you carry a weapon into my home?" he asked. "Should I be concerned regarding your motives for coming to see me?"

Sonja apologized and fumbled to remove her sword belt. Cejack and the teachers at his school made sure each student understood the rules of courtesy regarding carrying a sword. The first rule was to never enter a person's home armed unless specifically invited to do so, or unless the purpose of the visit was to kill the occupant. Habit from two years under the threat of punishment if she was ever seen without her sword had momentarily made her forget her manners. She was no longer in school. Had she stepped inside still wearing Brookstar, the owner of this home would have been within his rights to kill her in self-defense.

Well, he could have tried, she thought.

She propped her sword against the house, just outside the doorway. She felt uncomfortable, almost naked, being unarmed, but her choices were limited to removing the blade or remain standing on the porch. Refusing his offer to come inside might also be viewed as threatening, if not merely rude. As she had no idea why Rith had brought her to this place other than to speak to this odd little man, Sonja opted for remaining courteous and accepted the invitation to enter.

The inside of the shack did not look any better than its exterior. The entire living quarters consisted of a single large room. In one corner a wood-burning stove glowed warmly, almost cheerily, while beside the stove, a pair of rough-hewn wooden chairs bracketed a table that appeared to be covered with the remains of a recently eaten meal. Along the far wall rested a metal, six-footed tub currently full of soaking laundry, and hanging above the tub, a pair of crossed swords and a shield acted as the only decoration in the house. The man's bed – a straw-filled mattress covered by a tumble of tattered blankets – lay unmade in another corner of the shack, and in the middle of the room, a padded rocking chair waited, still moving slightly back and forth from being recently vacated. Sonja's host shuffled back to the rocking chair and settled into it. He motioned for her to have a seat as well. After glancing around and reviewing her choices, Sonja dragged one of the chairs away from the table and sat down.

"I guess the first thing we need is an introduction," said the man. "My title is Demarcus the Slayer. At least it was until a few years ago. Now I am called only Demarcus for … obvious reasons."

"My name is Sonja, and I've never had any title."

"Sonja," Demarcus repeated. "What can I do for you, Sonja?"

Rith chose this moment to fly up and reveal himself. The self-described slayer reacted to his presence with only a slight widening of the eyes. Whatever thoughts or concerns the man might have had regarding Rith, his body language revealed nothing.

"Demarcus, I want you to tell her how to slay a dragon."

"And what is your name, little flying beast?"

"Rithagarianaff," Rith answered. "I am with Sonja and I want her to learn to fight a dragon."

"Fighting a dragon is no easy task for one who is quick and skilled in the use of a sword," said Demarcus. "A young girl such as dear Sonja here would surely be killed."

"Sonja is better trained with the sword than most men you will ever meet. She can defeat a dragon. Her only handicap is that she does not know a dragon's habits or methods of attack. I need you to teach her these things so she will be prepared."

Demarcus did not respond for a long moment. He assessed Sonja once more, sizing her up as a potential warrior. Considering a girl as a potential dragon slayer was clearly a foreign notion to him, so he took his time.

Sonja felt the weight of his stare on her, and while there was nothing sexual or lascivious in the gaze, it left her decidedly uncomfortable. She felt like a calf at market, being appraised for what she might be worth as milk and meat. Struggling not to fidget, she gripped the arms of her chair and waited for his response.

"Maybe she is as good as you say, and maybe she isn't. Personally, I would like to see a demonstration."

Sonja stood up to meet his challenge. She said, "Demarcus, can you handle a sword?"

"Not as well as I used to," he replied, motioning with a nod of his head to his missing arm. "But I'm still good enough to hold my own in a fight."

Sonja removed the two swords from the wall and handed one to Demarcus. The one she kept weighed more that she was accustomed to, but the weapon had excellent balance. She cut the air a few times to test the feel and, satisfied, she looked at Demarcus. Sonja snapped the blade up in a salute as Cejack had taught her, then dropped into a practiced stance.

"First attack is yours," said Sonja.

Demarcus nodded and moved in to engage. Sonja deflected his first attack smoothly and went on the offensive. Her blade moved in a blur of bright metal, pushing Demarcus relentlessly backwards and threatening at any time to free the man of his remaining arm. It took only moments to become clear to both combatants that Demarcus' swordsmanship was greatly inferior to Sonja's own. Sonja pinned Demarcus to one of the bare wooden walls and, with a practiced ease, she trapped his weapon against his body, leaving the dragon slayer unable to attack or defend himself. With the fight decisively concluded, she stepped away, saluting once more as Demarcus lowered his sword with a small bow of acknowledgement at her skill.

"You are very good. Very good," he said. "Better than I have seen in a long time. Even in my prime, I believe I would have been no match for you."

"Then you will teach her?" asked Rith as Sonja placed the swords back up on their hooks on the wall.

"There isn't much to teach, but what there is I will tell her." Demarcus shuffled across the room and settled into his chair again. Sonja followed his example and sat as well. She felt a bit giddy over the slayer's praise but fought to keep her expression neutral. It would not do to prove herself a warrior only to then be caught smiling like an idiot over a simple compliment.

"To be a dragon hunter you must be fast, and you must be good with the sword. Dragons are stupid and very predictable, so a good warrior who pays attention will generally win. It was only a careless error that ended my career."

"What happened?" asked Sonja. "If you don't mind my asking."

"No. That's quite all right. It was during the dragons' mating season, you must understand. I had been hired to kill a rogue dragon that was raiding one of the larger towns and killing some of the residents. Because so many people had died, I was promised quite a bit of money to dispose of the beast. I was overly eager to find him and earn my fee.

"I hunted him to his lair and lured him out into the open where I would have the advantage. A dragon in his own cave is more than a match for any hunter. This particular dragon was bigger than most beasts I had faced previously, so I watched him closely. Too closely, in fact. He circled and I pivoted to keep him in front of me, leaving the opening of the cave to my back. I did not see his mate when she came out behind me. She trampled me, and he burned me. I suppose I am lucky they had matters on their minds more important than me, otherwise they would have made sure I was dead before returning to their cave. As it was, they came very close to finishing me.

"A small group of people came out from the town the next morning to make sure I had done my job. Needless to say, I hadn't. They found what was left of me and dragged me back home, bandaged me the best they knew how, then left me to live or die as I saw fit. I think I surprised them all when I lived. My left hand was so badly damaged however, it started to rot and had to be removed. I can never fight dragons again. Not successfully at least.

"To summarize, I didn't get paid, my career was over, and the dragon was still alive. He still is. I think about him sometimes. I wonder if somebody will ever get him. Perhaps you will be the one who next goes after him."

"Maybe I will," agreed Sonja. "But, if I do, what will I have to do to beat him?"

"The same as with any dragon. It isn't the mating season now, so he will be alone. Dragons tolerate each other's company only when they mate, otherwise they stay clear of one another's territory. You need not worry about being surprised as I was.

"His first attack will be a physical one. He will try to trample you under his claws or crush you with his tail. Dragons are big and clumsy, and once they start a charge, they can't stop or turn aside easily. All you have to do is step out of his way and

184

he'll run by you. But watch the tail. He may swing it as he passes, and you will need to duck or jump to avoid it.

"Let him make a few of these charges. Dragons are fire-breathers, but they can only do it a few times a day, so they save their flame until they truly need it. Blowing fire takes a great deal of effort, and they must rest afterwards. After the third or fourth time he charges you, he will realize he cannot catch you, and that is when he will try to burn you. He'll rise up onto his rear four legs – they have six, you know – and if you look closely you can see his chest expand as he takes in air. Watch carefully, because as soon as his chest stops moving you have only a moment before he drops his head and releases the flame. Watch his eyes. He will close them to protect them from the heat just before he drops and attacks.

"This part is very important. A dragon has only three vulnerable areas: both of his eyes, and a soft spot on his neck directly below the chin. He can exhale fire for up to five seconds, and while he does, he will stand absolutely still. This is when you have to make your kill. Unfortunately, because the dragon closes his eyes while breathing fire, the only way to kill him is to attack him at his soft spot under the chin. On a young dragon you might be able to stab through the eyelid all the way into his brain, but it is risky, and I don't recommend it. Stick to the throat. It is safer. You will have to dive forward, avoiding the flame and moving under his head. Strike fast and hard. You must push your blade deep enough to penetrate through to the dragon's brain. If you miss, it isn't likely that you will have time to get out of the way before he starts moving again. That's why you have to be deft with the sword, so you are able to hit your mark on the first try."

"What does the soft spot look like? How will I know I'm aiming for the right place?"

"It's located directly between the two jaw bones right near the center of the head. The scales are much smaller and usually a light, gray color. You'll know it when you see it."

Sonja nodded. "I have one more question, then I'll leave you alone. Where can I find a dragon?"

"I can show you where the one that got me lives, but it is quite a distance away. Besides, you should probably practice on something a bit smaller, first. There is a steamer holed up not very far from here. I'll take you to him."

"Steamer?" asked Sonja.

"A steamer is a young dragon that hasn't learned to breathe fire. He just blows steam. They're good practice. My first dragon was a steamer."

"How big is a steamer?"

"It depends on how old he is," said Demarcus. "The steamer nearby is small, and he should give you no trouble."

Sonja agreed to the hunter's offer to serve as escort, thinking they would set out sometime the following morning to seek the dragon. To her surprise, he stood and suggested they leave immediately.

With Brookstar once more secured to her waist, Sonja let the man lead her to the steamer's lair. Although several large hills dotted the countryside, Demarcus knew several pathways that bypassed the worst of them. The slayer walked with a slight limp as he travelled, and it made sense to Sonja that he would follow the trails around his home that required the least climbing. Trees and brush grew in abundance but offered no real obstacle to their journey, so the two travelers covered the distance at a respectable rate.

Demarcus talked little during the trip, saving his breath for walking. Sonja listened to him huff and wheeze despite the easy pace he himself had set. She wondered if the dragon that burned him had damaged more than just the outside of his body. Perhaps the heat or smoke had burned his lungs as well. Watching and listening to the man labor along the path she walked so effortlessly, Sonja marveled again at the fact he had survived the incident that had left him in such a state.

She wondered if a seasoned dragon hunter could be hurt so badly, what might happen to someone with no idea what she was doing. Rith told her he would never put her in a situation she was not prepared to face, and she trusted him. He had sent her to a school to train for two years in expectation of this very adventure. But, was she really ready for this? Despite Cejack's training, she had her doubts. After all, she would not be facing a human opponent.

The terrain passed by unnoticed as Sonja's thoughts continued to focus darkly inward. She pondered a hundred things that could go wrong. She imagined herself being bitten, trampled, and burned by a scaled monster breathing fire. The worst part of it, she thought, was she was the one seeking the monster out. The dragon hadn't come looking for her. *She* was initiating this ridiculous confrontation. Sonja almost convinced herself that this journey was a mistake, and she was about to tell Rith to end the whole thing, when Demarcus signaled a halt.

Too late, she thought, and sighed.

Demarcus pointed. The lair entrance glared from a stark, lifeless, rocky hillside. It was a black hole in a pale landscape. He explained to Sonja that plants could not survive anywhere near the dragon's naturally high body heat.

"The steamer is inside," said Demarcus. "You can see a heat shimmer coming from the mouth of the den. If he were gone, it would have dissipated by now. The easiest way to get him out is to throw rocks at him."

"Rocks?" asked Sonja, eyeing Demarcus as if he were joking.

"I know that sounds a little unsporting, but you don't want to go in after him, and he won't come out unless he is hungry or you goad him into leaving."

Sonja walked cautiously up to the opening and peered in. The darkness inside hid anything that might be lurking more than a few feet away. She could not see anything beyond the cool blackness, and a shiver ran up her spine as she wondered if whatever was inside could see *her*. She stooped to gather a few fist-sized rocks, and after a pause and a couple of deep breaths, she hurled them into the lair. Hearing an angry grunt following her second throw, she hastened to put some distance between herself and the cave opening.

A reptilian snout followed by a round scaly head poked out from the cave entrance a moment later. Two blood red eyes blinked against the bright sunlight as they tried to locate the source of the annoyance. A long, thick, heavily armored body supported on six powerful legs slid out of the protecting shadows, and a sinewy serpent's tail writhed behind, the last of the beast to clear the cave. Fully visible now, the creature stood five feet high at the shoulder and covered fifteen feet of ground from nose to tail. The massive head swayed from side to side as the monster scanned the area for its tormentor.

"Small!" shouted Sonja. "You said it was small."

"He is," called back Demarcus. "Wait until you meet a big one."

The young dragon reacted to the sound of Sonja's voice and turned towards her. A low growl rumbled from its throat, and six clawed feet scrabbled for a solid hold in the loose gravel, propelling the beast forward in a clumsy charge. Sonja waited for it to get up to full speed, then scrambled a few fast paces to her left. The steamer ran past her, never slowing or veering from its course. After passing by, the creature covered almost fifty feet before it could stop, turn itself around, and begin a second dash. Sonja repeated her maneuver, waiting for the dragon to gain speed and then stepping aside. This time as the dragon passed her, its armored tail whipped to the side, striking out at Sonja's head. Two years of sparring and training had sharpened her reflexes to a razor's edge, and although the tactic caught her completely by surprise, she reacted instinctively, bringing her sword up to deflect the brunt of the attack. The impact, though lessened, still drove her backwards and tumbled her to the ground.

"I told you to watch his tail," shouted Demarcus, but Sonja did not hear him. She scrambled to her feet and prepared for the next charge.

On the third pass, the steamer tried again to strike her with its tail, but Sonja saw the attack coming and ducked out of the way, letting it pass over her. The young dragon moved noticeably slower now, and after turning around one more time, it approached Sonja at a more careful walk.

Sonja saw the worm had worn itself out running and had decided to try a different tactic. According to Demarcus, the next assault would be fire. Sonja stood her ground as the dragon crept to within twenty feet of her and, exactly as Demarcus had predicted, reared up onto its four hind legs. It inhaled noisily and deeply.

"Watch the chest. Watch the chest," screamed Demarcus. "As soon as it stops moving, he's going to close his eyes. Then you have to move!"

The steamer's scaly chest continued to expand for several seconds, then stopped. The beast closed its eyes. Sonja saw the eyelids flick down and she began to run, closing the distance between them as fast as possible. The dragon's towering bulk toppled down like a felled tree as it prepared to release a burst of flame at its enemy. Holding her sword tightly in her right hand, Sonja dove the last few feet onto the heat-baked earth and rolled onto her back so, as the monster's massive head came down, she lay directly beneath it. She spotted a patch of light gray skin high up on the dragon's throat. Hoping she had guessed correctly she aimed her sword tip toward the paler-colored scales.

The toothy maw opened above her and issued a cloud of scalding vapor that passed harmlessly above Sonja's supine form. She stabbed up at what she prayed was the dragon's weak spot, driving her blade through the beast's flesh and up into its skull. The scales parted for the sword reluctantly and, for a panicked moment, Sonja thought she had missed her target. Then blood flowed, cascading over the guard of her sword to cover her hands and torso in a torrent of crimson. The dragon died instantly as Sonja's sword pierced its brain, but it took time for the huge body to realize it had been killed. Sonja rolled to the side to avoid being crushed as the animal thrashed around wildly, pulling Brookstar free and dragging the blade out of the way with her. At a safe distance, she rose to her feet and watched the mindless death struggles for a full minute before the doomed creature finally lay still on the bare rock.

Demarcus ran forward with shouts of congratulations and praise, clearly impressed with Sonja's performance.

"It was a clean kill," he said. "I've seen few done better. And on your first try, too! Your only mistake was when you forgot to watch his tail, but you recovered beautifully. I think you're ready to tackle a full grown one."

"He didn't breathe fire," said Sonja, panting heavily. She stood as if in a daze, her bloodied sword dangling, forgotten, from her hand.

"Of course not. He was too young. That's why they call them 'steamers.'" Demarcus took Brookstar from Sonja and began cleaning it on the rags of his shirt. "There's an adult dragon living only about a three-day march from here. I can take you to him if you think you're up to it."

Sonja walked over to the dead steamer and stared at the unmoving body. Once, it had pulsed with pure beauty and strength, but now ... all life had fled. Exposed to the sunlight, what had first appeared to be only a dull gray along the dragon's underside flashed in patterns of green, blue, and yellow.

She dropped down on the rocky ground next to the great head. The fiery eyes were closed, and the intimidating jaws now seemed morbidly comical as they lay partially open and slack in the dirt. Reaching out, Sonja stroked the hard muzzle. The blood on her hands left accusing red streaks across the glimmering scales. She looked over her shoulder at Demarcus. Her eyes glassed over, and a tear spilled down her left cheek.

"No," she said softly. "One was too many."

CHAPTER 13

Sonja sat on the toilet, staring at the ivory-colored wall of her bathroom. She was home. She had locked herself in the small room, closed the toilet seat lid and sat down just prior to returning to Cejack's school after her last visit with her family. Never knowing what state she might be in mentally or physically upon returning to her own world, it had seemed a good idea to isolate herself during the moment of transition.

Now that she was back, she was grateful for her own foresight. She took a second to remind herself what had been going on when she left. Although it was weeks later for her, nobody else had experienced more than a heartbeat while she was off chasing dragons.

Her father and brother were in the living room watching television. The three of them finished eating dinner – burgers her dad had grilled on the back patio – and Sonja had volunteered to clean what few dishes there were in the kitchen. When the dishes were done and the kitchen picked up, she had snuck off to the bathroom to return to her last weeks of training.

Before going back out to join her family, Sonja did a quick check of herself in the mirror, which proved to be a wise move. Although the sweatpants and t-shirt she wore were clean, her face was covered in dirt and her hair was a tangled mess. A glance at her hands revealed traces of blood still on her skin and under her nails.

She needed to shower before she risked seeing anyone.

Checking to be sure the bathroom door was locked, she turned the shower water to hot and stripped out of her clothing.

Fifteen minutes later, Sonja was clean and feeling presentable once more. She wanted to go straight to the living room to be with her father and brother, but a cautious part of her brain warned her she should put on some different clothing first. If any of the mud or blood on her body had transferred to her current outfit, it would not do to have anyone notice and start asking questions. So, reluctantly, she slunk off to her bedroom for something clean to wear.

In her room, Rith had a surprise waiting for her. Suspended from a peg set in the wall, hung a familiar, well-worn scabbard. Protruding from the top, a silver pommel displayed the decorative image of a stylized letter "R" in the palm of a gauntlet. Sonja held her breath, not daring to believe in her good fortune as she drew the weapon and hefted it in her hands. She ran her fingers lovingly over the delicate etchings on the blade: a bear on one side, a ceravit on the other.

"Oh, Rith," she cried happily. "Brookstar."

"Of course," replied Rith. "You earned it. It's yours. Why shouldn't you have it?"

Sonja made a few experimental cuts through the air, narrowly missing one wooden post of her bed. "Thank you, Rith.

But what am I supposed to tell my dad? Where would I get something like this?"

"Tell him you bought it from a friend. There is a Renaissance Faire next month. Say you wanted it for a costume to wear at the faire."

Sonja thought for a moment. The idea would probably work. Her dad had taken her and her brother to the faire last year and several people there had worn costumes. It was as plausible an explanation as any she could think of. She smiled broadly. "Thanks, Rith. I guess you're as smart as you are cute."

Rith fluttered around the room a few times before settling back on his ring, obviously pleased with her compliment. Sonja sheathed Brookstar and placed the blade back on her wall, then hurried out to spend time with the family she had been away from for so long.

Sonja passed the rest of the summer talking on the phone and hanging out with her friends as much as possible. Though she had known some of them her entire life, she felt as if she were just getting to know them for the first time. In a way she was. Although they had not changed while she was gone, she certainly had, and there were moments she found herself struggling to find the things that she still had in common with them.

When she found herself with free time, Sonja practiced with her sword and a homemade staff so she would not forget her training. Occasionally, she even went to a nearby archery range she found online and rented a bow and arrows to see if she could still shoot. She discovered her accuracy suffered a bit from neglect, but the muscle memory returned with steady repetition.

All too soon the summer ended. The long, sun-warmed days began to wane, and school started once again. Sonja was in her senior year, her last year of high school, and it did not take long for the workload to begin piling up. After only two months, she was sick and tired of homework, and she hated all her teachers. It wasn't the school's fault. After two years of essentially living on her own in a medieval castle and training daily in the art of warfare, mathematics and reading about who discovered how to make peanut butter no longer held her interest. Her attention began to wander in class, and she had to force herself to stay focused and keep her grades up.

November arrived. Only three months since she had come back home, and she found herself wanting to leave again.

One cold, rainy Saturday morning, Sonja sprawled in her bed staring up at the bedroom ceiling. Rolling her head to the right, she gazed at Brookstar hanging on her bracket on the wall.

"Rith," Sonja said. "I think it's time to go somewhere."

CHAPTER 14

A cold rush of air whipped through her hair, and the bustling sounds of industrious activity surrounded her. The ground beneath her shifted, forcing her take one awkward step to avoid falling.

Sonja stood on the raised wooden quarterdeck at the rear of a large ship. The craft was larger than any boat she had previously set foot upon, stretching a hundred or more feet from prow to aft and measuring thirty feet across at its widest point. Massive sails billowed above her. Wide swaths of yellowed canvas mounted in rows across three towering masts snapped and rippled with the changes in the wind. Arced to their fullest as they caught the available breeze, the sails pulled the ship along at top speed across the expanse of ocean far below.

The ship cut through the whitecapped water, sending plumes of salty sea spray across the exposed decks. Standing high in the rear, Sonja felt the sporadic geysers as little more than a fine mist that cooled her face with its touch. The sapphire blue sea lifted, dipped, and rolled beneath her, rocking the craft gently but determinedly back and forth and forcing Sonja to concentrate on her balance so as not to be thrown to the deck. Spreading her feet wide, she tried not to look as unstable as she felt.

A blazing noontime sun shone down from a cloudless sky, warming the day and casting a thousand scattered reflections of light along the moving surface of the water. Sonja gazed to the horizon but saw no indications of land in any direction. Water extended as far as she could see until it dropped from view with the curve of the planet. Wherever Rith had deposited her, she was going to be staying put. Unless she wanted to try swimming, this ship was going to be her home until whatever drama he had planned was played out.

Men wandered about the vessel attending various duties, talking and laughing loudly among themselves as they moved from task to task. They all looked hardened and unfriendly, with more than a few of them missing extremities such as a finger or a piece of ear. Although they appeared to be of a rough nature, they gave Sonja a wide berth. Only the gray-haired individual manning the ship's wheel a few feet from where she stood did not seem to be searching for a reason to move away from her location.

A few of the men glanced in her direction, but when she met their eyes, they immediately looked away. She wondered if they were acting out of some type of respect, or fear.

Most of the men were dressed in filthy clothing – some badly in need of repair and mending – but Sonja noted her own clothes were clean and well kept. She wore black, knee-length leather boots, cloth breeches, and a silk blouse covered with an unfastened leather vest. The comfortable pressure against her calf announced the presence of a dagger in her left boot. A wide-brimmed cloth hat perched on her head with the front edge folded down to shield her eyes from the bright sunlight. The brim flapped a bit in the wind, but it felt secure enough on her head that she did not worry about it blowing off.

Sonja's left hand dropped to rest on the hilt of a rapier strapped to her hip. Without looking, she could tell by the touch of metal under her palm that she was not carrying Brookstar. The knowledge she was wearing an unfamiliar blade made her sad, but she figured her broadsword would be somewhat out of place aboard a pirate ship. And there was no mistaking that a pirate ship was exactly where Rith had dropped her.

A shout from above caused Sonja to glance up. A man standing in the crow's nest pointed starboard and announced the presence of another ship. Above the man's head waved a black flag emblazoned with the symbol of a white skull and crossbones.

"Rith, what have you gotten me into this time?"

Rith hovered up to Sonja's eye level. "You're on the 'Blooded Dirk.' A pirate ship."

"I can see I'm on a pirate ship. *Why* am I on a pirate ship?"

"Haven't you ever wanted to be a pirate?"

"Not really. Think about this situation. I'm the only woman on a ship full of pirates. Isn't that a little unsafe?"

"You're armed," said Rith.

"So is everyone else."

"But you are better than they are. I made sure of that. Besides, you have rank over them. You're the first mate, and only the captain can give you orders."

Sonja was about to respond, but Rith suddenly dropped back onto his ring. A gruff voice announced the approach of someone behind her.

"Hey!"

Sonja wheeled around, startled by the shout, her sword out of its sheath and level in her hand. One of the crew stood before her, smiling even as her blade passed within a foot of his face. The man was short, though very broad in the shoulders, with a torso like a water barrel wrapped in dirty gray cloth. He was bald, with a few days-worth of black stubble on his cheeks that almost, but not quite, concealed a thick scar running from under his left eye and straight down to his jawline.

"I always knew you was a bit jumpy, but I didn't know you was so quick with the blade."

"If you ever approach me from behind again," said Sonja, sheathing the rapier with disgust at her overreaction, "I'll show you just how quick I am. Now, what do you want?"

"There's a ship been sighted on starboard. That means on your right."

"I know where starboard is, and I heard the crow man's call. Has the Captain been told?"

"No. That's your job," said the man, baring filthy yellow teeth in what barely passed for a smile.

"Very well." Sonja turned to leave but paused with her back to the pirate. "Incidentally, should you speak to me again, you will address me as 'sir' or I'll have you gutted and tossed off the ship." She left without looking back to see what affect her words had achieved. She hoped the comment sounded appropriate. The only experience Sonja had with pirates was in books and movies.

Sonja went to the captain's quarters below deck to inform him of the sighting of a new ship. She had no clue where she was going and might have wandered around lost for hours if Rith had not guided her to the correct door. Grateful for his assistance, Sonja figured it probably would not be good for her reputation if the first mate had to ask one of the crew for directions aboard her own ship.

When Rith assured her she had arrived at the proper location, she pounded a fist above the plaque marked "Captain Christopher Draw."

"What do you want?" responded an irritated male voice from inside.

"A ship has been spotted off our starboard side, Captain."

"What flag is she flying?"

I don't know, Captain. She's still too far off."

"Go above and keep things in order. I'll be up soon."

Sonja headed back to the main deck. At this point, everyone who could be spared from their work was lining the starboard rail trying to see what type of ship they approached. The men chattered excitedly among themselves and talk of a possible raid spread among them. Their last battle had apparently been only a few days ago, but a pirate crew was always ready for a fight, especially if the opportunity to gain a little wealth or prestige presented itself.

"What's her flag?" Sonja shouted up to the crow's nest.

"Can't see it, sir," the man called back. "As soon as I know, so will you."

"When do we move to attack?" asked an unpleasantly familiar voice. Sonja rested her hand on her sword and turned her stare on the crewman meaningfully. "Sir," he amended, though with no particular alacrity.

"We are not attacking. At least not until the captain says we are. We're going to stay on course until we have a make on that ship, and then we run or fight depending on what it is."

"You mean we're going to run from 'em?" The bald pirate's eyes narrowed unhappily.

"If we have to."

"I say we sink that tub no matter what flag she flies," he blustered.

"And I say you shut up and get back to whatever it was you were doing before you decided to bother me."

The pirate approached Sonja and stared down at her. He stood barely an inch taller than she, but somehow, he managed to look down his nose as though he were towering over her. His face flushed with anger and he moved in close enough for Sonja to notice he had green eyes. "I'm getting real tired of you ordering me around. You ain't the captain."

"No, but I'm the closest thing to it right now, and if you don't back off, I'll keep the promise I made earlier." Sonja's heart raced and she felt panic try to close her throat as she spoke. She wanted to turn and run away, but she knew she could not let the rest of the crew see her cower from this confrontation. If she backed down, she would lose any control she might currently have. She stood her ground and silently thanked Master Cejack for teaching her how to control her fear. Despite the turmoil inside, Sonja let none of her emotions show and she managed to keep her voice steady and calm.

"No girl talks that way to me. I don't care if you was a bloody admiral," the pirate growled. He moved to draw his sword, but the hand of another man dropped across his and held him back.

"Careful, Ski. I ain't never seen her lose no fight to nobody."

"Stick around then, Paulo," said the man identified as Ski. He pulled away from the restraining hand. "'Cause you're going to."

Before Ski's weapon came free of its sheath, Sonja stood ready with her blade bared. The belligerent pirate hesitated for moment, surprised by her speed, but he did not back away.

"First attack is yours," said Sonja, remembering her training.

"Sure. The sooner this starts, the sooner the fish get to eat."

Ski moved forward, slashing down and across with his sword edge. Sonja did not even bother to block the attack. She simply stepped back to let the blade hiss by, then countered with a thrust to the chest that Ski avoided only by jumping to his left and blocking wildly.

"She's too fast," shouted Paulo. "Give it up."

Instead of answering, Ski lunged again, and again was forced into an awkward retreat at Sonja's sword tip.

Shouts and cheers rang out from the men, but none of the cries seemed to be in Ski's favor. It was obvious to all that he was outclassed. He attacked over and over, but nothing got through Sonja's defense. Sonja even stopped counter attacking; she just deflected his attempts and let him tire himself out. Panting, Ski rushed in and back, hoping vainly to find an opening.

"Why don't you quit before I have to hurt you, or worse."

"I don't think you can hurt me," said Ski, breathing unevenly.

In reply, Sonja jabbed her sword toward Ski's face, dropped her aim at the last instant to avoid the parry, and slashed down across his chest, ripping his shirt and leaving a cut just deep enough to draw blood. Cheers roared out again. Ski paused in shock, realizing how easily she had gotten through to cut him. He shook his head like an animal trying to free itself of an irritation, then raised his blade again.

"First blood, Ski. Why don't you yield?" Sonja offered. Despite her dislike of this man, she did not want to do him any real harm.

"You'll have to kill me before I stop."

The combatants clashed once more. Ski's attacks were clumsy and wild, giving Sonja several openings to finish the fight, but she let them all pass. She did not want to kill him if she could avoid it. She did not even want to hurt him that much anymore. Despite her initial fear of him when he had challenged her, his ineptitude with a sword had quickly dispelled her concerns. As he continued to flail helplessly against her, she even began to pity him. Now, she only wanted the idiot to quit.

Finally, a chance to stop Ski presented itself. The angry pirate lunged forward and overextended on his attack. With a hard thrust, Sonja drove the tip of her blade through the wrist of his sword hand, cutting muscle and severing tendons. The pirate's sword clattered to the deck. Ski fell to one knee, cradling the injured wrist against his body. The injury was significant, he would probably never use that hand again, but at least Sonja had managed to keep him alive.

Sonja wiped the blood from her sword and sheathed it. She turned her back on Ski and looked at the faces of the gathered men. The show was over, and she needed to get everyone's minds back to the matter of the approaching enemy ship. Captain Draw was not going to be happy if he came up here and found the entire crew circled around her like spectators at a schoolyard fight.

She opened her mouth to order the men back to their stations, but a shout and several pointed fingers turned her whirling back around. She turned in time to see Ski charging across the deck directly at her. His shoulder slammed into her stomach, knocking the breath from her and bowling her to the wooden boards of the ship. With his good hand, Ski tried to achieve a stranglehold, his fingers locking around Sonja's throat. He straddled her chest, using the greater mass of his body to keep her pinned beneath him.

Struggling for air and freedom, Sonja twisted from side to side trying to find a way loose. Although his right hand hung useless at his side, Ski's grip on her neck did not falter and, combined with his weight crushing down on her ribs, Sonja was unable to draw a breath.

Drawing her sword was impossible at this angle, but Sonja remembered that the rapier was not her only weapon. Hunching her shoulders forward, she slid her left hand down her leg far enough to get her fingertips on the pommel of the dagger concealed in her boot. She pulled and the blade slipped a couple inches from its hidden sheath, allowing her to grasp the handle. She freed the blade from her boot, but Sonja found herself unable to move her arm enough to effectively use the weapon.

With the knife in her left hand, Sonja struggled to raise it high enough to strike. Ski's bulk made movement difficult as he continued to try to choke the life from her. There was no way to aim for anything vital on her attacker, and even if she could find something important to stab, she couldn't swing her arm with sufficient momentum to drive the point deep enough to cause damage.

Black motes swam at the corners of her vision and she realized she had little time left. She was moments away from passing out. Sonja did not know exactly how long the brain could function without oxygen, but she knew it couldn't be long. Ski was too heavy and too strong for her to push him off of her, and Sonja did not have the leverage to roll or crawl out from under his bulk. With her elbow pinned against her side, she could not use the dagger to save herself either.

In a final desperate move, Sonja raised her knees and placed her feet flat against the wooden deck. She bucked forward with her hips trying to lift Ski enough to topple him away from her. The man only lifted off her chest a few inches before crashing back down onto her already aching ribcage. That fraction of a second that Ski's weight was off of her was all she needed. Sonja squirmed deeper down between his legs. Not far, but enough that she could finally free her left arm.

Sonja raised her hand and angled the dagger toward the man who seemed so intent on trying to kill her. She still did not have enough room to choose her target, but she thrust the knife forward with every ounce of strength remaining to her. The blade met resistance as it parted skin and muscle. Sonja did not hesitate or flinch as she continued to drive the razor-honed tip forward. She stopped pushing only when the metal guard touched flesh, preventing any further movement. By sheer chance, the blade passed between Ski's fourth and fifth ribs, cutting through his right lung and finding his heart. The pirate grunted and his body tensed as he felt the blade go in.

Without another sound, Ski released his hold on Sonja's throat and slumped sideways, falling limp onto the deck beside her. He panted for a moment as he lay on the wooden boards, looking like a fish dragged from the water, gasping to pull air into his damaged lung. He was finished. Even if his lungs had still functioned properly, the damage to his heart was fatal. Ski wheezed out a final breath, drooling blood across his cheek, then went still.

Retching and coughing painfully, Sonja staggered to her feet, the bloody dagger still in her hand. She faced the rest of the crew, letting her gaze touch every man present. She was still lightheaded and dizzy, and she struggled to keep her feet, but she knew she could not show any more weakness than she already had. "Well, who else wants to try?" She rasped. Her voice was hoarse, and it hurt to talk, but the anger and deadly intent were clear. "This time I won't give you the opportunity to jump me from behind."

"Drommer," said a softly disapproving voice off to her left. She swung around to find an immaculately dressed man – even better dressed than herself – standing a few feet away with his hands clasped behind his back. Tall and lean, the figure stood motionless as a statue despite the rocking of the ship that threatened Sonja's own challenged sense of balance. Shoulder length blond hair cascaded from beneath a black three-corner hat, and under the low brim, hard gray eyes, empty of emotion, watched her intently. The face was too long to be handsome, and there was a curious lack of expression in his features that left Sonja chilled and uneasy. "Is this how you 'keep things in order?'"

Sonja guessed immediately that this was the captain. "Yes, sir. There was a, um … problem with one of the men. I took care of it."

"I see. Clean your knife and put it away, then brief me on what you know so far."

Sonja wiped her dagger on the dead man's shirt and replaced it in her boot. "We don't know anything more than I told you before, Captain. There's a ship out there heading in our direction and we don't know whose it is."

"Can you see her markings, yet?" shouted Captain Draw up at the lookout.

"Aye, Captain. I can just make 'er out. She flies a trade flag. Blue and red, sir. Merchant ship. And they're changing course. They sees our flag and they's running!"

"Then we give chase," said the captain to his men. "Stay with her. Whatever she's carrying, I want it. If we lose her, Ski won't be the only rotting carcass on our deck, I promise you that. Drommer, give me full sail."

She took the captain's order and relayed it to the rest of the crew. This turned out to be a completely unnecessary task. Everyone already knew what to do and where to be. Everyone, that is, except Sonja.

"Rith," she called when she had a second to herself with nobody watching. "What do I do now?"

"When the fighting starts, your place is next to the captain. Your job is to protect him, like a bodyguard. If he dies, the crew will kill you, too. Until the battle, though, you're pretty much free to do as you please."

Sonja chose to stand and wait with Captain Draw on the foredeck. They both stood silently, watching while the men checked sails, riggings, and hand weapons to be sure that all would be ready for the coming clash. The crew worked fast and efficiently, well-coordinated from the practice of many similar situations.

The pirate ship veered from its course to pursue the fleeing vessel. Men slid cannons and roped them into position along the sides, four to the right and four to the left. Each cannon held one round ready to fire and several more cannonballs – braced to prevent them from rolling away – stacked nearby to be loaded as needed. Once these preparations were completed, the pirate crew could only stand by and wait, anticipating the fight as the other ship came slowly within range. Sonja watched anxiously as the Blooded Dirk reeled in the trade ship. The pirates gained steadily, cutting swiftly through the choppy wake of the ocean as the wind blew them steadily onward. Capture was only a matter of time. Although the merchant ship appeared to be about the same size as the Dirk and it was currently running at full sail, Sonja figured the ship must be carrying a heavy load to be moving so slowly.

As they closed on their target, Sonja saw only two cannon ports protecting each side of the trade ship. Knowing their cargo must be attractive to raiders, she was surprised the ship was not better armed. She wondered about the crew that piloted her, and whether they would put up much of a fight. The pirates of the Blooded Dirk were experienced killers, but the upcoming battle came with no guaranteed outcome. A single well-placed cannonball could sink either ship. Sonja watched the distance between the two vessels dwindle and considered how many people might die, today.

Would she be one of them?

The trade vessel veered from its path, turning to angle its side to the chasing ship. Several of her sails folded and dropped, reducing her speed dramatically. Their prey had given up on escaping and now turned to fight. The tension that had been building among the pirates released with an almost audible snap and everyone moved as the captain's voice rang out. "Come about to port. Match speeds and man the cannons. Fire at will."

Less than a minute later, the Dirk had pivoted to align its starboard cannons against their target. The explosions of gunpowder sounded out and were answered in turn by the cannons of the opposing ship a hundred yards away. Water splashed as preliminary shots cleared their targets or fell short. The next volley would be better aimed, and the real damage would begin. Sonja's crew wanted to cripple the trade vessel, not sink it. Any valuable cargo aboard would be lost if the ship went down. The opposing ship had no such qualms. On the contrary, they would expend every effort to break and batter Sonja's ship until it disappeared under the water, never to be seen again.

Iron spheres rained down again. They tore into the sails, decks, and hulls of both ships. Wood splintered, and men died or were tossed overboard from the impacts. Captain Draw was thrown to the deck by the impact of a near miss. Sonja staggered, but kept herself upright by grabbing onto a railing. When she felt steady enough to let go, she extended a hand and helped Draw to his feet.

Shouts and screams echoed across the water from the merchant ship, and from the sounds of them, Sonja guessed that the crew was losing the ability or the will to continue fighting. Not everyone on board was ready to surrender, however. The cannons still sounded, and at any moment, there was still the risk of a lucky shot striking a fatal blow to the Dirk. Sonja knew they needed to end this attack soon, and Captain Draw apparently felt the same way.

"Raise all sails and come about," he called out to the Dirk's crew. For a moment Sonja thought the captain had decided to run, but she soon discovered he had something else in mind.

"Ram her!" the captain cried, pointing at the opposing ship.

Because of the short distance separating the two vessels, the Dirk did not gain enough speed to do any real damage. However, both crews tumbled to the decks as a loud hollow thud announced the ships had come into contact. Ropes flew from the Dirk, securing both craft to one another, and planks dropped across the narrow spaces between the two ships' railings, forming temporary bridges. Without waiting for further directions from the captain, pirates swarmed over onto the trade ship.

Captain Draw did not move from his position of observation. He watched the beginning stages of the fighting, perhaps making sure the struggle was moving in his favor before committing himself to any action. Sonja remained at his side. A few shots rang out as black powder pistols came into play, but the raid allowed no time for reloading and soon all fighting devolved into hand to hand and sword to sword.

With the ringing of metal against metal and the cries of injured combatants rising in the air, Captain Draw at last moved to enter the melee. The captain slid down the ladder from the quarterdeck to the main deck and bolted for the nearest plank linking the two ships. He boarded the trade ship with Sonja fast on his heels.

Striding toward the heart of the fray, Draw pointed to a swordsman fending off an attacking pirate. "Kill him," said the pirate captain, indicating Sonja should assist.

She drew her sword and approached the dueling pair. The man the captain had indicated had his back to her as she advanced, completely focused on the pirate he currently faced. It appeared the merchant was getting the better of the Dirk crewman and might at any moment deliver a final blow. Sonja tapped the top of his head with her rapier, and when the man turned, she ran her blade through his right shoulder. The merchant fell back, dropping his weapon and collapsing to the deck. His left hand clutched at his wound and Sonja could see blood seeping into his clothing between his fingers. She kicked away the fallen sword hard enough to send it skittering overboard and turned back to Captain Draw.

A look of disgust crossed the captain's face, drawing Sonja up short. She had only done what he told her to do. Why did he seem so angry? Captain Draw walked past her to the fallen swordsman. He stabbed the helpless man through the heart with his sword, then turned back to Sonja and held up his bloodied blade.

"I told you to kill him. When I give an order, I won't say it twice. Fail to obey me again and *your* blood will run on my sword."

"Yes, sir," said Sonja, too shocked to protest.

Draw turned and waded into the ongoing battle. After a stunned moment, Sonja hurried to follow.

The majority of the resistance had been dispatched by this time, and the fighting ended soon after Sonja and Captain Draw entered the melee. Most of the trade ship's crew lay dead at the feet of the victorious marauders. A few who had chosen not to fight or had given up quickly sat bound and gagged, huddled together at the prow of the ship. Also tied up and held prisoner were several male and female passengers, rounded up from the ship's quarters, storage holds and various hiding spots throughout the vessel after the battle. A few of the passengers had offered some resistance early on and died for their trouble. The rest learned from their example and submitted quietly to being bound about the wrists and ankles.

Sonja, Captain Draw, and one other pirate watched the captives while the rest of the Dirk's crew stripped the ship of all cargo, cash, jewelry, and anything else that might hold some value and could be easily carried away. Swords and pistols were collected as well and transported over to the Dirk. The pirates even took cannon balls and gunpowder to replace what had been expended during the confrontation.

Lastly, the Dirk's crew raided the ship of all food, fresh water, and alcohol before they finished. The survivors of this raid would arrive home hungry and thirsty.

If they made it home at all.

When the captain was satisfied that everything of value had been taken, destroyed, or tossed overboard, the pirates returned to their vessel. Sonja and Captain Draw moved to return as well, but Sonja paused when she noticed the third member of their group approaching one of the female captives. The girl was young, with dark hair and a pretty face. Her large brown eyes welled with fear as she watched the pirate looming over her.

"Let's see what you're hiding from us, love," the man leered. He grasped the edge of her bodice and pulled down on the lacings. Material tore, baring the girl's breasts, and the pirate cupped a hard, calloused hand over the exposed flesh. The girl began to cry, helpless tears spilling freely down her cheeks.

Before the pirate could do more, Sonja intervened.

"Leave the girl alone," she ordered. "Go back to the ship."

"Not yet," he replied, refusing to move away from his intended victim. "I got business here still."

Sonja drew her sword. "This is the last time I'll say it. Go back to the ship."

The pirate peered up at Sonja. Dropping a nervous glance down at her weapon, he decided his best interests lay with compliance. He rose to his feet and, without a second look at Sonja, strode cockily toward the Blooded Dirk as though it had been his intention to leave the entire time.

Sonja sheathed her sword and followed. She took a second to look back and check on the girl attempting unsuccessfully to cover herself with the torn material of her dress. In the process, Sonja almost walked directly into the point of a sword. If she had stopped a moment later, her momentum would have impaled her through the throat.

Sonja's eyes followed the length of the weapon to find an angry Captain Draw on the opposite end.

"Where are you going?" asked the captain in a level yet dangerous tone. He continued before Sonja could reply. "You are not fit to return to the Bloody Dirk. Twice, you put the interests of the enemy above those of your own shipmates. Since your concerns seem to lie with them, you shall remain with them. Perhaps they will even decide not to hang you when you reach land."

For a moment, his eyes softened. "I like you, Sonja. That is the only reason you are still alive right now. You are a strong leader and gifted with the sword, but you have become a liability for me. You do not have the heart of a pirate."

He turned and crossed back over to his ship, leaving Sonja confused and embarrassed aboard the vessel she had just attacked. She gaped mutely as the planks connecting the two ships lifted. Sails billowed and the Dirk drifted away, at first slowly, then rapidly gaining speed and distance. Sonja could only watch as the pirate ship on which she had so recently been a crewmember dwindled in size before disappearing over the horizon.

After what seemed an exceedingly long time standing at the railing of the crippled trading ship, staring over the now empty waters, Sonja remembered she was not alone. She turned to face her captives. Every one of them stared curiously and expectantly back. Sonja sighed and moved to untie them, wondering seriously if she might be releasing her own private lynch mob.

CHAPTER 15

The girl Sonja had saved from the unwanted attentions of her former pirate shipmate repaid the debt a hundred-fold as soon as she had been untied. While the majority of the freed hostages wanted to hang Sonja from the yard arm and use her body for a piñata in retaliation for the pirates' attack, the young woman – Sonja learned her name was Bethany – convinced them to leave her alone. Since most of the crew was dead and the ship had sustained a great deal of damage in the raid, she argued everyone currently on board would be needed to guide the ship safely to land. Once they arrived back home, they could let the local authorities deal with Sonja.

The angry passengers reluctantly agreed.

When Sonja's fate had been determined, Rith decided it was time to end the adventure.

Sonja wondered for an uncomfortable moment if Rith would have let her hang had the mob opted to go the other way, but she did not ask. She was home now and, ultimately, it did not matter. Besides, she was afraid she might not like his answer.

Sonja sat on her bed in her room, hugging her knees to her chin and pondering her latest adventure. "I guess I blew that one, too," she said at last.

Her throat still hurt, and she touched the fingertips of one hand to her injured neck. She cleared her throat painfully.

Rith perched on a supporting post at the foot of the bed, his tiny wings twitching occasionally to maintain his balance. He perked up when she spoke. "Why do you say that?"

"I got kicked off the ship. My own captain said he wanted to kill me and told me I make a lousy pirate."

"I agree with him. You are a lousy pirate."

"Thanks a lot, Rith. You're a big help." Sonja threw a pillow at him. Although he never moved to avoid it, it somehow missed him as it sailed across the room and flopped onto the bedroom floor.

"No, really. Think about it. He wanted you to kill a defenseless man and let a woman get raped. Would you honestly want to be a 'good pirate' in those circumstances? Do you think you and I would be friends if you were a 'good pirate?'"

"No. I suppose not," Sonja commented, pondering what Rith had said. "I didn't think of it that way."

"Besides, he never actually said you were a lousy pirate," Rith reminded her. "What he actually said was you don't have the heart of a pirate. Personally, I think he was giving you a compliment. I think he was saying you have a good heart and that you are a good person. I agree with that."

Sonja laughed but stopped when a sharp pain made her wince. "You're right. I suppose I handled myself pretty well out there. Didn't I?"

"I wouldn't go that far. You did get kicked off your own ship. I don't know that you can exactly call that outcome a win. Still, I think you did make the right choices when things got difficult. Maybe you just need more practice. Do you want to go try it again?" asked Rith, teasing.

"Absolutely not. No more pirates. Not for a very long time, anyway." Sonja touched her tender throat again. "I suppose I'm going to be wearing scarves and turtlenecks for a while. At least until this bruising goes away."

Thanksgiving, Christmas, and New Year's kept Sonja busy for several weeks. Shopping, eating, and visiting friends and relatives seemed plenty exciting for the time being without throwing in the possibility of getting killed by one of Rith's story ideas. Still, her desire for adventure would not be put on hold forever.

Early in February, on a dreary Thursday afternoon, Sonja decided she had had enough of the real world for a while. It was time to go adventuring once again. Outside, the sky hung gray and damp overhead, releasing intermittent bursts of a light but chilling drizzle. The weather matched her mood as semester progress reports had been posted earlier that day. In addition, she had been forced to walk home in the rain since her dad was working and could not pick her up. It had been an uncomfortable, miserable slog home, made infinitely worse by the fact she had forgotten to take an umbrella to school with her that morning.

With cold, shivering hands, Sonja grabbed the mail from the mailbox and hurried inside the house to dry off. Dropping the damp bundle of papers onto the kitchen table, she took a moment in her bedroom to first strip out of her wet clothes and change into a warm pair of sweatpants and a hoodie. After taking a towel to her hair to wick out the worst of the soaking she had received, she returned to the kitchen with her laptop computer in tow.

She plugged the computer's charging cord into a wall socket and touched the power button. When the machine finished its warmup process, Sonja pulled up the school's website and typed in her password to view her grades. As she had expected, they weren't great. Mostly B's and a couple C's, they were not terrible, but it was a definite step down from the previous semester. She swore, then sneezed loudly.

"Great," Sonja muttered. "I'm catching a cold on top of everything else."

Shutting the laptop with more force than absolutely necessary, she swore again. "The hell with this. I've had enough. Rith!"

"Yes," came an immediate response.

"I need a break."

"You're ready to go again?"

"Yes. But please, something non-violent, non-threatening, and definitely non-fatal." Sonja sneezed again. "And something warm. In fact, I know the perfect place for this trip, and I think you do, too."

"That doesn't sound very exciting," said Rith. "But you're the boss."

CHAPTER 16

Sonja lay on her stomach, stretched along the length of the cotton, beach blanket. She smiled at the sudden warmth radiating down on her back and sighed with contentment. Much better. Her friends and family could freeze and hide from the rain without her for a while. Not that they would notice she was gone, but it was still nice to imagine everyone she knew shivering, wet and cold while she basked in the glorious sunlight of her personal beach island.

Resting her head on her folded arms, Sonja closed her eyes and let the sounds of the nearby water lull her into a comfortable doze. She did not worry about the sunscreen this time. There was no need for it. From experience, she knew she would not burn regardless of how much time she spent lounging under the deceptively warm sun. She could remain here weeks and not get so much as the slightest bit of tan. Which was a shame. Although, upon further pondering, she realized it might be difficult trying to explain to people at home how she managed to maintain a lovely bronze glow in the middle of winter.

After a while – Sonja had no idea exactly how long since time had little meaning on this beach – she pushed herself up to her knees and reached for the picnic basket that Rith always kept close at hand. She flipped up the lid and found a pair of sunglasses sitting at the top of the pile of items inside.

"Thanks for remembering, little guy," she said, slipping them onto her face. Sonja paused, letting the basket lid fall shut. She glanced down at herself and noticed something that didn't seem quite right. She looked to Rith, who remained motionless on her ring.

"Hey, Rith?"

"Yes?" he answered.

"I know this may seem like an odd question, but how come I'm not naked?"

Sonja gestured toward the swimsuit she was wearing. She had on a blue bikini. Not the one she had in a drawer back home, but similar. "Not that I really care, but last time you told me there was no need for clothing here."

"There isn't," he told her. "I just thought you might be more comfortable since you mentioned not having anything to wear last time."

"That's when I didn't know that I was alone. If there isn't any reason for it, I can take it off, right?"

"Of course."

Sonja reached behind her back to unfasten the laces of her suit top.

"Except…"

Sonja paused at the word.

"Except?" she asked. "Rith? Except what?"

"Except this time, you might not be totally alone on the beach." Rith launched off Sonja's ring to flutter over her head; just out of reach in case she had an urge to swat at him. "Don't worry. It's fine. It's fine. No fighting and nothing dangerous, just like I promised."

"Who else is here?" Sonja asked, trying to keep her voice patient.

Rith risked moving closer, lowering himself to eye level. "I would rather not say. It needs to be a surprise. And, actually, no one is here now. He won't show up for a while."

"He?"

"Oops. I shouldn't have said that," Rith chastised himself. "It spoils some of the surprise."

Sonja shook her head in exasperation. "When is 'he' going to get here?"

"Later," Rith said, unhelpfully, then refused to elaborate.

Sonja flopped onto her back, clasping her hands together under her head and staring up at the cloudless, blue sky. "Fine. Keep your secrets. Just do me one favor, please? Let me know before he shows up so I'm not picking my nose or doing something gross when he gets here."

"Of course. I'll let you know."

The day passed leisurely for Sonja, just as she had hoped when she asked Rith to bring her here. She went for a run along the hardpacked sand at the waterline, swam, and played in the waves. In the later afternoon, she explored the narrow strip of forest that ran through the middle of the island. Occasionally, she rummaged through the basket for snacks or drinks when the mood struck. As the hours crawled by and the sun inched across the sky, sinking lower toward the ocean horizon, Sonja noted that no visitors appeared.

Evening arrived and dusk followed rapidly behind. Sonja pulled a soda from the basket and settled onto her blanket to watch the sunset. A narrow band of clouds gathering at the horizon blazed orange, yellow and gold as the enormous blazing orb touched, then slowly submerged into the water.

"I love this part of the day," Sonja said, as she watched the last glowing sliver of the sun disappear. The sky darkened to a deep purple. "It's always so beautiful."

She lowered herself flat on her back to stare at the fading sky around her and search for the first bashful stars to make their appearances. Letting her vision go unfocused, Sonja listened to the movement of the water nearby and wondered who Rith might have invited. Would it be someone she knew? A friend, perhaps? Or was it a complete stranger? Odd, that Rith wouldn't just tell her, but the flighty little guy really wanted it to be a surprise.

Sonja was not particularly sleepy, but she was tired from her day of play and exploration. She closed her eyes, slowed her breathing, and focused on the soothing evening noises. She heard a bird cry out from somewhere behind her, and a rush of wind rustled the tops of the trees in the forest nearby. She loved the experience, but her favorite part of being on her beach wasn't the sounds she could hear. It was the ones she could not. No traffic noises, electronic hums, or other manmade distractions. Just nature and the pervasive, blissful presence of silence.

Sonja bolted upright. She did not know if she had fallen asleep or, if so, for how long, but something out of place had prodded her subconscious, bringing her fully alert. A noise she could not place had reached her ears and now she sat rigid on her blanket, trying to determine if it had been real or merely a piece of a dream. Staring out toward the sea, she cocked her head and listened for a repeat of the sound that had awakened her.

A popping sound behind her caused her to jump. She spun around, hand reaching to her hip for a sword that was not there. A flicker of light on the beach between herself and the jungle pierced the gloom of the moonless night and caught her eye. Twenty yards away, a man in shorts and a t-shirt crouched over a slowly growing fire, feeding the small flame with driftwood and handfuls of dry seaweed to coax it to life. At Sonja's startled movement, he turned his head to face her.

"I thought you might like a fire," he said simply. "It might get cold later."

The voice was familiar. As the flames grew higher, she could begin to make out his face in the brightening firelight.

"Kevin?" Sonja asked, incredulous. "What are you doing here?"

Before he could answer, Sonja sprang to her feet and ran toward him. She leapt on him, throwing her arms around his neck and wrapping her legs tightly about his waist. Kevin staggered back a step as he caught her but managed to keep his feet.

He laughed at Sonja's greeting. "I guess you do remember me," he told her.

"Of course, I remember you." Sonja gave his neck another squeeze before letting her feet drop back to the ground and stepping back to look at him. "What girl forgets her knight in shining armor?"

Kevin's cheeks reddened, but Sonja could not be certain if he was blushing or if it was only a trick of the flickering firelight.

"Well, there doesn't appear to be anything you need saving from at the moment."

"No," Sonja agreed. "I'm fine. But I'm still really glad you're here. How long can you stay?"

"I guess that's up to you. Rith told me–"

"You know Rith?" Sonja blurted, cutting him off. "How do you know about him?"

"He … uh, he brought me here. He said I should spend some time with you when we weren't busy trying not to get killed. He also told me I should be a perfect gentleman while I'm here because the moment you get tired of me, he's sending me back home."

"I hope you aren't going to be too much of a gentleman," Sonja commented, thinking back to the interrupted kiss they had shared so long ago. It was not the first time she had thought about that kiss. Or even the one hundredth. Thinking about it now brought about a familiar warmth in the pit of her stomach.

Kevin smiled, and this time Sonja was certain he was blushing. She reached out and grasped his hand. "Come sit down. Are you hungry? There's plenty of stuff in the picnic basket."

"What about the fire?" Kevin glanced back over his shoulder. With him no longer feeding wood into it, the flame had begun to die back down.

"We don't need it. It doesn't get cold here. If you want the light, though, we can keep it going."

"No. Let's sit. That sounds nice, and if we want a fire, I can build another one later."

Sonja leaned into him, bumping her shoulder against his arm genially. "Sounds good. I guess I'll let you stay for a while after all."

They settled down on Sonja's blanket and stared out at the delicate ripples of starlight dancing on the waves of the ocean. Food and fire forgotten, they sat in companionable silence and listened to the world around them. Neither felt compelled to speak and there was no awkwardness in the silence. It felt natural for the moment.

Sonja rested her head on Kevin's shoulder and closed her eyes. She had a thousand questions for him. She wanted to know all about him; where he came from, what his family was like, and why he had agreed to come visit her. She especially wanted to know the answer to that last question, hoping he had been thinking about her as much as she thought about him.

All that could wait. There would be time for every one of her questions later. For now, it was enough to simply share her beach with Kevin. To be close to him.

Butterflies fluttered in her stomach and she was suddenly nervous as she wondered if she would get the chance to kiss him again. Perhaps sensing the change in her mood, Kevin turned to face her. Sonja climbed to her knees and took his face between her hands, deciding that the answer to this question was going to be yes.

The sun rose early on the morning of their fifth day together. Sonja lay asleep on her side with Kevin curled up against her, his hand draped over her waist. The previous night's fire had died hours ago, and only black ash remained to stain the unpolluted white sands. Waves rolled in from far out at sea to lap gently at the shore only a few feet away from the sleeping couple. From somewhere high above, a sea bird cried out dolefully.

A soft tickle in her ear brought Sonja to grudging wakefulness. "It's time to go," said Rith quietly when he saw her eyes flicker open.

Sonja shook her head, almost imperceptibly. "Not yet," she whispered. "It's too soon."

"It's been almost a week."

"Too soon," she repeated, but Sonja shifted Kevin's arm and rolled slowly away from him.

Careful not to wake him, she kissed his cheek lightly before rising to her feet. Several days of dark stubble brushed her lips and tickled her chin. She wanted more. Sonja wanted to shake him awake and kiss him properly; to start the morning with the feel of her body pressed tightly against his. Four days was not enough. She wanted to stay here on the beach with Kevin forever. It was only the knowledge that she had a life, family and friends waiting for her that gave her the strength to let him sleep.

Looking down at his relaxed features, she thought he looked like a child in his sleeping innocence, not the serious, attentive lover of last night. A small, satisfied smile played at Kevin's lips as Sonja watched him. She hoped his dreams were as pleasant as her own had been.

"Will I ever see him again?" she asked Rith, not looking away from Kevin's sleeping form.

"I have a feeling that you will," he replied. "After all, it was Kevin who gave me to you."

"What?!" she breathed, trying to keep her voice down.

"I belonged to him before I met you. Kevin's one wish was to meet the perfect girl. A soulmate, if you like. Someone he could love unconditionally that would love him back. I told him I could do it, but in exchange he would have to give me up. He agreed. I gave him your name, birthday, and address, and the rest you know. I'm sorry I couldn't tell you the truth sooner, but do you understand why I had to wait?"

A flash of conflicting emotions filled Sonja. She was angry at Rith and Kevin for hiding the truth from her. She felt like a pawn in a game she had no idea she had been playing. She still wanted to wake Kevin, but now she just wanted to slap his lying face. How dare he walk into her life simply expecting her to fall in love with him? How unbelievably arrogant to assume he just had to show up and she would throw herself into his arms.

Except…

Except she did care about him. Damn it, she might even be starting to love him.

Sonja sighed, still upset but willing to sort out her emotions later rather than throw everything away before she had a chance to think about how she really felt.

"I suppose I get why you waited. If I had known before I met him, I never would have given him a chance. I never would have gotten to know him. It would be pretty horrifying to be told 'this is the guy you will fall in love with' before I even saw him. No, you did the right thing. But I'm still mad at both of you."

"I know," said Rith. His tiny head drooped in contrition. "I hope we are still friends."

Sonja relented. "We are. Just, please, no more secrets."

"No more," Rith promised. "Not ever. That was the last one."

Sonja looked back at Kevin, her anger fading. Her expression softened. "So now he has his wish."

"And you have yours."

"So, I'll see Kevin again? I mean in the real world. You know, my world."

"It's his world, too. And, yes, you'll see him again. He actually doesn't live too far from you."

Sonja smiled. For the first time since Rith had whisked her away to distant Sherwood Forrest, she was excited about going back home. Whereas before, returning to her life always signified the end of an adventure, this time going back meant the real adventure could finally start. Today, home was not the end of anything.

It was only the beginning.

PART II

CHOICES

CHAPTER 17

Sonja fidgeted in her seat, desperately trying to remain awake and concentrate on the professor's lecture. The heat in the lecture hall, a recently eaten lunch still digesting in her stomach, and her instructor's monotone delivery of the material all combatted against her best efforts to stay alert and focused. The topic under discussion – researching market trends and target audiences – offered no real help either. For the five hundredth time in the past three years, Sonja questioned the wisdom of her choice of majors when she started college.

All through junior high and high school, she had loved to draw and paint. Every free moment, when Rith did not have other plans for her, Sonja spent time etching in her art book or experimenting with oils and watercolors on canvas or paper. Even training under Cejack she had found the occasional odd moment to draw or sketch. Many of her paintings had received compliments from family and friends, but Sonja had always wondered if she had the talent to actually make a living with her art. When she began mailing out college applications in her senior year of high school, she declared her major as Graphic Design, figuring she would have the chance to paint and also learn some marketable skills at the same time.

If it did not work out, she could always change her major.

Three years later, she found herself trying to stay awake in an advertising class, wondering for the five hundredth time if she had made the right choice, and for the five hundredth time she decided that despite her current predicament, yes, she enjoyed what she was doing and given the opportunity to choose again, she would still be in this exact same seat falling asleep.

Sonja lifted her head and forced herself to look around the huge lecture hall. Staring down at her notes only encouraged her eyelids to close and her head to nod, so she hoped a quick scan of the room would help wake her up. She happily noticed that hers was not the only forehead periodically tattooing dents into the desk in front of it. One poor student had lost the battle completely and now snored softly with mouth open and drool collecting on his chin as the professor proceeded blithely on with his tirade on timing market trends appropriately and recognizing current fads.

As she gazed at the thirty or so students randomly clustered throughout three hundred seats, Sonja wondered, not for the first time, at the waste of space the class represented. The small number of students would have been much better served in a smaller room. Although it would have been much harder to get away with sleeping while the professor hovered directly over them. She supposed even the teachers had to make do with whatever resources were available to them, and if a class of thirty students had to be placed in a hall with three hundred seats, so be it. It was better than the other way around.

232

Sonja glanced at her watch. One thirty. The class still had half an hour to go. She groaned inwardly. This day was crawling by much too slowly for her tastes.

At least she had her martial arts class to look forward to tonight. Master Toshida had promised to teach her a new advanced form and she could hardly wait to try it. Martial arts, she thought, had been another good choice when she started college. Wanting to keep in shape and maintain her weapons training, Sonja had sought out a small studio off campus early in her freshman year. When she met Master Toshida she explained that although she had received training with several weapons – she stretched the truth just a bit by stating that a friend of a friend taught her in high school – she wished also to learn unarmed combat and defense.

Master Toshida asked Sonja which weapons she had trained with. She told him she was familiar with sword, knife, and staff, figuring he would not care about either her archery skills or her experience with the mace. Nodding at her response, he produced what he called a "bo staff" from his equipment room. He handed the slender wooden pole to Sonja and requested a demonstration so he could gauge her present skills and decide where to begin teaching her. Sonja held the bo lightly in the palms of her hands, examining the weapon and testing its balance. Although more slender than the staff she knew, and despite a gradual tapering in diameter towards each end, the length and weight felt about right. After a few experimental motions to get a feel for how it moved, she began to pace herself through her beginning forms.

As she warmed up and adjusted to the slight differences in Master Toshida's staff, Sonja transitioned into the first of her advanced forms. She picked up speed and felt her body falling naturally into a rhythm perfectly in harmony with the motions of

233

the weapon in her hand. The staff whistled and hummed as it passed through the air. Sonja punctuated the sound of the wood as it blurred through each move with an occasional stomp of her foot or a violent expulsion of breath to emphasize specific attacks. Toshida merely watched silently as Sonja dodged, parried, and struck out at her invisible opponents. Sonja had only just begun an elaborate sequence of moves Cejack referred to as "chasing the dove" when Master Toshida called for her to stop.

She brought the whirling wooden scythe to an abrupt halt, standing rigidly upright and driving one end of the staff to the floor with a loud *crack*. She stood panting slightly from the exertion, a light sheen of perspiration forming on her face. Sonja saw from the mounted wall clock in the studio that almost ten minutes had passed during her impromptu demonstration. Enjoying the sensation of a weapon in her hands and the exhilaration of controlling it through a sequence of increasingly intricate maneuvers had caused her to completely lose any feel for the time.

Master Toshida gazed speculatively at her for a long moment before asking, "Who did you say taught you this?"

"Oh, I don't think you would know him. He lives pretty far away from here," Sonja offered lamely.

Toshida nodded. "I don't know what to say. I have seen very few people handle a Bo so beautifully, and I do not recognize any of the forms you just displayed. I don't think I can teach you anything that you don't already know. You say you are equally as skilled with a sword?" he asked.

"Yes." Honesty and pride warred briefly with modesty before Sonja added, "Actually better. But I don't know anything about unarmed defense. That's why I came here."

"Then I propose an agreement. I will teach you the art of Shorin Ryu, free of charge, and you will instruct me in the staff. Is that acceptable to you?"

Sonja's mouth had dropped. Master Toshida wanted *her* ... to teach *him*? She had taught students for Master Cejack, of course, but they had all been beginners. Master Toshida was a ... well, a master. But he had made the offer seriously. There was no evidence in his expression that he might be patronizing her.

Sonja agreed immediately.

Now, barely two and a half years after first stepping into Master Toshida's studio – or dojo, as he referred to it – she was preparing to test for her second-degree black belt; her *ni dan*. Master Toshida had also progressed markedly with the staff under Sonja's tutelage. He refused to accept any training with the sword or dagger except for a few techniques designed to disarm an opponent using one of the two weapons. Sonja offered several times to teach him some basic forms with the blades, but Master Toshida had politely declined each time and then redirected the conversation.

In exchange for the form Master Toshida promised to teach her tonight, Sonja had promised to show him the second of the four advanced Melee Drills. She looked forward to some light sparring as well. Master Toshida was a fierce competitor with the staff. Sonja remained superior in her handling of the weapon, but Toshida managed to occasionally take a match or two if she was careless. At times, he would abandon standard tactics and use his hands or feet to trip, tackle or sweep her to the ground. Once, he had grabbed her staff, dropping his own, and when she had attempted to pull it from his grasp, he pivoted and flipped her over his hip, throwing her completely out of bounds to win the match. It was techniques like this that she had so desperately wanted to learn.

Each time they faced each other, she realized Master Toshida became a little more devious and harder to beat. But then again, so did she. Toshida taught her that while skill and speed were important, experience more often than not would decide the outcome of a confrontation.

And experience could only be gained from practice.

No amount of practice or experience, however, could make her advertising class end any sooner. The instructor continued his droning diatribe and Sonja dutifully continued to take notes. She glanced again at her watch. One thirty-five.

Dammit, I'm going to grow old and die here, she thought. But I'm not going down without a fight.

"Rith," Sonja whispered. "It's break time. Do your thing, little guy."

CHAPTER 18

Sonja's vision blurred and doubled, leaving her dizzy and disoriented. Her stomach clenched, twisting inside her and threatening to empty its contents in revolt. In a desperate attempt not to vomit, Sonja squeezed her eyes shut and forced herself to take short, shallow breaths. The air felt dense around her, and in addition to her stomach problems, she found she was having some difficulty breathing in and out of her nose. It was as if she were suffering from some sort of sinus swelling that limited the amount of air she could pull into her lungs. She opened her mouth and tried taking a deeper breath. The restriction eased considerably. The nausea also began to pass.

Sonja felt her body relax as she kept her eyes closed and she focused solely on drawing oxygen into her lungs and exhaling it out. She thought back to the meditation techniques Master Toshida had taught her, letting her mind wander from sensation to sensation without dwelling on anything in particular.

"Rith, what the hell?" she asked, still taking long slow breaths.

"Sorry about that," came the immediate reply. "Don't open your eyes again for a minute. I have some things to tell you, first. I probably should have given you a bit of warning on this one."

"Okay," Sonja agreed. Her eyes remained closed as Rith had requested. Clearly, this adventure was something new, and if Rith thought she was better off blind at the moment, she wasn't going to argue. But … what was going on with her voice? She sounded like she was trying to talk around a mouth full of pudding. Where was she?

One more thing on the "not normal" scale suddenly registered in her mind. A concern that pushed all other thoughts to the back burner.

"Rith, why do I feel like I'm flying? I can't feel anything under my feet. It's like I'm floating or something. Are we in space?"

"No. No, we're definitely not in space," replied Rith's voice next to her ear. He at least sounded like himself. Her own speech remained muffled.

"Floating was a good choice of words, though. You are floating. In water. We are both currently under water. You can breathe just fine though," he said hurriedly to forestall any new panic from Sonja. "As long as we are here you will be able to breathe under water without any difficulty, so don't worry about that at all."

"Are there other things I *should* be worried about?" Sonja asked lightly, trying to sound nonchalant, though mostly failing.

"No. There really isn't, but I want to warn you that there will be a bit of an adjustment period on this one. If you think you're ready, go ahead and open your eyes. Just try not to get too upset."

"Try not to...?" Sonja began as she tentatively opened her eyes. "Oh, holy hell!" she cried out and squeezed them shut again.

"Rith, why can I see the back of my head?"

It was a bit of an exaggeration, but not by much. When Sonja opened her eyes, she had been met with a panoramic view that took in almost a full three hundred and sixty degrees around her; front to back, side to side, and up and down. She could see everywhere at once. No wonder her vision had been so blurry at first. Her brain had been unprepared to interpret the amount of information being thrown at it.

She closed her eyes to give herself another moment to orient herself.

Sonja drew in a long breath and blew it out. Then, a little more prepared for what to expect, she opened her eyes again. It was incredible. She could see in all directions without effort. Without moving, she could peer off into the distances behind her as easily as the area in front of her. The images she saw did come across as slightly blurry. It was like watching the world only through her peripheral vision. If something moved or drew her specific attention, Sonja could focus on it and see all details clearly, but most of her perceptions of her surroundings remained vague. With experimentation, Sonja discovered she did have a narrow blind spot directly behind her, but with a few slight moves of her head to one side or the other, she could effectively eliminate that gap in her vision.

As Rith had said, she was underwater. Plenty of light filtered through the water at her current depth, which meant that either she was close to the surface, or her new vision capabilities also included enhanced low light abilities. Perhaps both. There wasn't much around her to see at the moment, however. In all directions, the water just seemed to taper away into a murky fog after a few hundred feet. She could see sand and rock below her, perhaps a hundred feet down, and she spotted the occasional bottom dwelling fish making its way across that water-covered desert. Sonja cocked her head sideways and focused her vision above her present location. She could make out flickers of sunlight penetrating down in blue-colored beams. The surface appeared to be a hundred and fifty feet or so away.

"I had to make a few modifications for you," Rith explained. "Because you need to function underwater, you have to be able to see more than what is directly in front of you. To accomplish this, your eyes are bigger than they normally are, and they are closer to the sides of your head. That is a lot of visual information to take in all at once, and I can imagine it was a bit of a shock at first. Sorry about that."

"Uh-huh," Sonja agreed, simply. It had been a lot, and the unexpected breadth of her changed viewpoint had resulted in some rather nasty vertigo at first, but as she began to adapt to the new reality around her, the rest of her senses calmed down. Her nausea had all but disappeared, which was nice. She did not relish the idea of spending all her time here trying not to throw up. Especially since the altered gravity underwater meant that she would most likely be wearing anything she ejected. Not a pretty mental picture.

"I also had to make a couple changes so you could breathe," Rith continued. "You will probably find it better to breathe through your mouth since that allows the water to pass over your gills more easily."

"Gills?" Sonja echoed, her hands going to her throat. Her fingers brushed along three parallel ridges on either side of her neck. "Gills," she repeated.

"Yes. Gills. There are some other differences as well."

"I'm seeing that," Sonja interrupted. "Some rather drastic differences I would say."

Drastic was perhaps an understatement. As Sonja gazed down at herself, she could see that from the waist up she was still herself. Her own bare skin was visible from just below her navel all the way up as far as she could see to her neck. From the waist down however, she was … something else.

"I'm a fish?" she muttered, at first perplexed. Then a smile lit up her face. "I'm a mermaid!" She cried.

"You're a mermaid," Rith confirmed.

Sonja screamed with delight. She threw her arms out over her head and began dolphin kicking with her tail, driving herself forward through the water. She moved awkwardly at first as she tried to figure out the musculature of her fish anatomy, but she was soon rocketing about with abandon, seeing how fast she could go and reveling in the feel of the water rushing past her. She practiced turns and flips for the sheer joy of it. On a whim, she arced herself upward at full speed, breaching the surface of the sea like a dolphin and letting gravity drag her crashing back down. She allowed herself to sink back into the depths, giggling like a ten-year-old.

"I'm a mermaid," she said again. Setting off another burst of giggling. "I'm a freaking mermaid."

Sonja righted herself and looked about for Rith. "Hey, little buddy. I've got a question for you."

"I'm here," said Rith, appearing over her left shoulder.

"This whole mermaid thing is pretty cool," said Sonja. "But I couldn't help noticing that this is the third or fourth time in the last year that you've sent me somewhere either completely or partially naked." She held out her arms, highlighting her lack of any cover above her waist. "Is that just coincidence, or am I just now finding out that you're a little bit of a pervert?"

Rith did not answer. Sonja was shocked to discover that she had actually surprised Rith to the point of speechlessness. She pressed her temporary advantage.

"I mean, don't I even get a seashell bra? Or maybe really long hair that magically never moves away from my breasts?"

Before Rith could find an answer, Sonja bolted away, laughing.

The speed Sonja was able to generate with her powerful tail was exhilarating. She raced forward, pushing herself to go as fast and as far as possible. The feeling of skimming through the water rivaled that of flying, plus it had the added benefit of no sudden crash landings if she grew tired and wanted to rest for a moment or two. She swam with no particular goal in mind, alternating between mad dashes in random directions and slow, lazy loops.

When she found herself in deeper waters, she decided to see how far down she could dive. She had no way to gauge her depth as she descended, but she felt no discomfort from the increasing water pressure, except perhaps a slight sensitivity building in her ears. She felt perfectly comfortable and at home. She only stopped when she realized she had reached a place where no light of any kind penetrated to her location. The surrounding murky gloom had dimmed slowly for a while as she descended, but now it had become complete darkness. She paused when she realized that she could see absolutely nothing. Waving a hand in front of her face, Sonja felt a light wash of water on the skin of her cheeks, but that was all.

The sense of isolation and sensory deprivation created by the total absence of light left her feeling suddenly claustrophobic. Her hands shook as a sudden unreasoning panic filled her, a fear that if she did not immediately start moving back toward the light, she would become disoriented and forget which way was up. She would be hopelessly lost and doomed to wander in utter darkness forever. She turned around and pointed herself in what she prayed was the correct direction. Kicking her powerful tail, she raced toward daylight.

She forced herself to go slower than she actually wanted to, struggling to fight the panic that knotted itself in her chest and urged her onward. Fortunately, she did not have far to go before she saw the first stray beams of blue light in the deeps and she could once again make out pieces of her surroundings. The fear ebbed, and in its place came an embarrassment that she had allowed herself to be frightened so badly by mere darkness. She told herself she had been silly and there was no reason she could not try again to explore that dark emptiness at some future time. Although, she admitted to herself that she had no immediate plans to do so.

"Okay, Rith," she said when she was certain her panic attack had completely passed, and she was once again in control of her voice. "What's the game plan from here?"

"What do you mean 'game plan?'" Rith responded. Sonja saw that he had settled back onto her finger.

"I mean, where do I go? Which way should I be headed? I assume you weren't just going to let me swim in circles for a few hours and then send me back home. So, what now?"

"Now, you do whatever you want," was the response she got from the little creature. "That's how it always works. I don't tell you what to do. You have to choose."

Not very helpful. Sonja had to admit she was a bit surprised by his lack of input.

"However...," Rith continued after a long pause.

Sonja smiled inwardly. *That's more like it*, she told herself.

"...unless you have other more pressing plans, it probably wouldn't be a bad idea to start heading east."

"East sounds just fine," Sonja concurred. "But, um ... which way is east from here?"

Rith fluttered a tiny wing and pointed to Sonja's right.

Sonja pointed a finger in the same direction. "East. Right! That's what I thought, I just wanted to see if *you* knew where we were." She laughed at her weak attempt at humor. She got no response from Rith.

"Here we go. East." Sonja began to swim; not fast, not slow, but moving steadily in the direction Rith had indicated.

With no accurate method of gauging time, Sonja did not know how long she swam or how far she travelled. She estimated it had been about half an hour, but it could have been much longer. The landscape around her changed very little and gave her no feel for how much progress she was making, and the steady wash of water across her face and body acted as a soothing anesthetic, gently stroking her skin until the constant touch faded away to a background of general numbness. With nothing to see and no physical sensation of movement, she quickly zoned out from the monotony of her journey. Only the occasional school of fish disturbed into colorful flashes of frightened movement by her passage offered any relief to the scenery.

Despite her own lack of ability to estimate distance, Rith apparently had no such difficulty. When Sonja reached a location that looked exactly like every other place she had passed over the past thirty minutes – sixty minutes? More? – Rith spoke up.

"Stop here," he said. "Head up to the surface and take a look around."

With nothing better to do and no reason not to follow Rith's request, Sonja angled her trajectory upward.

"Do I need to hold my breath when my head is out of the water?" she asked, realizing she had no idea if she could breathe air in her current form.

"No," Rith reassured her. "You have gills and lungs. You can breathe water or take in air and you'll be just fine. You need to stay wet though. You don't want to be in the open air too long or you will start to dry up, and I don't think you would find that a very pleasant experience."

"Okay. Breathe air. Stay wet. Got it. Anything else I should know that you haven't already told me?"

"Only that you don't grow legs if you go up on land. You just flop around like a great big fish that was too stupid to stay in the water. This isn't a cartoon."

"That's awfully mean, even for you, Rith," Sonja commented. Then she laughed at the image of herself on land kicking and gasping like a stranded trout.

Still laughing, Sonja broke through the surface of the water and thrust her head up into the open air.

She immediately vomited.

Her first attempt to pull air into her lungs met with resistance leading to a coughing fit and an uncontrollable purge response. Her lungs were full of seawater and there was nowhere for that first breath to go. In reaction to her attempt to inhale, her lungs had attempted to expel the water clogging them, causing a violent gag reflex that pushed the water out through her mouth and dragged along the contents of her stomach for good measure.

Sonja retched again, coughed, and spat. With her lungs at last clear of saltwater, she sucked in a great gasp of air. The breath burned at first and caused her to cough more, but she was able to bring the fit under control and begin breathing more or less normally.

"Rith," she shouted when she could draw enough air to speak. "Remember when I asked you if there was anything else I should know? Well it would have been a nice heads up if you said I was going to throw up all over myself as soon as I opened my mouth."

"Sorry. Sorry. I'm sorry. I didn't know you were going to throw up," Rith said contritely. "I figured your lungs were full of water and it would need to come out, but I didn't think it would cause that much of a reaction."

Sonja's anger leaked away. She ducked back underwater, cleaning away the worst of the mess before returning to the surface. "Not your fault, buddy. It just surprised me, and I took it out on you. Sorry I yelled."

With the immediate drama over, Sonja looked around to see what might be in her vicinity. The water extended unbroken to the horizon in three directions. Further off to the east however, she spotted the outline of land jutting up above the sea. In the middle of the land mass appeared to be the remains of a massive, hopefully non-active, volcano. Trees and other greenery covered what she could see of the mountainous outcropping of rock, suggesting it had been a long time since the volcano had last erupted.

"Is that where I'm headed?" she asked Rith, gesturing with a nod of her head. "Toward the shore over there?"

"That's it," the hippoganth agreed. "It's an island. A really big one I'll admit, but still an island. Head for the left side of the volcano, away from the beach. Can you see the small cliff? You want to go there."

"I see it," Sonja said, then ducked down below the surface.

Back under water, Sonja paused to take a careful breath. There was a moment of discomfort, but her lungs quickly adjusted to the change. Apparently, it was much simpler to fill the lungs with water than it was to clear them out. When she was completely convinced there was not going to be a repeat of her earlier reaction, she headed off toward the island.

After a few more minutes of swimming, Sonja noticed that the ocean floor was once again visible beneath her. The water grew shallower the closer she moved to the island. When the ground appeared to be only about one hundred feet down, she decided it was once more time to head for the surface and take a quick look.

This time Sonja anticipated the need to clear her lungs. Just before she broke the surface, she inhaled deeply, filling her lungs to their full capacity. When her head and shoulders were out of the water, she blew out hard, as if trying to extinguish all the candles on a very large birthday cake. Water spouted from her mouth in a steady gout. When she risked inhaling, she did cough and sputter a bit, but it went much more smoothly than her first attempt at breathing air.

Sonja glanced around, locating the island and orienting herself. She was on the correct side of the beach, not far from the cliffside she had been aiming for. Sonja was still a short way off from land, but she could see the side of the cliff clearly from where she bobbed in the light swell of the surf. Motion caught her attention and drew her gaze to a point about twenty or thirty feet up the rock wall. The movement continued as she stared toward it, although it took her some time to figure out what she was watching.

It appeared to be a person moving around on the cliff face. The figure shuffled slowly, carefully, on the steep hillside, and Sonja realized it was holding something in its hands. The loose brown and black clothing flowing around the figure in the breeze made Sonja think it must be a girl, although she did not know for certain due to the distance. Also, clothing styles might be vastly different here.

Sonja could see from the way the person was hugging the item tight against their chest that the object in question must be very heavy.

Sonja swam closer to shore to get a better look. She glided forwarded, keeping her head above water so she did not lose sight of the subject on land. When she was close enough to be confident that the figure on the cliffs was indeed female, she paused and prepared to call out to announce her presence.

Suddenly, the girl fell. No, not fell.

She jumped!

Sonja saw the figure kick out away from the small ledge on which she had been standing, leaping forward, out to the water below. As the girl dropped, she released the object she had been holding and let it fall a short distance away from her. Sonja still could not identify the item, but she saw some kind of tether running from the unknown object back to the girl. She was tied to it.

Without consciously deciding to act, Sonja slipped underwater and darted forward toward the spot she assumed the girl would land. She was there in seconds, but she could see by the air bubbles and agitation at the surface that the girl had already struck the water and begun to sink toward the bottom of the sea. Fortunately, it was not deep here, no more than a few dozen feet to the bottom, and she quickly spotted the girl below her.

The girl looked peaceful. Her eyes were closed, and she was calmly allowing herself to be pulled down by the weight tied to her leg. She appeared perfectly content with the situation as it was. Sonja hesitated a moment, wondering if she should help or let the girl be.

Then Sonja saw the first signs of distress. The girl had expended her air, emptying her lungs as she initially hit the water, and now she was starting to feel the tightness in her chest as her body searched for oxygen that was not available. She flailed her arms in the first throws of growing panic, clawing against the water to pull herself back to the surface. The rope around her leg held her in place. Sonja decided it was time to step in.

Sonja attempted to grab the girl's leg and loosen the cord tied there. The knot was pulled small and tight and did not want to move under the manipulation of her fingers. Adding to her difficulty, the girl was twisting and kicking in her attempt to swim upward and Sonja's hands were repeatedly batted away by the frantic movement.

Giving up on the leg, Sonja next followed the rope down to locate the object to which the girl had tethered herself. It proved to be a large, flat stone the girl must have found on the cliff. The knot around the stone also proved to be too well tied for Sonja to easily undo, and in the time it would take Sonja to search for something sharp enough to cut it loose, the girl would already have drowned.

Sonja forced herself to stop and reassess the situation. She could not untie the knots and she did not have anything that would cut the rope. Those were dead ends, so she had to look for other options. She examined the rock itself. It was a large flat stone, shaped roughly like an oval. The rope had been wrapped twice around the widest portion of the rock and then been tied back onto itself. It was wrapped snug, but there did appear to be the smallest amount of space between where the knot had been tied and the surface of the stone.

Grabbing one edge of the rock, Sonja braced her lower body against the sandy sea bottom and pulled up with all the strength she could muster. If the girl had been able to pick up and carry this thing on dry land, surely Sonja could lift one side of it under water.

It moved. Success!

Sonja levered the rock onto one of its smaller sides, balancing it by letting the opposite edge rest against her body. With both hands, she grasped the rope wrapped around it and jerked back, trying to move the knot toward the narrower end of the rock. It did not budge.

She kept pulling, dragging the rope at one edge of the stone then moving to the other until she felt the tiniest of motions under her fingers. The rope had shifted, only a bit, but at least now she knew it could be done. She alternated from side to side on the rock, left to right and back again, moving the line around it a fraction of an inch at a time. Left, right, left, right. Each pull moved the rope slightly further than the last until, all at once, the rope slipped completely free, coming away in loose coils in her hands.

Sonja looked up at the girl suspended in the water above her. She was still trying to swim, but her struggles had weakened. Unconsciousness could not be far away. Sonja darted for the surface. With no time to be gentle, she grasped a handful of the girl's hair as she swam by and pulled her unceremoniously behind her. Both of their heads popped up into open air two seconds later.

The girl in Sonja's arms drew in a deep desperate breath, then doubled over in a coughing, sputtering fit trying to clear her lungs of the small amount of water she had inhaled. Sonja held the girl, making sure her head remained above the water as she sucked in a deep lungful of air. When it was safe to do so, Sonja went through her own unique hacking and gagging routine to expel the water from her lungs and get them working again. Once both of them were breathing more easily, Sonja swam them to shore.

When the water was no more than a couple feet deep, and Sonja could no longer move forward without having to drag herself along by her hands, she released the girl. With a small push, she encouraged her to crawl the remaining distance to dry land. The bedraggled figure complied.

The girl reached the beach, rolled over and sat upright, her hands propped in the sand behind her. She and Sonja stared at each other, both getting their first good look at the other. At first glance, the girl appeared young, maybe a little less than Sonja's own 21 years. Large, almond-shaped black eyes dominated her pretty face, and peered intently back at the mermaid that had rescued her. The girl had a broad, flat nose over a small mouth with curved, full lips that Sonja would have killed for. A soft jawline and rounded chin gave her face a delicate oval shape that may have caused her to appear younger than she truly was. It gave a childlike innocence to her expression, and the heavy black locks of hair currently plastered to her cheeks only added to the illusion.

Her skin was deeply bronzed from regular exposure to the sun, several shades darker than Sonja's – although Sonja felt her own tan was quite respectable considering that back home winter was only a couple months gone. The girl's limbs were long and lean, her shoulders and back heavily muscled, suggesting a life of hard labor.

"Can you understand me?" asked Sonja, deciding it was time to break the silence.

The girl nodded.

Okay, Sonja thought, that's one hurdle down.

"Are you okay?" Sonja asked. She immediately regretted the question. It was stupid. Of course, the girl wasn't okay. She had just tried to kill herself.

Still, the girl nodded her head, indicating she was fine.

"You are one of the People of the Deep," the girl responded. Her voice was quiet, respectful. "I never thought I would meet one of the People. I truly did not know if you actually existed or were just a story my mother told me."

"I suppose I am. My name is Sonja. What's your name? What should I call you?"

"I am Mirrenata. My family and those close to me call me Mirren."

"May I call you Mirren?" Sonja said. The girl nodded again. "Okay, Mirren. Why did you just try to kill yourself?"

Sonja knew the question was brutally to the point, and she was not surprised when Mirren recoiled as if physically slapped, but she had just saved the girl's life and felt she at least deserved an honest answer as to why she had to drag a half unconscious person out of the water today. Apparently, Mirren agreed with her assessment.

"I am ashamed of my actions, and I thank you deeply for saving me. I was not thinking clearly." She paused a moment before continuing. "There is a man. He and I are very much in love and want to marry. His family is wealthy and very respected by the people of my village, while my family are fishermen. We are important to the village because of the food we provide, but we do not have much status otherwise.

"The man I love, Nijoko, has been forbidden by his father to marry me. Nijoko has threatened to leave his family and marry me anyway."

Mirren dragged a hand through the sand next to her, scooping up a palmful of the wet, gray grit and tossing it away with a disgusted look on her face.

"He is a fool. But I do love him." Her expression softened again.

"I thought if I was dead, he would stay with his family and he could eventually marry someone of whom they approve."

"Are you out of your mind?" Sonja shouted at Mirren. The words were out of her mouth before she realized what she was going to say. "You tried to kill yourself because of some *guy*? That's got to be the stupidest thing I've ever heard of. Listen to me, Mirren," Sonja said, jabbing a finger in the startled girl's direction. "There is not a man in the world worth dying for. No one is so important you should ever consider giving up your own life."

Mirren dropped her head and slumped her shoulders, shrinking in on herself. The reaction made Sonja feel like she had kicked a puppy. She regretted yelling at the girl. The words were true and needed to be said, but she could have delivered them with a little more compassion.

"Mirren," she said in a gentler tone. "Why don't you just marry the boy anyway? You said he was willing."

Mirren did not raise her head when she answered. "If I marry Nijoko, his father would declare me an insult to his family name and have me killed. If Nijoko renounces his family and marries me, then his father could have us both killed."

Sonja's mouth dropped open. "He could do that?"

"It would be within his rights," Mirren confirmed.

Sonja swore quietly. "What if you kill him first?" she asked, more out of curiosity than with any real plan in mind.

"We would be charged with murder and executed," said Mirren, finally looking back up to meet Sonja's eyes.

Sonja shook her head in outrage. She opened her mouth to speak then closed it again, not sure what to say. "He can kill you, but you can't kill him?" she finally blurted out.

"He is important to the village. He has status. I do not," Mirren said, as if it were the most obvious thing in the world.

"Well, how the hell do you gain status? Why does he have so much of it and get to treat everyone else like shit under his boot?"

The expression was probably not familiar to Mirren, but she seemed to grasp the sentiment.

"Status is based on how important you are to the survival of the village," Mirren explained. She stated it like an elementary school student repeating facts out of a textbook. She did not react to the complete unfairness of the statement. It was a simple truth and therefore nothing to get angry over.

"Nijoko's family owns and runs the smoke houses and salt storage. They take all the fish caught by my family and the meat hunted by other families and prepare it so it will last. They store the food and are essential to feeding the entire village during the colder months when all other sources are scarce. They are vital to the survival of all of us. This gives them status."

Mirren might see this as a basic fact of existence and be resigned to her place in the chain of power, but Sonja was angry enough for both of them at the injustice of it.

"And why don't you have status. You fish. You bring in food for the village. They just save what you catch. I mean, what if you and your family decide one day to stop going out and catching fish. Everyone starves, right?"

"No," Mirren shook her head. "It is not that simple. My family is one of many that fish. There are several others that hunt, and many that farm. All of the food is good for several days and then it goes bad. Nijoko's family is the only one that takes food and preserves it so it is available for a long time."

"Smoking and salting fish can't be that hard," Sonja continued to argue. "Why doesn't your family do it, too? That way Nijoko's family isn't the only one doing it and you can gain some more status."

Mirren shook her head again and smiled sadly. "Thank you for trying, but that would not work. Preserving food takes time, buildings, and resources. All our time is spent fishing. Especially now because the fishing has been so poor for so long. We do not have the time to learn the techniques and gather the materials necessary. By the time we did, we would have starved because we would have caught no fish to eat or trade.

"Besides," she said, gravely. "Nijoko's family would never tolerate the challenge to their status. As soon as they discovered what we were attempting, they would make sure that no one else in the village would bring their meat or fish to us."

What initially had sounded like a simple problem to Sonja, was now taking on much more serious weight. Mirren did have a problem. She was being told to keep in her place by a more powerful family and it seemed she had little alternative other than doing what she was told. Still, Sonja had one more argument to try.

"What about Nijoko? If his family has status, doesn't that mean that *he* has status? Why can't he just tell his father that he wants to marry you?"

"Nijoko has status," Mirren agreed. "I do not. Even as his wife, I would hold no status until I was accepted by his family. His father has made it clear that will not happen. If Nijoko leaves his family, he will lose his place with them and that will be worse because it will not be just me that his father will retaliate against."

Tears welled up in Mirren's eyes. It was the first time during her explanation that Sonja saw the true depth of the feelings within the girl. She had not completely accepted the situation, despite her words. Not yet.

"Nijoko is telling everyone who will listen that he is going to defy his father anyway. The fool is going to get us both killed because he has no brains in that rock-filled head of his. That is why I did what I did. I figured if I am going to die anyway, perhaps if I do it quickly enough, Nijoko can go back to his family and be safe."

Sonja still believed that Mirren trying to kill herself was stupid, but she had to admit her reasoning did make a kind of tragic sense. If the choice was dying alone or cause the death of someone you love, then choosing the lesser of the two evils had merit. But there had to be another way. A third option that didn't leave anybody dead and maybe even allowed Mirren to marry Nijoko.

"Let me think about this for a second," Sonja said. "You mentioned that the fishing has been bad here lately. What if that improved? What if you catch more fish? Would that increase your status?"

"No," said Mirren, shaking her head. Her hair had begun to dry in the sun and wind, and she pushed it back absently from her face, tucking the loose strands behind her ears. "There would be more food for the village and that would be a good thing, but it would not improve my status. All the fishing families would be catching equally, and no individual family could claim to be responsible for the change in fortune. Even if only my family was catching fish, the other families would claim we were hiding secrets from them. They could say because we did not share our methods with them, we put the entire village at risk. That would be bad for us."

"Dammit!" Sonja swore. She slammed a palm down onto the water, making a less than satisfactory splash. "There has to be some way to get past this. Some way that elevates you or your family without making it look like you're hiding anything from the rest of the village."

Sonja began pushing herself backwards, worming her way into deeper water. "I'm not done with you, Mirren. I just need some time to think about this a little more." She glanced up at the position of the sun in the sky. "Is the sun setting or rising?"

Mirren looked at Sonja with profound surprise, as if she had just been asked where on her face she kept her mouth. Sonja figured it was probably an incredibly ignorant question since every child from this planet knew which way the sun crossed the sky. But damn it, she wasn't from this planet and she didn't want to make an assumption.

Mirren quickly schooled her expression, not wanting to offend the creature that had saved her life. She answered Sonja's question with a studied seriousness. "The sun is on its way down. It is late in the afternoon and it will be getting dark in a few hours."

"Meet me tomorrow, here on this beach," Sonja said. "First thing in the morning, when the sun comes up. I'm not making any promises, but I want to help. Try to stay alive until I can talk to you again."

Mirren nodded, solemnly. "I will," she promised.

Sonja slipped beneath the water and swam out toward the open sea.

"Seriously, Rith?" asked Sonja, swimming short distances back and forth; her mermaid equivalent of pacing. "'I want to marry the man I love, but his father has forbidden it?' Isn't that storyline a little played out?"

"Well, not every story can be Anna Karenina," Rith huffed, fluttering his tiny wings from where he sat on Sonja's finger. "If you don't like it, we can just go home."

"No, no. I'm sorry. I'm not mad at you. I'm frustrated that I can't come up with some way to fix this. The whole 'his dad is going to kill us both' part is a bit of a tricky twist. What am I supposed to do?"

"What do you want to do?" Rith asked.

"That's the whole problem. I don't know." Sonja turned again with a flick of her tail and began swimming in the opposite direction. "I need to do something that gives Mirren status in her village at least equal to Nijoko's family. Something that is specific to her and not necessarily to all the fishing families in the village. And it has to be something that isn't a secret, so nobody thinks she's hiding anything. I need something that will be totally unique to Mirren, but as far as I can see, there isn't anything unique about her. She is a perfectly ordinary girl, from a desperately ordinary family, in a depressingly ordinary village."

Sonja coasted to a stop and let herself drift. "Completely ordinary, except…"

"Except what?" Rith encouraged when Sonja did not immediately finish her sentence.

"Except for one thing. What does Mirren have that nobody else in the village does?"

"I don't know," stated Rith, "but I assume you are going to tell me."

"She has nothing unique, except ... me." Sonja rested the fingertips of one hand on her chest. "I'm the unique factor in this equation. From what Mirren said, the people on the island think mermaids – or what did she call me? People of the Deep? – anyway they think we are just creatures in a story. I'm guessing from that statement that nobody in her village has met one of my kind in a very long time."

"Seems a reasonable conclusion," Rith agreed.

"Rith?" Sonja asked.

"Hmmm?"

Are there any more mermaids around here? I'm not the only one, am I?"

"Well," said Rith, taking his time answering. "I suppose where there is one, it would be logical to conclude that others must be somewhere nearby."

Sonja held Rith close to her face where she could get a good look at him. "I need you to take me to them," she said. "I need to talk to them and get their help, and I'm afraid if I just swim around blindly searching it will take more time than Mirren has right now. Can you...?"

"Who in the blistering sun are you? What are you doing here?" A deep, rumbling voice interrupted Sonja. She had been so focused on Rith she had not noticed anyone approaching.

She spun and discovered another mermaid floating above her in the water, glaring at her intently. No, not a mermaid. It was a mer*man*. He was huge, almost twice Sonja's size, with a heavily muscled chest that tapered into a narrower, scale-covered waist and fish tail. Long blond hair drifted in the water around a face that was basically human shaped, but decidedly odd. His eyes were large bulging ovals of deep blue placed far back toward the sides of his head. His nose was an upside-down V-shaped opening over a mostly normal looking mouth. Lips, pink and delicate, parted slightly as he breathed water in through his mouth and pushed it out through triple row of gill slits along both sides of his neck.

Sonja's hand went to her face, slid down her chin and moved to one side of her own neck. No nose, she realized, and three flapping gills on the side. This man must be how she looked to others. She had not previously had an opportunity to view her own reflection or do any real inventory regarding her appearance.

"I'm waiting for an answer," the man growled. "Or do you not know how to speak?"

"I can speak," she replied, lowering her hand. "My name is Sonja, and I'm here searching for the People of the Deep."

The large man scowled. He drifted closer to Sonja. "People of the Deep is a human term. Why do you use it? And where are you from? I do not recognize you, so you are not from my clan."

"No, I'm not," Sonja agreed, edging backward away from the imposing figure looming over her. She tried not to be too obvious in her retreat. "I'm from a clan a long way from here. I need help and I was hoping you might be able to assist me."

He did not respond to her statement. He merely stared at her, appraisingly; perhaps assessing if she was any sort of a threat.

"What's your name?" Sonja asked, hoping to put this conversation onto more comfortable footing.

"Mot," he said.

"Mot? Just Mot?"

"Mot is all you need," he retorted.

Sonja raised her hands placatingly and smiled. "Okay, Mot. Can you help me? There is a girl living on the island east of us that needs assistance. I was hoping, with your help, I could give it to her."

"We don't help the humans," Mot said levelly. "They stay away from us, and we stay away from them."

"Are they dangerous?" asked Sonja. "Are they a threat? Is that why you avoid them?"

Mot appeared insulted by the statement. He slashed his hand through the water in negation. "They are no threat. They are a nuisance in our waters, and we are better off ignoring them."

This was going nowhere, Sonja thought. It was time to stop sparring and get to the point. She gathered up her courage and, keeping her voice as bland and neutral as possible, she said, "Well, I want to help this girl, and I need you to do it. But I don't want to seem unreasonable. I don't expect something for nothing. So, what's it going to be, Mot? What do you want? What do I need to do to make this work?"

Mot stiffened and cocked his head to the side, puzzled. "What do I want? I want nothing. I do not wish to help this girl of yours, and I do not wish to help you. What I want is for you to leave here and return to whatever clan you came from."

Sonja maintained her calm and lowered her voice to a more conspiratorial level. "C'mon, Mot. Everybody wants something. Just tell me what you need and maybe I'm the one that can get it for you. I've already been talking to the humans.

Maybe there's something up on land that you have been dying to get your hands on. Now's your chance. Just tell me what it is."

Mot's demeanor changed abruptly. His face grew pensive. Sonja thought she saw hope in his eyes, but there was still doubt there as well. Before he could decide she was bluffing and send her away, Sonja spoke again.

"That's it, isn't it? There's something on land that you can't get to on your own. Just tell me what it is and I'll fetch it, or have someone make it or grow it, or whatever the hell needs to happen to get it. Just take a chance," she pushed. "What have you got to lose?"

Sonja watched as Mot debated internally over her offer. She could see she had struck a chord with him, even if she did not know exactly why, but he was still unsure if he should be speaking to a stranger. Was he uncertain she was telling the truth? Or was he hesitant because it was something shameful or embarrassing and he didn't want her to laugh or ridicule him?

"Go ahead. I will try to get whatever it is you want, and I won't speak to another soul about it. It will just be between you and me."

This was apparently what Mot had been waiting for. "Okay," he said at last. "There is something. If you can recover it for me, I will help you. If you can't, I expect you to leave and never come back."

Sonja nodded her agreement. "Name it."

"Follow me," said Mot. He pivoted and swam away.

Confused, but hopeful that she had created an ally during her negotiations with Mot, she followed, swimming at her top speed just to keep pace with the huge merman.

Sonja had no clue where Mot was leading her. She saw no landmarks underwater to help her orient herself, but Mot seemed confident in his sense of direction. She also had not yet figured out a reliable method of gauging her speed as she flew through the unchanging blue-green landscape, so she had no idea how far they were going. Fortunately, Mot's final destination was not too far away. Sonja had feared she might be swimming for days, chasing the flashes of light glinting off Mot's tail as she struggled to keep up, but in truth it was only twenty or so minutes before he stopped. Sonja pulled up short behind him.

Mot led her to the surface where they both took a moment to clear the water from their lungs. Mot seemed to have the process figured out from long experience and Sonja envied the casual effort he displayed while purging his lungs. Sonja went through her usual hacking and coughing routine before she could take in her first clear breath and, when she finished, she noticed Mot staring at her, disapprovingly. The merman said nothing of what he was thinking.

Mot pointed. Sonja followed the direction of his finger and found a small atoll rising out of the ocean. A remarkable azure lagoon sat at the center of a ring of pink and white coral. The exact distance was difficult to determine, but Sonja would have bet the lagoon was at least a mile in diameter. The reef rose above the water by only a few feet, but the sharp stony ridges spanned an area fifty feet across at its narrowest, with larger stretches of sand and rock perhaps three hundred feet wide.

The beaches were beautiful, with alternating swirls of pink, white, and even green where some form of stubborn plant life had taken root and managed to thrive. The lagoon was a serene presence in the middle of the island, smooth as glass, protected from the surrounding agitation of the sea by the ridge of living rock around it. As attractive as they were, these features were not exactly inviting. Sonja could see razor sharp outcroppings of coral and jagged rock all along the edges of the land mass. Anyone foolish enough to try swimming into that lagoon or climbing up onto the beach would pay dearly in blood and skin for the privilege.

"Do you see it?" Mot asked.

"The beach? Yes, I see it."

Mot shook his head. Water beaded and cascaded from his hair. "Not the beach. *On* the beach." He pointed again. "Do you see the spear thrust into the sand?"

Sonja put her hands over one eye to shield it from the sun and cocked her head to peer at the patch of pink sand Mot had indicated. A slender, yellow-white pole poked upright from the sand, looking like a sickly tree that had not managed to form any leaves or branches. It was not far from the shore, maybe thirty feet from the waterline, but anyone trying to get there would first have to swim through a forest of jagged coral trees, then drag themselves across the razor's edge of the atoll itself. To someone like herself, or Mot, it would be excruciatingly painful. Perhaps even fatal.

"I see it," she said. "That's what you want?"

"That's what I want," stated Mot.

Sonja sighed. "Mind if I ask what's so important about a white stick on the beach?"

Mot did not move his eyes away from the beach. "That spear has been in my family for nine generations," he said. "We are the guardians of the clan, and that spear is a symbol of our lineage. When the oldest male child of each generation reaches maturity, his father casts the spear onto that beach. It is the child's responsibility to reclaim the spear and return it to the family."

Mot at last pulled his gaze away from the distant weapon to glare at Sonja. "My father is not the oldest male of his generation. His brother died on that beach attempting to recover the spear. The task then became my father's. He managed to bring it back, but it nearly cost him his life as well.

"Twenty storm seasons have passed since I reached maturity and my father cast the spear onto the beach. I have made three attempts to recover it but have been unsuccessful. The last time I tried, I almost died."

Mot touched his chest and indicated a silvery scar that ran down the length of his torso and several inches into his scaly lower body.

"I have been afraid to attempt it again since my last injury, although I dearly wish to recover the spear before my father passes so he knows the tradition lives on. In addition, I have a son. He is yet very young, but I would like him to one day complete the ritual. Yet, how can I expect him to attempt what his father was never able to accomplish?"

"I think I understand," said Sonja. "What are the rules?"

"Rules?" asked Mot, confused.

"Yeah, rules. Does someone need to almost die to get it? Do I sneak the spear to you later so you can pretend you pulled it off of the beach by yourself? How does this work?"

"There are no rules," said Mot with a laugh. "The only requirement is that the spear must be reclaimed and returned to my family. My grandfather passed his test by convincing a friend of his to crawl up onto the beach and tie a rope around the spear. His friend died trying to get off the beach, but my grandfather was able to pull the spear out of the sand and bring it home."

Sonja grimaced, appalled by the story. "Okay, so no rules. That actually makes things easier. I think I can get you your spear, but first we have to come to an agreement. Can you drive fish from the deeper areas of the ocean toward my friend's fishing boats and into their nets?"

"I can, with help. We often hunt by chasing large schools of fish into traps. The technique isn't difficult."

"Great. Then here's my offer: I will get your spear and you will fill the humans' fishing nets with fish. You will do this as soon as I recover the spear, and then again once every year for as long as my friend, Mirren, lives."

"What?!" Mot bellowed. "Absolutely not. Ridiculous!"

"Wait a minute," said Sonja, putting a hand on Mot's shoulder to calm him down. "Okay, so not quite that long. How about ten years? Sounds like a good trade to me. And don't think of it as ten years, think of it as ten fish hunts. Doesn't sound so bad that way, does it? Besides, I think I'm offering you a bargain. How many years have you been staring at the spear sticking out of the sand up there? You said twenty, right? Well, if I don't get it for you, how many more years do you think it will be before you find another way?"

Sonja leaned in closer, lowering her voice to just above a whisper.

"Do you want your son to grow up without it? What I'm proposing will have the spear in your hands tomorrow. Isn't that worth one day out of the entire year?"

"It is," Mot agreed. Sonja could hear his reluctance, but the chance of having the spear back after so much time was too much to let slip away. "I accept your terms. First, I receive the spear, then your human has my commitment for the next ten years."

Sonja left Mot and, with Rith's guidance, returned to Mirren's island. She spent a long, anxious night curled up in shallow water, dozing fitfully as she waited for sunrise. Sonja believed her plan could work, but there were so many things that could still go wrong that her mind would not quiet itself enough to let her sleep. What if Mot changed his mind, or reneged on their agreement as soon as he had what he wanted? What if Nijoko's father could not set his pride aside long enough to recognize an opportunity? Anything could happen, including the girl simply refusing to participate.

At the appointed time, as the sun crested over the landward side of the island, Mirren appeared on the beach. Sonja surfaced to meet her and, a half hour later, had laid out her proposal in detail. Mirren was not immediately convinced, but her fears regarding the plan were tempered by her desire to find any potential solution to her current predicament. She was also hesitant to say no to Sonja and possibly offend one of the People of the Deep.

At Sonja's direction, Mirren procured the smallest of four, wood fishing boats belonging to her family. She raised the single sail into the morning breeze and set out for the atoll holding Mot's spear. The distance was not great but the wind that day was slight and intermittent, so it took Mirren and her boat several hours to travel. Still, with Sonja providing a helping push whenever the wind gave out completely, the two arrived at their destination well before the sun was at its highest point for the day.

As they had discussed that morning, Mirren furled the sail well clear of the first coral outcroppings. With one hand on the tiller, she steered the boat to the beach of the atoll with Sonja easing the craft along from behind. The fishing craft crawled forward until it nosed up against a preselected length of the reef ringing the island. The jagged branches of coral were more than sharp enough to punch through the fragile hull if they moved too fast, so Sonja was careful to keep her forward progress slow and steady. She stopped pushing as soon as the boat met resistance.

They had arrived.

The constant movement of the tide pushing the boat over and over against the living barrier could cause damage over time, so Sonja had planned for that possibility as well. The moment the prow of the small craft touched the shoreline, Mirren stepped out. She wore soft leather slippers and several wool rags were tied around her feet for added protection against the sharp stones. When she was safely on the beach, Sonja pulled the boat away from the reef by a mooring rope tied to the stern for exactly that purpose. Sonja's job now was to keep the boat at a safe distance until Mirren was ready to re-board, then return it to land to retrieve the girl and the spear.

Sonja waited outside the corral ring with the boat and watched as Mirren maneuvered along the worst of the jagged reef. Holding her arms out from her sides to help maintain her balance, the young girl traversed the uneven ridges of living rock, quickstepping and hopping from one precarious step to another. Sonja held her breath during the handful of seconds it took to reach the smoother, pink sands of the atoll's beach.

Mirren reached secure ground, turned, and waved happily at Sonja. Sonja returned the salute. Once on the beach, only a short trek separated Mirren from the sun-bleached staff of Mot's family spear. The girl strode purposefully across the intervening space.

When Mirren reached the weapon, Sonja realized the spear was much taller than she had originally guessed. From a distance, with no frame of reference to judge, it had not appeared all that impressive, but now she could see it was huge. It had to be ten feet long. The length of the shaft towered at least three feet over Mirren's head, even at the canted angle it protruded out from the sand. The girl grabbed the weapon and awkwardly pulled the point loose from the ground. In addition to being tall, it appeared to be terribly heavy. Mirren strained visibly, holding it with both hands as she marched back toward the coral ridge of the island, moving at a much slower pace on the return journey. From her position in the water, Sonja could see the newly freed spearhead was a lethal-looking, shiny, black blade almost as long as Mirren's forearm.

"It is beautiful," said Mot, rising up out of the water behind Sonja.

This time she saw him coming and was not startled by his sudden appearance. She merely nodded in agreement with his statement. "Delivered as promised," she told him.

Sonja slid the boat back to the beach and Mirren climbed in carrying the ungainly weapon. For a moment, the girl almost overbalanced and fell into the water. The weight of the spear pulled her forward as she stepped into the boat causing her to momentarily lose her footing, but she was able to catch herself against the sail mast before toppling completely over. Mirren sat heavily on one of the wooden benches and exhaled noisily in relief.

Sonja grasped the mooring rope and towed the boat back out to open water. With Mirren and the boat away from the dangerous coral reef, Mot held out a hand in anticipation.

"The spear. Give it to me."

"The spear is yours," Sonja told him, "but I have a question first. In order for you to fulfill your part of the agreement, Mirren will need to have a way to contact you. How will she find you when the time comes?"

In response, Mot glowered at Sonja then disappeared beneath the surface of the water. He did not immediately return. Ten minutes passed with no sign of the unhappy merman, and Sonja began to wonder if he was gone for good. But no, she reasoned, he wouldn't leave the spear behind. Not after coming this close to finally getting it back. There must be some other reason for his prolonged absence. He would come back.

She hoped.

They waited. Another five minutes passed. And another. Then, as suddenly as he had left, Mot's giant mop of blond hair erupted above the surface of the water. He shook his head to cast the damp locks from his face, coughed the water from his lungs, then held out his left hand to Sonja, palm up. In his hand were ten smooth, black stones. They looked like ordinary pebbles gathered from the ocean floor and Sonja did not understand their purpose right away.

Mot placed his right hand over his left and blew a breath between them. When he removed his hand, the stones shone with a bright silver light that rippled over their surface before slowly fading away and returning them to their original glossy black color.

"The human can contact me with these. Each year she will need to come here to this island and toss one of the stones into the sea. I will know when the magic returns to the water and I will come meet with her. As you and I discussed, I will talk only with this girl–"

"Mirren," Sonja interjected.

"Mirren. If anyone else comes in her place, I will leave. I have no agreement with them and therefore will have no discourse with them either."

Mot held the stones up to Mirren who took them into both of her much smaller hands. The girl bundled up a thin outer layer of her skirt and dropped the stones into it forming a sort of pouch. She then freed a ribbon of cloth that had been holding back her hair and tied it around the pouch, cinching it closed and secure. *A neat trick*, thought Sonja. Instant pocket. She was going to have to remember that one.

"Mirren, the spear, please," Sonja said.

Mirren levered the spear up from where it lay on the bottom of the boat and slipped it over the edge to Sonja. Sonja grabbed the weapon, avoiding contact with the wicked looking blade. It was obsidian, she realized. Carefully chipped and shaped into a massive, razor-sharp instrument of war. It was as heavy as it looked, and Sonja made haste to hand the spear over to Mot before the weight of it could begin to drag her down.

"Here is your weapon. I've met my part of the agreement," she said. "It looks like the handle is damaged, though. It's started to crack and split."

Mot shrugged. "Whale bone," he said. "The sun has damaged it while it sat on the beach all those years. No matter. That can be replaced. The important part is the head, and that is unharmed."

Mot dragged a meaty thumb across one serrated edge of the obsidian blade, testing its keenness. He seemed pleased with the result.

Mot reluctantly dragged his eyes away from the spear to gaze up at Mirren. "Have your people's fishing vessels lined up tomorrow morning when the sun is three fingers high in the sky, nets in the water. My clan will fill them all. I will keep my promise."

Mot disappeared beneath the water again, and Sonja knew this time, he was not coming back.

"Well, we're one step closer to getting you and Nijoko together. Tomorrow morning is going to finish this plan, one way or the other." Sonja splashed water up at Mirren playfully. "Raise your sail, girlfriend, and let's get you back home."

The next morning Sonja bobbed in the water several hundred feet from shore and watched as a line of fishing boats boiled with activity. Men and women dragged at full nets teeming with flashes of silver and gold sea life, trying to pull the overladen traps onto the decks of their vessels. A few of the smaller boats had given up for fear of capsizing and turned back toward shore, towing their catch behind them and hoping to have better luck with it on land.

It was an amazing sight. The village would have fish to feast upon over the next few days, and still have plenty to preserve and put aside for the harsh storm season when it wasn't safe to put boats in the water. Mot had more than delivered on his end of their bargain.

Mot's clan disappeared as soon as the villagers' nets were full, not waiting around to see the results of the hunt or if the villagers needed anything further. They had done what they came to do, then left. Sonja did not think anyone from the island had actually seen any of the merfolk as they drove the schools of fish toward the boats. That was too bad. It might have been more effective if the villagers had seen an entire clan, but she understood their reluctance to stick around. One solitary mermaid would have to be enough.

It was almost time for Sonja to make her first appearance and remind the villagers that the People of the Deep were not just myth.

Along with the fishing families, Sonja made Mirren promise that Nijoko's family would also be on the beach today to witness the catch. For the final step of her plan, it was critical that Nijoko's father – A man called Barrado – was present to see the gift the merfolk offered, and that he know it was only because of Mirren that it had happened.

It was show time.

"Rith, I need to talk to the village, but I don't know if I can yell that loud. Can you make sure that they hear me, and that I can hear them?"

"Absolutely," came the immediate reply. "They will hear whatever you have to say, and you will be able to hear whomever you please."

Sonja nodded her thanks, then squared her shoulder as she mentally ordered herself to get moving. The next few minutes would determine if her plan would work or if the last two days had merely been a great big waste of everyone's time. She swam forward until she was confident she was close enough for those on shore to see her and know who – and what – she was.

She spotted Mirren on the deck of one of the larger fishing vessels, wrestling with her catch with the rest of her family.

"Mirren," Sonja said. Everyone on board the boats and standing on shore startled and looked up at the sound of Sonja's voice. She waited a moment longer until she was sure that most of those searching for the source of the call had spotted her in the water. When she had everyone's attention, she continued.

"As I promised you, I have delivered full nets for every family that placed boats on the water today. I hope you are pleased with my offering."

That took care of step one. Now, everyone knew the fishing bonanza was because Mirren had somehow built a friendship with a mermaid. Step two was going to be letting them know this wasn't a one-shot deal.

"Also, as I promised, I will deliver the same bounty next year and each year thereafter."

"Thank you, Sonja!" Mirren called back from the railing of her family's boat. "This is truly wonderful!"

Sonja held her arms out toward Mirren like an old friend waiting for a hug. "I am blessed by your joy."

Okay, that might be laying it on a bit thick, she thought. *Everyone gets it. The mermaid likes Mirren.*

It was the next part that was going to get a bit tricky. She needed to broker a marriage and not get anyone killed while she did it.

"Where is Barrado?" Sonja asked.

There was surprise and some confused conversations on the beach. Finally, a fat, dark-haired man stepped away from a small cluster of people and approached the shoreline. He fairly waddled as he walked, his skinny legs seemingly barely able to hold up the enormous round belly they supported. Being the top supplier of food to the village came with some obvious perks, Sonja mused. Perhaps if Mirren and Nijoko bided their time for another year or so, this man's fat-laden heart would burst in his chest, solving all their problems. Ah, well. It was too late to back out now. Perhaps that could be plan B.

"I am Barrado," the man called back to Sonja. He bowed, and Sonja feared for a moment that he was so top heavy he would topple over. He managed to right himself without any apparent difficulty. "I am honored that the People of the Deep know my name."

"They don't." Sonja snapped, not wanting to give this egotist any reason to think he was more important to her than he was. "We know Mirren. And Mirren knows your son."

"My son?" Barrado asked, glancing back up the beach, confused. "Nijoko? What is his part in this?"

"Mirren has told me she is in love with your son. She wishes to marry Nijoko. Do you consent to this?"

Barrado stared at his feet for a moment, thinking. He could feel a trap closing in the wake of her question, and he searched for a way out. "What if Nijoko does not wish to marry the girl?" he asked, not even willing to speak Mirren's name. "Are you compelling him to enter into a marriage he does not agree to?"

"Fair argument," said Sonja, keeping her voice calm and unworried. Barrado was trying to make her request appear as an unreasonable demand. That way if he stepped in later, he would be doing it to rescue a beloved son, rather than for his own pride. "Of course, Nijoko has a choice. No one should be forced to marry someone they do not love. Or kept from someone they do," she added. "If Nijoko wishes to marry Mirren, will you give your blessing to the union?"

"I would never wish to come between anyone who wishes to marry. However ... I am concerned that perhaps Nijoko and the fisher girl are not an ideal match. While I myself do not put much weight to it, there is a small matter of unequal status between the two of our families–"

"I agree with you completely," Sonja cut in before Barrado could finish his appeal. "I am pleased you recognize the inequality. Nijoko is absolutely not worthy of my dear Mirren. But she tells me she loves the boy, and for that reason I have given her my blessing."

Sonja smiled. She had enjoyed dropping that bombshell on the fat, self-important blowhard. She had just let the entire village know that in the world of the merfolk, Mirren held status. Nijoko – and by extension Barrado – did not.

"Do they have yours?" Sonja asked again.

"They of course have my personal blessing for the union," Barrado stated. "Although before the actual marriage can occur there will need to be some private discussions between our families and many details to be worked out. It could take some time, but I will personally oversee the negotiation."

A negotiation that would immediately fall apart the moment Sonja was gone, she had no doubt. Barrado was trying to appease her and still leave himself room to weasel out later. Sonja needed to nail this wedding down, and she needed to do it now.

"Perfect!" agreed Sonja, intentionally misunderstanding his waffling. "Then the wedding shall be held tomorrow since there is already plenty of food for a feast. That should also be enough time for you to sort out the details you mentioned. And as you have taken responsibility, I will hold you personally accountable. Mirren knows how to contact me if there are any problems. Let me be perfectly clear: if she is unhappy with you for any reason, then I too will be unhappy with you."

Sonja decided she needed to drive in one more stake to hold the deal in place.

"Barrado, just so there are no secrets between us, I must tell you that my clan greatly dislikes humans. They have only allowed you to exist on this island because I have asked it of them. If anything should happen to Mirren for any reason, I will withdraw my support of your village. You will be the cause of your people's downfall. For that reason, I suggest you take very good care of your new daughter-in-law."

That last part wasn't true. She had no control over what the local clan of merfolk did or did not do regarding this village, but Barrado didn't know she was lying. Mirren herself didn't even know it was a lie. Barrado had just lost a significant amount of status today by being forced to allow a lesser family to join his own, and he could not afford to let himself fall further by being perceived as the one who personally caused his village to lose favor with the People of the Deep. Even if he thought Sonja might be bluffing, she did not believe it was a risk he would take.

She prayed is was not.

Once Mirren was married to Nijoko – with Barrado's very publicly announced support – she would be part of his family. From that point forward, any harm committed against Mirren would be an attack on Barrado's own status. With Mirren's status greatly elevated because of her friendship with Sonja, he should recognize the asset she could be for him. It would be in his best interests to keep her safe.

"Okay Rith, you can turn off the bullhorn effect. I'm done talking."

Sonja swam close to Mirren's boat and waved the girl toward her. Mirren's trust in her was such that she jumped overboard to join her without the slightest hesitation. Landing feet first, Mirren plunged underwater, then popped back up immediately, a bright glow of elation plastered on her face. Sonja glided over to her and embraced her in a fierce hug.

"I have to say goodbye," Sonja said into Mirren's ear, still holding her tightly. "It's time for me to go."

Mirren pulled away far enough to look into Sonja's eyes with a shocked, hurt expression. "You're leaving? Now? Will you come back? Of course, you will. You must come back for the wedding. You are the only reason it is happening."

Sonja shook her head, sadly. "I'm not from here. Mot will honor his agreement with you, but I am not from his clan. I can't stay," she hedged, telling only a partial truth. She really wasn't from here, and she needed to go home, but Mirren didn't need to know everything.

"You have done so much for Nijoko and for me. Is there anything I can do for you before you must go?"

"No," Sonja told her. "Just … be happy."

Mirren nodded her agreement, her face splitting once more into a wide grin. Her eyes glistened wetly, but Sonja was unsure if it was unshed tears or merely seawater.

"I have to go," Sonja said again. She gave Mirren a small nudge toward land. "And you need to swim to shore and find your new husband."

Mirren glanced back toward the beach. While she was momentarily distracted, Sonja slipped underwater and bolted away. She had said her goodbyes. She did not wish to prolong the parting any further.

It hurt too much.

Sonja was surprised by how much she had come to care about this girl she had only known for a few days. She didn't want to leave.

When she was far enough away and she felt she had her emotions back under control, she stopped swimming. The last thing she wanted was to go back to a lecture room and let everyone see her bawling, so she took another moment to compose herself before she touched the ring on her left hand.

"Okay, Rith. Let's go home."

CHAPTER 19

Sonja swung her staff in a vicious downward arc, hard enough to crack the skull of the man in front of her. He countered her swing with a short, practiced movement of his own staff, stopping her weapon's progress with a loud *tak!* Sonja stayed on the offensive. She shuffle-stepped forward with each attack, varying her technique with every flurry of the weapon in her hands.

High. Low. High. Low. Low.

Her opponent countered every move. He gave ground grudgingly under her assault, and he successfully blocked each strike as it was launched. Sweat beaded and ran down her face with the effort of the melee. Her hair plastered itself against her forehead and across her cheeks. A small part of her mind longed to mop her sleeve across her face and wipe the hair out of her eyes, but the rest of her was laser focused on the task at hand.

Sonja swung low, toward his knee, then reversed the swing to attack the other leg. Neither landed. Her staff blurred in a helicopter spin over her head – a showy move with no real purpose other than to distract or intimidate an opponent – then dropped a hard slash at his collar bone. She followed this with two blows to the body and a lunging thrust toward his head. Nothing got through his defenses.

Tak! Tak! Tak!

The sound of the staves clashing echoed through the room.

Sonja paused for only a moment. Her opponent converted his last block into a fast thrust toward her chest. Sonja shifted back and, with a slight tap from her own weapon, deflected his attack harmlessly past her body. But he had the offensive momentum now. He pressed forward with fast surgical strikes designed to disable and potentially kill. Sonja was the one giving ground this time.

She allowed nothing to get through. None of the attacks touched flesh, but they came in a steady, rapid-fire rhythm, giving no quarter and no window to escape.

High. Low. High. Low. Low.

Sonja shuffled back again and watched her opponent raise his own weapon in a helicopter spin above his head followed by a downward blow toward her shoulder. He lashed out, two strikes to her ribs, then a final thrust toward her face. Sonja lightly tapped the incoming staff to deflect it neatly past her right ear.

Both of them relaxed from their crouched defensive postures, rolled their shoulders back straight, and struck one end of their staffs on the floor with a loud, percussive bang. Sonja bowed and her opponent returned the gesture.

"Master Toshida, that looked almost perfect. Be careful with the overhead spin, though. You're still releasing with both hands. If I had put my staff up and countered you, your bo would have gone flying across the room. Make sure at least one hand is fully controlling it at all times."

Master Toshida bowed again. "I will work on that," he said.

"Otherwise, I have no corrections. You've got number one pretty much nailed down. It looked smooth and you definitely increased your speed from last time. I almost couldn't keep up with you."

Toshida offered a wry smile, knowing Sonja was exaggerating but appreciating the compliment, nonetheless.

"Okay, dealer's choice," she said. "Do you want to work on the newest form, or would you like to start learning Melee Drill Number Two?"

"Master Sonja, I think I would like to see some new material today. Let's begin the next melee drill."

When Sonja was teaching, Master Toshida insisted on referring to her by the title, Master, even though it made her uncomfortable. He explained that it was a sign of respect to someone that was willing to impart knowledge or skills to a student. He also told her in no uncertain terms that, despite her age, her abilities with a staff more than entitled her to the honorific.

"You got it. You know, at this rate I'm going to run out of things to teach you in another year or so. Are you sure you wouldn't like me to show you a few basic sword forms? I've got a bunch of those that you've never seen."

"Thank you, but no," Toshida said as politely as always.

"Are you sure?" Sonja pressed. "Wouldn't you like to have something new to show off to your other students? A nice flashy sword form could really get their attention. And what about doing some demonstrations? I bet it would pull in some new students for the dojo…"

"Stop!" said Master Toshida, his voice low but firm. He pointed to a spot on the floor in front of him. "Sit!"

With a bemused smile, Sonja immediately dropped to her knees then settled back to sit on her heels. She placed her staff on the floor in front of her and placed her hands palms down on her thighs. Master Toshida spoke with a serious tone when he ordered her to sit so, although Sonja wanted to ask what was going on, she remained respectfully quiet.

"You have been coming to this dojo for over two years now," he began. He stood over Sonja, his staff held upright in his right hand, his left hand resting formally behind his back. "For two years I have taught you unarmed combat techniques that you insist you have never seen before and yet you repeat them as though you have been doing them all your life. Then you demonstrate skills with weapons that students three times your age have yet to master. There are days I wonder why you come to this dojo, as I think I have nothing to teach you. Perhaps you just coddle this old man. Make him feel useful."

Master Toshida's normally slight accent grew a bit more pronounced as emotion crept into his voice. Sonja had only heard him address her this earnestly a few times in the past and she knew something important was bothering him.

"Whatever your reason, today I realize I do have at least one thing still to teach you. You understand motion like few I have taught, but you do not understand *choice*. You act, but you do not decide."

He started to pace in a circle around Sonja. She remained staring directly forward, listening. She did not need to see him to hear what he was saying.

"Everything you do must be a choice, or else you must accept the consequences of something out of control that you started because you simply reacted. I try to live my life making choices. I make choices when I train. I make choices when I fight. I make choices when I select a weapon."

Master Toshida stood in front of her again. "Stand up," he ordered.

Sonja rocked her weight forward preparing to stand. Master Toshida placed the butt of his staff against her chest and pushed her back down. She looked up at him, confused.

"With a staff, I choose control. You want to stand. I want you sit. So, you sit. I have control."

He spun the staff and struck her on her right bicep. The blow was not meant to seriously hurt, but it still had some impact behind it. "I choose to injure." He swung the bo again, stopping it inches from her temple. "I choose to kill."

"I choose my outcome. It must always be my choice. Without conscious choice, when I just allow things happen, there is chaos." Master Toshida dropped the staff, letting it crash loudly to the floor. Sonja winced at the sudden noise. Next, he marched to the east wall of the dojo where an assortment of weapons was always displayed and available for students to train. He grabbed a wooden practice knife. He returned to where Sonja remained kneeling on the floor, brandishing the new weapon in front of her face.

"With a knife, with a sword, there is no choice. There is only kill. There is only action and consequences."

"But Toshida Sensei, I can control the knife," Sonja argued. "I can still choose my outcome."

"No. You only have choice to cut, or not cut. That is not controlling the outcome. In fact, with a blade you do not even have that much choice. You have given over the choice to your opponent. Does he run, or make you cut him? You can only react and accept what comes next. A gun, a knife, a sword, they are all the same. Shoot. Don't shoot. Cut. Don't cut. These are not choices. These are reactions, because you have already lost the opportunity to choose."

Toshida replaced the practice knife in its holding pegs on the wall. "I will not train with a blade because I will not surrender my ability to choose. I will not teach a blade to a student because I will not teach them to limit themselves." He walked back and knelt beside Sonja. "I am not asking you to give up the sword. You are quite skilled with it and perhaps for you it serves a purpose. I am only asking you to recognize the choice you make – or fail to make – when you use it. I am asking you to think about what you do when you draw a blade, and let it be an informed, intelligent act, rather than just a mindless reaction."

Sonja nodded her understanding. She did not fully agree with what Master Toshida was saying, but she knew he believed it and she was willing to consider the argument.

"And I am asking you to stop trying to teach me how to use a damned sword." He rose once more to his feet, waving with one hand for Sonja to do the same.

"Now, about that melee drill."

CHAPTER 20

Gazing around at her surroundings, Sonja took in the ambiance of the quiet little restaurant she and Kevin currently occupied.

The college campus so near to this neighborhood dictated that most of the shops and restaurants that wished to stay in business did so by catering to the younger, twenty-something dynamic. This meant that pizza, delis, and fast food dominated the dining choices, and upper echelon establishments were scarce or, in many parts of town, non-existent. The Original Steakhouse, where they found themselves tonight, at least made an attempt to resemble fine dining.

The staff dimmed the lights enough to be intimate but not so much as to make the customers struggle to read menus or see their food. The chairs and booth cushions were comfortable, clean, and well maintained, and the tables were spaced apart sufficiently to give diners a feeling of privacy during their meals. Conversations around the restaurant stayed generally subdued as most of the people present enjoyed the peaceful atmosphere and wished to preserve it.

Each table came with its own candle in a round, red glass holder, and a narrow vase holding a single purple and yellow flower that Sonja had thus far been unable to identify. The careful illusion was only ruined by the plastic, red-and-white checked tablecloths trying unsuccessfully to mimic real fabric. Sonja brought her attention back to her own table, a smile pulling at her lips as she poked a finger distractedly at the flower. She touched the delicate petals then watched as the bloom rocked gently back and forth in its vase. At least the flower seemed real.

"What are you thinking about?" asked Kevin. His own eyes never left Sonja's face, staring at her intently while she played with the flower.

"Nothing, really," she admitted. "I'm just happy to be here with you. Actually, I'm happy to be anywhere with you. We haven't had a lot of time together lately with our class loads and your internship."

Kevin had completed his undergraduate degree in civil engineering the year before and was in his first semester of graduate school. He had also recently been hired part-time by a local construction company that specialized in road and street design. Between work, school, studying and sleeping, his schedule allotted him little free time. With Sonja's own class schedule thrown into the mix, that didn't give them many opportunities to see each other.

"I know. I'm glad to be here, too," he said, reaching across the table and taking her hand. "I wasn't about to miss your special day."

"Is today a special day?" she asked, feigning confusion and rolling her eyes as if searching her memory for something she might have forgotten. She tapped a finger against her chin, thoughtfully.

"Special enough that I'm not cracking a book tonight even though I'm a couple chapters behind on my reading. I am planning on doing some studying after dinner though."

"Oh?" asked Sonja, her brows furrowing in disappointment. "I only get dinner with you?"

"I was hoping you would help me with my studying. I need to put in some practice time on the finer points of female anatomy." Kevin leered at her playfully, his eyes dropping to stare meaningfully at her chest. "You appear to have the expertise necessary to tutor me in that particular field."

"Hey," Sonja laughed. "It's *my* birthday. How come you just assume that you're the one going to get a gift tonight?" The black t-shirt she had chosen to wear for their dinner date did not show her off to her best advantage, but Sonja rolled her shoulders and arched her back to give Kevin a better view. "Maybe looking is all you're going to get to do."

"That would be a shame," he lamented, bringing his gaze back to meet hers. "But, speaking of gifts, I do have something for you." Kevin leaned back in his chair to reach into his pocket.

"You didn't have to get me a birthday gift," Sonja told him. "You're already taking me to dinner. Besides, I think you are exempt from having to get me a birthday gift ever again. You gave me Rith, remember?"

"How could I ever forget?" Kevin asked. "How could anyone forget Rith?"

Sonja could hear a slight edge in his voice. It wasn't new, either. She had begun noticing the darker tone a few months back. Any time she brought up the subject of Rith, Kevin would grow irritated and change the topic, although she wasn't certain why. She had hoped she was imagining it, but it was getting harder to ignore.

"Here it is," said Kevin triumphantly, removing a black, plastic square from his wallet. The object resembled a credit card. He held it out to Sonja, who took it and examined it closely, not sure what she was looking at.

"It's a gift card from Aspen Spas Retreat. It's for a full-day getaway for two. It's not really a couple's retreat, so either I can go with you or you can bring one of your friends. All you need to do is pick a day that you're free and you get six hours of pampering for you and one other person."

"This is really sweet," Sonja said, reading the raised, silvery number code on the card. She looked toward Kevin and smiled brightly. "Thank you. Maybe I will help you out with that anatomy studying after all. I mean, a good education is important."

Sonja set the card on the table beside her napkin. She fidgeted, sliding the card back and forth as her mood grew more serious. "But, um … I wanted to ask what you meant when you said, 'how could you forget.'"

"What?" Kevin asked, his brows pulling together in confusion. "What did I forget?"

"I mentioned that you gave me Rith, and you said, 'how could I forget.' You sounded kind of upset though when you said it. What's wrong with Rith?"

"Nothing is wrong with Rith. He's great," he told her. But Sonja could see the irritation back in his face. "Everything is fine, I guess. Unless you kind of zone out for a moment, and then I find out later that you actually disappeared for a year in the middle of our conversation."

Sonja sat speechless for a moment, not sure how to respond. "I… That only happened once. I've only been gone that long one time, and it was before I even knew you. You know I've never disappeared on you. I wouldn't do that."

"Actually, no, I don't know that. But I appreciate you saying it, and I hope it's true," he told her. He smiled, but Sonja could tell it was forced. "I don't want to talk about Rith. This is your birthday celebration and we should just focus on having a good time."

Sonja wanted to push him, to try to figure out what was really bothering him, but she decided that Kevin was right. Maybe tonight wasn't the time for this discussion. It was her birthday and they finally had an evening together, the first in a long time. They should enjoy it.

"Okay," she conceded. "Maybe you're right. We should have a nice dinner, some pleasant conversation, and later, anatomy practice."

"Anatomy practice. Right." Kevin smiled again, and this time it was more genuine. The expression lit up his face.

A waiter approached their table, a younger man wearing black pants, a black button-up shirt and a pocketed apron tied around his waist. He set down two red, vinyl-bound menus with "Original Steakhouse" embossed in gold letters across the front.

"Can I get you anything to drink while you look at our menu? Or would you like to hear about our specials tonight?"

"Actually, I would like a bottle of the best champagne you have," Kevin told him. "And by best, I mean something under twenty dollars."

"Wow. You really know how to treat a lady," Sonja muttered with a laugh.

"Not a problem," the waiter told Kevin. "Can I see some ID first, please?"

Kevin already had his wallet out and showed the waiter his driver's license. Sonja dug into her purse for a moment before finding her own identification. When she held it out for the waiter to see, his eyebrows rose.

"Twenty-one today," he said. "So, this is a celebration dinner. Happy birthday, Miss Drommer. I'll go get your champagne."

Sonja slipped her driver's license back in her wallet and dropped the wallet into her purse. "Shit," she swore quietly.

"What?" asked Kevin, surprised by the small outburst.

"He knows it's my birthday," she said to Kevin, indicating their waiter who had wandered over to the restaurant bar and was now talking to the bartender. "Do you think he's going to bring out a cake after dinner? All the waiters are probably going to sing to me. How embarrassing."

"I'm counting on it," Kevin told her with a wink. "The champagne will calm you down, though, so you don't have to run screaming from the room when they start to sing."

"Oh? I thought the champagne was to get me drunk so you could take advantage of me later."

"Can't it be for both?"

Sonja leaned toward Kevin, conspiratorially. "Maybe we could just skip dinner altogether and get right to that anatomy lesson," she suggested.

Kevin's eyes twinkled at the offer. Sonja enjoyed the look of genuine joy in his face. She loved staring into his eyes when he was happy, especially when she knew that she was the reason for it.

"As much as that idea tempts me, I have to say, no. We are not going to run out of here just so we can rut like animals in the woods. We are going to have a nice, civilized meal to celebrate your birthday."

"And then after dinner, go rut like animals in the woods," Sonja said, opening her menu and perusing the appetizers.

"Yup," Kevin agreed, opening his own menu. "Just like animals in the woods."

CHAPTER 21

Sonja skipped down the concrete steps of the campus' history building, the books in her blue, canvas pack jostling and bouncing against her back. She leapt the final three stairs and landed with a satisfying stomp on the sidewalk. She was still in a good mood from her dinner date with Kevin two nights ago, and not even a ninety-minute midterm on the indigenous peoples of Australia had dampened it.

Peering up at the unseasonably clear blue sky, she let herself bask for a moment in the warmth of the early afternoon sun. The past winter had been cold, dreary, and persistently wet, so this break in the unpleasant weather felt long overdue. Most days, Sonja rode her bike to classes, but today she had opted to walk, choosing to take advantage of the promising spring morning. This left her on foot for the afternoon as well, which suited her just fine. Classes having now finished for the day, it seemed a perfect opportunity for a leisurely stroll home.

The previous school year, she had aged out of the dormitory housing and in the fall, she had to seek one of the off-campus housing alternatives. She found a single bedroom for rent in a house close enough to the school that she didn't need a car to get around, but still far enough off campus she could pretend she was just another member of the community rather than part of the student invasion that occurred every year. She thought of it as her first "grown-up" place, although she had to share it with a family she barely knew, and she wasn't allowed to have anyone spend the night.

Even in the worst weather, she did not mind her daily walk or bike ride through the small downtown community from her house to campus and back home again, but on clear days like this one, the trip was an absolute pleasure. She drifted along the paved city streets in no particular hurry, taking the time to observe the people along her path and window shopping at the various stores on her route. She smelled fried food in the air and contemplated turning into one of the restaurants or sandwich shops nearby to grab a late lunch. She had not eaten since eight o'clock that morning and food sounded very attractive to her at the moment.

She shifted her backpack from her right shoulder to her left. Her textbooks were heavy and if she didn't occasionally shift the load from side to side, she would start to develop a pain in her back and neck. *There must be an easier way to lug these things around*, she thought as she worked the kinks out of her shoulders.

She paused at an intersection and debated whether to turn right or left. Left would take her to a family owned pizza shop that did killer personal sized pies, but right would take her to her favorite deli. The staff knew her there and her sandwich was usually more than half completed before she even made it to the counter to order.

While she pondered, she heard the slap of tennis shoes pounding the sidewalk, growing louder behind her. A sudden jolt on her left side knocked her partially off balance and she felt her backpack sliding down her arm. She instinctively grabbed at the strap, arresting its fall. Oddly, it continued to pull away from her. She turned and saw a young boy holding the backpack's other strap, trying to run off with it.

The boy was maybe sixteen years old, with a light brown complexion and dark black hair. His hair had been shaved close to his scalp except for a three-inch fringe grown out from the base of his hairline. At first, she thought someone she knew must be pulling a prank on her, but she did not recognize this kid, and what he was attempting to do was certainly no prank. When she realized that someone was trying to steal her property, she jerked it back toward her, arresting the boy's momentum and spinning him around to face her. Sonja's free hand slipped behind her back and under her shirt, grasping the polished grip of the dagger she kept concealed in her waistband. As her fingers closed around the handle, she froze.

Jesus, she thought, getting her first good look at the would-be thief. She downgraded her assessment of his age from sixteen to maybe fifteen. The kid had wide, dark eyes that looked equally fearful and determined. On his upper lip was a wisp of black down that might someday become a mustache. If Sonja didn't kill him first.

The thought caused her to recall her conversation with Master Toshida. If she pulled the knife, what did she think she was going to do with it? Maybe she could draw the blade and show the boy, then he would release her backpack and run off. But what if he didn't run? What if he also had a weapon? Or what if he was just too stupid to recognize the threat and he tried to fight her? Was she really ready to cut him for something as petty as a backpack and a pile of books?

Yes, her wallet was in the pack, but that stuff could be replaced. What if she hurt this kid? How would she feel about that?

The boy saw her hesitation. He had no way to know about the knife at Sonja's back or what was going through her mind, but he did recognize an opportunity. He stepped back and pulled with all his strength, popping the strap out of Sonja's hand. He was running before she even realized she had lost her hold on it.

"Damn it," she swore. It had only been three weeks since Master Toshida's tirade on edged weapons and making choices, and now the next time she went to his class she was going to have tell him that he had been right. Even though she had lost her backpack, she knew in her heart leaving the knife in its sheath had absolutely been the correct choice.

With a frustrated sigh, she started walking in the direction the boy had run. He disappeared behind a convenience store at the next corner, darting down a side alley that would give him access to one of the local neighborhoods without requiring him to stay on busy main streets. Fewer witnesses to worry about that way. When she reached the store, Sonja turned into the same alley.

A few feet into the alley, she saw her backpack tossed onto the ground outside the side exit of the grocery. It lay next to a dumpster, pulled open and rummaged through. Sonja picked it up and did a quick inventory. All three of her textbooks were present. That was good. The darn things cost a couple hundred bucks apiece. Her wallet was gone, however.

Of course, she thought. *Nothing could ever be that easy.*

"Damn it," she said again, zipping up the pack and slinging it back over her shoulder. "Damn you, Toshida, and damn your enlightened thinking. If I had just stabbed the kid, I would have my wallet now."

She might also have a dead kid on her conscience, she knew, but that wasn't the point. She was angry and needed to vent.

"Rith?" Sonja glanced at her ring. "Do you know where that guy went?"

"I do," said Rith, still perched unmoving on her finger.

"Can you take me to him?" she asked.

"I don't think so. I don't think I'm supposed to do that."

Sonja cocked her head, surprised at the response. "Huh? What does that mean?"

"Well, finding him for you would kind of be like granting you a wish. You want to find him, so you ask me to do it, then I do it. You see? And since you only get one wish, and I already granted that one, I don't think I can do this for you."

"I..." Sonja trailed off. "But... Damn it, Rith! Now you have to get a stick up your ass about following the rules?"

Sonja realized she had gone too far and forced herself to calm down. "Okay, sorry. Sorry. I didn't mean it. This isn't your fault. I'm just upset that I got robbed by a four-year old."

"I understand. I'm sorry you're upset," said Rith, sounding genuinely contrite.

"Let me try running a different kind of logic past you and see if you agree with it. All right?"

"Sure."

"The wish you granted me was for a life of adventure. That's what you've given me so far. Up until now..." Sonja stopped talking as she noticed a couple walking hand in hand down the sidewalk approaching her. She thought she recognized the girl from one of her classes, and the last thing she needed was one of her classmates seeing her talking to herself and spreading stories about the crazy girl at school.

Sonja smiled and waved. They both smiled back as they strolled past. When they were far enough away that they could no longer overhear her conversation, she continued.

Um … where was … Oh, yeah, up until now you have created the story lines and brought me there. But is that the only way this can work? For example, can I have an adventure right here in real time?"

"I suppose that could be done," Rith allowed.

"Great, then why don't we consider this one of my adventures? I am going to confront the bad guy that stole something from an innocent victim and get it back for them."

"You, being the victim?" Rith clarified.

"Well, yes. I'm the victim *and* the hero in this story. But the story can't really progress unless I confront the bad guy, and I can't confront him if I don't know where he is. So, what do you say?" Sonja was waving her arms, getting into the argument. She hoped there was no one watching from inside any of the nearby shops. If there were, they would probably be calling the cops at any minute. "Can you tell me where he is?"

"I guess that does make some sense. If I consider this just a piece of your initial wish and a way to push this storyline along, then I guess I can tell you." Rith fluttered his wings with excitement as he considered the argument.

"Great, so which way did he go."

"North," Rith answered immediately.

Sonja's shoulders slumped. She sighed audibly. "Rith, we've been over this before. Remember? Can you...?"

"Oh yeah, sorry." Rith raised a tiny hoof and wiggled it toward Sonja's left. "North is that way."

A few minutes later, Sonja stood outside an ice cream and frozen yogurt shop, trying not to be noticed as she watched the customers inside through the front glass. The boy who had stolen her backpack sat inside at the counter ordering a double scoop of some flavor of green ice cream.

"What kind of a thief robs a stranger in broad daylight so he can go buy ice cream?" she muttered to herself. "I don't know if I should be pissed off or feel sorry for him."

She watched him pay for the ice cream with cash from a blue, cloth wallet, then slip the wallet back into the rear pocket of his jeans. "That's probably my cash." She said, glowering through the window. "I think I'm leaning toward pissed off."

The boy took his ice cream and wandered around the shop for a moment. Sonja thought he might be looking for a place to sit down and prepared herself for a long, drawn out surveillance. Fortunately for her, the boy located a napkin dispenser, grabbed a handful of paper sheets, and headed for the front door.

Sonja sidestepped to the next store on the street and stared in at a window display of denim dresses, hats, and purses. She kept her back to the sidewalk just in case the kid remembered her face. She needn't have worried. The boy exited the ice cream store, turned right, and strolled past her without a second glance.

If the kid was going to make it as a thief, he really needed to be more observant, she thought. He didn't even recognize the backpack slung over her shoulder. It was the same one he had just stolen less than fifteen minutes ago, for crying out loud.

As soon as the boy passed by, Sonja stepped away from the window, slipped up behind him and matched his pace. Without a sound to warn him what was coming, Sonja reached out with her left hand and grabbed a handful of the longer hair at the kid's hairline. She pulled him back, taking him off balance then dropped the instep of her right foot into the back of his knee. The affected leg collapsed. Pushing forward with the hand holding his hair, she placed a knee on his lower back and rode the boy to the sidewalk. As soon as he struck the concrete, she reached into his back pocket and yanked out his wallet before bouncing back to her feet and skipping a few steps out of reach.

The kid rolled over onto his back and stared up at her in surprised disbelief. When he fell, his ice cream had hit the sidewalk and rolled to the curb, stopping just before it flopped into the gutter. Sonja felt a smile pulling at her lips as she remembered an old comedy routine she had once heard by a comedian named Eddie Murphy. The joke was about a boy who dropped his ice cream and all his friends began taunting him. The kids had been laughing and chanting, "you dropped your iiiiiiiiiiice creeeeeee-eeeeeam."

Restraining her urge to laugh, Sonja flipped open the wallet in her hands and looked for the identification pocket. There was no drivers' license. The boy must not be old enough to drive, or else he just hadn't bothered to apply for a license yet. Behind the plastic window where a license should have been, Sonja found a blue and yellow student ID card from one of the local high schools. On the left side of the card was a picture of the boy on the sidewalk in front of her. On the right was the name Julio Gutierrez.

"Hey, Julio." Sonja waved the wallet at the boy. "Do you remember me."

Julio's eyes widened. *Oh, he remembered all right*, she thought. But he controlled himself quickly and just shook his head.

"Who the hell are you?" he asked. "I've never seen you before in my life. Give me back my wallet."

"I'm hurt you don't remember," Sonja pouted. "I thought I meant something to you. Turns out you're just a hit it and quit it guy like all the other boys. Oh well. Let me remind you: you took something from me, and now, I have something of yours. If you want it back, we are going to have to trade." Her voice lowered; the friendly bantering tone gone. "What did you do with my wallet you little creep?"

Julio stood up, brushing at his pants and shirt. "You're a crazy bitch. You know that?" he said. Then he charged her.

The boy was young, but he was easily as tall as Sonja and maybe thirty pounds heavier. If he got his hands on her he could potentially cause serious injury. Unfortunately for him, he had no idea how to fight, and Sonja could see that fact as soon as he lowered his head and rushed at her. He was going to try to grab her and wrestle her to the ground, which is what larger opponents often tried with smaller targets when they had no idea what else to do.

Sonja, on the other hand, did know how to fight. She had training and more experience than anyone her age had any right to have, and that experience told her in an instant that this kid was not really a threat. She did not even try to avoid his rush. Instead she shuffled back a couple feet, braced her left foot behind her and lashed out with a fast, right jab to Julio's face. The force of the punch along with the boy's forward momentum created an impact harder than Sonja had intended. She felt cartilage break under her knuckles. Julio's head rocked back but his body continued toward Sonja, who pivoted to her right and pushed her extended hand against his lowered shoulder, redirecting his uncontrolled attack. The boy stumbled, his feet coming completely off the ground before he crashed back to the sidewalk.

Sonja straightened up, shaking her right hand. Her knuckles stung and ached. A human skull was extremely hard, and the bones of the hand were surprisingly delicate. She realized with mild surprise that Julio's wallet was still in her left hand.

Julio sat up on the sidewalk but did not try to get to his feet this time. He placed a hand over his nose, which had begun to bleed profusely. "Oh, fuck! You broke my nose."

"Probably," Sonja agreed. "And please watch your language. There's a lady present."

She felt bad about the nose, but Julio had initiated the attack, not the other way around. She was sure he intended to do a lot worse to her than just break her nose if he got his hands on her, so her regret at his injury was somewhat mitigated.

"You bitch!" he shouted. I'm gonna call the cops. They're gonna take you away for hitting a minor."

Sonja shook her head. "Yeah, I don't think you're actually going to do that. You don't get to steal my shit and then call for the cops when it starts to go really bad for you. That's a pussy move. Besides, if you call the cops they're going to need to talk to your parents. You know, because you're 'a minor' and all that. Do your parents know that you've been pulling strong-arm robberies for ice cream money? Because if they don't, they're going to find out."

Sonja paused, then added, "And if they do know what you're doing in your spare time, then I'm guessing that they're the kind of people that would get really upset if you brought cops into their house. They probably wouldn't be too keen on the fact you let yourself get beat up by a girl, either. So, I'm pretty sure this is just between you and me."

Julio didn't respond. He remained where he was, glowering up at Sonja. A great deal of blood had leaked through his hand and it was beginning to drip onto his shirt.

"Where's my wallet, Julio? You can even keep the cash. I just want my driver's license and credit cards back."

"I don't know where it is," the boy said, his voice muffled by his hand.

"Sure, you do," Sonja encouraged. "Where was the last place you saw it?"

"I threw it away," he said. He dropped his eyes to his feet, unable to meet Sonja's gaze any longer.

"Good. So, you do remember what you did with it. Where did you throw it?"

"It's in a garbage can. I went through a neighborhood behind the grocery store and dumped it in front of one of the houses. I don't remember which one."

Sonja nodded. "Okay, that helps. About how far did you go from the alley before you dumped it, and did you go right or left?"

Julio scrunched up his face, thinking about the alley and trying to remember which direction he had run. "I turned right. I think I went about two or three houses then I dumped it. I threw it in a brown garbage can."

"Thank you, Julio. You've been surprisingly helpful for a lousy little thief."

"Fuck you," he responded. "Give me my wallet."

"Not just yet. When I get mine back, I'll leave yours in the same garbage can. You can pick it up later. If my wallet isn't there…" Sonja flapped the cloth wallet in her hand. "Well, you and I are going to have to have another chat."

Sonja started to walk away. She heard Julio climbing to his feet behind her.

"If I see you again, I'm gonna kill you, bitch."

Sonja stopped. She turned around to face the boy, but he had already expended whatever courage he had left in him by making the statement. He was running in the opposite direction.

CHAPTER 22

"…and I actually found my wallet right where he said it would be. The cash was missing, but I already figured that would happen. The credit cards and driver's license were all there, though. I grabbed my wallet and dropped his in the trash, with his money – my money probably – still in it. I have no idea if he's ever going to go looking for it, but I told him what I was going to do."

Sonja stabbed another bite of salad with her fork and brought it to her mouth. As she chewed, she glanced up at Kevin who sat on the other side of the small, round metal table, drinking from his water glass. He peered at her over the rim of the glass, brows furrowed in concern.

"That sounds incredibly stupid," he said, setting his glass back on the table.

"I know. Can you believe that little rat? He ran right at me. He was asking to get punched."

Kevin shook his head. "No. I love you, Sonja, but I was talking about you. You should have just let him go. Credit cards can be replaced. There was no reason to go looking for him."

Sonja's eyes widened and her eyebrows arched in surprise at Kevin's reaction. She swallowed her mouthful of lettuce and wiped her lips with a paper napkin. "He was just a kid," she said. "He wasn't any threat to me. He was just a punk that needed to know stealing isn't a game. It comes with a risk of getting caught."

Kevin barked a rueful laugh. "That's funny," he said a little too loudly, shaking his head at her.

Sonja set her fork down on her plate and met his gaze. His expression was so serious, she wondered what part of this conversation she had missed. They were having a nice lunch and, up until now, a light-hearted chat about their day. She felt something was off with Kevin this afternoon, but she couldn't quite figure out what it was. She was fairly sure, however, that it wasn't about her wallet or the fact she went after the kid to get it back.

Even Kevin's black hair, usually so perfectly groomed, was a bit tousled today as if he had showered then gone outside before it had completely dried. He had also forgone his customary contact lenses and was instead wearing an old pair of thick-rimmed glasses. Normally, Sonja didn't mind when he wore glasses. They gave his dark eyes a deep, soulful look. Now, however, all she saw in those eyes was sadness and a growing anger.

"What's funny?" she asked, keeping her own voice at a conversational level, though a note of warning crept into the question.

Before Kevin could answer, their server, an overweight young woman in a button-up white blouse and a pink and blue apron tied tightly around her middle, arrived at the table. She set down two plates laden with food. She wore a large plastic name card pinned over her left breast that said, "Welcome to Bertie's," and "Heather" handwritten below it in black sharpie.

"Here are your sandwiches," she said, placing a chicken burger with fries in front of Sonja and a club sandwich next to Kevin. Sonja pushed her salad plate aside and the server scooped it up. Next, the woman fished a small stack of brown table napkins from the front pocket of her apron and set them on the table.

"Some extra napkins for you," she said. "Is there anything else you guys need while I'm here? Ketchup? More water or iced tea?" Her round face pulled into a pleasant smile as she looked back and forth between Sonja and Kevin. She did not appear to be wearing any makeup and her face was naturally pale except for a flush of pink high on her cheeks where she had either gotten too much sun or was possibly just tired from running tables all afternoon.

"No, thank you, Heather," said Kevin, while Sonja indicated with a shake of her head that she was fine.

"Okay. Enjoy your lunch and just wave me down if you need something later." The woman moved away purposefully and slipped through the diner's front doors to check on her guests seated inside.

Sonja had been meeting Kevin for lunch at this same spot every Wednesday since the new semester started. It was the one day during the week that both of their class schedules opened up from one o'clock to three in the afternoon. When available, and weather permitting, they always elected to sit at one of the five outside tables on the patio. The patio was separated from the sidewalk by only a waist high, wrought iron fence, and the location gave them a chance to enjoy the fresh air and to people watch while they ate.

Sonja looked forward to their weekly lunch date and ordinarily enjoyed every moment of it. Something in Kevin's tone today, though, had her edgy and on guard.

"So, what do you find so funny?" Sonja asked again, picking up a french-fry from her plate and taking a small careful bite.

"You. You talk about the risk he took stealing from you so calmly, but do you ever consider the risks that *you* take?" Kevin shook his head, staring down at his food although not really seeing it. "You hunt down a thief and confront him alone in the middle of the street. And this is right here in the real world. I can't even begin to guess the kind of risks you take when you're gone."

"Shit," Sonja said softly, closing her eyes. "This again."

"Gone" was the euphemism Kevin used to refer to her travels with Rith. He rarely discussed it anymore, because when he did it usually resulted in an argument between the two of them.

"No. No, not this again. This still. There has never been any closure to this discussion, I just try not to bring it up because it hurts too much. I never know when you disappear so I can't even prepare for it. My stomach is always in knots because I know that at any time you might get hurt or killed, and I won't even realize that you were in danger until it's already happened.

"And it doesn't help that you take crazy chances with your safety that I know about. It just makes me worry more."

Sonja smiled, trying to keep the conversation calm. "You don't need to worry about me…," she began, but Kevin cut her off.

"I do," he said, harshly. "I absolutely do need to worry. But do you know what the worst part is?" He looked at her intently. His eyes glinted, wet, not from anger this time but from something more primal. More painful.

Grief.

His voice lowered, heavy with unexpressed emotion. "What bothers me the most is that I can't do anything about it. I can't help. I can't stop it. I'm just a spectator, and I get absolutely no say in that part of your life. I'm a complete outsider."

"How can you say that?" Sonja leaned forward and reached a hand across the table to touch Kevin's arm. He pulled away. "You're not an outsider. You're a huge part of my life. You're very important to me."

Kevin forced a smile, but it fell away after a moment. "You say that, and I think I believe you, but for some reason, it doesn't always feel that way. I see you almost every day, and I look forward to it. It's important to me. But you, I have no idea how long it's been since you last saw me. You might be gone days, weeks, hell, maybe even months at a time, and you never seem to mind the time away from me.

"It must be like maintaining a long-distance relationship with someone you only see on rare occasions. How do I know that you aren't going to get tired of that before too much longer? Tired of me?"

Sonja's mouth dropped open. She had never heard Kevin talk about his feelings toward Rith like this. Except for occasional flare ups of jealousy or anger, he had always seemed so accepting of her arrangement with Rith. "You can't honestly believe that would happen?" she asked. "I'll never get tired of you. I love you, Kevin. I hope you know that."

"Let me ask you something." Kevin ran a hand over his mouth, pausing to think, or perhaps second guessing whether he should continue talking. He gazed around the restaurant patio as if the answer to his question could be found under one of the tables. After a moment, Sonja could see his eyes harden as he came to a decision. "If I told you that I wanted you to get rid of Rith, would you do it?"

Sonja sat bolt upright in her seat. "We are not having this discussion," she said, her voice flat and cold.

"Just a hypothetical," Kevin pressed. "If I said it was him or me, which would you choose?"

Sonja's eyes flashed. She felt her face grow hot with anger. "Damn it, Kevin! You gave Rith to me." She realized she had spoken louder than she had intended and immediately lowered her voice. "I won't even dignify your question with an answer."

Kevin held his hands palm out in surrender. "You're right. Forget I asked. I'm sorry for dumping all of this on you without warning. I know I'm doing this badly."

"Doing what badly?" Sonja asked, still working to control her temper.

"I'm tired of just pretending that I'm okay with things the way they are. I can't swallow my feelings anymore. I love you, Sonja, but I need to know that I'm important to you. Not just because you say it. I need to see it. And yes, this is my insecurity talking, but that doesn't change the way I feel.

"I don't know what the future looks like. I just know that if things stay exactly like they are, we don't have one together."

"What?!" Sonja felt gut-punched. Breathing became more difficult as her stomach clenched into a tight ball. "What are you telling me?"

Kevin didn't answer. He stood up and reached into his back pocket, retrieving his wallet. He removed two twenty-dollar bills and slipped them under the plate holding his untouched food.

"Kevin?" Sonja said. She did not move from her chair.

"I'm sorry," he told her. He stepped over the small railing separating the restaurant diners from the sidewalk. "I have to think about this a little more carefully. I'm making a mess of it right now. Please don't call me tonight. I need some time to figure it out."

He walked away without another glance in her direction.

Sonja watched him go. Too stunned to react or to even call out after him, she simply stared, watching his figure grow smaller with distance before he turned down another street and vanished from her sight completely.

"Are you okay?" asked a voice directly behind her. Her server had returned unexpectedly.

Sonja realized she was crying. Tears spilled down her cheeks in fat, glistening trails, forming briefly into drops at her jawline before falling and creating a dark pattern of stains on her shirt. She wiped quickly at her face with her fingers, avoiding the gaze of the waitress.

"I'm fine," she blurted, standing abruptly and hopping over the iron fence. "Keep the change."

She broke into a run, heading for home in the opposite direction from where Kevin had disappeared from view.

CHAPTER 23

Sonja stood alone on a wide-open road of pale, hard-packed earth. She wore what she referred to as her "working clothes:" a soft, long-sleeved cloth shirt, under a leather vest. The leather had been tanned and treated until it obtained a hardened consistency that gave some protection against edged weapons. It was long on her, with a flared hem that shielded her hips and upper legs. She also wore cloth breeches that were tucked into knee-high, calfskin boots. The boots were supple and comfortable but had stiff leather plates stitched along their length to offer additional cover to her shins and calves.

In her right hand, Sonja held a long staff, and slung along her left hip was the familiar weight of Brookstar. She stroked her fingertips along the pommel of the sword.

This is exactly what I needed, she thought to herself.

After Kevin walked away, Sonja had locked herself in her room and dropped limply onto her bed. The family renting her the room was not currently home so there was no one around to hear her crying. Convulsive sobs erupted from her, wrenching and painful and demanding to be released. A tightness had formed in her chest that, despite her best effort to cry it loose, would not relax its grip on her. Instead, the discomfort condensed until it became what felt like a solid ball of misery. She could not swallow it or cough it out. It remained, hot and barbed, lodged deep inside of her.

"Is that it?" she asked aloud. "Is that how he ends things after four years?"

Rith, not knowing if Sonja was speaking to him or to herself, remained still and silent.

Sonja cried for ten minutes before she began to calm. The sadness still filled her chest like a gaping hole, but depression and fatigue were now taking their turns as the dominant emotions while she attempted to understand why her life had just been turned upside down.

What had she done? Why hadn't she seen any signs that this was coming?

Next, came anger, fast and intense, burning away all other feelings in its way. She turned that rage outward, pointing it toward the cause of her pain.

Kevin was a coward for running away. Sonja promised herself she would tell him that the next time she saw him. How dare he ask her to choose between him and Rith? Was he *trying* to make her mad? Maybe he wanted her to break off the relationship first, so he wouldn't have to be the bad guy. What a child he was. A child *and* a coward.

"Rith," Sonja said suddenly, sitting up in the bed.

"Yes?"

"Let's go somewhere. Right now. I need to get the hell out of here."

Rith had not responded verbally to the request. He fluttered up from his ring and…

...and now here she was. Wherever "here" might be. The good news was she was fully outfitted to do damage, and still angry. A perfect combination to wreak some havoc.

She glanced around, checking the roadway in both directions, but she was the only person visible along this solitary stretch of dirt. To either side she spied countless undulations and hills covered in prairie scrub and dry grass. They seemed to go for miles before giving way to a darker line of mountains far off on the horizon. The road directly in front of her rose in a slight incline for about a quarter mile, then dipped down into a decline she could not see. Dust rose up from within that valley, indicating some sort of activity. A few stray noises reached her ears from the same direction: animals lowing, the occasional bang of metal striking metal, and a human-sounding voice shouting out above the other sounds, although she could not make out what was being said.

With a shrug, she rested her left hand on Brookstar and began walking toward the only signs of civilization she had so far been able to locate.

The hill was a deceptively long climb. The barrenness of the surrounding area made judging distances difficult and Sonja walked most of a mile before she finally crested the top of the rise. Fortunately, although she had no shelter from the sun directly above her, the temperatures remained mild and she was not unduly discomfited by the protracted walk.

Reaching the ridge, she gazed down into a broad, flat valley. To the right of the road she spotted a small town, consisting of a dozen or so flimsy-looking buildings lined side by side, facing the street. Another two dozen shacks had been erected further back from the roadway with more space left between them. Several of these structures farther from the road had fences around them, and the large yards they delineated contained grazing animals of various types.

A small river meandered from Sonja's right to a point a mile or so from town, then veered off away from her, following a path parallel to the road she stood upon. At the bend of the river, the waterway had widened to form a slow-moving eddy the size of a large pond, which likely explained the location of the town. During the rainy season, the pond probably expanded into a respectable lake.

Just outside of the far end of town, settled along the riverbank, Sonja could make out a gathering of wagons drawn into a large circle. She counted at least twenty of the wheeled carts clustered together – some covered, some open to the air – with a respectable gathering of people moving among them. The wagons did not currently have animals hitched to them, but several dozen horses stood placidly tethered nearby, most of them nosing through the opportunistic greenery sprouting up near the ready water supply.

"Am I headed for town?" asked Sonja. "Or should I check out the wagons?"

Rith buzzed in small loops next to Sonja's left ear. "Go to the wagons," he said. "They are going to be leaving soon and you need to get a job with their security escort before they go. You are going to hire on as a mercenary and help them get to the next town."

"The wagons," Sonja repeated. "They're farther away, so of course that's where I'm going. Ah, well. At least it's downhill from here."

Sonja took her time during the walk down. She figured there was no sense arriving hot and sweaty when she started asking around for a job. It wouldn't help her prospects any if she looked ready to fall down from exhaustion and smelled worse

314

than the horses that pulled the wagons. She used the extra time to observe the people bustling around the wagons. Much of the crowd appeared to be doing business with the owners of the vehicles. Two or three people stood at the back of each cart, pulling out merchandise for demonstration or handing items to the customers for examination. The customers in turn either returned the item or passed over what Sonja could only presume was some sort of currency.

The people wandering the grounds appeared to be farmers or laborers that she assumed came from the tiny town or perhaps homesteads nearby.

The journey took no more than an hour, even at Sonja's glacial pace, and she soon found herself strolling among the venders and buyers and getting her first closeup look at the merchandise for sale.

Each wagon tended to focus on only one type of product, such as tools, bolts of various fabrics, or cookware. The assortment made sense since the town did not look advanced enough to have much of a manufacturing industry. Most people here would be dependent upon bartering items they could make or grow for themselves to obtain more advanced equipment or luxuries from other areas of the world. The bazaar represented by all these tradesmen in one place was probably a rare enough occurrence that everyone for miles around would make a point of visiting.

Sonja walked from cart to cart viewing the goods displayed and getting a feel for her surroundings. She passed wagons carrying clothing, farming tools, weapons, and even some elaborate blown glass figurines for sale. One wagon carried horse and oxen tack, with an on-site blacksmith offering quick fixes and alterations not requiring a fully functional forge to complete. There were also several different merchants specializing in food items, from sugar, salt, and flour, to various jerked meats. A few fresh items could be found as well; Sonja discovered apples and some hard-skinned squash among the venders. The display that drew her in, however, was next to a wagon loaded with racks of salted meat. Just outside, the vendor had set up a homemade spit where he turned some kind of mid-sized animal over a low fire.

Sonja couldn't tell if the animal was a large goat or maybe a small calf, but whatever it was, it smelled amazing. She suddenly realized that she hadn't eaten anything for several hours. She had walked – okay, ran – away from her lunch without taking more than a couple bites.

She looked longingly at the fire, but without money she could do nothing to fill the hole in her belly. She turned away, planning to begin her search for the caravan master so she could beg for a job.

"Master Sonja?" asked a deep basso voice from behind her. "I'm sorry miss if I am mistaken, but you look very much like someone I used to know."

Sonja turned, shocked that somebody had recognized her. She looked back, then up at a tall, dark-skinned man towering almost a foot over her own five-foot, seven-inch frame. The man had broad, pleasant features with high cheekbones and a long, sharp jawline. His thick, black hair was pulled and tied into a wild ponytail that lay across his back, and he had three heavy, gold loops pierced through his right ear. Sonja saw he wore leathers like her own and he was one of only a few people she had seen in this gathering that carried a weapon. On his left hip rode a formidable looking, two-handed broadsword.

Despite his height and size, the feature that grabbed Sonja's attention immediately was his eyes. They were a pale gray, the color of a fast-moving thundercloud, or the whitecaps on a boiling sea, and they shone like two icy beacons piercing the dark backdrop of his face. Sonja remembered those eyes. She remembered they were the first thing she noticed about him five years ago when she observed the cocky new recruit strutting the grounds of Master Cejack's training school.

The man's name was Rolan Kowdi. His friends and fellow students called him Rolan. The other instructors just called him recruit. For the first three months that he had been Sonja's student, he had been a royal pain in her ass, and she had come up with her own name for him.

"Rowdy," she said, facing him with her hands on her hips. "You son of a bitch."

"By all the gods in the ground, it really is you." His face broke into a wide grin and he stepped forward to meet Sonja's headlong rush.

She crashed into Rowdy and her hands wrapped tightly around his waist. Rowdy's own long muscular arms enfolded her, pulling her against him in a crushing embrace.

"My fierce little teacher." He laughed, still holding her against him. "What are you doing here?"

Sonja squeezed Rowdy around the middle one more time before stepping away. "I'm not exactly sure," she admitted. "I guess I'm looking for work."

Rowdy gestured in the direction of the roasting fire behind her. "Well, we need to go buy a couple beers and talk. I want to know what you have been up to since you left Cejack's camp. And by the way you were eyeing that meat a moment ago, I'll bet you could use something to eat."

"I would love to," Sonja said, honestly. "Maybe a little later? I really need to try to find the caravan master here and ask for a job."

"So that's it?" Rowdy asked, taking on a sour expression. A sudden tick pulled at one corner of his mouth, ruining his attempt at looking angry. "You're going to walk away from an old friend to look for someone you've never met? You are just going to abandon the princess?"

Sonja paused, her brow furrowing. "Abandon who? I have no idea what you're talking about."

"Apparently." Rowdy nodded, sagely. "It's an old story my grandmother used to tell me. I guess it's my turn to tell it to you. Come with me. I'm going to feed you, get us both a strong beer, then tell you the tale of the princess and the lost key."

"Please, Rowdy. I really think I should take care of business first. We can talk later."

"We can talk now," said Rowdy, his voice low and firm. "I promise you Sonja, you will have time to talk with the caravan master. The wagons are not going anywhere before tomorrow morning. If you spare me the time, I will absolutely make it worth your while." He pointed at the meat turning slowly on the spit behind her.

Sonja realized that she was being foolish. She had not seen Rowdy in years and here was a chance to talk to the lovable jerk she had become fond of so long ago. Plus, he was offering to feed her. The job hunting could wait.

"You're right. You are going to feed me and buy me a beer. We are going to talk, then I'm going to try to go get a job. In that order." She grabbed Rowdy's left wrist and slipped her hand around his arm. "Lead the way. I hope you have money."

Rowdy's smile returned as he walked her to the man tending the spit. He held up one finger to the merchant who in turn reached into a basket balanced on the back of his wagon and retrieved half of a hollowed-out loaf of crusty bread. He produced a thin, wicked-looking knife from a sheath on his belt and cut off a generous, steaming strip of meat from the cooking rack next to him. He dropped the meat into the bread and handed it over to Rowdy.

Rowdy handed the trencher to Sonja and pulled a small leather purse from under his vest. The man tending the spit chuckled and waved Rowdy away. Rowdy thanked him, recovered Sonja's arm, and led her off to find something to drink.

A few minutes later, Sonja and Rowdy were seated comfortably at a row of benches placed outside of the main flow of people prowling the sales grounds. Sonja happily chewed at her rustic meal while Rowdy sipped from a massive pewter mug.

"I guess they know you around here," Sonja said between bites. She had observed the beer vendor also refusing payment from Rowdy when he ordered their drinks.

"I guess they do," he responded, noncommittally.

"I hope I'm not being rude by asking this, but while I was still at the school, I remember you earned your sword right before I left."

He drew his sword partway out of its scabbard and displayed the school emblem in the pommel. The staring eye Sonja remembered gazed out at her from the palm of an open gauntlet. Grinning, he told her, "I did."

He smiles so easily, Sonja thought. She liked the look on him. Relaxed and content, comfortable with the world around him.

"And...?" Rowdy prompted when she did not immediately continue.

Sonja mentally shook herself, embarrassed at being caught staring at him. "And I was just wondering if you stayed and earned your bear after I was gone?"

Rowdy turned the sword over, revealing shiny, bare metal on both sides of the blade. "I was not asked to stay."

"I find that hard to believe," said Sonja. "You were an amazing swordsman. The other students looked up to you. Even if you were a cocky bastard most of the time. I think you would have made an incredible teacher."

He sheathed his sword and gazed off into the distance, the smile still on his face. Sonja found herself staring again, admiring the strong lines of his face.

"To be honest, Master Cejack did offer to let me stay and teach. I refused. I was honored by his request, but I know myself too well. The first time some recruit tried to prove himself by insulting me or challenging me, I would have gutted him. It would not have looked good for the school. I don't have the patience for people like that."

"You mean people like yourself?" Sonja needled, laughing softly.

Rowdy turned to her, mock horror in his expression. "I was never a problem, was I? I thought I was the model student while I was there."

"If by 'model,' you mean asshole, then yes. You were. I asked Master Cejack a dozen times in the first couple weeks if he would reassign you to someone else."

Rowdy laughed. "But he did not move me."

"No," Sonja agreed. "He told me that you would be a good learning experience for me."

"And what did you learn, Teacher?"

"Like I said, I learned you were an asshole. But you had a sense of humor that kept me entertained, once I stopped being pissed off at you all the time. I also found out how talented you could be if I could only find a way to keep you focused on your training. I hope I did you justice."

320

Rowdy's pale, gray eyes fixed on Sonja, taking in her serious expression. "You did Master Cejack proud," he assured her. "I learned more from being your student than I did from any other instructor. Most of the training I received taught me to use my strength and size to break down an opponent, which I admit works for me most of the time. But you taught me that even someone my size needs finesse. Not every opponent I meet is smaller than I am, and when I have come across someone bigger and stronger, it is your lessons that have kept me alive."

"Um. Thank you, Rowdy." Sonja hastily grabbed her mug and put it to her mouth to hide the pleased flush that had come to her cheeks.

Rowdy's eyes flashed and he chuckled lightly to ease the somber mood that had settled over the two of them. "Now that you have food and something to drink, I believe it is time for that story I promised you."

"What story...? Oh, right. The princess thing," Sonja remembered. She took one more swallow of her beer and set the mug down. She took a bite of her trencher, nodded at Rowdy, then mumbled around the huge mouthful of food, "Go for it."

Rowdy gazed into his own mug as if searching for something hidden just under the surface of his beer. "My grandmother was the storyteller in our family. She made this tale come alive for me and my two brothers. I am sure I am going to ruin it by forgetting something or just explaining it badly, but I will share it as best I can. As a lot of stories do, this one begins far away and a long time ago. There was a kingdom as vast as any that has ever existed. It is gone now, but while it flourished it covered half of the known world. Because it was a kingdom there was, of course, a king who ruled over it."

A LIFE OF ADVENTURE

The king's name is unimportant. It has been lost to the dark reaches of time. What matters to this story is that the king had a daughter; a young woman of seventeen who was the most important thing in the world to him. He would do anything for her if she asked it and if it was within his power. When she desired new clothes, he would hire the most talented dressmakers in the kingdom to create them. When she wished to throw a party for her friends, he would organize a lavish ball and order everyone who lived within a hundred miles to attend.

Her slightest desire was his greatest joy to give.

One day, the princess told her father, that she would like to saddle her favorite horse from the royal stables and take a ride through the Carderian countryside. She had heard that the flowers and trees in the area were in full bloom, and at that moment it was the most beautiful place in the world to ride and have a picnic.

The king desired to grant her wish, but the territory she wanted to explore was not safe and carried significant risks for those travelling through it. Carderus was a small settlement miles to the east, and though it was indeed beautiful at that time of year, the king had received reports from his soldiers that bandits were active in the area, robbing travelers and strangers unwary enough to cross paths with them. The king refused to put his only child at risk, but he also did not want to forbid her from going.

The king called for one of his closest knights to attend him. When the knight arrived, the king ordered him to take fifty mounted soldiers into Carderus and sweep the area clear of anyone they came across that might pose a threat to his daughter. The knight did as he was bid but took his orders too far. Rather than risk any harm to the king's daughter, he made no attempt to distinguish the harmless residents from the dangerous ones. After he and his soldiers went through the area, there was not a traveler, farmer, or settler left alive in Carderus.

The princess took her ride, had her picnic, and passed a lovely afternoon. She came home safe and happy, and the king did not give the incident another thought.

Until three days later.

Three days after the princess spent an afternoon in the shadows of a Carderian hillside, an old woman came to the castle. This was, of course, not just any old woman, but a witch of immense power. She had been away from her home in Carderus during the slaughter, and when she returned, she found her house burned to the ground and her family dead. All at the orders of the king. A few stray survivors of the massacre who were lucky enough to have avoided the soldiers' attention on that day told her what had happened. The witch promised them the king would not go unpunished for his murderous actions.

The witch found the king's daughter wandering through the flower gardens planted outside the castle walls for her enjoyment. When the princess noticed the strange old woman intruding in her private garden, she demanded indignantly, "Who are you? What right do you have to be here?"

The witch replied, "I am here by the right of the aggrieved who seek justice against you and your father."

She touched one finger to the princess' temple, and the young girl immediately fell into a dreamless sleep.

The princess awoke to find herself lying on a simple straw mattress and confined in a small stone structure. The building was the size of a peasant's cottage, with four walls of brick and mortar, a roof of slate, and only two openings. There was a window through which one could see the outside world, but it was much too small to climb through and escape. There was also one doorway, sealed by a thick, iron-banded, wooden door.

Confused as to why she was in such an unfamiliar little house, she sat up to look around. She was startled to discover she was not alone. The witch was inside the cottage with her, sitting on one corner of the same mattress upon which the princess awoke.

"We need to talk, child," the witch said when she saw the princess had noticed her.

"Who are you? How dare you bring me here," the princess cried out.

"Quiet. You will not speak again until I allow it," the witch commanded.

The princess, indignant at being addressed so rudely, attempted to chastise the witch further, but hard as she tried, she could not utter another word. She could not make so much as the tiniest squeak. The witch had indeed silenced her.

"Much better," the witch said. "This will be much easier without your foolish outbursts. There is only one way in or out of this house. The door, however, is locked and there is only one key to unlock it. This key."

The witch held up a gold key as long as her hand and as slender as the princess' smallest finger. She placed it on the bed next to where the girl sat.

"This key can only unlock the door from the outside, and it can only be used by your father. To anyone else, it is useless. I have placed a curse on you, so listen carefully. When your father comes here, and he will come very soon, you will be unable to speak to him. In fact, you will not be able to speak to anyone for one day and one night. You may not give your father the key. You may not show it to him. You may not communicate in writing or in any other fashion that you have the key, again for one day and one night. If you go against any of my rules, your heart will stop in your chest and you will be dead before your father can open the door."

The old woman offered a yellow-toothed smile and leaned forward to pat the princess on one knee. The girl shrank back in revulsion at the touch.

"But I am not so cruel as your father or his men," the witch continued. "I will give you a chance, even though they offered none to my family. If your father asks you to give him the key, you may give it to him. After one day and one night have passed, you may even tell your father that you have the key and you may toss it out the window to him."

The witch held up a gnarled finger, "But you may mention the key only to your father. You may only give it to him. If you give it to anyone else, or you tell anyone else about it, you will die. Other than those restrictions, tomorrow you may say what you wish to whomever you wish. I do not care."

The princess opened her mouth trying to speak; trying to ask a question. Only the hiss of her breath came out.

"It is time for me to go. Your father will be here soon, and I do not wish to be in the way of your reunion."

The witch rose from her chair and walked to the door. She pulled it open and stepped through the doorway. She glanced back at the shocked princess still seated on her bed. "Of course, it opens for me, child. I'm not going to trap myself in here with you." The witch laughed as she crossed the threshold into the daylight and pulled the door closed behind her.

The princess leapt from the bed and dashed to the door the moment the old woman was gone. She pulled at the handle, but it was no use. The door would not budge under her hand.

Less than an hour later, she heard the voice of her father calling from outside. She went to the window and saw him standing on the path leading to the front door. The princess waved and, seeing the motion in the window, her father rushed to her.

"What is this note I received," he called in to her, waving a sheet of paper in her direction. The princess did not speak. She could not. "It says, 'Find the key to set her free,' then it gives directions to this location. Is there a key I'm supposed to find?"

The princess thought carefully about the directions the witch had given her, then she nodded to her father once. Her heart did not stop in her chest. She still lived.

"The man who brought me this note said it was given to him by a witch who wanted revenge on me and my kingdom. Was it the witch who brought you here?"

Another careful nod from the princess.

"Where is this key?" the king asked.

The princess stood motionless, frightened by the question into complete immobility. Any action on her part might be a subconscious attempt to communicate an answer to her father's question and she did not wish to die.

"It does not matter," her father assured her. "We will have you out of there very soon. Stand away from the door."

Thirty men with war hammers and axes attacked the cottage walls and door. The princess sat on her bed and listened to the noise of the assault for an hour, maybe longer. When it ceased, she returned to the window. The men stood around her prison with broken and dulled tools, but they had not managed to

326

put a single chip on any brick, nor had they caused so much as a splinter to separate from the door.

The king looked away from his exhausted men to see his daughter gazing out at him. He approached the window once more. "Do not worry, my daughter," he said to her. "I will get you out. I will find the witch that put you here and I will have the key from her, or I will have her head."

The king reached a hand in through the window slit, the narrow aperture permitting him entry only to his elbow. The princess, surprised that the witch's magic had allowed the intrusion, clutched her father's hand desperately. She kissed his fingers, her frightened tears wetting them as she did.

The king pulled away. The princess clung desperately to him, but she was terrified of what might happen if her own hands passed through the window so, reluctantly, she was forced to release him.

"I must go," the king told her. "I promise you I will not come back to you empty handed. When you see me again, I will have the witch or the key, or both."

The princess shook her head desperately, willing him to stay, but she could do nothing more. She watched in horror as he walked away, leaving her behind.

The king left men to watch over his daughter, to feed her and provide basic comforts. Whatever she wished that could be passed through the window, she received. But the king kept his word. Without the key or the witch in his possession, he did not return.

Instead, he traveled across the known world searching for the vile woman that had imprisoned his child, chasing down the slightest rumors of where she might be. He travelled by boat, by horse, and by foot when necessary, but as he arrived at each new location, he always found the same thing. He had missed her by weeks or days, sometimes less, but regardless, she was gone.

While he travelled, he occasionally received messages from his daughter begging him to come home, to come visit her. He desperately wanted to go to her, but his pride kept him from returning. He had promised her he would find the key. How could he return to her without it?

He ignored her pleas, and he chased the witch.

For ten years.

Finally, broken hearted and defeated, he returned to his kingdom and went to see his daughter. He had for the one thousandth time chased after a story of the witch's whereabouts only to find he had been misled. At last, with no further leads to follow and no idea where to go next, he surrendered to the inevitable. His precious daughter was going to be imprisoned for eternity and there was nothing he could do to change it.

With his head hung low in misery, he walked the lonely path to his only child's prison. When he reached the stone cottage, he stood outside her window and called out to her.

Something small and heavy struck him in the chest, then fell at his feet. He looked down to see a gold key laying on the ground. Confused, he picked it up and walked to the iron bound door. The key slipped into the door's keyhole and turned without resistance. The door swung inward.

The king's daughter waited in the open doorway, and with a shout of pure joy he spread his arms and moved to embrace her. She slapped his face and stormed past him into the daylight.

In shock and in pain, the king turned to her. "Why did you slap me?" he asked. "I freed you. You are no longer imprisoned."

"You left me!" the princess shrieked. "You walked away and left me a prisoner in that house for ten years."

"For ten years, I searched for a way to rescue you," the king told his daughter. "For ten years I thought of nothing else but you."

The princess slapped him again. "Then why did you abandon me?"

Rowdy tipped his cup to his lips, then eyed it with displeasure as he realized it was empty. He set it on the bench beside him. "Whenever my grandmother would tell that story, she would always ask what we learned from it. I always figured it had several meanings. For instance, the best intentions can still lead to the worst outcome. Or caring about someone is no excuse for thoughtless actions."

"Don't kill a witch's family," Sonja chimed in.

"Another good one," Rowdy agreed with a laugh. "Anyway, my grandmother believed that the story's most important lesson was that life can be very difficult if you always try to do things on your own. You have to ask for what you want, even if you don't believe you are going to get the answer you hope for. Even if you think you are talking to the wrong person, you still must ask. If the king had asked his daughter for the key instead of assuming she wouldn't know where it was, his quest would have been over before it began.

"My grandmother would tell us, 'If you don't ask because you think the answer is no, you're going to be right every time. If you open your fool mouth and try, you might be surprised time and again.'"

"She sounds like a wise woman," Sonja said with a nod.

"So…?"

"What?" Sonja replied, unsure what Rowdy was fishing for.

"Why did you say you were here?" he asked.

"Um … I think I said I was looking for a job," Sonja told him, understanding dawning in her eyes.

"And…?"

"And, Rowdy," she said sweetly, putting a hand on his arm, "can you get me a job with the caravan?"

Rowdy raised his eyebrows as though surprised by the question. "Well, it just so happens that I do know the man in charge of security for the merchants. Would you like me to introduce him to you?"

Sonja laughed and stood up. "I would like that very much," she said. "Which way are we going?"

Rowdy stood up beside her and dropped one large hand onto her shoulder. "Hello, Sonja," he said. "My name is Rolan Kowdi. I understand that you need a job."

The following morning, the merchants stowed and secured their goods, preparing for travel. The animals were collected from the fields and hitched to the wagons in preparation for the three-day trek to the next town. The noise and bustle woke Sonja from a sound sleep. She opened her eyes and poked her head out of the bedroll Rowdy had given her, trying to orient herself and recall exactly where she was. Directly above her, she saw rough cut boards and a metal axel. Beside her head, she spied a metal-banded wagon wheel.

Right, she recalled. *The armory wagon.*

The previous evening, as the sun set and the local residents left to seek their own homes and beds, Sonja had joined her new co-workers for dinner around a communal pot simmering over a low-banked fire. The stew inside the pot was provided by the caravan members for the men – and woman – hired to provide security on the road. It was hot and well-seasoned, and when she saw others going back with their empty bowls, Sonja had joined them for seconds.

After eating, Rowdy checked to see what gear Sonja possessed. She opened her arms to show him the clothes on her back and the weapon on her hip. He gathered extra blankets for her to create a bedroll, and he advised her that each mercenary on the team typically slept underneath one of the wagons. The wagon owner would often tip the guard in the morning out of gratitude for the extra protection during the night, and the best tippers generally got the more frequent guests.

"Take the armorer's wagon tonight," Rowdy had told her. "That's usually my spot, but I should move around a bit. I don't want to be too predictable." He winked at her. "By the way, we all have shifts during the night to stand guard. You get a pass tonight, but we'll talk tomorrow about your shift."

Sonja thanked him and crawled under the indicated wagon. She arranged two blankets into a comfortable nest, balled a third into a passable pillow, and settled herself in for the night.

As she attempted to fall asleep, her mind would not quiet. She felt lonely, even surrounded by the sounds of several dozen people talking and moving around her. In the past, she always enjoyed sleeping alone, but that was because she knew that she was alone by choice and that the condition was temporary. With no more than a phone call, she could be next to Kevin's warm, softly snoring form, contentedly curled up in his bed. Now, that was all gone. She still did not fully understand what had happened to trigger him like that. She only knew that her life had irrevocably changed in the blink of an eye.

Sonja felt her throat tighten as she thought about what he had said to her on the restaurant patio. The words felt so final. A tear escaped, running across her cheek and into her hair. She rolled her face into her makeshift pillow and as silently as possible, she had cried herself to sleep.

The bright light and brash noises of this new morning were a welcome relief from the empty hours she had so recently endured. Last night she had only her own miserable thoughts to keep her company. Now, she had a job to do and other people to help keep her mind occupied.

Sonja sniffed. Her nose was stuffy from crying and her eyes were crusty and partially glued shut from sleep. She wiped at her face with her sleeve and desperately wished for an opportunity to wash her face before having to talk to anyone. She wriggled free of her blankets and crawled out from under the armorer's wagon.

"I guess you're not dead after all," a voice called from above her. "You were lying there so long several of us had a bet going. I lost."

Kneeling on the ground, Sonja slipped her vest on over her shirt, then began pulling her blankets out from under the wagon and rolling them more or less neatly into a single thick tube of cloth.

"Shit," she muttered under her breath. So much for cleaning up first. She pasted on a smile and gazed up in the direction of the voice. "Hey, Rowdy. Sorry if I overslept. Is there anywhere I can wash up a bit and, um … take care of a few things?"

"You have to piss?" he asked, bluntly.

"Like a prize bull," Sonja replied. If he felt no need to be delicate, why should she?

Rowdy laughed at the imagery. He jerked a thumb over his shoulder. "There is hot water over the fire and two bowls nearby if they aren't already being used. The bowls are for the hot water only. Not the bull thing. You will have to deal with that situation in the pit at the edge of camp. Someone put up some temporary walls, so you'll have a bit of privacy."

Sonja nodded, then held up her blankets. "And where can I stow these, so I have them tonight?"

"Anywhere you like," Rowdy answered, shrugging. "It's your gear, you need to deal with it."

Sonja glanced around, at a loss. "You mean carry it? Or … or what?"

The smile she liked so much reappeared on Rowdy's face. "Like this. Hey, Lerrin!" he shouted.

A wiry, middle aged man turned from where he had been hitching horses to the front of the armorer's wagon. He was wearing a dirty grey shirt with tan suspenders holding up a baggy pair of brown breeches. "Oy, Rolan. What d'ya need?"

Rowdy indicated Sonja standing next to him. "The lady here looked after your sorry hide last night. Right generous of her, I think. She needs a place to store her bed for the day. Can you help her out?"

The man flapped a hand dismissively at Rowdy. "Wherever she can find space in the cart. And you can stuff y'damned head in there w'it. Botherin' me w' blankets when I got horses to tend to." He continued muttering similar sentiments as he turned back to hitching his team.

"Lerrin's a good man. He'd carry you on his back if you asked him. Don't let the way he talks fool you. Anyway, put that away," he said, pointing at her blankets, "clean up, then grab some breakfast. They are almost done eating, so don't get lost chasing clouds."

Sonja followed Rowdy's advice. She located the pit and made use of it, then got hot water to wash her face. Next, she hurried to the guards' communal food pot for a bowl of some sort of thick chewy oatmeal. It was not the tastiest meal she had ever eaten, but it was certainly filling. She gulped it down, surprising herself with how hungry she was, then dropped the bowl and spoon into a bucket where the cook was starting his cleanup. As she thanked the man for her meal, she heard Rowdy calling for his team to gather.

She joined the other mercenaries as they circled around their leader. There were eleven in the team, including Rowdy, all men except for Sonja herself. She had been introduced to them the previous evening at dinner, but she did not remember most of their names. She decided she needed to rectify that today.

"Most of you have been working with me since we left Arentown last month, so you already know how this works. Tallon and Brin, you are both assigned to scout. Albus and Alren, you take rear. The four of you go grab the horses and be ready to go when we move out. The rest of you are on foot. I want two teams of two and take either side of the caravan."

Rowdy pointed at Sonja and another man standing to his right. "Micka and Sonja, you are both new, so split up and join one of the teams on foot."

"The girl can go with me," said one of the men whose name Sonja had forgotten. "As long as she knows how to keep her mouth shut." He grabbed his crotch and added, "Or open, as needs might arise."

The others in the group laughed at the crude gesture. Rowdy did not seem to find any humor in the gibe, but he also said nothing to put the man in check. Sonja understood his silence. If she shrank away from this kind of behavior, or was unable to stand up for herself, it was going to be a long, uncomfortable journey. In addition, if Rowdy had to run to her rescue every time someone made a rude comment towards her, that would only make the situation worse. She needed to earn their respect, and she could not do that hiding behind Rowdy for protection.

Fortunately, she had experience dealing with this kind of situation, as a teacher for Master Cejack, and many times since.

"That works for me," she said to Rowdy. "If the little head in that guy's pants is as worthless as the big ugly one on his shoulders, I have nothing to worry about. Besides, I'm sure his partner would appreciate the help babysitting him."

A few of the men chuckled at the comment, and the man identified as Tallon slapped the target of Sonja's joke on the shoulder. "She just called you ugly, Ronni," he chided.

"And stupid," added Sonja. "Don't forget I also called him stupid. Although somebody might need to explain that part to him."

More laughter followed, and Sonja felt the tide start to turn in her favor. At least the group did not appear to be openly hostile towards her. Ronni scowled for a moment, not appreciating being the focus of amusement, but soon even he was laughing along with the rest, grinning ruefully. He had prodded at Sonja, and she had poked right back. That was how this game was played. Sonja was happy to see that he did not appear to exhibit any animosity toward her over the exchange.

She glanced at Rowdy. His expression did not change, but she caught the quick wink he threw in her direction.

"Well, if we are all done acting like children," Rowdy broke in when the laughter had faded, "we do have some work to do."

The caravan of wagons set off less than an hour later. Twenty-two wagons in two rows of eleven travelled abreast of each other, filling the wide, packed-clay road out of town. For security, two of Rowdy's team rode on horses scouting the territory ahead. The rest stayed with the wagons. The next town was two and a half days of steady travel away through the rolling hills of scrub and grass Sonja had observed on her first day here.

Sonja walked to the left side of the wagons with Ronni and another mercenary who went by the nickname Dancer. Dancer's features were sharp, weather-worn, and as hard as the career he had chosen. Carefully tailored leathers wrapped his slender torso and revealed lean, sun-browned arms with wiry-muscled biceps and broad forearms. He was in his early thirties, but the hollow curves of his cheeks and the frown lines deeply etched around his nose and mouth suggested it had been a hard thirty years.

Ronni informed her that Dancer's name came from the way he handled his sword in combat. Those who had seen him fight claimed it looked like he was dancing with his opponents rather than battling to the death. Dancer spoke little as he walked, which seemed fine with Ronni, who had barely stopped talking since the caravan started out that morning. Sonja followed Dancer's stoic example, saying little while nodding or shaking her head as appropriate to Ronni's constant chatter.

The animals pulled the wagons at a manageable pace, covering no more than three miles an hour and allowing for the people on foot to keep up without too much difficulty. Occasionally, a member of the caravan needed a rest, or just wanted to escape the sun for a while, and they would hop up onto the back of one of the wagons and ride in shaded comfort for a few minutes. When they felt able, they clambered back down to resume walking. As it was nearing the middle of the day and the sun was high above them, these brief riding breaks were becoming more frequent as fatigue set in.

Sonja and the rest of Rowdy's crew, however, were not permitted this luxury.

Rowdy spent most of his time at the front of the column of wagons. He was mounted, which allowed him to drop back and circle the caravan several times each hour to check in with his security team. Ronni was talking, as usual, when Sonja spotted him trotting up to their trio from behind.

"...when he told me that was his girl I spent the night with, I says he shouldn't be so mad. At least she was still shoutin' out his name all night long. She kept yellin' 'Willem, Willem,' like she was gonna die. Then he says his name ain't Willem. So, I says, then we gots to go find this Willem feller and tell him to keep his hands off'n our girl. Oh, hey, boss," Ronni said as he noticed Rowdy approaching.

"I've got something for you three," said Rowdy, pulling his horse to a slow walk beside them. He held out three, handmade straw hats. He tossed one down to each of them. "It appears today is going to be a hot one, and I'd rather my people didn't boil out what few wits they have."

Dancer flipped his hat onto his head with barely a grunt of acknowledgement. Sonja did the same. Ronni, however, eyed his hat warily as if it somehow offended his personal sense of style and he was unsure if he wanted to be seen wearing the ungainly thing.

"Oh, wear it or don't," snapped Rowdy, watching the display Ronni was making. "Just stop acting like I tossed you a horse flop."

Ronni dutifully mashed the hat over his head, crushing flat most of the curved top with his meaty hand.

"Good enough," said Rowdy. "We are going to be stopping in about an hour to water the horses. We can grab something to eat at the same time if you're hungry. Sonja, fall back with me for a moment, please?"

Rowdy reined his horse to a stop and Sonja paused beside him. Dancer and Ronni didn't break stride and quickly outpaced them, Ronni already warming up to his next story. When they were far enough ahead that they could not likely eavesdrop on his conversation, Rowdy cleared his throat as if mentally addressing an uncomfortable topic.

"Sonja, I just wanted to let you know that last night, after you settled in, I came by to check on you. To see if you needed anything. I, uh, I heard you crying."

Sonja's heart raced, embarrassed at having been caught in such a weak moment. Her cheeks grew hot, but she kept her voice steady as she replied. "Sometimes girls cry. I'm sorry if that disappoints you, but I promise it will not affect my ability to do this job."

"No, I…" Rowdy growled in frustration. He dismounted, dropping from his horse to be closer to Sonja.

Sonja glanced away, not wanting him to see the heat in her face. Besides, this was not a conversation she was prepared to have just now. When Rowdy remained silent, she chanced a glance in his direction and found him staring intently at her. Before she could look away again, his pale eyes locked onto hers and would not let her go. His gaze was so open and vulnerable Sonja could not pull away. She saw no judgement there, no disappointment. Only concern and a desire to help.

"I don't care that you were crying," he said. "I mean, I do care, but not because I hired you. I care because I care about anyone when I know they're in pain. I only wanted to let you know that I'm aware something is going on. You don't have to tell me why you were crying. You don't have to say anything to me at all. But, if you need anything, please tell me. If there is something I can do to help, just ask. Even if you just need someone to listen. I know I'm not much, but I'm here. Don't abandon the princess."

This reminder of Rowdy's story eased Sonja's embarrassment a little. She exhaled a soft snort of laughter.

"Come find me anytime. Or pretend we never had this conversation. Your choice. I promise I will not bring it up again."

Rowdy straightened and waited quietly for a moment. When Sonja said nothing, he nodded to her, gave her another of his quick winks, then moved to climb back onto his horse.

"Wait," Sonja said. Rowdy paused with one foot in the stirrup. "I don't really want to discuss it right now, but I will tell you that I just ended a relationship with someone I cared about. A lot. He and I have been together a long time, and I thought we would be together forever. That all ended yesterday, and it left me a little fragile."

Rowdy pulled his foot from the stirrup and approached Sonja. He placed a hand on her arm. She liked the feel of his touch. The human contact, when she had been feeling so disconnected from everyone around her, was comforting.

"Any man you care enough about to cry for, should care enough about you to never make you cry," he told her.

Sonja laughed again, but she felt the tears building behind it. "That's very wise," she said, swiping a hand at her cheek and trying to bring the conversation back to a lighter footing. "Or just asinine. I'll let you know when I figure out which."

"My grandmother would say wise."

"Well, who am I to question your grandmother?" Sonja said, holding her hands up, palms out in surrender. "But we both have jobs to do, and this emotional crap isn't accomplishing either one of them."

Sonja's tone softened. "Thank you, Rowdy. I'm fine."

"If you need to talk…" He said again.

"I know where to find you. Now, shoo." Sonja flapped a hand at him, urging him on his way.

Without any further conversation, Rowdy climbed up into the saddle, put his heels to his horse and rode off to rejoin the front of the caravan.

While the wagon owners paused to give their animals water and the opportunity to crop whatever grass or plants they could find, Sonja sat in the shade of a stubby oak tree with Ronni and Dancer. The three of them passed around a skin of water and gnawed on rock-hard, white cakes of something Ronni called 'trail bread.' It wasn't particularly appetizing, but it eased Sonja's hunger pangs and chewing on it gave her something to do while they waited to move on.

"I counted twenty-two wagons," Sonja said, making conversation. "Two or three merchants per wagon, a few family members, I figure about sixty civilians."

"I guess that number sounds about right," agreed Ronni, although the way he said it made Sonja briefly wonder just how capable he was with basic math. Dancer merely nodded.

"There are eleven of us. Is that enough? Or too many? How do you figure how many people you need to guard a wagon train like this?"

"Eleven is plenty," Dancer said.

"Twenty-two wagons of merchandise would require at least twenty-two bandits to drive them away," Ronni explained. "Bandits don't want to be merchants. They just want money or things they can sell quick-like. Nobody is gonna pay enough for the stuff we're watchin' to make it worth the while of twenty-two bandits to attack us. Not anythin' close to twenty-two."

Sonja's estimation of Ronni's math and logic skills ticked up a notch at his explanation.

"What about our weapons? Or the money the merchants have with them?"

"Eleven is plenty," Dancer said, again.

"Yeah," agreed Ronni. "The money we have and even some o' the nicer stuff in the wagons would make five or six people real happy for a while. Starts to get a little thin past that. Ten people attacking this ... what did you call it? Train? Ten people splittin' this stuff up might get 'em a couple nice days in town. Food, drink, women. But only a couple days. And ten is still pretty even odds with eleven of us. I'd be good with that tussle."

Ronni stretched and groaned loudly. "Hasn't happened yet, anyway. I been with Rolan since he hired me 'bout a month back, and I ain't see'd nothing to swing my sword at 'cept a couple o' trees."

Sonja sighed. "Well, keep that blade sharp. I have a feeling you're going to be swinging it sooner than you think."

Ronni eyed Sonja closely. Even Dancer seemed to take notice of her comment.

"You know somethin' you should be tellin' us?" Ronni asked.

"No. Not really. I just know that I have really shitty luck most of the time, and I don't usually get to enjoy peace and quiet for very long." Which was an understatement. If Rith put her here in this caravan, it probably wasn't to take a nice three-day jaunt and enjoy the scenery.

Sonja heard the recognizable sounds of the merchants climbing onto their wagons and readying their animals to move. Their rest break was over, and it was time to take up their posts once more. She stood, brushed at the dirt on the back of her pants, then recovered her staff from where she had propped it against the tree. Dancer and Ronni stood and dusted themselves off as well.

Harnesses creaked and whips snapped. Sonja heard the vocal complaint of several large animals and, just like that, the caravan was in full forward motion. The dust kicked up in the roadway was significant due to the number of wagons in the group, but fortunately for Sonja and her two travel companions, what little wind there was blew the dust away from them and across the unlucky trio of guards that walked the opposite side of the caravan.

The sun was warm as Rowdy had predicted, but not cruelly hot, and the pace set by the wagons at the front of the caravan was relaxed enough that Sonja did not feel overworked to keep pace. When she found a comfortable stride, she lowered her head to stare at the ground in front of her and let the unchanging terrain lull her into a mild state of highway hypnosis. Time passed unnoticed, and Sonja found that the miles they travelled were slightly less tedious when she let her mind wander. Ronni continued his non-stop narrative of past exploits, but Sonja tuned most of it out as useless background noise.

"Something is wrong," said Dancer. He looked up at the sky then glanced back to the rear of the caravan.

Sonja came fully alert in an instant. By gauging the current position of the sun, she guessed no more than two hours had passed since the wagons had stopped for their midday break. She looked around her in all directions but could not see what had caught Dancer's attention.

Rowdy had only minutes ago ridden past them on one of his regular checks of the perimeter. He had made no mention of any problems before returning to his post at the front of the group. If something were wrong, wouldn't he have warned them?

"What do you see?" she asked Dancer, still whipping her head back and forth to scan the horizon.

"Nothing," the slender man admitted. "Just a feeling. I'm going to the back to talk to Albus and Alren."

"Want me to go with you?" asked Ronni.

"No. Stay with the new girl. I'll be back soon."

Without any further explanation, Dancer turned on his heel and strode off to the rear of the caravan. Ronni and Sonja walked on, exchanging confused looks regarding Dancer's odd behavior.

"Has he done this before?" Sonja asked Ronni.

"No, but Dancer is a bit strange, if you get me. Keeps most to himself. Like you seen already, he's just … Dancer, I guess."

True to his word, Dancer returned after being gone no more than a few minutes.

"Everything okay?" Ronni asked him.

Dancer simply nodded. Then he asked, "While I was behind the wagons, did either of you hear anything? I thought I heard a shout."

Sonja had heard something while Dancer was gone, but it had been muffled by the constant noise of the animals and wagons so she could not tell where it had come from. She assumed it was one of the drivers cursing at his animals.

"The wagons are so loud you couldn't hear y'self shittin' glass," Ronni told him. "I only heard Sonja talkin' to me. Nothin' else."

"Good," said Dancer.

Dancer drew his sword from its sheath in a practiced draw and drove it point first through Ronni's chest. The razor-honed blade punched easily through Ronni's body and protruded more than a foot from his back before Dancer pulled it free again. The blade came out as smoothly as it went in. As soon as the point cleared Ronni's torso, Dancer slashed sideways toward Sonja's throat.

If Sonja had not already had her staff in her hand, the blow would have taken her head off before she could move to defend herself. It was only luck and years of carefully trained reflexes that saved her. As Dancer's sword cut at her neck, Sonja shifted her staff ten inches to the left, catching the edge of the blade on the thick wooden post. It took Dancer only a fraction of a second to pull the blade free from where it had stuck in the wood, but it was the fraction of a second Sonja needed to pull her wits together and recognize that she was in a fight for her life.

Ronni was down. Dancer had pierced his heart and the poor, garrulous mercenary had been dead before his brain even registered that he was being attacked. Sonja shivered at the thought of how close she had come to joining him.

Dancer did not give her time to dwell on his attempt to kill her as he was still actively trying to finish the job.

Dancer shuffle stepped forward, his blade cutting the air back and forth in a zigzag pattern designed to push open an opponent's defenses and lay open their chest and stomach. Sonja did not recognize the attack or Dancer's style of fighting, but the intent was clear, and she countered with basic left and right parries from her staff.

The attacks continued to come, too fast for Sonja to effectively do much more than defend herself. She found no openings through which to attempt one of her own assaults so had to content herself with a steady retreat and keeping that flashing edge from finding her flesh.

"Ho, drivers!" she cried out, never taking her eyes from Dancer's whipping blade. "Raise the alarm. Call for Rolan!"

She repeated the cry several times, hoping someone would hear and spread the word that there was a problem.

Dancer pushed forward, continuing the odd serpentine attack: feint left, right, thrust. Left, right, thrust. Sonja tried timing his moves and anticipating them, but every time she thought she had figured the pattern, he would alter it just enough to put her back on the defensive. He kept his weapon close to his body, allowing him to drive his assaults forward without giving up the ability to defend; not that Sonja had found an opportunity yet to test those defenses. She noticed the way he kept his elbow bent and his wrist loose was ideal for covering his chest and torso, but it would increase the time necessary to bring the blade up to protect his head.

At least she hoped it would.

Dancer's tactics were designed to combat an enemy holding another sword. Sonja was using her staff. Maybe that would be an advantage. She had more reach with the staff than she would with a blade, and she could attack with either end of her weapon with equal efficiency. This should allow her to try a few maneuvers he might not expect.

Dancer's attacks kept coming. It was time for Sonja to test that hypothesis.

Dancer leapt forward, stabbing straight then cutting in a backward slash from Sonja's hip to her shoulder. Instead of meeting the attack directly and stopping its momentum, Sonja rocked her weight onto her back foot and swept her staff up and to the left, tapping Dancer's blade and adding momentum to it, causing it to sweep wider than the man had intended. With the slight opening this created, Sonja brought her weapon horizontal and drove one end forward with everything she had, driving for his throat. A killing blow.

It never landed.

Dancer did not even try to counter her attack with his sword. Instead he turned his shoulders, blading his body in Sonja's direction, and with an almost casual shift of his head he moved from the path of the strike. Sonja's staff drove harmlessly past his neck, less than two inches from its intended target. Before Sonja could pull back to regroup her defenses, Dancer shifted right, recovering his former positioning and slashing his sword to the left. The blade caught Sonja across the ribs, just above her waist.

She felt it bite through her leather vest and find skin beneath. She gasped at the icy flash of pain high on her left side. Sonja spun with the attack, hoping to minimize the damage from Dancer's blade, then took several running steps away from the mercenary to gain distance and buy herself some time. She felt something warm and wet running across her stomach. She was bleeding.

There was no way to know how badly she was cut without looking, and she did not have the time to pause and examine the injury. She would just have to push on and pray that the blood loss wasn't so severe that it might cause her to pass out anytime soon.

She also didn't have the luxury to keep fighting with her staff. The weapon offered her better defensive options, but if she was going to beat Dancer, she needed a strong offence as well. Dancer might be able to weather several hits from the staff before succumbing, and she couldn't risk further injury to herself while she attempted to wear him down. One well-placed strike with a blade was what Sonja needed now.

"Sorry, Toshida," Sonja said aloud through gritted teeth. "But at least you'll be happy to know I'm making a conscious choice this time."

Sonja flung her staff at Dancer. The man barely flinched as it flew past him.

Brookstar glimmered as it cleared her scabbard and caught the light of the afternoon sun. The blade felt good in her hand. Solid and comforting. It felt like meeting an old friend she had not seen for a very long time.

Dancer flicked his weapon left then right, unimpressed by Sonja's decision to draw her sword. Sonja smiled. Her odds of winning had not improved, she knew that, but she also knew that the blade in her hand meant the rules had changed. The shackles were gone, and control was no longer a concern. The choices were as limited as they were clear.

"Cut, or don't cut," Sonja growled, then launched herself forward.

A LIFE OF ADVENTURE

Brookstar whipped through the air and cried out clear and loud as it met Dancer's own blade. Sonja followed her first cut with a flurry of attacks, stepping and shuffling in a slow circle to her left. Using a pattern learned from years of practicing basic forms, she struck, slashed, and cut without pausing between moves. Sonja knew she needed to stay on the offensive as long as possible, and she prayed that her fighting style was as foreign to Dancer as his had been to her. If it took him a while to figure out her patterns, she might just have a chance.

If Dancer took the initiative away from her and regained the advantage, Sonja might not ever be able to get it back.

Just as his name implied, Dancer was fast and light on his feet. He moved and countered Sonja's attacks without apparent effort. So far though, he had not been able to turn her attacks away enough to build any forward momentum of his own. That would not last for much longer. Sonja knew he was better than she was, and her only real hope was that maybe she was just a little smarter.

Sonja stepped left again, raising her blade high and raking two quick downward blows. Dancer met them each with his odd zigzag cuts: left, right. Sonja shuffled right and slashed horizontally across his middle, but instead of blocking the attack, Dancer merely leaned his weight back, causing her blade to part only empty air. Sonja pushed forward, afraid to let up for even a second lest Dancer gain the initiative, but now an idea was beginning to form on how she might possibly end this confrontation. It wasn't a guarantee, but it might be the best chance she had.

Shuffling to her left, Sonja repeated the two downward raking blows. Dancer again met them with his loose zigzag defense. This time, as Sonja had done with her staff, rather than meet Dancer's backhand cut with equal force, she dropped her own attack then popped her blade back up, tapping Dancer's sword and adding enough momentum to it to cause it to swing slightly wider than he had intended.

Lunging forward, Sonja thrust the point of her weapon directly at Dancer's throat. As she hoped, he chose not to parry, again defending by blading his shoulder toward Sonja and shifting to his right. The blade passed through empty air where his head had been just a moment before. Dancer whipped his blade in a horizontal cut designed to give Sonja a second wound to match her first. With her vest already damaged, another cut across her ribs could well end the fight. And her.

When Sonja had tried to crush Dancer's throat with her staff, both of her hands had been on the weapon guiding it toward its intended target. When she lunged with her sword, however, Sonja kept her left hand free.

Expecting Dancer's cut, Sonja grabbed out with her left hand and touched Dancer's right wrist. She was not fast enough to grab onto him, but the contact slowed his attack. Brookstar hissed through the air. Even as Dancer's blade made contact and sent a fresh wave of agony through Sonja's tortured side, Brookstar flashed between the combatants like the arm of a windmill, striking Dancer's right arm below the elbow. Bone and muscle parted.

The man screamed and staggered backward. Sonja let him move away. He was no longer an imminent threat. She had his sword … and his arm.

"What's going on?" Roared a voice from behind Sonja.

"Watch out, Rolan!" Dancer cried. "She turned on us. She killed Ronni and then tried to do the same with me." He turned so Rowdy could see the bloody stump of his right arm. "Kill her before she murders us all."

Sonja spun, indignation screwing her face into an expression of rage. "What the hell?" she shouted.

Rowdy pulled his horse to a stop and dropped from his saddle to the ground a few feet from Sonja. He drew his sword as soon as his feet struck earth and he leveled the blade at her. "Drop your weapon," he ordered.

"I will not!" Sonja spat. "That crazy bastard–"

"Drop it!" Rowdy ordered. His voice was the rumble of nearby thunder. "Or be prepared to use it."

Was this really happening? Sonja thought. Did Rowdy believe Dancer? Or was he working with Dancer? No, that wasn't right. He couldn't be working with Dancer or else Dancer wouldn't have tried to shift the blame of Ronni's murder onto her.

So, now the question was, did she keep her sword and risk a confrontation with Rowdy, or trust that he was smart enough to figure this out before Dancer tried something else? "Shit," she said. Rather than drop Brookstar to the ground, she stabbed the weapon point down into the soil, leaving it upright beside her.

Rowdy nodded at Sonja and ordered her to take a step away from the sword she had relinquished. She did as she was told, still angry but not having much choice other than to comply.

Dancer moved around Sonja, giving her a wide berth as if desperately afraid of her, and sidled up to Rowdy.

"Thank you, Rolan," he said. "You came just in time. She caught us by surprise, and I was afraid she was going to kill me like she did Ronni. If you hadn't–"

Sonja fumed impotently, staring at her feet, unable to look Rowdy in the eyes. She did not see what happened, only heard the wet 'chuff' of a blade cutting through meat. There was a hollow thump on the ground and Sonja looked up in time to see Dancer's head rolling across the ground toward her. She took an involuntary step back. Dancer's decapitated body collapsed to the ground a moment later.

Rowdy knelt and wiped his sword on Dancer's clothing before placing it back in its sheath. He picked up Brookstar and cleaned it the same way. When it was free of blood, he brought Sonja's blade to where she remained standing a few feet away.

"Here," he said, handing it to her.

She accepted Brookstar and numbly placed it back in its scabbard. "How did you know he was the one lying?"

"You surrendered when I asked you to. We both know you are better with a sword than I am. If you wanted to kill me, you would have attacked."

Rowdy placed a hand to the side of her face, brushing her cheek with his thumb. "Besides, forgive my directness in saying so, but the woman I heard crying alone in her bed last night is not a woman who was planning to murder eleven men in cold blood today."

"Thank you," she said. Sonja touched his arm, holding his hand to her cheek a moment longer.

The intimacy was short lived as shouts rang out along the length of the caravan. Drivers passed along word that the scouts were back and they had company with them. Rowdy ran to his horse and mounted up.

"Go to the front of the caravan and meet the scouts," he called to Sonja. "I'll see you there. I am going to make sure the rest of the men heard the warning."

"Rowdy! I think Albus and Alren are dead. Dancer went to the back of the wagons a few minutes before he … before he killed Ronni."

Rowdy gave her a quick nod, acknowledging that he had heard her before spurring his horse into a run. Sonja watched him go, then sprinted for the front of the wagon train.

The wagons had ground to a halt, stopping as soon as the drivers in the front spotted the scouts off in the distance riding hard to return to the caravan. Four men on horseback raced after them less than a quarter mile behind. Sonja stood in front of the first two wagons, Brookstar again in her hand. She had forgotten her staff but did not figure it would be much use anyway. She was soon joined by Rowdy and the three guardsmen from the opposite side of the caravan.

"Albus?" Sonja asked softly, as Rowdy dismounted and stepped up beside her.

He shook his head, not meeting her eyes. Instead, Rowdy kept his gaze on the approaching riders. They were only a few seconds out.

The two scouts reached the wagon and reigned their horses to a stop. They turned to face the pursuing riders and positioned themselves one to either side of Sonja and the other mercenaries on the ground. Together, the seven remaining guards faced the incoming riders.

The four strangers slowed their mounts to a walk and continued approaching until they were close enough to get a good look at the caravan guard lined up in front of them. They brought their steeds to a sudden stop. The animals fidgeted, tossing their heads and stamping hooves in agitation, still excited from their run. The riders turned to look at one another as though they were confused. Or surprised.

"Are you looking for Dancer?" shouted Rowdy. "He is no longer with us, but I would be happy to send you to meet him."

Rowdy drew his sword. The guardsmen who did not already have their blades in hand, followed his example. The four strangers wheeled their horses about and left as fast as their mounts would carry them.

"I think they expected Dancer to have killed us all before they got here," said Rowdy, watching the would-be bandits disappear into the distance. "I think he might have done it if Sonja hadn't joined us when she did. I've never seen a better fighter than Dancer. Although, come to think of it, I guess I have."

He smiled at Sonja. She smiled back, enjoying the compliment.

A hollow roar filled her ears, like an ocean tide rushing in. Sonja felt dizzy and silver motes hovered at the edge of her vision.

"Um, Rowdy," she said, bringing a hand up to the cut across her ribs. She had forgotten about the wound during the confrontation, but now the pain was back, and she was afraid that she might be experiencing the first stages of shock. "Is there a doctor in this travelling circus?"

Sonja lay curled in her bedroll trying to fall asleep. It was dark outside of the wagon except for the light of a few campfires. Grateful for what she had done to save the caravan, one of the merchants had given up his own bed, allowing her to sleep *in* the wagon, rather than under it.

The caravan did not have a doctor riding with it, but one of the women travelling with the group had some experience caring for injuries. She cleaned Sonja's wound, made a few rough stitches to hold it closed and wrapped it with clean bandages. The cut, though long, had not been deep. Her vest had taken most of the impact and the blade had struck a rib, turning aside whatever momentum remained and preventing the cutting edge from penetrating far enough to do any real damage. Sonja had been incredibly lucky.

The light of a lantern suddenly bathed the interior of the wagon. "Are you asleep? Do you need anything?" It was Rowdy's voice.

Sonja rolled over and sat up in her bed so she could see him. She brushed her hair from her eyes and shook her head. "No, I'm fine. Thank you for checking on me."

"Oh ... ah ... yes, of course."

Sonja furrowed her brow, puzzled. Rowdy suddenly appeared uncomfortable, and he wouldn't look directly at her. A cool breeze from outside reminded her.

Sonja had removed her bloody shirt earlier, not wanting to sleep in it, and she did not yet have a replacement for it. When she sat up in the bed the covers had fallen away leaving her bare from the waist up except for a narrow cloth bandage wrapped a few inches below her breasts. She pulled the blanket up high enough to cover herself.

"Oh. Sorry about that."

"No need to apologize," Rowdy assured her, the confident smile back on his face. He stared at her chest under the blanket, perhaps imagining the sight he had glimpsed earlier. "It was my pleasure."

His smile faded, and a new concern filled his face. "I'm very happy that you were not badly hurt. I would never want to see any harm come to you. Especially since it was my fault."

"Your fault? How could this have possibly been your fault?"

"I hired Dancer. He had a … reputation. But I still hired him because of his skill with a sword. Three good men died because of that decision."

"You had no way of knowing any of this was going to happen," Sonja told him. "You gave him a job and you gave him your trust. Just like you did for me. Dancer made the decision to betray you. This was his choice. His fault. Not yours."

"Thank you for saying that. I'm just glad you are safe. I … well, I care about you. Very much. I think I have since I met you back at Master Cejack's."

Rowdy gave her a wide grin, trying to dismiss the solemnity of his confession, but the expression looked forced. "I will be up for a while longer, so if you need anything, please let me know." He turned to go.

"Rowdy," Sonja said.

When he turned back toward her, she released the blanket she held, allowing it to fall into her lap. She saw him freeze, a sudden hunger growing in his eyes, but still too unsure to act on it.

"You wouldn't abandon the princess, would you?" she asked him.

Rowdy extinguished the lantern and set it down. The wagon shifted under his weight as he climbed inside. Sonja raised the blanket to make room and felt him slide in beside her.

"No," he promised her. "No, I would not."

The next two days were uneventful. The bandits did not return, and the caravan meandered its way to its next stop unmolested. The second night on the road, Rowdy again joined Sonja in her bed. They talked, shared their greatest regrets, and offered comfort to one another.

Rowdy asked how long Sonja would stay with the caravan, and she admitted that as soon as they reached their next destination she would have to leave. He did not plead with her to stay. He only nodded with a stoic acceptance, leaned in, and pressed his lips softly to her cheek. Sonja grabbed his head in her hands and pulled him into a fierce kiss before rolling on top of him. They made love twice more that night.

The following day, as the new town came into view on the horizon, Sonja found Rowdy at the head of the caravan.

"It's time," she told him.

"Now? You won't wait until we reach the town?"

"No. It's time to go. I ... need to go."

Rowdy simply nodded his understanding. Again, he did not beg her to stay or ask to come with her. He stroked the side of her face with his thumb and placed a kiss on her forehead. She looked up into his soul-stealing, gray eyes and lost herself there for a long moment. There was so much life and emotion there to see, she could spend forever gazing into that abyss.

Sonja expected the tears on her own cheeks. It was the one on Rowdy's cheek that surprised her.

CHAPTER 24

The display on her phone said "Kevin," and a picture of his face popped up over the name on the screen. Sonja debated not answering. He had told her not to call him, now maybe she should enforce a little radio silence of her own. Her reticence quickly faded, and she sighed. She was going to answer the call. She was being childish and she knew it, but it didn't change the fact that he had hurt her, and she wasn't quite ready to forgive him. At least she had given herself a couple extra days to process her feelings and come to some level of acceptance – even if to Kevin the breakup had only happened yesterday. She felt she would be able to speak with him while keeping the contact civil.

Sonja swiped the green accept button.

"Hello?"

"Hi, Sonja. It's me."

"Mmm-hmm." It was all she could manage. All she felt he deserved.

There was a short silence on the line as Kevin tried to read her response. "Look," he finally said. "First, I wanted to apologize for how I handled things yesterday. It was wrong for me to just walk away. I shouldn't have done that. I'm sorry."

"Are you saying you didn't mean what you said?" Sonja asked, a small amount of hope growing inside her.

"No, I meant it," Kevin told her, extinguishing the tiny flicker. "I just said it badly. I wanted to explain myself. Explain better what I was trying to say. Are you free? Can we talk?"

"Go ahead and talk," Sonja told him. She could hear the coldness in her voice, and it made her flinch, but he had hurt her once already. She wasn't going to open herself up so he could do it again.

"No, not on the phone. Will you meet me? Please? Anywhere you want."

Sonja almost said, no. It would be best to just cut him off, hang up and put him out of her head completely. But to close out the biggest part of her life over the past four years in that manner seemed wrong. It was just too sad. She needed to see him, she decided. She needed to face him and tell him exactly what his words had done to her; how much they had crushed her.

Most of all she wanted to see his expression when she told him. She needed to know he still felt something, too. It might not change the outcome, but maybe it would give her the chance to figure out what had happened. How had a relationship that felt so comfortable, so strong, die in flames like that without ever giving her a hint that the end was coming? Had she done something? *No.* Sonja shut down that line of thinking as soon as it popped up. Kevin had made the decision to walk away. This was on him.

"Are you still there?" Kevin asked into the silence.

"I'm here," she told him.

"I really would like to talk to you in person."

"That's very big of you," Sonja said, keeping her voice level and trying not to let any of the thoughts or emotions roiling through her slip out over the phone. "I suppose I could meet with you. I'm skipping my classes today, anyway."

Sonja took a deep breath. She felt a thick lump lodge in her throat and her heart began to race. She tried to swallow the painful knot and her eyes started to water. *Damn it!* She thought she had gotten past this.

"I'll be at Bertie's again today at one, o'clock. If you want to talk to me, meet me there." Sonja hung up the phone before Kevin could reply. It wasn't that she didn't want to hear his answer, but rather she was afraid if the call lasted any longer, she might break down. She did not want Kevin to hear her losing control of herself.

Sonja wiped at the wet streaks on her cheeks. "I need a hot shower," she told herself. "A hot shower, a good cry, and then a little bit of makeup."

Sonja arrived at Bertie's at a quarter before one o'clock. Kevin was already standing outside the front door, waiting. That at least was a good sign. If he really didn't care, he would come late. Or not at all.

Kevin broke into a huge smile when he saw her. Sonja smiled back but the cheery expression felt tight and artificial.

"I'm glad you came," he started. He moved close to kiss her, but Sonja turned her head slightly forestalling the attempt. He stepped back, regret crossing his features briefly. He recovered his smile the best he could, then pulled the restaurant door open, gesturing for Sonja to precede him.

"I'm buying today," he told her.

"That sounds fair. I didn't really get to eat lunch yesterday."

Kevin dropped his eyes to his feet and his cheeks reddened. "I … know. I'm sorry about that. Let's find a spot on the patio again."

"Why?" Sonja asked. There was unintended heat in her voice. "Do you think you might need to make another quick getaway?"

"I deserve that," Kevin admitted. "I deserve everything you're going to say to me and everything you're thinking that you want to say to me. I'll listen to all of it, I promise. Can we sit first?"

Sonja nodded. They both stepped up to the wooden podium at the front of the restaurant and allowed a smiling hostess to seat them outside at one of the patio tables. It was not the same table they had the day before, but it was close enough. Sonja eyed the spot as they passed, as she might stare at the location of a particularly gruesome traffic accident she had witnessed.

When they had been seated and handed menus, the hostess promised their server would be with them shortly, then bounced away to meet the next customers coming through the front door.

Kevin watched her go. When he was sure she wasn't coming back, he turned to Sonja. "Thank you for agreeing to see me. It would have been perfectly understandable if you told me to go to hell."

"I'm still holding onto that option," Sonja told him, opening her menu and glancing through it.

Kevin's lips curled up tightly, accepting the statement graciously. "Let me say this fast, before I start to ramble and screw everything up all over again."

Sonja put the menu down and looked across the table at Kevin. She noticed he was sweating, and his hands were shaking slightly where they rested on the table in front of him. *What the hell is wrong with him?* she thought. *Is he sick?*

"I hurt you yesterday," he said, staring at his own unsteady hands rather than meeting Sonja's eyes. "I think I hurt you badly. Last night I realized that hurting you is the last thing I ever want to do. In fact, I want to spend the rest of my life with you doing everything I can to make up for hurting you."

Kevin leaned back to reach into the front pocket of his jeans. He removed a small, gray, felt-covered box and held it up in both hands. "I bought this a few months ago," he told her. "I was waiting for the perfect time, but I think that ship sailed. I think it sailed and then I sunk it in the middle of the ocean."

Sonja's eyes widened. Her mouth opened, then closed, as she tried to speak. "Oh, God. Don't," was all she managed to say.

Kevin cleared his throat, pushing forward despite the unexpected reaction. "Sonja, I love you more than you will ever know. I want you to be my wife. Will you marry me?"

He opened the box, flipping the hinged lid back with a tiny pop. Inside was a gold ring with three solitaire cut diamonds mounted at the top of the band. Sonja did not immediately move or react to his question, so he placed the box on the table between them and slid it a short distance toward her.

Sonja balled her hands into fists and jammed them into her lap as if Kevin had placed a poisonous spider onto the table and she was terrified she might touch it.

"What the hell is this?" she asked, her eyes never wavering from the ring. "What happened yesterday? What happened to 'we have no future together' and you running off telling me not to call you anymore? What the fuck are you doing right now?" Sonja clamped her teeth together. She felt hysteria rising inside of her, and if she kept talking, she was afraid she would scream.

Kevin leaned forward, holding his hands up in surrender and acknowledgement. "I know what I said. And I meant it. I didn't see a future for us if things stayed the way they were. You have this entire life separate from me, separate from everyone actually, and I was jealous of that. Rith isn't going anywhere, I accept that, but I still didn't like feeling like an outsider in your life. I needed to know, somehow, that I was important to you. Important enough that I could stop worrying about losing you to Rith, knowing that we each had a part of one another that nobody else could ever have. Something we never had to share. Something that was just ours.

"Maybe I'm saying this badly again but," he pointed toward the box, "I think this is it. I want to marry you. I want to know you care enough to say, yes."

Sonja's shoulders slumped and her hands relaxed in her lap. She did not know how to respond, so she stayed quiet. Kevin said nothing, letting her have the time to think.

If he had asked her this question yesterday, what would she have said? *I would have told him, yes,* she thought. *Probably without hesitation. I loved him. I still love him,* she admitted, *with all my heart.*

The wall of anger and sorrow that she had built to shield herself was not based on the fact she had stopped caring for him, it was there because she needed to protect herself from how bad the idea of losing him had hurt. It was there because of how desperately she *did* love him. Now she needed to decide if she could take that wall down and forgive him for what he had done to her.

Sonja placed her hands on the table on either side of the ring. She still did not quite dare to touch it.

She felt the wall breaking away, a little. But it was still there. Kevin had hurt her deeply. He had abandoned her at the restaurant. She had spent the night crying into her blankets. She had...

"Oh, my god. *Rowdy!*"

Sonja bolted to her feet, driving her chair backward. It overbalanced and crashed to the cement with a loud metallic bang. "I... I need a minute," she sputtered, then fled for the bathroom before Kevin could ask what was the matter.

Flinging the patio door open, Sonja forced herself to slow to a hurried walk through the main section of the restaurant. She found the bathroom door and pushed through. It looked empty. Stepping up to the sink, she stared at herself in the mirror. The woman gazing back at her looked haunted, terrified. Her eyes were wide and wild. Sonja's heart stampeded in her chest as if it were trying to break free of her ribcage. She wanted to run, to fight. Something truly awful was happening and her brain had responded the only way it knew how. Adrenaline flooded her body, and with nowhere for that rush to go, she began to shiver. Nausea boiled inside of her, twisting her stomach into knots. She was panicking, and with no opponent for her body to fight, it was fighting itself.

"Rith," she said, beginning to pant in shallow labored breaths. "Beach. Now!"

A LIFE OF ADVENTURE

In an instant, the restaurant bathroom was replaced by the shore of her private beach. The white sand shifted beneath her bare feet, soft and warm, and the sounds of the waves lapping the shoreline a few dozen feet away were as steady and constant as ever. She had first met Kevin on this beach; the *real* Kevin, not the role-playing character in one of her adventures. It was where she began to understand him as an actual person, and where she started to fall in love with him. This was also the same beach she had come to many times before whenever she needed quiet or was looking for a place to relax.

It felt different now.

Nothing about the beach had changed, but today, it felt not merely secluded, but empty. The roar of the waves sounded more ominous. Instead of soothing her anxiety, they rumbled accusingly at her.

Her sanctuary, a place of tranquility and peace, had become a desperate refuge, a place of escape to avoid the nightmare her life had just become.

Sonja raised her face to the sky and screamed. She did not try to control it, she just let her body vent the rage, fear, and misery locked inside. Piercing and raw, it was the howl of a lonely, injured animal. When her lungs had emptied, she gasped air back into them in ragged gulps and screamed again.

She did not stop until her throat choked closed from the harsh treatment and she was left coughing violently. Sonja collapsed to her hands and knees, her back bowed as she began to dry heave. Her stomach was empty, she had eaten nothing the entire day, and she could only choke up small streams of bile, gagging and spitting repeatedly. Her insides convulsed several times, but still she could not free herself of the knot in her chest and the painful, bitter lump at the back of her throat.

Exhausted and sobbing she collapsed to her side, pulling her knees to her chest, and wrapping her arms tightly about herself.

"What have I done? What have I done?" she repeated, over and over in a litany of recrimination.

Rith remained silent. Sonja expected no answer from him. The question was not meant for him.

"Oh, Kevin. I'm so sorry. I'm so sorry. I thought you were going to leave me and now I've thrown away any hope we had left."

Sonja closed her eyes, feeling the tears push through her lashes and track across her face. She let them fall without attempting to wipe them away. She wanted to disappear, to just lie here in the sand until she melted into it, becoming part of it. Maybe she could fall asleep and never wake up, or she could stay here forever, leaving the real world frozen in that one horrible moment and never go back to face it again.

She almost convinced herself that staying curled up on the beach for eternity was an option, but reality eventually reasserted itself despite her attempts to push it away. After several agonizing minutes passed, Sonja sat up and wiped at her face with her arm. Sand stuck to the back of her hand and scratched at her cheek. She glanced around and located the blanket and picnic basket that were always waiting for her. Pushing herself to her feet, she brushed the sand off her body as best she could with her hands as she trudged forward a few steps to the waiting items. She twisted around and sat back heavily onto the blanket.

Sonja sighed, hiccoughing softly as her gaze trailed out over the rippling blue-green water of the ocean in front of her.

"Rith, what am I going to do?" she asked.

Rith left his perch on her left hand and fluttered upward to hover above her shoulder. "I don't know. What are your choices?" he responded.

"I can't hide here forever, so I know I've got to go back and face him. The problem is what do I tell him?"

"What are your choices?" Rith asked again.

Sonja released another long breath. The choices were pretty simple. Deciding on the right one to pursue was what was so hard.

"I tell Kevin what happened between me and Rowdy, or I don't. Those are the options." She paused, then said, "I think I need to tell him."

"Why?" asked Rith.

"Why? What do you mean, why? Because it's the right thing to do. It's the honest thing to do."

"Okay," agreed Rith. "But won't telling him hurt him? What if you didn't tell him what you did and agreed to marry him? Wouldn't that make him happy? Don't you want to make him happy?"

Sonja stared at the hippoganth, appalled by his statement. "What are you doing, Rith? Do you think I shouldn't tell him?"

"I don't know what you should do," he replied honestly. "I don't really understand relationships enough to know what the right thing is. I'm trying to understand, though, why one decision is better than the other. What would happen if you didn't tell him?"

Sonja gave the answer a moment of serious thought. "If I don't tell him, we would get married and I could just pretend the whole thing with Rowdy never happened. If I don't say anything, there's no way he would ever find out. I mean, he's never going to meet Rowdy. I'll probably never see Rowdy again either."

"That sounds okay," said Rith.

"But," she continued. "*I* know what I did. By not telling Kevin, I'm allowing our marriage to be based on a lie. I would feel like garbage knowing that I was keeping something this important from him. I already feel so guilty my stomach is twisted into knots. I think it'll only get worse if I hide it from him."

"You can tell him and make him sad, but you would feel better. Or you can not tell him, and he would be happy, but you would feel bad. Do I have that correct? So, by telling him, you would feel better about yourself, but it would be at the expense of his happiness. Isn't that selfish?"

Sonja clambered to her feet and started walking along the beach, following the shoreline. She wanted to be moving, hoping that the activity would help her while she processed her thoughts. "Damn it, Rith. It's not that simple. Yeah, I guess it is kind of selfish, but if I marry Kevin and don't tell him I'm afraid it's going to put a wedge between us that eventually breaks us up anyway. Or worse, maybe I convince myself that it wasn't really such a big deal."

"Why would that be worse?" asked Rith, keeping pace with Sonja.

"Because if I convince myself that cheating on Kevin is okay, I might do it again. I hate admitting that, but that's what I'm afraid is going to happen. That means marrying Kevin and lying to him is not an option." Sonja turned and strode in the opposite direction, working her way back toward her blanket. "If I don't tell him what I did, then I can't marry him. I have to break up with him. And when I break up with him, I can't tell him why I'm doing it. I'll just tell him that we're done and let him wonder why. Maybe he'll think I'm still mad at him for leaving me at the restaurant yesterday."

Sonja paused, staring out at the water lapping against the beach in slow, rhythmic motions. She walked the few paces toward the damp sand delineating the ocean tide from the rest of the beach. When she felt her feet sink slightly into the wetness of the shoreline she stopped again, letting the saltwater splash gently against her ankles as it rushed past her, then again as it slid back out to sea. As always, it was cool, but not cold.

"Except…" She said, quietly.

"Except?" repeated Rith.

"Except I still love him, and I don't want to leave him. If I'm going to lose him anyway, I want him to know the truth. That way he can hate me for the right reasons. Maybe, if there is any hope of us getting past this, he will know that despite whatever else I may have done, I've never lied to him. That has to be worth something. Right?"

Sonja lowered her head, her eyes staring sightlessly at the water gliding past her feet. She had made her decision. She would tell Kevin. Whatever happened next was completely out of her hands.

Taking one more moment to wipe at the wetness around her eyes, she realized she needed to act while she still had the courage to do so. If she waited any longer, she would begin to doubt herself and the entire internal debate would start up again.

"Okay, Rith. Take me back."

The beach disappeared. The bright afternoon sun overhead winked out of existence to be replaced by a harsh bare lightbulb mounted in the ceiling of a public bathroom. Sonja was once more staring into a mirror at her own reflection. The wild panic in her eyes had faded and she discovered only a resigned acceptance in her features now. It was time to go outside and face Kevin.

Sonja's heart accelerated in her chest at the idea of confessing her infidelity. The thought of running away started to sound appealing again, but she took a few deep breaths, forcing herself to calm down. "Let's get this over with," she told herself in the mirror.

When she returned to the table, Kevin was still seated. He immediately stood when he saw her, a concerned expression furrowing his brow and tightening his jaw. She waved him back to his seat. Sonja noticed that somebody had picked up her chair from where it had fallen and replaced it by their table. The gray jewelry box with the gold ring nestled inside remained where she had last seen it. It sat open, like a tiny mouth laughing at her.

Or shouting accusations.

Sonja sat down and looked directly at Kevin. Before she could lose her nerve, she said, "I love you, Kevin, more than anything, and I do want to marry you."

"That's great!" he exclaimed, a broad grin splitting his face.

Sonja cut off whatever else he was about to say.

"I cheated on you."

Kevin shook his head, not able to immediately absorb what she had just told him. "You ... what?"

"When you walked away yesterday, I thought you were done with me, leaving me for good. I thought I lost you, and that devastated me. That's not an excuse, it's just the truth. I was crushed and completely empty inside. I needed … comforting. I didn't go looking for it, but I ended up sleeping with someone. He was kind to me."

"How did this even happen?" Kevin asked, his hands pressed together in front of his mouth like he was saying a small prayer. "It's been one day."

"It's been three days," Sonja said.

Kevin sat back in his chair and closed his eyes. He understood immediately.

"I'm so sorry. I know that's not enough, but I mean it. I love you and I would never do anything to hurt you. I want to make this up to you. I'll do anything you want, if you can just tell me that there might be a way we can get past this." Sonja was rambling. She knew it, but she didn't care.

Kevin leaned forward and stretched one arm across the table. For one brief instant, Sonja thought he might be about to take her hand and tell her that everything was okay and that he forgave her. His hand closed around the jewelry box. The crack of the box snapping closed in his fist rang like a gunshot in her ears.

Standing up, Kevin placed the small, gray ring box back in his pocket. "I don't know what to think, right now," he told her. "A moment ago, I was ready to marry you. Now, I'm not sure I know who you are. I think… I…" His throat closed, choking off his voice for a moment. He shook his head and coughed before continuing.

"The scary thing is I still love you. But this is a lot even for you, Sonja. I want to get past this. I really do. But I don't know if I can. I don't know."

Kevin climbed over the patio railing and stepped onto the sidewalk. Sonja experienced a painful flash of déjà vu.

"I have to get away from you for a little while. I don't think I can be around you right now. But we are going to talk later." He turned as if to leave, then turned back around to face her.

"Damn it, Sonja! It was one day. You couldn't wait one day? Try not to fuck anyone else while I'm gone this time."

Sonja flinched back, the words slapping her with an almost physical impact. She saw on Kevin's face that he regretted the statement the moment he said it, but he did not take it back. Instead, he turned and stormed away from her for the second time in as many days.

This time was different though, Sonja knew. This time she had no one to blame but herself.

"Rith, as soon as we get home we are going on another little trip," she muttered under her breath. "Something good and violent that makes me forget how much I hate myself."

CHAPTER 25

The first thing that struck Sonja was the noise. It was deafening, drowning out all other immediate sensory input. She ignored the uproar as best she could, cupping her hands to her ears, and forced herself to look carefully at her surroundings. She stood on the manicured, dirt grounds of a large outside arena. Dozens of people wandered around the main floor of the arena, and hundreds more, maybe thousands, packed the bleachers encircling her. The raucous noise was all those people talking, shouting, and cheering.

As she watched the activity bustling around her, Sonja noticed that many of those closest to her seemed a bit odd. Many were abnormally tall or short, and they moved in a manner that left her with the feeling that something was terribly out of place. With a shock, she realized the problem: some of the people around her were not actually people. To be more precise, they were not human.

Now that she was paying closer attention, she could see that most of those around her were quite alien. Sonja, and anyone resembling anything remotely human were the clear minority in this crowd. Creatures walked, crawled, and slithered across the dirt as their anatomy dictated, and Sonja saw beings that reminded her of various insects, lizards, and amphibians, as well as a host of furry mammalian shapes. Some of them appeared so strangely constructed she had to stop herself from staring lest she draw unwanted attention upon herself for being rude.

A longer glance through the bleacher seating surrounding her confirmed the audience was an assortment of life forms closely representing those on the field.

As Sonja's ears adapted to the crowd noise, the sense of disorientation began to fade, and she was able to focus on the activity around her. There did not seem to be any direction or pattern to the creatures wandering the grounds other than a general flow that moved to and from five distinct points within the arena.

On the arena floor, were five stages: one central stage raised onto a platform and surrounded by some sort of mesh netting and four more performance areas set up in a loose square situated around the main stage. The four outer stages had been erected at ground level and had only a series of three layered ropes delineating their boundaries. They reminded Sonja of boxing or wrestling rings she had seen on television, though these were more rounded, supported by multiple posts instead of only four.

Next, Sonja took stock of herself. She was wearing a black sports bra that wrapped tight around her upper torso and some sort of elastic compression shorts that covered her snuggly from waist to just above the knee. The only other material on her body, was a wide bandage wound around her ribs a few inches below the bottom hem of her sports top, a reminder of the painful present she had received from Dancer.

She was barefoot, but the dirt beneath her was soft and appeared to have been raked free of any rocks or objects large enough to cut into the soles of her feet. Many of the creatures were dressed similarly, with patches of skin-tight clothing over various parts of their anatomy. Although, Sonja noted, some wore nothing at all.

"I hope you have something good planned this time," Sonja told Rith. "This might be our last adventure and I want it to be memorable."

"What do you mean by last adventure?" asked Rith, flying in agitated circles around Sonja's head.

"Nothing. I'm just prattling. Don't sweat it. What do you have on the agenda for today?"

"Death match!" squeaked Rith. "Two combatants enter the cage, only one lives to walk out."

"What!?" shouted Sonja. Her eyes widened and she stared in panic at the assortment of claws, spines, horns, and teeth on the fighters around her.

"You looked like you were ready to kill something when you asked for another adventure, so here we are."

"Rith, what were you thinking?" she hissed. "I mean, you aren't wrong, but I didn't want anything like this. Look at the size of some of these guys."

Rith squealed and nickered happily. "I'm kidding. I'm kidding. No death matches today. Just some barehanded fighting and you can quit anytime you want. Nobody dies. Well, probably not. I suppose it could happen, though. Maybe."

Sonja put a hand to her chest, trying to get her breathing back under control. For a moment, she had considering breaking into a run and trying to find the nearest exit. "That wasn't funny," she said when her heart rate began to return to normal. "You better give me a quick rundown of what's happening. How is this going to work?"

"Eight species are competing today. Each species is allowed two competitors. The first round is kind of a preliminary fight and it will be with your own kind. Subsequent rounds will be against opposing races. After the first round, it is single loss elimination. You lose and you're done. See how simple it is?"

"Simple," Sonja echoed. "Should I go join them?" she asked, pointing toward a group of four humans standing outside one of the roped stages.

All four were men. Three were much older than Sonja, fully dressed in t-shirts, what appeared to be sweatpants, and laced sneakers. Each of them had a thick, neatly combed beard covering his face, giving them all a very homogeneous appearance. The fourth, a well-muscled young man in his mid or late twenties, was garbed in only the elastic shorts similar to those Sonja currently wore. He was tall and lean, with curly black hair and pleasant-looking features. He did not have facial hair, but Sonja could make out a dark shade of stubble that he probably had to shave frequently to keep under control. His deeply tanned skin had a slight, olive-green tone to it, and his bare chest and torso were covered by a T-shaped thatch of dark hair that trailed down his abdomen into the waistband of his shorts.

"Yes. You should go introduce yourself," Rith agreed.

Sonja tried to project more confidence than she felt as she marched across the arena to meet the small group of humans. As she approached, they all turned to face her. One of the older men said something that sounded like a greeting – he was smiling, at least – but she could not understand the language he was speaking.

"I'm Sonja," she said, smiling back. "I'm sorry, but I don't know what you're saying. Does anyone here speak English?"

The younger man nodded his head. "I speak English," he said. He spoke with a heavy accent that Sonja could not identify. Italian? Spanish? Maybe something not spoken on Earth. "I'm Paulo."

Well, that certainly sounds like an Earth name, Sonja thought.

"I'm Sonja," she said again, holding out her hand. Paulo shook it, taking her hand in both of his then kissing the back of her wrist lightly. Sonja almost laughed at the gesture, surprised by the simple gallantry. "It's very nice to meet you, Paulo. Who are the guys behind you?"

"I only just met them a little while ago." Paulo lowered his voice, conspiratorially. "I must admit I have already forgotten their names. No matter. They will be our judges."

"Judges?" Sonja asked.

"Yes. They will oversee our fights when we are matched up with the other combatants. Each of the species represented here is allowed three judges to make sure the rules are followed and the pairings are fair. These gentlemen are our judges."

Sonja took a moment to nod at the men behind Paulo. They bowed slightly in acknowledgement but said nothing.

"So, when do the fights start?" she asked, turning back to Paulo.

"The ranking fights have already started," he told her.

Sonja glanced around and saw that, just as Paulo had said, two of the ground level rings had contestants inside squaring off. In each ring, the combatants both appeared to be of the same species.

"When the ranking fights have finished, the competition will begin. All fights will then be in the cage at the center of the arena. For now, we have been assigned this stage," he continued, gesturing at the roped area closest to them. "We were just waiting for you to arrive so we could begin our match."

"Now?" Sonja asked, a little startled at the informality of the arrangement.

"Yes, if you are ready," Paulo told her. "If you need some time to prepare, we have a few minutes. But, please do not take too long. We must hand over the stage in a half hour or so to the next fighters."

Sonja did a few stretches and ran in place for a minute or two to get her heart rate up and warm up her muscles. Paulo waited politely, chatting amiably with the judges. When Sonja had managed to break a light sweat and she figured she was as ready as she was going to get under the circumstances, she clapped her hands together twice and jerked her thumb at the roped combat space.

"Okay, Paulo. Let's do this." Sonja climbed between the bottom and second rope into the ring. Paulo followed her example from the opposite side. "Are there any rules?" she asked as she twisted her head from side to side, popping the cartilage in her neck to loosen it.

"This is not the actual competition yet, so the rules are whatever we wish them to be. What do you suggest?"

"I suggest you stop being so damn polite," Sonja said with a smile to show she did not mean anything by the comment. "Um ... how about no biting? That would be a good start."

Paulo nodded his agreement. "Of course. And I would ask..." He waved a hand around the area of his groin.

"Hands off the delicates," Sonja said with a laugh. "Fair enough."

"Other than that, I think we fight as we see fit. Please keep in mind that ultimately we are partners and should not cause any injury that may impact our ability to fight in the tournament."

Sonja was surprised by this statement, but quickly agreed to it. "How do we start, and how long is each round?"

Paulo's face twisted in consideration of her question. "There are no rounds, and we start when we start."

"Okay. Then I guess: ding, ding."

Paulo cocked his head and raised an eyebrow.

"That means start," Sonja clarified.

Paulo laughed. "Ding, ding," he repeated, then moved toward her.

Paulo held his hands in tight fists, high to either side of his face and close together. His shoulders hunched forward and he walked with a side to side, bouncing gait that kept his head constantly moving. Sonja guessed from his posture that he had extensive boxing training. Striking was not her strength, and Paulo had an obvious reach advantage, so she was going to have keep moving and try to keep out of punching range.

Sonja's own stance was looser than Paulo's. Her hands were more relaxed in front of her body, kept lightly curled so she could punch or grab with equal speed. Her feet were also wider apart, and she kept her weight evenly distributed between them, allowing her to shift and kick with either foot if the opportunity presented itself.

Paulo shuffled closer, trying to force Sonja against the ropes. Fortunately, the rounded shape of the ring permitted her to shift out of his line of attack and move away whenever he tried to hem her in. He threw a few experimental jabs with his left, gauging his distance and testing her reaction. Sonja stepped back and shifted to her left but did not counter with anything offensive. Not yet.

If she moved in close enough to throw a punch of her own, Paulo could easily counter with much more force than she could generate. It was not an exchange she would win. Sonja knew she needed to be patient, let him keep coming to her, and hope to spot an opening.

Paulo crowded close again, jabbing twice with his left hand. Sonja again slipped to her left and kept her distance. She watched his hands as he followed her. They stayed high, close to his head. Even as he punched with his left, his right stayed close to his cheek, protecting his face. With his hands that high, though, his lower ribs were open. Sonja might be able to throw a few kicks at his side and midsection. These were not knockout strikes, but they hurt, and they might slow him down later if this fight lasted for any length of time.

Paulo moved in for the third time. He again led with a left jab. Instead of going left, Sonja moved right and stepped in closer. With a light slap from her right hand, she deflected Paulo's jab just enough to protect her face from impact, then lashed out with her right foot in a roundhouse kick.

The kick landed, but rather than try to move away from the impact, Paulo dropped his left arm and caught her leg around the calf. He pivoted to his left, pulling her closer, and threw a right cross at her extended leg. Paulo's knuckles struck Sonja's inner thigh just a few inches below her hip. She gasped at the sudden pain and retaliated with a wild punch at Paulo's head. He had already released her leg and danced back, so her fist met only empty air.

Sonja stepped back, limping slightly. The initial pain had already subsided, but what was left was a dull ache that radiated outward throughout the muscles of her upper leg. The limb throbbed and her footwork felt sluggish. She shuffled around the ring, trying to walk through the injury. If she could keep the blood circulating, maybe she could work through the pain before it became a major liability.

Taking the center of the ring, Paulo watched Sonja pacing her way around the ropes. He observed her limp. Sonja could see him thinking about how to best take advantage of her temporary loss of mobility. He came at her again, not rushing, but moving quickly. Sonja saw his shoulders tense and she shuffled left to avoid the punch she knew was coming. She never saw the kick.

Pain lanced up her right leg again, starting six inches above the knee and rocketing up into her hip. Paulo had used a roundhouse kick of his own that struck her right thigh where he had punched her just a few seconds ago. Sonja put her right foot down and her leg immediately collapsed out from under her. She went to the ground, catching herself on her hands and knees. Fearing a follow up kick or punch to her head, she dove and rolled away from the last place Paulo had been standing. Rising back to her knees, she brought her hands up to protect her head from whatever came next.

Paulo did not follow. He moved back to the center of the ring and watched her closely. Sonja tentatively put her weight on the injured leg. It held, and she was able to rise to her feet, but her thigh felt like so much dead meat. She did not trust her balance on that leg, and she knew if Paulo rushed at her right now, she would not be able to get out of the way.

"How is the leg?" Paulo asked, politely. Sonja did not hear any mockery in his tone.

"Hurts like hell. Thanks."

"Do I need to knock you unconscious?" he asked. Again, Sonja did not detect any teasing or cruelty in his voice.

"I don't know," she answered, peering at him through a sweaty lock of hair that had fallen over her eyes. She brushed it away. "Do you?"

"Some fighters are too proud. They would rather be beaten to unconsciousness than admit they are losing. Are you one of these?"

"Not usually," Sonja admitted.

"Remember, this is just to determine who fights in First Rank and who is in Second."

"What's the difference?" asked Sonja, still trying unsuccessfully to get full use of her leg back.

"First Rank is usually the better fighter. There is more prestige in winning First Rank."

Sonja slumped onto the ground, landing hard on her bottom but not caring. Her ass didn't hurt half as much as her leg did. "I don't really care, either way," she told Paulo. "If you want First Rank or whatever, it's all yours."

A grin lit up Paulo's face, revealing two rows of even, white teeth. He marched over to Sonja and extended a hand, helping her to her feet.

"Maybe you should have paid a little closer attention during Master Toshida's lessons," said Rith at a volume that only Sonja could hear. He remained motionless on her ring.

"Oh, shup up," she fired back at him.

"I'm sorry. Did I say something to upset you?" asked Paulo, pausing before slipping an arm about her waist.

"No. I wasn't talking to you. I'm just conversing with an annoying voice in my head."

Paulo nodded his understanding, as if it were every day that someone told him they had arguments with themselves.

With Paulo's assistance, Sonja climbed out of the ring, limped a few feet away to find an open area of the arena, and promptly sat back down in the dirt. There were no benches or chairs to sit on, and Sonja didn't want to stand at that moment, so the ground seemed a perfect alternative.

Paulo knelt down beside her and, without a word, took her injured thigh in his hands and began to knead the muscle. At first Sonja tensed at the familiarity of Paulo's touch; his hands were dangerously close to some more sensitive portions of her anatomy. After a moment, she relaxed. Her shoulders slumped and her head lolled forward. *Damn, that felt good*, she admitted to herself.

After a few, much too brief minutes of bliss, Paulo stopped. He patted her leg and stood up. "I'm sorry if this slows you down in your next match. Just take it easy, keep moving so it does not stiffen up, and you should be okay. We are paired with the O'paahan in the first round which should start in about an hour. After that we will not need to fight again before tomorrow."

Sonja shrugged. "That's good, I guess," she said, not having any clue what Paulo was talking about. Who were the O'paahan?

"I am going to eat something. There are two vendors at the edge of the arena with food and drink. They usually have something that humans can eat. Do you want anything?"

Sonja shook her head. "I'm fine. I'm just going to stay here for a while and rest."

Paulo headed off with a wave. When he was gone, Sonja glanced around, but she did not see any other humans nearby. Even the three judges had disappeared. Despite Paulo's recommendation to keep moving, Sonja stretched out on her back and closed her eyes. The physical exertion, the pain in her leg, and the emotional storm she had endured over the past few days had left her completely drained. Her last coherent thought was that she hoped none of the creatures wandering around the arena grounds accidentally stepped on her.

"Wake up. Your match is starting soon. You need to get up."

Sonja opened her eyes. It felt like she had only closed them a moment ago, but when she gazed up at the pale blue sky above her, she realized the sun had moved several feet from its previous location. Paulo stood above her head, bent over far enough to peer down at her.

"Sorry, I must have fallen asleep. I didn't– Ahhh!"

Sonja had rolled over and tried to stand up. The muscles of her right leg immediately clenched into a white hot, fiery knot, spilling her back to the ground in an ungainly heap.

"Oh, shit. That really hurts," she whimpered.

While she had slept, the muscles in her thigh must have stiffened as Paulo warned her they might. The leg no longer wanted anything to do with holding her upright. Woodenly, Sonja forced herself to her knees, then her feet. When she was sure she was not going to fall again, she hobbled in a small circle, trying to get the blood flowing back through her legs and ease the painful cramping.

"Hold still," said Paulo.

He knelt in front of her and again put his hands around her leg. He used his thumbs to push deep into the knotted muscle. Flashes of pain exploded upward, threatening to topple her over again with each movement of his hands. Sonja hissed through her teeth, trying not to scream obscenities at the man who was only trying to help her. The muscles finally, reluctantly, began to relax enough for her to stand up straight and take a few normal steps.

"We are fighting the O'paahan," Paulo said, watching Sonja critically as she walked a tentative circle around him. "My match begins immediately after yours ends."

"In the same ring we were just in?" asked Sonja, pointing at the roped area closest to them.

"All fights from now to the end of the tournament will be held one at a time in the main cage."

Sonja glanced over her shoulder toward the raised platform in the center of the arena that she had noted when she first arrived. Black, metallic mesh surrounded the circular stage. The spaces in the black pattern were open enough to allow the spectators an easy view of the combatants inside, but the barrier still appeared sufficiently rigid to prevent anyone inside from getting out prematurely. Most of the creatures on the arena floor were currently busy arranging themselves outside the cage where they could get the best view or making their way across the field toward it.

"How long do I have before it starts?" she asked.

"The judges sent me to find you. You have only a few minutes before you need to be in the cage."

"And if I don't make it?"

"We will be disqualified and the O'paahan move to the next round," Paulo told her.

"We," Sonja repeated. "So, I don't show up, you get the boot, too."

"I'm not sure I understand the boot, but yes, if you are disqualified then so am I."

Sonja sighed. She had been considering sitting out this fight. Her leg still hurt like hell and she had temporarily lost her taste for combat. Her nap, in addition to tightening her muscles, had cooled the self-directed anger that had fueled her thus far. She did not want to be the reason that Paulo got tossed out of the competition, however. He genuinely seemed to want to be here.

"Okay. Let's go."

Paulo directed her to the main stage, taking her arm and guiding her to the small cluster of three human judges waiting for her near one of the two gates that led into the cage. The three men turned to her with obvious relief on their faces. One of the men – Sonja decided to call him bearded judge number one – began to talk. Sonja glanced at Paulo for translation.

"He said you are almost late. He has spoken with the O'paahan judges and they have decided on the rules that will govern the fight. There will be no biting, as the O'paahan have an unfair advantage in that area. They also have very sharp claws, so you are given a choice of options. You may elect to wear artificial claws that match your opponent's natural ones, or you may require him to wear gloves that nullify them as weapons."

"I think I like the idea of the gloves," Sonja stated. The mental image of her and another creature ripping huge pieces out of each other caused her to shudder slightly.

Paulo nodded. "I agree. I also requested the gloves." Paulo relayed her preference to the judge who in turn hurried away, presumably to pass along the decision to the O'paahan judges.

Watching him go, Sonja asked, "Should I get in the cage now?"

"As soon as your opponent is gloved, he will go in. So, yes, you should already be in there."

Paulo and the two remaining human judges formed a small escort around Sonja and walked her toward the cage.

Seeing the procession, the other creatures clustered around the center stage moved aside to let her through. When she reached the cage, she found four wide, heavily reinforced metal steps leading up to one of the gates which was already open and waiting for her. She climbed the steps with the determined finality of a condemned prisoner making their way up to the gallows.

Sonja stepped into the cage, paced off the distance to the far end – she figured it was about twenty feet across – then turned around to wait for her opponent. She jumped up and down a few times and dropped into some deep squats to bring her heart rate up and loosen the muscles in her legs. Her thigh complained at the treatment. She felt sluggish. After only a few seconds, another figure joined her in the cage: a small, hairless creature with wrinkled gray skin. Sonja thought it looked like a monkey because of the way it moved, but no monkey she had ever seen possessed six eyes and chitinous horizontal mandibles for a mouth the way this creature had. It walked on two legs, using its long arms to assist itself along, and was no more than thirty inches tall from foot to head.

Sonja let her hopes rise for a moment. She might just be able to beat this tiny freak show. If she could get one good hit or land a solid kick she had a chance. Then her heart sank as she realized it was not wearing gloves and it did not have claws. This could not be her opponent. The way the creature scampered to the center of the stage then turned to watch the open gate confirmed it was probably some sort of referee or neutral judge for the fight.

Sure enough, as soon as Sonja realized this was not her adversary, her real opposition approached the ring. The beast was massive. It looked like a dragon climbing into the cage. The head was blunted, rounder than an actual dragon's, but with a mouth full of dangerously pointed teeth. Its body was thick, heavily muscled, and layered with some sort of scales or overlapping plates. *Terrific*, thought Sonja, *it has its own personal body armor.*

The creature crawled up the steps and through the gate on all fours, then raised itself onto its hind legs, supplementing its balance with a long tree-trunk-sized tail. When fully upright, it towered over Sonja by almost two feet. Desperately, Sonja peered around to see if anyone else was coming into the cage. Maybe this was just another referee and the real fighter was still coming. That was when she noticed the blue, leather gloves covering the monster's hands.

"Shit. I'm dead," she muttered. "Any ideas, Rith?"

Rith remained unhelpfully quiet.

So, who was calling out to her? Through the crowd noise, Sonja could swear she heard someone shout her name. She dared a moment to look away from the creature at the far end of the cage and search among the spectators in the arena. She spotted Paulo, who had squeezed closer to the stage and was waving to get her attention.

"Watch the Callipac. The little one inside with you," he shouted. "When he claps his hands, the fight has started. Don't do anything until he claps his hands."

Sonja nodded her understanding. Not that it really helped matters. It just meant she wasn't going to get her head caved in until the gray monkey clapped.

She waited patiently, trying to keep her breathing under control. She saw the human judges just outside the open gate, conferring with three more of the massive dragon things. They only spoke to each other briefly before one of the O'paahan reached over to the gate, closed it, and secured it in place with two metal bolts affixed to the cage's framework. The scaled monster nodded once to the little referee inside the cage.

Without a word, or any further delay, the Callipac slapped its hands together twice and rapidly moved to press itself against the mesh of the cage.

The O'paahan charged at Sonja. The creature did not move quickly. Its hind legs were too short to allow much speed while moving on two legs, but the effect was still that of a freight train coming straight for her. Sonja dodged right then dove forward, giving the monster no time to compensate and change direction. As the O'paahan passed her, she threw a punch with her left hand into what she figured was its ribcage. It was like hitting a bag full of wet sand. She was not even sure if the creature noticed the strike.

Sonja shuffled backwards giving herself some space. Her opponent did not pause. He turned around and initiated a second charge. Sonja jumped left this time, not bothering to try another punch. She would break her hand before she did any damage to this monstrosity. As the O'paahan ran by her, its massive tail raised up and flailed at her head.

It had been years since Sonja faced an actual dragon, but that lesson was not forgotten, especially since her current opponent reminded her so much of one of the reptilian creatures. She saw the tail coming as soon as it left the ground. She dropped flat and rolled away from the attack, allowing it to pass harmlessly over her head. The moment she was clear, she bounced back to her feet and prepared for the next charge.

The O'paahan changed tactics. It was apparently intelligent enough to recognize a fast rush would continue to be ineffective against a significantly quicker opponent. This time it chose to lumber in more slowly, attempting to hem Sonja in and eventually pin her to the metal mesh at the edge of the cage.

Rather than wait to be trapped, Sonja opted to try a charge of her own. She lowered her head and rushed the creature. As she drew close, she leapt into the air, pivoting her body and driving both feet forward into the massive, scaled chest with every bit of strength and momentum she could gather. She felt the creature take a step back. With a cry of success, she hit the ground and rolled backward, rising to her knees as she came to a stop.

She had made an impact that time. She knew he must have felt that kick and, maybe, with any luck, she had done a little damage. If she could get to her feet quickly enough and repeat the maneuver, she might have a chance.

Too late, she understood the creature had not backed up because of her attack. Her kick had done nothing other than create an opportunity for the big lizard. The O'paahan had used the momentum of her push to step away, turn, and bring its tail back into play. Before Sonja could get out of the way, the armored club masquerading as a tail caught her across her left side, swept her up, and sent her flying.

She tumbled like a rag doll, her feet flipping up over her head. The awkward tumble fortunately ended with her legs taking the brunt of the impact as she struck the wall of the cage. The out of control collision could just as easily have resulted in a broken neck. Sonja crashed to the floor onto her shoulder and cried out in shock. She tried to get her hands under her and push herself back to her feet, but her brain was unable to get the message to her limbs.

Her lungs hitched, and Sonja realized she wasn't breathing. The creature's tail had driven the air from her lungs and done who knew what kind of damage to her ribs or internal organs. She tried again to suck in air but her diaphragm spasmed, making it impossible to inhale deeply enough to ease the growing pain of oxygen starvation in her chest and head.

Rolling onto her stomach, she coughed. It was a sickly, wheezing cough that gave no comfort and no relief. Tears of pain and frustration filled her eyes. She tried once more to push up with her hands.

Something warm and rough pressed against her neck and the back of her head. She could not see what was happening, but she felt the claws of the O'paahan's foot pricking her scalp as the creature applied its bulk to the fragile bones of her neck. The pressure built gradually. He was giving her a chance to quit before he killed her outright, but his intention was clear: if she resisted, he would crush her spine.

Sonja tried to call out. She tried to surrender, but she still could not get air to move in her lungs. She could only gasp short, honking exhalations. Despite her growing panic, a small part of her thought it would be okay if the monster finished the job, if he just snapped her neck and put her out of her misery. She wouldn't have to go back home and face Kevin. She wouldn't have to think about her betrayal and the pain she had caused him, or about the damage she had done to their relationship. Death would be so much easier than facing what she knew must come next.

She pushed the thought away. That was the coward's way out, and Sonja might be many things, but a coward was not one of them. Desperately, she slapped the floor with her hand. She prayed the referee here understood the significance of the action.

In a flash, the Callipac swarmed onto her back and began to slap the scaly leg holding her down. The tiny referee chittered loudly. She did not understand what it said, but slowly, like the tide moving away from land, the pressure on her neck eased.

Sonja coughed again, more forcefully this time. The muscles of her diaphragm and rib cage were at last beginning to cooperate with one another and she could pull in a few shallow breaths. Before she was ready to move, she felt several hands – human hands – grabbing at her and pulling her to her feet. She looked up to find the bearded judges glaring at her unhappily as they guided her none too gently toward the reopened gate.

She was pulled outside of the cage, assisted down the steps to the arena floor, then released. The sudden lack of support caused her to stumble and fall to her hands and knees. As it turned out, her current position was making it easier for her to breathe, so she stayed where she was.

"Are you okay?" It was Paulo's voice.

"Nope," was all she managed to say to him.

"I have to go fight. I'll check on you afterward."

Sonja simply nodded, too focused on breathing and staying alive to respond.

After a few more moments of shallow panting, the muscle spasms ceased, and Sonja was able to draw her first full breath. A sharp lance of pain stabbed through her ribs on her left side. She placed an arm across her chest and applied pressure in an attempt to ease the discomfort. When she pulled her hand away, there was blood on her palm. Disoriented, she wondered if the O'paahan had clawed her through the gloves or perhaps torn her open with its tail. Then she realized where the blood came from. The cut she received from Dancer had reopened.

"Shit," she said softly. "What was I thinking."

Feeling slightly more stable, Sonja climbed to her feet. She did not believe that anything was broken, but her ribs – and probably several other parts of her – were definitely bruised, and she was going to need to change the bandages over her cut as soon as she had the opportunity. Going head to head with the

O'paahan had been a colossal mistake. She should have just forfeited for the both of them. Paulo was never going to be able to defeat one of the things.

Paulo!

Sonja spun toward the cage in time to see Paulo and his own opponent circling each other in the ring. The O'paahan on the stage was even larger than the monster that had nearly killed her. It towered over Paulo. He was going to be destroyed.

Paolo lowered his head and charged. Leading with his left shoulder, he bulled into the larger creature causing it to stumble back a half step. Paulo dropped to his knees and executed a fast roundhouse punch into the lizard's right thigh. He immediately bounced up to his feet, grasped the creature around the waist in a bearhug and delivered two fast knee strikes to the thigh in the exact same spot. The O'paahan flailed its upper limbs, trying to pull Paulo off. From the loud hissing the monster made, Sonja figured it did not enjoy the leg attack any more than she had.

Paulo released his hold after one more knee strike, dropped and rolled safely away from any counterattack.

Paulo popped back to his feet, a fierce grin spreading on his face. The creature eyed him wearily. The lizard dropped to all fours, protecting its sore leg, and charged him. Much faster on four legs than two, the O'paahan covered the distance quickly. Paulo's smile never faltered. He held his ground until the giant lizard was only a few feet away, then he vaulted onto its back.

At first, Sonja thought he meant to ride the creature around the cage like some sort of cowboy, but she realized quickly that Paulo had other plans. He locked his legs around the lizard's thick neck, tucking his right foot behind his left knee to give himself more purchase. Next, he wrapped his arms around its head so he could not be thrown off. The O'paahan grabbed at

Paulo's legs, trying to pull free, but with the heavy gloves effectively blunting its claws, it could not gain any purchase.

Sonja saw the strain in Paulo's body as he clamped down on his opponent's neck; the muscles of his thighs were working overtime to compress the heavily armored throat. The monster in the ring flailed its limbs, its movements growing more frenzied and wild as Paulo refused to be dislodged. In a final bid for freedom, the massive lizard fell to the ground and rolled, crushing Paulo under its significant mass. It had to be painful for the smaller human, but Paulo never loosened his hold.

The O'paahan slowed, growing lethargic. Unable to shake the human from its back, it tried again to stand but it staggered unsteadily, its balance even on four feet seeming precarious. With a final shudder it toppled, crashing heavily to the floor to lie unmoving. Paulo held his grip around the creature neck, in case its fall proved to be a ruse, until the referee rushed up to pat his chest several times, chittering loudly. Paulo let go and climbed to his feet.

Sonja thought the arena was loud before, but when Paulo raised his hands in victory every creature in the audience was on its feet cheering and screaming in shocked amazement at the human's accomplishment. Sonja found herself joining in, shouting with surprised joy, even though it caused her damaged ribs to ache.

Paulo walked a victory lap in the cage, escorted by the three human judges who patted him vigorously on the back and shouted praises at him. Sonja gave him one last congratulatory wave, although she did not think he saw her. She turned and pushed her way through the throng, away from the main stage. When she was far enough from the majority of the crowd that she could move freely again, she raised Rith up to eye level.

"I think it's time to go," she told him. "I was hoping we could do a couple days on the beach before we go home. I should rewrap this cut and let myself heal a bit. I don't want to bleed in my clothes or freak anybody out if they see blood all over me.

"Besides," she said, her face lighting up, "I'd like to spend a couple days where it's just you and me. Would that be okay?"

Rith flapped his tiny wings, happily. "That would be wonderful. We haven't done that in a while. Are you ready now?"

"Yeah, buddy," Sonja responded. "I'm ready."

CHAPTER 26

Sonja paced the length of her rented bedroom. The digital clock on her bedside table showed 8:15 AM, but she had already been up for several hours. She had showered, dressed, eaten, and even watched some Saturday morning television to try to quiet her mind and get a few more minutes to pass without thinking about how messed up her life was.

And how it was all her fault.

Every free second seemed to be an exercise in guilt and self-loathing. Attending classes the past couple of days had been a complete waste of time. As the instructors had babbled through their canned material, all she could focus on was the way she had betrayed Kevin and praying that he might one day be able to forgive her. Two painful losses in the arena had not beaten her up as badly as the mental abuse she now heaped on herself.

Sonja and Rith had returned home three days ago. Three days, with no word from Kevin. Sonja wanted to give him his space and as much time as he needed; she knew pushing him would not help their chances of repairing their relationship. She didn't even go outside except to walk to classes and then go straight home. She did not want to accidentally run into him and force a conversation neither one of them was ready for. But now she was beginning to worry that if she waited too much longer, Kevin might believe she didn't care enough to check in with him.

Damned if you do, and damned if you don't, she told herself.

Sonja pulled her phone out of her back pocket and opened Kevin's contact info. Thinking that she would rather fight the O'paahan again than make this phone call, she braced herself and tapped the green call icon. The phone started to ring. And ring. And ring.

Kevin's voice came up announcing that he was unable to answer the phone, but if the caller left a message, he would get back to them as soon as possible. When the tone sounded, Sonja almost hung up without saying anything. He would know who had called. That was probably enough.

For him maybe, but not for her.

"I love you," she said. "I hope I get to talk to you again."

She disconnected the call. She hadn't thought about the message before she said it. She just spoke from the heart and that was what had come out. Was it enough? It would have to be. It was the best she could do right now.

Sonja slipped the phone back into her pocket and it immediately began to vibrate. Pulling it back out, she saw Kevin's face on the caller identification. Her hands began to shake, and she actually debated not answering, even though she had called him only seconds ago and he knew she could not possibly be unavailable to pick up. With a large part of her wanting to throw the phone across the room and crawl under the bed to hide, she slid the answer icon to the right.

"Hi, Kevin," she said, trying to sound bright, or at least not quite as frightened as she felt.

"Hi," he responded. His voice was subdued, but not hostile. Sonja hoped that was a good sign. "You called me."

"I did. Yeah, I…" Oh, god, this was even harder than she expected. She was terrified that anything she said would be the wrong thing, that she would set off another argument that only crippled her hopes further. "I … guess I just wanted to hear your voice. I wanted to see how you were doing. If you were okay."

"I'm a long way from okay," he told her. "But I am glad you called."

Sonja's heart soared. She quickly fought down the excitement, as it was much too soon to get her hopes up. "Glad you called" was a long way from forgiveness. This was a very promising start, however.

"I'm really glad you called back," she told him, honestly. "I wasn't sure you would."

"I wasn't sure, either. I almost didn't."

Sonja nodded, even though she knew Kevin could not see the acknowledgement. "I love you, Kevin, and I'm sorry I hurt you. I never meant to. I know I've already said that, and you probably don't want to hear it again, but it's true. I also know that words alone aren't going to fix us."

"Sonja–" Kevin began, but she cut him off.

"No, please let me get this out while I can. Then you can hang up, or yell at me, or do whatever you have to. I know words can't fix anything this time, so I am going to give Rith away. You asked me once if it came to a choice between you or Rith, which would it be, and I'm choosing you, Kevin. I choose you.

"If you think there is even the tiniest possibility that you and I have a chance together, I promise you Rith will never get between us again."

Rith drifted up from his ring to hover beside Sonja. He did not say a word or offer any indication of his feelings regarding her statement. Sonja covered her phone with a hand. Tears spilled uncontrolled down her cheeks. "I'm sorry," she sobbed to the tiny creature that had been her friend for so long. "I have to do this." Then she turned her back to him.

"Kevin? Did you hear me? Please say something."

PART III

A NEW ADVENTURE

CHAPTER 27

The moldering leaves and foliage of the forest floor made no noise as Sonja's calfskin boots pressed it down underfoot. With each silent step, she slipped carefully through the underbrush and moved closer to her prey. She watched the path in front of her, making sure she did not place her foot onto a dry twig or brush against a low hanging branch, knowing the slightest noise would alert her quarry to her presence and send it flying off into the surrounding trees.

She could see it now, up ahead, just visible through a tangle of small tree trunks that had grown close together: a hovering ball of blue light drifting in a lazy figure eight pattern about four feet from the ground. The ball was about twenty-four inches across so did not offer much of a target, especially from where Sonja crouched a little more than a hundred feet away.

Sonja brought her longbow up in front of her, the arrow already nocked. As she pulled the bowstring back, the bow arched and creaked lightly. She froze at the sound, breathing shallowly and watching the light carefully. It did not divert from its repetitive behavior. Relaxing again, Sonja drew the arrow all the way back, letting the fletching brush against her cheek. When she felt her aim was true and she had correctly anticipated the light's path, she released.

Her aim was good, but not perfect. The arrow passed through the ball of light near its edge. The light flickered a bright yellow.

"Yes!" Sonja shouted. "A point!"

A second arrow, appearing to come from nowhere, pierced the light directly through its center. The ball flashed an angry red then popped out of existence.

"That would be two points for me." The voice, whispery soft, came from directly behind Sonja.

Sonja whirled to find a tall female figure gazing off toward where the light had flickered out, lowering her own longbow. The woman was as slender as the bow she held in her hand, with long graceful limbs. She wore multiple colorful drapings of silk and gossamer that seemed very out of place in the middle of a forest, although she herself clearly belonged there. Sonja looked up to the beautiful, pale face towering more than a foot above her own. She took a moment, as she always did, to admire the sharp, narrow lines of the woman's cheeks and jaw as they trailed up to meet the soft curves of her pointed ears.

"Eli, you surprised me," Sonja told her. "I didn't hear you come up behind me."

"Which I believe is the whole point to this game. Yes?" the elf asked her with a mischievous smile and a regal nod of her head.

Elianda – Eli, as Sonja more familiarly knew her – took a few steps between the trees, casting her gaze upwards and gauging the position of the sun. "I believe the hour is up. The game is over. You did quite well, today, Sonja. You are improving nicely."

Sonja had been introduced to the elves by Rith a little over a year ago. They had invited her to join in a wisp hunt during that first meeting, and she had enjoyed the opportunity to return and hunt with them three times since. The rules of the game were simple: fifty wisps were released into the woods and the hunters had one hour to hunt down as many as they could find. A "touch" with the arrow was worth one point, while a "kill" was worth two. Today's was a small turnout; Sonja had only been competing with Eli and two other elves.

"I don't know if I'd call it improvement," Sonja responded with a shrug. "I got three points. I had three points last time, too."

"Tsk," Eli said, with a quick wave of one long, elegant finger. "Last time you tracked three wisps. You missed one and scored the other two, including a kill with what I can only surmise was an incredibly fortuitous shot." Eli smiled to show she meant no offense by the comment. "Today, you tracked five wisps. You missed two and scored three. Your tracking is much better. Your aim... Well. But yes, I still would call that improvement."

Sonja nodded, accepting the compliment gracefully. "How did you do, today?"

Eli rolled her eyes and placed a hand to her cheek dramatically. "Not one of my finest performances," she admitted. "Only eighteen points on this hunt. I fear that Aurio may have bested me this time. He had twenty-two at my last count."

Sonja shook her head in bemused amazement. Assuming that the elves had scored two points per wisp, and Sonja knew the elves almost never missed, Eli had tracked nine wisps and Aurio had found eleven. Sonja definitely needed more practice.

"Thank you for the hunt, Eli. Please pass my appreciation on to the others as well." Sonja held out her bow and stripped off the quiver holding her remaining arrows. Eli accepted the items.

"You must go?" asked the elf. "Will you not stay for the celebration and dance tonight?"

Sonja almost laughed, but politely kept her reaction under control. Every night was a celebration and dance for the elves. Some mornings as well. It seemed all they ever did was play games or throw parties.

From past experience, she knew elven celebrations were always an amazing spectacle and she was sorely tempted to stay a while longer but, unfortunately, a party was not on Sonja's agenda for tonight.

"Thank you, but no. Not this time."

"You will visit us again." Eli phrased it as a statement rather than a question.

"Of course. Hopefully soon."

"Then I wish you safe travels and a joyous journey's end." Eli leaned forward and kissed Sonja once on each cheek. The elf turned, her gown dancing with a flurry of color, and disappeared among the trees.

Sonja gaped. Although she had seen it many times before, it still surprised her how quickly the elves could be gone from sight. Even with all the contrasting colors of their clothing, they blended into the surrounding forest like another one of the trees.

"I wish I could learn that trick," muttered Sonja, enviously. "Okay, Rith. Are you ready?"

"Always," said the hippoganth, appearing in front of her almost as fast as Eli had disappeared. "Just say the word."

"How would you feel about one day at the beach before we head home? Can we do that?"

Apparently, they could. One moment, Sonja was standing in the cool, shaded recesses of an elven forest, the next she was on her favorite, white sand beach staring out at the brilliant blue-green ocean. The sun shone above her in all its glory with not a cloud threatening to shade its warmth. Sonja, too, stood in all her glory since her own private beach enforced a no-clothes-permitted policy. It was always plenty warm here, even after the sun went down, and there was never anyone else around to make clothing, or lack of it, an issue.

She found the blanket and picnic basket that were always here waiting for her and settled in for a quiet afternoon. Opening the basket, she rummaged around until she found the bottle of sunscreen. Rith always made sure the bottle was on top because, although pointless, Sonja had insisted that she found a sense of comfort from a good slather of SPF 150. Nothing said day at the beach like sticky skin and a layer of sand clinging to every part of you.

When she felt sufficiently coated – she couldn't reach everywhere on her back, but she did the best she could – she returned the sunscreen to the basket and pulled out a can of soda. The can was cold, although there was no cooler or ice in the basket. She had learned not to ask Rith questions about things like this, however, and popped the can open without another thought.

After setting her can aside in the sand, she sat on the blanket and watched the waves rushing up the shore and gracefully receding. The unchanging sound of the water made her feel calm and safe.

Sonja held up her right hand and gazed at Rith sitting on his ring. "I'm glad you're here, Rith," she told him.

Rith said nothing, merely fluttered his tiny silver wings at her.

Sonja held up her left hand and stared at the three solitaire diamonds mounted on a gold band. A narrower, plain gold band had been added to the first ring eleven months ago. She and Kevin had an anniversary coming up soon. Their first anniversary. She was going to have to start thinking seriously about what to get him.

Looking back out toward the water, she let the reflected ripples of sunlight and the gentle splashing sounds take her thoughts wherever they cared to drift. She found herself thinking back to a phone conversation five years ago when she thought she had lost everything. Kevin had walked out on her after learning she cheated on him, and she had called to tell him she was sending Rith away, knowing that it might mean losing both of them. It was the only thing she could think of to show him how much he meant to her.

She told him if there was any chance they might still be together, Rith would never come between them again.

Kevin's answer had surprised her.

"No," he said.

"No?" asked Sonja, unsure what he was referring to. "No, what? No, there's no chance?"

"No, you're not giving away Rith," Kevin told her. "You can't give him away."

"But, why not? You told me–"

"I gave him to you. Rith is the reason we met in the first place. I will not allow him to be the reason our relationship ends. When I asked you if you would get rid of Rith, I was being horribly unfair. I thought about it later. A lot. And I realized that even if you were willing to do it, you would eventually resent me for it."

"But you aren't asking me this time. I'm offering to do it."

"Stop!" Kevin barked at her. "You had your chance to talk. It's my turn, so just listen. Even if you don't think so right now, you will still eventually resent me for making you get rid of Rith. Resent me and maybe even hate me. I am not about to poison our future together before we even have a chance to figure out today."

"We have a future?" she asked, her heart beating in her throat.

"Look, Sonja. I don't know what's going to happen to us. I don't know if we'll make it past this phone call, but what I do know is that you're keeping Rith."

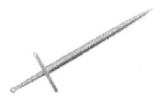

They did make it past that phone call. They made it five more years, and with luck, they had many more ahead of them. It had not been easy. Not at all. There was a lot of anger and sadness for Kevin to work through, not to mention Sonja's own self-destructive guilt that kept telling her it would be easier to run away than to look at the pain in Kevin's beautiful face every day and be reminded of what she had done to him, reminded of the worst thing she had ever done to someone she cared so deeply about.

The love was still there. It was always there. That wasn't the hard part. Love did not go away even when you injured it so badly. Love was unconditional, irrational. The hard part had been regaining his trust. Kevin loved her, but he no longer trusted her. In one thoughtless act, she had shaken his faith in her until it broke. That could not be repaired easily or quickly. She spent years building that foundation back. Step by step, and brick by brick, she tried to prove herself worthy of him. She would happily spend the rest of her life continuing to prove it to him if he let her.

Sonja stretched luxuriously on the beach towel, feeling the warm sand shift beneath the movement of her body. She propped herself up on her left elbow and glanced down the length of her bare torso. She smiled at the odd little lump protruding low on the right side of her tummy, then covered it protectively with her right hand. The tiny bulge fit neatly into her cupped palm. At just nine weeks, the fragile life within her was not visible when she was dressed, but at moments like this she could see the initial changes her body was making to accommodate the new member of their family.

"I guess I have to start being a lot more careful with this little guy to look after," Sonja told Rith. "That means you and I won't be heading off on any more crazy trips for a while."

"I suppose not," agreed Rith.

"We can still hit the beach once in a while, though. Right?"

"Absolutely. Just say the word." He nickered.

Sonja settled back on the towel. She gazed up at the blue sky above her as a few wispy clouds drifted by, and she listened to the steady wash of water breaking on the shoreline. Her hand drifted back to the slight rise in her belly, stroking it lightly with the tips of her fingers.

With a contented smile on her face, Sonja closed her eyes and drifted off to sleep, thinking about the amazing new adventure in front of her.

About the Author

G. Allen Wilbanks was born and raised in northern California. He is currently still there, living a quiet life with his wife and a ridiculous number of animals. For twenty-five years he worked in law enforcement while writing horror and fantasy fiction during his free time to keep himself occupied and stay sane. In 2016 he decided to retire from real life and live in a fantasy world of his own making full time. *A Life of Adventure* is his second published novel. For additional information about G. Allen, including where you can find more of his writing, please visit his website at www.gallenwilbanks.com.